FLASHPOINT SERIES

TINDERBOX

RACHEL GRANT

Books by Rachel Grant

PRAISE FOR
TINDERBOX

"This first novel in Grant's Flashpoint series offers a multilayered, suspenseful plot that's strengthened by its appealing characters, strong attention to detail, and a healthy dose of romance. The story kicks off with a bang, literally and figuratively, and Grant keeps the momentum going through a series of plot twists and well-staged action sequences that plunge the heroes into the path of a vicious warlord who'll stop at nothing to consolidate his power in the region."

- *Kirkus Reviews (starred review)*

"Tinderbox is raw and energetic, thrills-wise and sex-wise, and offers an exceptional combination of humor, suspense, romance and archaeological details that are always intriguing and never intrusive. This first book in Rachel Grant's Flashpoint series is unexpected and intense from the get-go. With irresistible characters, a rare setting and an inventive, high-powered plot, it's a smartly crafted gem of a story."

- *USA Today* Happy Ever After

This one is for Dave,

One of a select few professional archaeologists to work in Djibouti and the love of my life.

Chapter One

Morgan Adler's gaze darted between the cloud of dust in her rearview mirror and the road in front of her. Two more miles. She was going to make it. With the American embassy closed, Camp Citron, a US military base, was her only hope for refuge. The bones would be protected.

Adrenaline still coursed through her system after she'd faced down a warlord's henchmen armed with machine guns. They'd arrived moments after she'd received the text from the embassy, stating a credible threat had been made against the US ambassador and the embassy was going into lockdown. Her local field crew of five had fled as soon as the militants arrived, leaving her to face the armed men alone.

The warlord's message—apparently memorized, as the men repeated the words, and nothing else, at least half a dozen times—was clear: "Etefu Desta controls this land. Everything you find here is *his*."

Etefu Desta was an Ethiopian warlord looking to expand his territory into Djibouti. Apparently, he'd heard about her astonishing paleoanthropological find.

But how?

Officially, only Charles Lemaire, the Djiboutian minister of culture, knew the details. Which meant turning to the local government was out.

Djibouti—pronounced "juh-booty" by Americans and "jey-bootay" by the French—sounded both funny and sexy, but she'd learned once she arrived in the tiny nation on the Horn of Africa that the country was neither. Djibouti had third-world aspirations, with a long way to go to reach even that level of affluence.

Her find could help the Djiboutian government achieve those goals, and she'd be damned before she turned over the fossils to a warlord.

Another glance in the rearview mirror. No one followed. Her hands still shook as she gripped the wheel. She was going to be fine. She'd get on the base, explain the situation, and they'd help her. The US military had a vested interest in her project. She simply hadn't reached out to the powers that be on the base before now because she knew how the military worked and would not relinquish one ounce of control of her project.

She rounded a bend in the road that hugged a low plateau, and slammed on the brakes. A tire spike strip stretched across the road thirty meters in front of her. Another twenty meters beyond that, a Humvee blocked the road.

She twisted the wheel and skidded to a halt just shy of the spike strips. Her heart pounded as two men with big rifles stepped from behind the Humvee.

The vehicle indicated they were with the US military. Why had they blocked the road with tire-shredding spike strips?

A moment of panic ripped through her. What if these men had stolen US equipment and really worked for Desta?

As they approached, that fear subsided. There was no mistaking their American-ness, right down to their M4 carbine rifles, which each man carried with one hand on the stock and the other on the barrel, aimed down and to the side. Not pointed at her, but ready to aim and fire if warranted.

She'd seen far too many automated weapons already today. But then, she was more the Sig P226 type.

Both men wore desert combat camouflage—better known as Army Combat Uniform or ACU, according to her father. One was fair-skinned, the other dark. They moved like so many soldiers she'd known growing up. These were the good guys. They could help her.

They separated, the taller, white soldier rounding the bumper to her side of the car, while the black soldier paused in front and hitched up his weapon. Covering his partner without being too threatening, she guessed.

She kept her hands on the wheel, in view of both men and reminded herself she'd done nothing wrong.

Well, nothing except taking the fossils from the site. But she was protecting them. They'd be handed over to the Djiboutian government as soon as she knew if she could trust Charles Lemaire.

The soldier to her left signaled for her to lower the window. His name tape on the right breast said BLANCHARD. The branch tape on the left said US ARMY. The familiar reverse US flag patch on his right sleeve signaled friend.

Camp Citron was primarily a Navy base with Marines providing security, making her wonder if these guys were Special Forces, and if so, why they'd set up a roadblock two miles from the base.

Everything about the soldier's stance was meant to be intimidating.

I've done nothing wrong.

She gingerly lifted one hand from the wheel to comply with his signal. These guys didn't mess around. She pressed the button, and the glass slid slowly downward, releasing precious air-conditioning to the sweltering March day.

"ID?" the man asked.

"Why did you stop me?" she asked, hearing a tinge of fear in her voice. She cleared her throat, hoping to expel the panic.

"I'm not at liberty to say. ID?"

She reached for her passport from the pouch she wore under her shirt, next to her belly. She glanced up at the soldier, but dark sunglasses covered his eyes, telling her nothing of what he thought of her mild striptease.

She handed him her passport and rebuttoned her shirt. Her hands shook harder now than they had before. She gripped the steering wheel again in an effort to control the shaking.

"Please state your business"—he lifted his dark sunglasses to inspect her ID—"Morgan Adler." His face was expressionless to the degree that he might as well be addressing an acacia tree. Perhaps that was how he practiced the blank look, talking to the thorny plant that had destroyed her favorite pair of work boots. Either that or the intense heat had sucked all the life out of him.

"Right now, I'm heading to Camp Citron and trying to figure out why you have the right to stop and question me two miles from the gate."

"Please state your business on the base."

"Are you some sort of advance screen?"

"If you cooperate, we might permit you to approach the base."

"You might permit me to drive on a public road. That's very generous of you."

"We aren't in the US, ma'am. For the most part, Djibouti is lawless, so forget your notions of public and private when it comes to roads and pretty much everything else." His jaw tightened. "Please step from the vehicle."

She tightened her grip on the steering wheel. Could they really do this?

I've done nothing wrong.

She didn't want to be stupid but feared it was too late—she was starting to believe she'd been stupid when she took the contract to begin with, but then the weight of student loans from her newly minted PhD meant she didn't really have a choice.

When she made no move to exit the vehicle, Blanchard opened the door and said, "Now, *Dr.* Adler."

She startled at his use of and emphasis on her title. Her passport, several years old, didn't indicate her advanced degree. *What the hell is going on?*

She shut off the engine. Blanchard moved back so she could step out. The other soldier slowly paced the passenger side of her rental car, his head tilted down, looking at something.

Between the seventy-eight percent humidity, and the eighty-eight-degree day, the heat index was pegged at a hundred and five, and she felt every thick, blistering degree as she faced the soldier. "How do you know who I am?" she asked.

"Raise your hands, please."

When she made no move to do so, he barked a sharp "Now!" and gestured with the butt of his M4.

She tried to stifle her squeal of terror as she raised her arms. She'd wanted to get herself and the fossils safely inside the perimeter fence of the military base, under the protection of machine guns, instead of being threatened by them.

Although technically, he hadn't pointed his rifle *at* her.

"There's a cell phone in my bra," she said when he began to frisk her. Her ample cleavage hid the bulge, making the warning necessary. "In the front."

Thankfully, he was perfunctory in the pat down, finding and extracting the phone without fuss. She'd been groped enough to know the difference, and this man kept it professional.

He slipped her cell into his pocket along with her passport and continued the search, pausing on the pouch against her belly, but a quick hand inside proved it was empty. He circled her and repeated the process on her back. "She's clear," he said to the other soldier.

She turned to face him. "Was that necessary?"

"We received a tip Etefu Desta was sending Camp Citron a message with one Dr. Morgan Adler. So yes, it was necessary." His brows lowered, making her wish she could see his eyes behind the shaded lenses. "However, the tipster specifically indicated Dr. Adler was a man."

She couldn't contain her shock. She'd faced that issue more than once when she arrived in Djibouti—Morgan was a name that could be male or female, and she *might* have used that to her advantage when bidding on the project, because East African nations weren't known for their progressive attitude toward women—but the fact that her name had been mentioned in conjunction with a warlord's was far more alarming than the lack of correct gender identification. "That's bull! I don't know, nor am I working for, Etefu Desta. I have no clue what that even means."

Behind her, the other man swore. She turned to see what triggered it. He had a mirror mounted to a long pole and was scanning the undercarriage of her car. "Shit. Found the message. There's a package on a timer."

Blanchard stiffened. "Can you see the countdown?"

"No, just the Timex." He looked down the road, toward the base. "If it's set to go off when she reached the base—"

Blanchard grabbed her arm, yanking her forward, away from the car. "Move!" he shouted as he dragged her behind him. She yanked her arm from his grasp and turned to the other soldier. "Do you mean there's a bomb?"

"Yes. C-4. Lots of it. Right under the gas tank."

She took three quick steps back to the car and leaned inside. Her finger hit the trunk release as hands snatched her from the vehicle.

She struggled against the soldier's grip. "I have to get the fossils! They're in the trunk."

Blanchard's grip only tightened. "No time."

She kicked at him and broke free, but he caught her again before she took two steps. With a curse, he scooped her up and threw her over his shoulder, which hit her diaphragm and knocked the wind out of her. She gripped his back and tried to breathe as he ran at shocking speed.

"Stop!" she shouted when she finally caught her breath. A stream of invectives escaped her mouth, which she followed up with "Let me grab the bones!"

The other soldier ran on a parallel course, ignoring her yells and shouting, "Go! Go!"

She clawed at his shoulder—not that he'd notice through the thick combat fatigues—and cursed. "Dammit! Let me grab the bones from the trunk!" Her eyes teared as the distance between her and the rental car widened. The surge of bile in her throat could have been caused by the Heimlich-maneuver-type abdominal jolts she received with each bounce as he sprinted across the rocky desert ground, but the tears were undoubtedly caused by the fact that the fossilized bones were in danger of being destroyed.

She'd taken them from the site to save them from a warlord. She pounded on his shoulders again, spewing more curses. "Stop!" Her voice trailed off as tears of frustration and anger won the battle.

They'd covered at least a hundred meters when the soldier slowed. His heavy pack protected his back from her frustrated fists, so she tried to knee him in the chest, only to meet body armor.

He let out a low growl. "Stop it! I'm trying to save your damn life!"

"I need to get the fossils!" She shoved at his shoulder, throwing him off-balance and giving him no choice but to set her down. The moment her feet touched earth, she pushed away from him. He had no idea how important the bones were, how they could enhance—even change—current evolutionary models.

He caught her around the belly and yanked her backward. Her breath left in a rush with the force of the blow to her diaphragm.

She saw the explosion before she heard it—a quick flash of orange followed

by a percussive wave of heat. She managed to get air in her lungs just in time
to scream.

Pax Blanchard twisted as he dove, so the woman wouldn't take the brunt
of impact with the hard, dry ground. He rolled, tucking her under him as
a secondary—and bigger—explosion shook the earth. A wave of heat—
noticeable even at eleven degrees north of the equator—washed over him.
Fortunately, they'd cleared the blast zone. His legs were peppered with debris,
but it was more akin to a spray of gravel kicked up by a passing truck than
being pelted with hot, sharp shrapnel.

He held Dr. Adler beneath him as the echo from the blast faded. He'd had
to fight her every step from the vehicle, which pissed him off. If she'd
managed to escape his grip and made it back to the car, he'd have had to
follow, blowing them both to bits. That didn't sit well with him.

He glared at her as she struggled beneath him, her face contorted with grief
and rage as if someone had just stolen her baby. With hearing dimmed due to
the explosion, cursing her out for her stupidity would have to wait.

Damn, that had been close. If they hadn't stopped her, she'd have made it
to Camp Citron. She never would have made it through the screen, but the
explosion would have taken out more than the foolish woman and whatever it
was she'd been desperate to get from the trunk of her car.

Hell. He owed Callahan fifty bucks. He'd been certain the tip was bullshit.

Dust filled the air, limiting sight distance, but shielded as she was by his
body, he could see every bitter emotion that crossed Dr. Adler's features. He
had a feeling this was her first rodeo and would be braced for waterworks
except she was too angry to realize she'd just come very close to becoming the
source of a blood rain in the desert.

He peeled his body from hers and got to his feet. Five yards away, Callahan
also stood. "I'm getting too old for this shit." Cal's voice was muted but firm,
indicating he was uninjured.

She flopped backward when freed of his weight and closed her eyes. Her
chest rose with two deep breaths.

Maybe she'd launch into hysterics after all.

Pax radioed the base, informing them of the explosion while keeping his
eye on Dr. Adler. The conversation was frustratingly short, as he didn't know
exactly who the woman was and why she'd carried a package from Etefu
Desta. Their Humvee had been damaged in the explosion, so the base was
sending a convoy to pick them up. A second team would investigate the
explosion and recover the Humvee.

He clipped the radio to his belt and faced Dr. Adler. He needed answers. Now. He offered her a hand, but she ignored it and instead pushed herself up from the ground. "Dammit! The fossils are gone!" With her gaze fixed on the smoldering vehicle, she cursed again, as creatively as she had while he carried her.

Pax glanced from the woman to the wreckage. "I've never heard the word jizz used in quite that way."

Cal grimaced. "I'm never going to look at a goat in the same way again."

The woman glared at Pax. "Why didn't you let me grab the box? There was time! I could have saved—" Her voice cracked on the last word, and finally an emotion besides anger slipped through. Tears began to roll down her cheeks.

Shit. He'd take anger over tears any day. Even anger that pissed him off.

"Maybe you could have grabbed whatever it was from the trunk," Pax said. "But we had no idea how much time we had. No idea if we'd be able to clear the blast zone at all. Grabbing crap from the car was a risk I wasn't willing to take."

"But *I* was," she said.

"I couldn't leave you. In going back for whatever it was you wanted to save, you risked *my* life too." His voice hardened. "I'm not okay with that, Dr. Adler."

Her jaw snapped shut. All at once she deflated. Her knees buckled and she dropped to the ground again. She stared at her smoldering, annihilated vehicle. Color leached from her face—something he'd have thought impossible in the intense desert heat—and she covered her mouth as though she was trying not to hurl.

"What was it? What was so important you risked your life for it?" This from Cal, who sounded genuinely curious and not nearly as pissed as Pax.

She met Cal's gaze, giving Pax a chance to take in her profile. She had pretty—almost angelic—features, and the pat down had revealed impressive curves hidden under the loose field shirt. But it was her mouth that really caught his attention. She had the sweetest lips that said the foulest things. The woman was Barbie's raunchy alter ego.

"What just blew up?" she repeated Cal's question as she swiped away tears with a trembling palm. Her hand dropped, revealing a smear of red desert dirt across her cheek. "Only a piece of the biggest paleoanthropological find in East Africa this millennium. A bigger find than Lucy."

"A piece?" Pax asked, curious now. He knew about Lucy.

She nodded. "We lost Linus's dinner."

Chapter Two

Morgan couldn't take her eyes off the wreckage. Gone. All gone. Bones that had been butchered by an australopithecine male over three million years ago, the only find of its kind, destroyed in an instant.

"We still have Linus," she said under her breath, as if saying the words was a talisman against losing the hominin remains.

"*Who* is Linus, and why do we give a fuck about his dinner?" the soldier who'd dragged her away before she could grab the bones—Blanchard—said.

"Have you ever heard of Lucy? She's an australopithecine fossil found in the seventies in Ethiopia by Donald Johanson and his team. She's estimated to be about three-point-two million years old—"

Blanchard cut her off. "Skip the lecture. I know what Lucy is."

She shook her head to clear it. "Sorry. I'm—" Her voice cracked again, and she cleared her throat. "Two weeks ago, I found a male fossil that likely dates to the same epoch, similar in age to Lucy. It's hard to estimate in the field, and it's too early for us to have dates back from the lab, but several characteristics of the skeleton are consistent with the Lucy fossil. It seemed natural to name him Linus."

The name had been her own private joke, because while the field workers provided by the Djiboutian government all knew of Lucy the australopithecine, they weren't familiar with Lucy van Pelt and her little brother, Linus, from the *Peanuts* comic strip. She met the gaze of the soldier who'd been—understandably—glaring at her because she'd fought him as he carried her away from her car and the fossils.

He cracked a smile, and she enjoyed the moment of sharing the joke with someone at last, but she'd been abominable toward him. Kicking. Scratching. And the things she'd said… It was a wonder he hadn't tossed her to the compacted ground and continued running.

She'd thoughtlessly endangered him and the other soldier. Shame flooded her. She'd been unable to think of anything beyond saving the fossils. They were so much more than the find of a lifetime. The remains and associated artifacts would change what was known about *Homo sapiens sapiens'* hominin predecessors.

She hadn't wanted to save them for personal glory—although that would come when the find was announced to the world. The fossils had been pure information. Scientific data about a period of human evolution that was represented by scant few fossils. And the bones were now lost forever.

She met the gaze of the other soldier, noting his name tape said CALLAHAN, then faced Blanchard again. "I'm sorry," she said. "I shouldn't have risked your life—either of your lives—by fighting you." She shook her head. "I just couldn't think about anything other than the fossils. I took them from the site to protect them from Etefu Desta." The car smoldered in the distance. The scent of burned rubber reached her on the hot wind. "And now they're gone. Frankly, I'd rather Desta have them than they be destroyed. And I never, ever thought there'd be a reason to wish a warlord had possession of any artifacts or fossils."

"You said Linus's dinner was destroyed. Not Linus?" Callahan asked.

"No, thank goodness." She stood and brushed off her pants, trying to recapture some dignity. "One thing that makes Linus special is he—unlike any other fossil of his age—has tools. An entire assemblage. And—" Her voice broke again. So much for dignity. "He'd butchered an animal. A meal. No one has ever found a hominin with tools, let alone with the butchered remains of a protein source. The butchered bones were in a box in the trunk. That's what I was trying to save."

"Why did you take those from the site and not Linus?" Blanchard asked.

"Because Linus is still in the ground. He's exposed and vulnerable—which is partly the reason I was going to the base—but removing him quickly would have destroyed him. So I took the fossils that had already been excavated and left Linus and his tools, hoping, praying, Desta's men wouldn't steal him while I was at Camp Citron pleading for help."

"What happened with Desta's men?" Blanchard asked. His voice hardened as he said the warlord's name. She guessed he was more on her side now than against her.

The enemy of my enemy is my friend.

And Desta was most certainly a shared enemy.

She explained how Desta's henchmen had shown up at the site and declared the find theirs. "Linus is a secret. The only official who knew about him is the minister of culture. I can't imagine why he would tell Desta, but if he did, I can't trust him. Basically, with the embassy closed, Camp Citron was my only hope."

"What about your field crew? Couldn't one of them have told Desta of the find?"

She couldn't hold back her gasp at that. In the two months she'd been in

Djibouti, the five men who worked for her had become like family. Ibrahim had learned so much about archaeology and was a natural in the field. He had a new career ahead of him. The idea that one of her crew could have betrayed the site to a warlord brought the return of bile to her throat. "It's possible," she said so softly she could barely hear her own words over the ongoing ringing in her ears. "But right now, I'm more afraid *for* them than afraid of them."

If her car had been bombed, what did that mean for her crew?

Callahan pulled his radio and spoke to someone on the base again, using jargon she didn't understand. Her thoughts wandered to the plight of her crew. Had Ibrahim gotten them safely away? Could a bomb have been planted under his car as well?

It was an open secret that the US military launched lethal drone strikes from Camp Citron, making it strategically important—and a high-priority target for enemy states. She'd never wished death from above on anyone before—hell, she'd been opposed to the drones on principle—yet she wouldn't bat an eyelash if the US had the coordinates for Etefu Desta's base of operations and opted to use that knowledge for a deadly strike.

The warlord had tried to blow her up, after all.

He'd threatened her crew.

And he'd destroyed Linus's dinner.

Callahan clipped his radio to his belt and said to Blanchard, "Double or nothing Desta was behind the threat to the ambassador that triggered the embassy lockdown."

Blanchard gave him a terse shake of his head. "No bet."

She wondered what the original bet was. The sequence of events paraded through her aching head. The armed goons at the site, the closed embassy, her mad drive to Camp Citron. If Blanchard and Callahan hadn't stopped her, there was no doubt she'd have reached the gate just in time to explode.

And die.

Who had called in the tip that saved her life? Had Desta been both tipster and bomber? Did he intend for her to be stopped outside the camp, or was there a traitor in his midst?

The thought of her body shattered in a thousand pieces and littering the entrance to Camp Citron sent a shudder through her.

It finally began to sink in, how close she'd come to dying. Horror at losing the fossils had clouded her brain, making her stupid.

She could have *died*.

Would have died, if not for these two men.

"We need to head back to the road to meet the convoy that's coming to pick us up," Callahan said.

She nodded and took a step toward the road, toward her decimated rental car. *Does the rental insurance provided by my credit card cover bombing by warlord?*

As soon as she was alone, her panic attack would be epic.

Blanchard's hand on her arm stopped her. "We aren't going near the wreckage." He pointed east. "We'll meet up with the road if we go that way."

They walked in silence, the soldiers flanking her. She assumed this was to protect her, and was again chagrined at the things she'd said as Blanchard carried her away from her vehicle. She needed to work on her people skills.

After a half mile, she requested they stop so she could catch her breath. She usually avoided working during the highest heat of the day, and this walk without water had taken a toll. Her head—already aching from the explosion—now throbbed with an unforgiving dehydration headache. The water bottle she always kept handy in this country, where water was far more precious than oil, had blown up along with her laptop and Linus's dinner.

She dropped onto a boulder and tried not to think about the loss of her computer or thirst. While she was at it, she might as well not think about the omnipresent heat. Or the fact that she'd just driven fifteen miles across a desert with a bomb attached to her fuel tank.

Blanchard appeared in front of her, and she shaded her eyes to look up at him in the bright, hot sun, wishing she still had her boonie hat. At least her sunglasses had stayed on her face in the midst of the dash and tumble.

I still have sunglasses. She couldn't even muster fake cheer at the pathetic positive note.

"Drink," Blanchard said, and she realized he was holding out the bladder for a hydration bag. Blinded by the sun, she hadn't seen it. So much for the glory of Ray-Bans.

"Thank you," she croaked, her throat too dry for smoother speech. She took only a small sip. She wouldn't deprive the man who'd saved her life of precious water. The convoy would arrive soon. She could wait.

She handed him back the bladder, but he shook his head. "It's a spare. Keep it. You need it."

Both men wore heavy, bulky packs, which couldn't be pleasant in the heat. She glanced at each in turn. Both were big—tall and muscular—and handsome. Blanchard was the taller of the two, at least three inches above six feet. With the exception of the slight smile at her explanation of the name Linus, his expression had remained largely cold—impressing her with his ability to pull off a chilly demeanor in the sweltering heat of midday—while Callahan had a much more congenial air. But then, she hadn't compared

Callahan to slug jizz while he carried her across the harsh landscape.

The US ARMY label on Callahan's uniform caught her eye again. "I thought Marines provided security for Camp Citron."

"We're not the regular security detail, ma'am," Callahan said.

When he didn't offer more, she glanced at his rifle and cataloged his other gear. "Special Forces?" she asked.

He nodded. "I'm Sergeant First Class Cassius Callahan. Call me Cal. And"—he nodded toward Blanchard—"the hulk looming above you is Master Sergeant Pax Blanchard."

Blanchard didn't even acknowledge the introduction. Instead, he pulled out a water bottle and removed his sunglasses to splash water over his face before taking a long drink. He had heavy, dark brows that capped brown eyes framed by thick lashes many women would kill for, but combined with his long straight nose and strong chin, his face was hard and masculine. And hot, which wasn't a reference to the water that mixed with the sweat dripping from his hairline.

"Special Forces," she repeated, pulling her mind back from the unwelcome thought. He was exactly the type of man she didn't want to find hot. She'd devoted herself to avoiding men just like him for a dozen years. "Capitalized, as in Green Berets?"

"Yes, ma'am," Callahan replied.

"How did you get the job of stopping me?"

"Just lucky, I guess," Callahan said.

Blanchard made a sound that was suspiciously like a snort. "We were meeting with our XO when the tip came in." He cocked his head. "Ready to go?"

"Yes." The bladder had a strap, which she slung over her shoulder. It must've been nearly frozen when he set out earlier, because the water was still chilled and felt heavenly against her skin. She hurried to take her place beside him, and again both soldiers flanked her.

"How did you end up working in Djibouti, Dr. Adler?" Callahan asked.

"Please, call me Morgan." She took a deep breath of air so hot, she feared it would sear her lungs. "A few months ago, I landed a contract with the Djiboutian and Ethiopian governments to locate and clear sites along the planned route for the Ethiopian railway expansion at the Port of Djibouti. It's a private sector contract, and the Djiboutian government is paying me, but the US Navy has a vested interest in the project because the government of Djibouti agreed to allow for an expansion of Camp Citron if the US helps expedite the construction of the railway, which is being paid for by China. Djibouti is desperate for the cash the railway will bring, and frankly, they're playing our country off China to get it done quickly."

It was a tangled web of bureaucracy that had her on edge, not knowing if the project would happen until she'd boarded her flight. And even then, she'd wondered if she'd arrive in Djibouti, only to be turned back due to the fact that she was the proud owner of a vagina. She'd been tempted to pack a strap-on, but didn't think the customs inspectors would be amused.

"I thought they were breaking ground on the railroad next week?" Callahan said.

"At the Ethiopian border, yes. A geologist who specializes in this region cleared that portion of the line months ago. I was brought in to investigate two proposed routes that meet up with the cleared portion. I've only investigated one APE—Area of Potential Effect—so far, which is where I found Linus. I was supposed to start surveying the second APE weeks ago, but finding Linus delayed us. If the second route is clear, then the railway will go that way, avoiding Linus. If not, then the government will have to decide which route, and do a full-scale data recovery excavation of all sites along the chosen route."

Would she be the one who surveyed the second route? Someone had planted a bomb under her rental car. That was a strong argument for going home.

Her PhD was in New World archaeology; she'd never expected to work as a paleoanthropologist, but this project had come together thanks to friends in the right places, and all that had mattered were the letters "PhD." No one cared that she'd never worked in Djibouti. But then, few had; there were only eight professional archaeologists who'd ever reported on digs in Djibouti, and she'd consulted with the ones who were still alive before she arrived.

She was as qualified as anyone and better suited than most.

But as thrilled as she was with having found Linus, she liked breathing more. And as much as she felt like the tool-making, meat-butchering, three-and-a-half-foot-tall hominin who was akin to a hairless, bipedal chimpanzee was hers, if her life was at stake, she could—and probably should—walk away.

Or, as she should have done when told by Callahan there was a bomb under her car, she could run.

They reached the road, but there was no sign of a convoy. Blanchard radioed, and a driver responded. He was midsentence when she heard a boom in the distance.

The crackling of the radio went silent.

Chapter Three

Motherfucker! The convoy on Bravo route had hit an IED. Pax met Cal's gaze. "We need to get Dr. Adler out of the open." He nodded toward the dry riverbed. "The wadi is our best bet."

With a sharp nod, Cal changed directions and led the way down into the dry valley. Pax followed, behind Dr. Adler, his attention on the radio, listening for updates on the situation on Bravo. The second convoy—the team that would investigate the explosion and retrieve the damaged Humvee—was coming the long way around, via Charlie, but HQ opted to reroute them to provide aid to the Bravo team.

"Injuries to personnel in the convoy are minor." Cal translated the chatter for Dr. Adler's benefit.

"Thank God." Her voice was shaky. Pax had a feeling the seriousness of the situation had finally eclipsed her anxiety over losing the fossils.

He understood the significance, but still, his life, her life, and Cal's life were worth way more than some damned fossilized bones, and anger still simmered over the way she'd fought him as he carried her to safety.

He had no time for myopic civilians, no matter how angelic their features.

Djibouti hovered on the edge of a flashpoint. The country was no place for anyone who couldn't grasp that. It was a massive tinderbox, baking in the sun. One tiny piece of glass catches the light just right, and the region would be engulfed in flames.

Cal traipsed down the steep slope at a rapid pace. Dr. Adler surprised Pax by keeping up, but then she'd said she'd been in country and working in the field for months and was probably acclimated to both the climate and the terrain. Her earlier exhaustion was likely due to shock and that they were out during the highest heat of the day.

Cal reached the bottom of the wadi and turned to give Dr. Adler a hand. She froze in front of Pax with a suddenness that forced him to stop short to avoid slamming into her.

Cal's brows furrowed. "Dr. Adler?"

"There's a Northeast African carpet viper sliding over your boot." Her voice was low and so dry, it was more breath than sound.

Very slowly, Cal looked down. Pax shifted so he could see around a boulder protruding from the slope and watched as the highly venomous snake took its sweet time slithering over Cal's boot. Thankfully, the leather was thick and went well above his ankles. The snake would have to strike high if it wanted to break skin.

Cal and Dr. Adler stood frozen as the snake slithered past. It disappeared under a large rock several feet away. She drew in a deep breath and swayed back on the release, leaning into Pax's chest. She stayed with her back pressed to the hard plate of his body armor as she took another deep breath. "That's the second one I've seen since I arrived."

"First one for me," Cal said. "Thanks for the heads-up."

She nodded and gingerly stepped down to the floor of the wadi.

Some sections of the dry riverbed were wide and open. Here, the wadi was fifty yards across bank to bank, but much of the desolate valley, including parts of the winding two-mile stretch that would take them to the Gulf of Tadjoura and the US Navy port at Camp Citron, was constricted and riddled with massive boulders they'd have to navigate around. US forces heavily patrolled the section closest to the base, but the Djiboutian government frowned upon the appearance of the US military controlling more territory than they'd been granted, so this far from base, the wadi was a no-man's land.

Wadis—the beds or valleys of streams that remain dry except during the rainy season—were a cruel taunt in Djibouti, which had no actual rivers and only seasonal streams. They were a promise of water that never delivered. But as far as Pax could tell, everything about Djibouti was cruel.

Cal took the lead with Pax walking backward, covering their six with his M4 at the ready. They'd find a protected, viperless position to hole up in and await orders. If they didn't have Dr. Adler, they'd go directly to the base, but the woman was more than a hindrance, she was an unknown.

A spy with the perfect cover, or an innocent targeted for death by Etefu Desta?

Once they found a safe position, Cal radioed their commander. The news wasn't good. The second convoy, the one that had taken the Charlie route, was pinned by sniper fire. They were dealing with a coordinated assault orchestrated by Desta.

"Desta's never had the organization or firepower to launch an attack like this before," Cal said.

Pax nodded. He'd been thinking the same thing. His gaze traveled up and down Dr. Adler. Desta's messenger. What the hell did that mean? "What if Desta isn't the one behind this three-pronged assault?" he said. "Who else is gunning for Camp Citron?"

Cal snorted. "We can narrow it down to pretty much everyone in East

Africa and on the Arabian Peninsula."

He grimaced at the truth in Cal's statement. "I'll rephrase: who has the means to organize an assault like this? Both the timing and the money?"

Cal shrugged. "No clue. Maybe China?"

It was true that China was working awfully hard to gain a toehold in East Africa, but a direct attack on a US military base seemed far-fetched, even for them. Again Pax's gaze landed on Dr. Adler. Her reaction had been extreme. *Too extreme?*

Possible. But his gut said she was just a shortsighted fool.

Radio chatter increased as the marines on Charlie estimated the sniper's position. Cal perked up. "If the sniper is west of Charlie, between the wadi and the base, we're behind the asshole."

Pax pictured the location in his mind. "The sniper could be above the wadi a half klick northeast. We can sneak up on the prick and take him out." His gaze turned to Dr. Adler, and he frowned. This wasn't the sort of op in which a civilian could tag along.

Cal could read his thoughts. "I'll forget the fifty you owe me if you take babysitting duty," he said.

Pax snickered and was tempted to demand a hundred, but he'd rather go after the sniper. "No deal."

"I'm a better shot at distance, and this is likely to be a long one." Cal's gaze slid to the archaeologist. "And you're better with the ladies."

Dr. Adler snorted, then glanced up and down the narrow, dry-as-bone riverbed. She met their gazes in turn. "If you can get him, you should. I can hide and wait."

As much as Pax liked that plan, there was no way in hell they'd follow it. He gave Cal a sharp nod. Pax was no slouch at sniping down snipers, but Cal was an ace. "I'll stay with Dr. Adler, but you're buying tonight at Barely North."

Separating was far from ideal, but since when was combat ever ideal? And sure as shit checking out the tip about Dr. Adler as a favor to the XO had turned into a full-blown combat mission. "This is not how I pictured spending my day off," he added.

"Think of the overtime pay," Cal said.

"You're going to need it, because I intend to blow past the two-drink limit tonight." He pulled out a map and spread it on a rock between him and Cal.

The sun beat down, glaring off the plastic sheet that protected the paper map. Sweat dripped from his hairline onto the plastic. He'd start with a frozen drink. He didn't give a damn what kind, so long as it had a lot of ice.

Cal pointed to a ridgeline above the wadi. "Along here"—he traced the contour with a fingertip—"he'd have a line of sight on Charlie. It's long, meaning this sonofabitch has skills. Plus, he's feeling smug because no one on the ground can get a line on him."

"Time to take the smug bastard down a notch," Pax said, tucking the map away. "Dr. Adler and I'll continue up the wadi. See you on base."

Cal cracked a grin. "Not if I see you first." He turned to Dr. Adler. "Ma'am, it's been terrible meeting you. I hope when we meet again there will be fewer explosions and snakes."

Adler laughed. "Agreed."

His gaze flicked to Pax. "Don't let Pax scare you. He's a teddy bear. Brooding means he likes you. It's how he flirts."

"Don't you have somewhere to go?" Pax asked in exasperation.

Cal grinned at her, then turned to Pax, and in a flash, the soldier returned. Cal could change from congenial buddy to Special Forces operator with a speed that would give some men whiplash. "Barely North at eighteen hundred. I'm buying." He turned and jogged up the wadi, not slowed in the slightest by the heavy pack on his back.

Adler met Pax's gaze. "A teddy bear? Somehow I doubt that."

Pax kept his face blank as he studied the woman who had seriously screwed up his day. "Grizzly, teddy. Cal gets those terms confused."

Her mouth twitched, but she didn't smile. Her gaze turned serious. "I'm sorry I was an ass earlier."

"Not so much an ass as an idiot."

She nodded. "That too. I was awful. And I'm sorry."

He gave a sharp nod. "Apology accepted."

She tilted her head down the wadi, opposite from the direction Cal had gone. "I take it we're heading that way?"

"Yes. We don't know what's waiting for us. So we'll take it slow. Play it cautious."

She nodded and took a step forward. He stopped her with a hand on her arm, ignoring the zing of contact. "I go first."

"Sorry."

He led the way, scanning the wadi with his gun barrel with each slow step. Pretty much everything about this situation sucked. The sun had reached zenith, humidity was at about a thousand percent, Cal had gone off to take on a sniper by himself, and Pax was stuck with Morgan the Foul-Mouthed Fairy.

As if cued by his thoughts, Dr. Adler let out a stream of curses. "What's wrong?" he asked.

"I started mentally cataloging everything that was in the car: my computer, field notebooks, camera. All my site notes, all the excavation photos, all the strat drawings. Gone." More curses escaped her lips, her invective directed at Desta and his ancestors, followed by "Arugula served with goat spunk on moldy toast is too good for that pig-faced dung beetle."

"You must hate arugula."

"Arugula is Satan's lettuce."

Since she couldn't see his face, he allowed a full smile. He wasn't a fan of arugula either. "Did you have backup for the data?" Pax asked.

"The minister of culture has copies of some of the field notes—preliminary findings, project updates, but not the detailed maps and drawings. Not the hardcore data."

A noise up ahead had Pax stopping short. He held up a fist at shoulder height to signal a halt and hoped Adler knew the sign. She stopped immediately and caught on to the need for silence.

He listened, knowing he'd miss the softer notes because his hearing was still muted by the blast. But even so, the sound of gunfire was unmistakable, as was the basalt spall that hit his shoulder, having been dislodged from the rock to his right by a bullet.

He grabbed her and dropped down, dragging her behind a boulder. He cursed silently. He'd caught a glimpse of at least two men before one had squeezed off the shot.

"Give me a gun," she whispered.

He startled and met her gaze.

Her eyes flicked to the Sig on his belt. "Give me the Sig."

"Are you nuts? You know what would happen to me if anyone found out I gave a civilian my gun?"

"I'd feel safer with a gun, you aren't using it, and we've got at least two militants shooting at us from forty feet away. This isn't the time to worry about what your XO will say."

He placed his hand on the Sig. Shit. She had a certain logic. And if something happened to him, she'd be facing down armed militants alone. They'd kill Pax, but Dr. Morgan Adler? She'd be kept alive. Spoils of war. In Somalia, which was less than ten miles away, ISIS stripped adolescent girls, stood them on auction blocks, and sold them into sexual slavery. Adler would almost certainly suffer the same fate if taken.

"I don't suppose you know how to shoot?" he asked.

She gave a sharp nod. "I'm a good shot."

Pax hoped she wasn't lying.

He handed her the Sig, and she checked the load like someone who was well versed. She rammed the magazine back into the handle. "I'm rusty, but I know what to do." She glanced down at the weapon. "Are the sights true?"

He nodded.

"Good."

"You won't be shooting at paper. Can you shoot a person if you have to?"

"Do you think these men had anything to do with the explosion?"

"Yes." He did, but he'd have said yes either way.

"Then I will blow the motherfuckers' squirrel-sized peckers off."

He smiled, for the first time thinking he might like this woman.

He pulled out a mirror on a telescoping pole and extended it until he had a fix on the shooters' position. They'd have a better shot at the bastards if they took cover behind a boulder fifteen feet to the left. "I'm going to lay down cover fire while you run to that boulder there." He pointed. "Can you do that?"

He could see the fear in her eyes. It was one thing to shoot at targets in a range, another thing to run across a fifteen-foot opening when there was potential for bullets to fly. She straightened her spine. "I can," she said firmly. The alarm in her wide blue eyes disappeared behind a veil of courage. She meant it.

Even more important, she *believed* it.

He gave her a pair of earplugs and inserted his own. Things were about to get loud.

They both moved to a crouching position, and he counted to three with his fingers. On his signal, he opened fire with the M4 and she ran. Short to average height for a woman—he guessed five-four or five-five—she ran in a fast, low crouch, becoming a tiny target with lightning speed. She moved like this was something she'd trained for, making him wonder if she participated in paintball wars or something similar back in the US.

She reached the boulder unscathed and signaled to him. She tucked herself into the cover like a pro and positioned herself to take a shot. He realized she intended to lay down cover fire for him. He shook his head. He'd fire his rifle all the way across. It would be more effective, and he had far more rounds for the M4 than he did for the handgun.

But he couldn't help but grin at the thought of her laying down cover fire for him. Dr. Morgan Adler was a woman full of surprises.

With quick bursts of gunfire, he crossed the opening. The sound echoed through the wadi, the vibration moving the humid air. Again by her side, he nudged her over, into the deepest cover, and he again used the mirror to scope out the enemy.

A crevasse split the wadi wall, and at least one gunman had taken refuge in the fissure. He could see a toe peeking out from the cleft at ground level and the barrel of a rifle poking out at hip height.

Sloppy. These weren't trained soldiers.

A relief, as his A-Team had been training locals, and the idea that they could be under attack from one of the men he'd been teaching to be a guerrilla fighter was a repugnant but ever-present concern.

With his gun fixed on what he estimated was the shooter's head height, he waited. He'd give this poor excuse for a solider five minutes. If he didn't show himself, they'd crisscross to the next boulder.

But the bastard did Pax a favor and peeked around after only thirty seconds. Pax squeezed the trigger as the gunman raised the barrel to his eye. The prick might as well have held up a sign. Blood splattered the boulder.

One tango down, at least one more to go.

Behind him, he heard the scrape of Adler shifting her position. He turned, hoping she wasn't freaking out over the bloodshed. *Shit.* The other man had circled around. He lunged as he aimed his gun at Dr. Adler.

She squeezed off a shot before Pax could raise his weapon.

The man dropped and curled into a ball.

Holy Christ. She really had shot him in the pecker. The man howled in agony.

"You should have aimed center mass."

"I *was* aiming center mass. As I said, I'm out of practice. Plus, he was charging."

Pax pulled out his earplugs and approached the writhing man. He kicked the man's weapon away from his hand and searched his body quickly. No more weapons. This guy couldn't hurt anyone. "How many more?" he asked in French. "How many men are in the wadi?"

The man sobbed denials that there was anyone else blocking their path to the base, and begged to be taken to a US medical facility.

No way would Pax risk himself and Dr. Adler to save a man who'd been charging in for the kill. They would continue down the wadi, heading for the base, hoping there weren't more militants in position. This orchestrated attack on Camp Citron was unlike anything that had been attempted so far, and he feared further treats Desta had in place.

He stood and brushed off his ACU. He'd gotten blood on the uniform. "Let's go," he said to Dr. Adler.

The militant's sobs turned to wails as they walked away, leaving the man to die in the hot wadi. "Desta," the man said. "I can give you Desta." More words tumbled out, but Pax spoke little Arabic, so they were meaningless. The man switched to French, which Pax did speak. "I know where Desta's encampment is. Save me, and I'll tell you. You can send the drones that bring death from the sky."

Chapter Four

Blanchard stopped short and stared at the wailing, babbling man. His flushed face was closed, expression unreadable.

"What did he say?" Morgan asked. She was fairly certain the man's last words were French, but her French was limited to cuisine.

Blanchard unbuckled the straps of his heavy pack and dropped the load at his feet. "He said he can give us Etefu Desta. He knows where the man's encampment is." He knelt next to the wounded man. "He said he'll give up the location in exchange for medical care."

Morgan's whole body came to attention. Etefu Desta had been listed as the most wanted man in the region on every security bulletin she'd received from the embassy.

"Bombing your car was minor compared to the things Desta has done to seize power in Ethiopia and Eritrea," he added.

He was right. They couldn't ignore any lead to Desta's location, even if it came from a dying man who was angling for medical care. She dropped to her knees next to Blanchard. "Know anything about patching gunshot wounds to the groin?"

"Stop the bleeding." He removed the man's hands from his wounded genitals. "Did you *have* to shoot him in the junk?" He turned to his pack and pulled out several pouches marked with red first-aid crosses. "Put pressure on his femoral artery. That will help stem the bleeding. I've got bandages filled with a clotting agent."

She moved and settled on her knees across from Blanchard and unbuttoned the man's pants, trying to decide the best way to pull them down without aggravating the wound.

Bones, dirt, insects, and reptiles didn't make her squeamish, but she'd never had her gag reflex tested by torn flesh and bloody wounds before. She steeled her spine. She could do this.

She took a deep breath. In a flash, the scent of blood baking in the hot sun caused her to gag. *Okay. Breathe through the mouth.* She reached again for the man's waistband and tugged at the cloth.

Blanchard produced a sharp knife and split the man's pants with a quick slice starting at the hip and going all the way to the hem at the ankle. He handed her the knife. "Do the other side," he said, then returned to grabbing medical supplies from his pack.

She copied his action, then peeled the pants down from the front. She grimaced at the sight of blood-covered genitals.

"Do you know how to find his femoral pulse?" Blanchard asked.

"I think so." She'd recertified in CPR and first aid as part of her prep for the trip to Djibouti. She could do this.

She *would* do this.

She centered herself like she did before practicing kata. When she did karate, it was all muscle memory and focus. She could apply that here.

Blanchard handed her surgical gloves and antiseptic wipes. She poured water from the precious bladder he'd given her over the man's crotch to clear away some of the blood, donned the gloves, then used the wipes to find the wound. The bullet had grazed his scrotum and lodged in his inner thigh. Good. It was in the leg, below the artery.

She was breathing normally again; the scent no longer bothered her. She'd dialed in her focus. Nothing mattered but the task before her.

She found his femoral pulse and pressed with the heel of her hand, digging in deep. The man shrieked, likely because the pressure caused blinding pain given the proximity to his wound.

She pressed harder.

The man's wail cut out midstream. He'd passed out from the agony, leaving them with blessed silence.

Blanchard pressed a thick bandage over the wound. It soaked through, but the clotting agent and pressure seemed to be working, because when he removed it to swap out with a fresh bandage, the wound didn't immediately pool with blood. She increased the pressure on the artery as he applied the second bandage. Her arms shook with the effort to maintain pressure.

"You're doing well," he said as he wound gauze around the man's thigh, securing the bandage. He tied off the end.

She relaxed her arms and sat back on her heels, massaging her wrists, which ached from the strain.

"You can't tell anyone you shot him," Blanchard said. "My gun. My bullet. My shot. Unless you want to tank my career."

"I won't tell," she promised.

"Shit. A groin shot. I'm going to be teased about this for months. You said you were a good shot."

She couldn't help but smile at his complaint. "Sorry. It's been over ten years since I fired a gun. I'll hit the next guy center mass. I promise."

"Let's hope there is no next guy."

She let her gaze fall on the unconscious man. "Do you really think he knows where Desta is?"

Blanchard shrugged. "I'm not willing to take a chance and assume he's lying. We've been after Desta too long to let this opportunity pass, and given this assault, we need to take the asshole out. I'll carry him out of the wadi and call for a medic helicopter."

"Won't the copter be at risk from the sniper?"

"Hopefully, Cal will have taken care of the sniper by then."

Morgan stared at the bandage, watching for deep crimson to saturate the bright white, but no red soaked through. If the militant bled out before he reached a medical facility, it wouldn't be because they hadn't tried to save him. She took a deep breath and stood, stretching cramped legs and arms that were tight from the strain of maintaining constant pressure on the artery.

A glance downward showed her favorite field clothes were covered in blood. She probably looked like blonde bimbo number three in a horror movie, and Blanchard definitely looked like he should be the one wielding the chainsaw.

She shucked the gloves, putting them in the bag Blanchard had used for other medical waste, and rubbed down her hands with sanitizing gel. Marginally clean, she grabbed the bladder from the ground and saw she'd gotten blood on the bite valve. She grimaced. No way would she drink from that.

Blanchard offered her the mouthpiece for his hydration pack, and she took a grateful sip of water, then tucked the valve into the sleeve on his pack. "So, I'll take one arm, you take the other, and we'll drag him?" she asked.

"No. That could make the bleeding start up again. I'll carry him."

"Out of the wadi?" She glanced toward the slope. The dry riverbed had narrowed in this area, requiring a deeper valley. "The wall is steep here."

His mouth curved in a cocky smile. "I can handle it. I carried you—while you were kicking and fighting me."

She flushed at the reminder. "I think I'm the one buying tonight."

He looked at her over the top of his sunglasses. His eyes no longer held anger, but then, their truce had been solidified with gunfire. She glimpsed warmth in his gaze, and his lips held a hint of a smile. "You owe me more than that."

It was like he'd flipped the switch to her libido. Sure, she'd noticed he was attractive before, but it had been an abstract perception, like seeing a good-looking actor in a movie and enjoying his looks in a passive, impersonal way. But with one faint smile and a trace of humor, his appealing features went from theoretical to concrete. She went from thinking *he's hot* to *I want a piece of that.*

Did she want a piece of that?

Her eyes landed full stop on the words "US ARMY" over his left breast.

He wasn't *just* military, he was Army. A Green Beret, no less. Her father would *love* Sergeant Pax Blanchard.

Which put the soldier high on her no-way-in-hell list. She definitely did *not* want a piece of that.

She cleared her throat and inserted a chill into her voice. "Well, I'm afraid a drink is all you're going to get."

He cocked his head. "Relax, Dr. Adler. I was kidding."

"Morgan," she corrected again.

"Call me Pax. Hell, call me anything except Hulk. Not even Cal is supposed to call me that." He nodded toward his gear. "Can you carry my pack?"

She nodded.

"Good." He pulled out his radio and spoke in the foreign language of military radio code. Task complete, he tucked it away and nodded for her to don his pack while he lifted the wounded militant.

Holy hell, his pack was heavy. She contained her curses, having no desire to show him what a weakling she was.

He'd carried her while wearing this thing? In this heat? The guy wasn't the Hulk, he was Captain America.

Captain America just so happened to be her favorite Avenger.

Burdened with the wounded militant who was undernourished and probably weighed a hundred and twenty pounds, Pax climbed the steep wall of the wadi.

Trailing behind, she tried to hide her labored breathing as she hauled a pack that was only one third that weight up the same slope. Pebbles rolled out from under her feet, threatening to trip her as the sun beat down on her head.

This was why she'd never joined the military, in spite of her father's intense pressure. Her dig kit was heavy enough, thank you very much.

Just when she thought she might pass out from the heat and exertion, she reached the lip and collapsed on the ground. So much for masking her wimpiness. Vomiting sounded really good right now, except she was too dehydrated for even that.

"Go on without me," she muttered as Blanchard—*Pax*—continued forward without breaking stride.

"No time for a rest break, Adler." His voice oozed disdain. "We're exposed and need to take cover while we wait for the helo."

He sounded just like her father. Bastard.

She surged to her feet, finding strength in the desire to avoid embarrassment and the need to prove herself to this stranger.

He reached an alcove at the base of a mesa and tucked the unconscious man in the enclosed space. Morgan dumped his pack at his feet and dropped to the ground, desperately hoping she wouldn't hurl.

Her entire body was flushed, and she could barely breathe in the thick, hot air. Her sunglasses slipped off her sweaty face, and, too tired to retrieve them, she closed her eyes against the blistering sunlight. Her heart pounded as blood pulsed along her occipital nerve. She was one step shy of a migraine, and her heart felt ready to explode.

"You did well," Pax said.

She cracked open one eye to see the accompanying smirk but was surprised to glimpse nothing of the sort. He looked sincere. She drew her brows together. This man made no sense.

"You did. I figured you'd react more strongly if I was an ass. Stopping there wasn't safe."

He'd manipulated her to spur her out of danger?

Cunning, yet embarrassing that he'd correctly guessed how to get her moving. Her father had wielded humiliation too, but she supposed this was different. Pax's taunt might have saved her life.

He'd get a pass on his methods. *Once.*

Her pounding pulse slowed to a more normal rhythm. Breathing became less of a chore. Maybe she wouldn't die of heat exhaustion. Speaking of dying, she twisted to look at the unconscious militant. "How is our patient?" she wheezed out the words.

"Still breathing."

"How long until we can get a copter?"

His shrug was anything but casual, and she realized he was worried. About Callahan.

On a conscious level, she knew today's events weren't her fault. She was a victim. But the brain didn't always accept logic as fact, and in fighting Pax to get to the fossils, she'd made the situation worse.

It *felt* like everything was her fault.

The explosion. The IED. The sniper. She was responsible. The catalyst. Or maybe Linus was. Regardless, it fell on her shoulders, which was a heavy, horrific weight to bear.

What if Callahan was injured or killed? He was out here because of her. Because she'd stepped right into Desta's trap and acted exactly as he'd expected her to.

A single gunshot reported in the distance.

She met Pax's gaze as he stiffened, holding his radio in a tight grip. The silence broke with a rustle of static, then a voice she suspected was Cal's.

She heaved a sigh of relief as a wide grin broke out on Pax's face.

She felt his smile low in her belly.

Oh yeah, I definitely want a piece of that.

Less than five minutes after the militant was whisked to a Navy ship via helicopter, a Humvee rolled up to take Morgan and Pax to the base. It had been less than three hours since he and Cal had laid down the tack strip in the roadway and set up their roadblock. He pulled off his helmet and settled into the rear seat beside Morgan. He scanned her as she leaned back and closed her eyes.

Long blonde hairs had escaped her braid and now adhered to her flushed, sweaty brow and neck. Her clothing, arms, and hands were splattered with blood, and dust had settled into the damp creases of her skin, giving a hint to how she'd look years from now, when facial wrinkles would be more pronounced.

She'd be a beautiful, aging fairy.

She looked so delicate, yet it had been made more than clear in their short acquaintance she was no fragile blossom. She'd escaped an explosion without hysterics—well, except for the part about being pissed at him for saving her—shot a man without flinching, and then proceeded to help save that man's life.

His anger at her had evaporated in the scorching heat and been replaced by something entirely different.

Simple, basic lust. A side effect of adrenaline that usually had no focal point when a combat mission was completed.

She was feeling it too. He'd seen it in her eyes as they waited for the copter, felt it in the charge that rippled through her when she'd accepted his help climbing into the backseat of the armored vehicle.

And, like him, she was trying to ignore it.

Did she know adrenaline was the cause, or was that new for her?

He doubted her work usually got the adrenaline pumping in quite this way. But then, she'd moved through the wadi like a seasoned soldier.

"The base commander wants me to take you both straight to HQ," the marine in the driver's seat said.

"She needs to be checked out by a medic first."

He could see the driver's frown in the rearview mirror, but he didn't argue. How could he when she was covered in blood? Sure, it was someone else's blood, but that needed to be confirmed. The woman needed to be hydrated and checked for signs of shock.

On the base, they entered the medical clinic together, and Morgan was quickly whisked into an examining room. Pax turned to leave, intending to head straight to the commander's office, but Janelle, a pretty, petite African American medic with a heavy Brooklyn accent stopped him. "Not so fast, Blanchard. You step into my building after an explosion and exchanging gunfire, and you get examined like everyone else."

"I'm fine."

"You aren't fine until I tell you you're fine."

Ten minutes later, Janelle tucked away her stethoscope. "You're fine," she said with a wide grin. She scanned him from head to toe. "But don't tell Dion I said that."

Pax laughed. Dion, a fellow Special Forces operator, and Janelle had been having a not-so-secret fling for the last month. Given that they were in different branches of the military and neither was an officer, fraternization rules didn't apply, but it would be damn hard to maintain the relationship when one or the other was sent home. A reason to avoid in-country flings.

Or maybe a reason to have them.

Pax reached for his blood-coated shirt and pulled it on, wondering if he had time to take a shower and change before Dr. Adler would be released, but she was in the waiting area when he stepped out of the examination room. She clutched a thirty-two-ounce bottle of blue Gatorade to her chest and made a face when the doctor admonished her to drink the whole bottle.

Dr. Carson turned to Pax. "Make sure she finishes it, Sergeant. If she refuses, I want her back in here for an IV."

It appeared he was once again Dr. Morgan Adler's babysitter. Given the adrenaline-fueled thoughts that ripped through his brain every time he looked at her—dirt, sweat, blood, and all—he didn't find the role nearly as annoying as he had in the wadi.

"Yes, sir," he said. He led Morgan out of the building. The early afternoon heat hit him in a wave, and that fast, he was sweating again. He took the sport drink from her hands and twisted open the top, breaking the seal. He handed it back to her. "Drink."

She frowned. "I don't trust beverages that are colors not found in nature."

"Flowers are that shade of blue."

She rolled her eyes. "Not found in *food*. Did you know blue is a sign something is poisonous or spoiled? We're hard-wired by evolution to avoid blue food. Even blueberries aren't really blue—they're green inside with purple skin, which is why they *look* blue but have purple juice, not Smurf-vomit blue."

The adrenaline had a tighter grip on him than he thought, because he even found her obstinance appealing. And obstinance was never appealing. "You've put a lot of thought into this."

"I wrote a paper on it as an undergrad." She studied the bottle. "They were out of red at the clinic."

He placed a finger under the bottle, tilting it up to her mouth. As she drank, he leaned into her and spoke softly. "After we meet with the base commander, I'll take you to Barely North—the bar on base—and spike your Gatorade."

She lowered the bottle and swallowed. There was a sheen of blue on her lips, and he had the urge to lick the moisture away. "I don't think the doctor would approve," she said in a husky voice, and it took a moment to realize she was responding to his words, not his thoughts.

But then, the doctor probably wouldn't approve of his thoughts either. "He said to make sure you finish the Gatorade." Pax shrugged and flashed a not-very-innocent smile.

She smiled back, and he felt heat that had nothing to do with the sweltering day and high humidity.

A horn sounded behind him, and he turned to see Cal at the wheel of an open-top utility vehicle. "Get in."

Even though he'd known Cal was okay, Pax felt relief at seeing him just the same. Morgan made a beeline for the back. Pax took the front passenger seat.

Cal's gaze scanned Morgan before he turned to face the road. "Damn, Pax, you had one job. What the hell sort of babysitter are you?" Then he glanced sideways at Pax. "And I hear you hit a guy in the nuts. Do we need to send you back to remedial shooting school?"

Pax rolled his eyes. "I was aiming for his balls so he'd live and give up Desta's lair."

"Right." Cal put the Gator in gear and gave them a brief rundown of his encounter with the sniper as he drove them to the CO's office. He buzzed with energy and looked ready to run a 10K, which was how he usually burned residual adrenaline.

Pax usually went to the gym and beat the hell out of a punching bag to dispel it. But today, proximity to a foul-mouthed fairy had led to a different adrenaline reaction.

Put simply, he wanted to fuck.

He'd get through the meeting with the base commander and head to the gym. Showering would have to wait. He needed to get the adrenaline out of his system before it made him completely stupid.

Morgan tilted her head back and filled her mouth with the vile blue stuff as they neared the CO's office. The nausea was gone, and the doctor had given her a strong painkiller for the headache. With aches and pains at bay, her body wanted a different sort of release.

Damn adrenaline. She'd experienced this type of rush before, but it was after white-water rafting, not after shooting a man.

Jesus, she'd shot a man.

And now she wanted sex.

What kind of monster did that make her?

She studied the Green Berets in the front seat. Cal seemed hyped up. Floating on adrenaline. Pax turned and met her gaze, but his expression was shuttered. Locked tight.

No doubt both men knew how to deal with this adrenaline ride.

She sucked in a deep breath and told herself sex was not an option. It wasn't like she was rocking the bloody, sweaty, disheveled look. She needed to focus on the upcoming meeting with the base commander, then she needed to return to her apartment, pack her bags, and catch a flight.

No way in hell was she staying in Djibouti after today. Not even for Linus.

She'd have to move back in with her parents and face her father's crowing I-told-you-so lecture. He hadn't been supportive of her decision to major in anthropology, and when she'd decided to quit her job at a large architecture and engineering firm so she could work on her PhD full-time, he'd vowed she'd regret going into debt for a useless degree.

She and the general had difficulty getting along on a good day. It sucked even more when he was right.

It would only be made worse by the fact that he'd finally praised her when she'd landed this military-related contract. He'd gone so far as to say her education might not have been a complete waste of time, given that her work would make it possible for the US Navy to expand the boundaries of Camp Citron and thereby increase the capacity for rapid-response deployments throughout all of North and East Africa.

But now she'd be going home with her tail between her legs and carrying an even greater debt load. Her one-woman archaeological consulting firm would declare bankruptcy after only six months in business, and she would be the only PhD serving wings and beer at Double D. The chain restaurant's name was supposed to refer to drumsticks and drinks, but everyone knew what the Ds really stood for.

Her father would burst a blood vessel, but hopefully he'd lay off the scorn when he understood that someone had tried to kill her.

Again, her gaze fixed on Pax. He was the type of man her father had always wanted her to bring home, which was why Morgan had gone instead for the soft-spoken poet type. The peacenik environmentalists, those were her people. Plus, they irritated the hell out of the general, which made them even more attractive.

So she was shallow and out to piss off her dad. At least the guys were nice, and they always respected women. Some were even stauncher feminists than she was.

They were caring and determined to prove they understood the discrimination she faced and always went above and beyond to ensure she came first. The sex was good, and they pitched in for birth control and volunteered their sexual health history. Some of them would probably take on the burden of menstruating if they could. But sometimes she hated to admit she might be attracted to a guy who wasn't so insistent on being understanding. A guy who admitted to liking guns because it was scientifically proven that just touching one upped a guy's testosterone level.

Just once she wanted to date a guy who was as pro-testosterone as he was pro-estrogen.

She wasn't about to dis estrogen—some of her best friends were loaded with estrogen, and some might say she had more than her fair share—but she was also a fan of testosterone.

A big fan.

God, she missed testosterone.

The way Pax had carried her while wearing a heavy pack and body armor in a hundred-and-five-degree heat. That required some serious testosterone.

No. Absolutely not. The general would approve too much.

"Morgan?" Pax asked.

She shook her head to clear it. They'd reached headquarters, but she'd been too lost in thought to notice. Okay, so maybe she was more rattled than she wanted to admit over the day's events. She took a last gulp of the Gatorade and set the bottle on the seat, then climbed out, taking Pax's proffered hand, trying to ignore the jolt his touch gave her.

Contact testosterone. Lovely, lovely testosterone.

She was led through the front offices directly to the base commander's door. The man's aide asked her to wait, while the two Green Berets met with the Navy captain first. She dropped into a seat and closed her eyes. The explosion flashed in her mind. A viper slid over a boot. And she pressed her hands against a man's bleeding groin. She'd washed her face and hands in the medical clinic, but her clothes were still covered in dust and blood.

Why had a bomb been planted under her rental car? Was this about Linus or something else?

Finally, she was admitted to the captain's office. Captain O'Leary greeted her with a handshake and bade her sit in the lone visitor's chair in front of his desk. She glanced back to see Cal and Pax remain standing, flanking the door. Their blank faces resembled the soldiers she'd first met a few hours ago on the road.

She described in detail the arrival of Desta's henchmen at the site and everything that had followed after. She also admitted—to her chagrin—that she'd tried to save the fossils. She glanced over her shoulder and met the gaze of the man who'd saved her life and again apologized to him.

The Navy captain sat impassively and listened. When she finished, she asked, "Has there been any word on the condition of the militant who was shot? Is he going to be able to provide Desta's location?"

Captain O'Leary shifted forward in his seat. "He's in surgery. He lost a lot of blood, and he's malnourished. The surgeon didn't give good odds of him surviving the night. Only time will tell."

If he didn't survive, it would mean the bullet she'd fired killed him. On one level, she knew she didn't have a choice, but on another…she'd never had a man's death on her conscience before. She cleared her throat. "Now that I've told you everything I know, is there more you need from me?"

"For today, no. You've had a difficult day. You should rest. For your protection, you've been assigned a private CLU here on base."

"Clue?" she asked, wondering if she'd misheard him.

"Containerized Living Units—Camp Citron's housing. It's not safe for you to return to Djibouti City. You'll live here on base while you complete your project."

She startled at that. "That's very kind of you, sir, but I was planning to return to my apartment in Djibouti City and start packing. I'd like to fly back to the US as soon as I can. I'm done here." She placed her hand against the empty pouch at her belly and glanced back at Pax. "Do you have my phone and passport?"

Pax remained silent until the Navy captain inclined his head, giving him permission to speak. He pulled both items from his shirt pocket. He stepped forward to give it to her, but the captain stood and said, "I'll take the passport."

Pax didn't break stride and handed the commander her passport, then he gave her the phone. She grimaced when she saw the screen. Busted. It must have hit the ground when they'd rolled after the blast. She tried to power it up without luck. Another item for the list of things she'd lost in the blast.

She faced the commander. He studied her passport, then tucked the blue booklet into his desk.

Alarm shot through her at the simple gesture. *What the hell?*

"You'll get your passport back tomorrow. You're in no condition to leave the base tonight."

He was keeping her passport. With the embassy closed, he was effectively trapping her in Djibouti. "I'm afraid I don't understand, Captain. Am I being detained?"

"Not at all. I just want to ensure you give your decision whether to stay in Djibouti or go home serious consideration. You're rattled after the day's events. Naturally, your first impulse is to leave."

"A bomb was planted under my car," she said, allowing her anger and frustration to enter her voice. This man wasn't *her* superior officer.

"I understand how upsetting that must have been."

"I was shot at by militants. That doesn't happen often in my line of work."

O'Leary smiled. "Finding a three-million-year-old hominid with tools doesn't happen often in your line of work either."

His words gave her pause, but all she had to do was close her eyes to see and feel the heat of the blast that should have killed her. "I'm a one-woman consulting firm. I can't take on a warlord's armed militia."

Captain O'Leary sighed. "You signed a contract, Dr. Adler. You promised the governments of Ethiopia and Djibouti you would survey the two proposed routes. There is no one else available to do the work, and the railroad can't proceed until your project is done."

"A *bomb* was planted under my car, Captain."

"You were made aware you could be targeted when you signed the contract."

True, but she hadn't really *believed* it.

The captain leaned his elbows on his desk. "The US Navy has a vested interest in you completing your contract. You know this. We're assisting the local government with the expansion of the port and expediting the work on the rail line. In exchange, we'll get to expand Camp Citron. This base is strategically important to the War on Terror, but we're packed in and unable to advance our operations because we don't have the land we need to conduct the necessary trainings and build our own airstrip and control tower. Air traffic control is a joke at the Djibouti airport. It's only a matter of time before US military personnel die in a civilian-caused air traffic accident. If you leave now, those deaths will be on your head." He fixed her with a glare. "Do you really want that kind of stain on your soul?"

The man's words were a low blow. So low it practically knocked the wind out of her. She simmered with rage even as his words found fertile ground in her mind.

Her stomach rolled. Military personnel wouldn't die because she didn't finish her survey, they would die because a warlord was gunning for everyone who had a role in making the base expansion happen. The warlord was the enemy, not her.

But right then, she felt like the enemy.

She cleared her throat to deny his point, but the officer interrupted before she got a word out. "You need time to think about it. You've been assigned a single wet CLU—a luxury many of my sailors would be grateful for—for the duration of your time in Djibouti. My aide will show you to your quarters. I'll expect an answer from you at sixteen hundred tomorrow. You are dismissed."

She gripped the arms of the chair. She'd been commanded and dismissed her entire life, but she sure as hell wasn't part of this man's chain of command. She was a civilian and not employed by the Navy. "I'll call my father." She'd never, ever played the general card before.

"General Adler? Wrong branch of the military."

So. He'd done his homework today. She narrowed her gaze. "He has friends at the Pentagon."

The captain shrugged and picked up his phone. He punched a button and said, presumably to his aide, "Get General Adler on the line again."

Again?

Fuck.

Moments later, the captain hit the button for the speakerphone, not bothering to hide his smirk.

It wasn't yet dawn in Fairfax County, Virginia, where her parents lived. But her father was wide-awake and gunning for her with the same ferocity as Etefu Desta. "Dammit, Morgan, if you'd been born with balls, you wouldn't be trying to turn tail and run. That project was the first time since you were eighteen you were actually doing something right. You think you can abandon your project and hightail it home? Think again. It's about time you used that wasted education for something worthwhile."

Her belly churned. This was dear old Dad. "General,"—she'd stopped calling him Dad when she was eighteen and still wondered if he'd noticed or even cared—"they placed a bomb under my car."

"All the more reason to fight back! Christ, girl, if every soldier went crying home after someone tried to shoot them, we'd all be speaking German right now."

"I'm not a soldier."

"Damn right, because you don't have the balls."

Her face had flushed with his first insult, knowing the two Green Berets overheard her humiliation, but now she'd passed embarrassment and moved into rage. Since she was eighteen, she'd gone for rebellion instead of outright telling her father off. No more. "Why would I want balls?" She tried to get a grip on her anger as she adapted her favorite Betty White quote. "Have you ever seen a woman taken out with a simple kick to the crotch? Hell no, because a vagina can take a beating. I'd like to see you squeeze a baby out of your precious, fragile balls." *You intolerant, jizz-headed ass.*

One of these days, she'd get the courage to say the last part aloud to the man. She'd been polishing her cursing skills as diligently as she'd once practiced her karate kata, preparing for the day she'd have the courage to let loose on her father.

She could forget moving in with the folks while she begged for her old job at Double D. Maybe Staci would let her crash on her couch. They could carpool to the restaurant, which would be necessary because Morgan had sold her car to buy her plane ticket to Djibouti.

She stood without a word and turned toward the door. First she met Cal's gaze, then Pax's. His eyes were hard, cold. His jaw clenched, he positively radiated resentment.

She was taken aback by the hostility in his gaze.

Just what she needed. Captain America had sided with her father. She fixed him with a glare.

Behind her, O'Leary said good-bye to her father and shut off the speaker. "You can't simply leave, Dr. Adler."

She whirled to face the man who'd just blithely triggered what could well be the end of her relationship with her father—and by extension her mother, because even though Mom didn't always agree with the general, in the end, the two were a package deal.

She opened her mouth to speak, but no words came out. She'd been rendered speechless.

"Go to your quarters. Take a shower. Think about it. Return here at sixteen hundred tomorrow, and tell me your answer."

She gave the man a sharp nod, spun on her heel, and left the office without meeting either Green Beret's gaze again.

Chapter Five

It wasn't the best shower of Pax's life, but it ranked in the top fifty. He scrubbed the dried blood from his skin, the stain of an enemy combatant, and tried not to think about the pain in Morgan Adler's eyes after her phone conversation with her prick of a father.

Christ. She was a general's daughter. That should put her on the do-not-touch list for all time, but the fact that the relationship between father and daughter was a wreck made her a possible exception to the rule.

He'd been shocked but relieved when she said she was heading home. He'd have happily helped her pack her bags. Djibouti was no place for idealists who didn't understand the explosive nature of the region. A civilian like Morgan had no business getting in the way.

But Captain O'Leary didn't see it that way, and he was the man in charge.

After Morgan left, O'Leary asked for Cal's and Pax's take on her. They both had played it simple. *Just met her, don't know her. Seems competent.* They both admitted to being surprised she wanted to leave, given her feelings toward Linus the australopithecine.

The commander had probably filed that away as another screw to tighten. Captain O'Leary might be Navy, not Army, but it was his base, and Cal and Pax had been in the Army long enough to know better than to second-guess a commander's already-issued orders.

He'd left the meeting and gone straight to the gym, where he beat the crap out of a bag. Cal joined him for a change, skipping his usual run in favor of unleashing aggression on an inanimate object. Pax had a feeling Cal was exorcising the same outrage, but said nothing on the subject—not in the public gym. That conversation would wait until they were in their shared CLU.

Workout complete, he showered, then finally went to their CLU and collapsed on his cot. The units all had air-conditioning, making the metal box he called home bearable, but theirs was a dry CLU. No shower, no bathroom. No privacy.

He slept for an hour, a quick, rejuvenating nap as he was trained to do. Cal returned sometime while he slept, and he was deep asleep when Pax rose from his cot. He had a sneaking suspicion that Morgan Adler would make her way to Barely North tonight, either hoping to drink her way into oblivion or looking for action to release adrenaline and escape from the horrors of her day.

Like a fool, Pax dressed in his civvies, not knowing if he intended to stop her or help her achieve her goal.

B arely North was crowded, but then, it had been a day of action for many on the base, with the explosion, the attack on the convoy, and the roadside bomb. A lot of people needed to blow off steam, making Morgan wonder if the two-drink limit would be firm tonight or not.

Not that it mattered, because she wasn't here to drink. No, she was here to find someone to take her off the base. She needed to check on Linus and find her crew leader, Ibrahim. She needed to make sure he and the rest of her crew were okay.

Captain O'Leary had made her all but a prisoner here, but she wasn't the type of person to make an important decision uninformed. She needed to know if any of her crew had been harmed and to make sure they received care if they had. She had to know what happened to them before she could decide whether or not to stay in Djibouti.

She tugged at the tight Camp Citron T-shirt she'd found on the cot inside her CLU. The T-shirt had been accompanied by lightweight pants, bra, and underwear, and assorted toiletries. The bra was at least one D too small and the T-shirt rode up thanks to her oversized bust. All items sported tags from the base store, and she wondered if they'd been out of her size or if the person who'd acquired the items had simply made a mistake. Regardless, she was thankful she didn't have to wear her sweaty, bloodstained clothing and had crammed herself into the bra without complaint.

The fact that the bra and T-shirt were tight could work in her favor. She hadn't put the twins on display since she quit waiting tables at Double D, but tonight she needed to talk to sailors and marines to find a ride off base, and the girls would come in handy.

At least her years as a server had made her comfortable with the reaction her curves triggered. She knew how to ignore the creepy leers and enjoyed the generic appreciation—after all, it would be hypocritical of her to use her physical assets for bigger tips if men and women enjoying the view bothered her. But the disgusting tongue wagging? That she could do without.

She made her way toward the bar, grabbing an empty stool near the end. She ordered a tonic with lime. A drink would knock her on her ass, especially given the painkiller the doctor had prescribed, but she could at least *look* like she was drinking—and therefore approachable.

She scanned the club. Who could she convince to help her?

She needed a sailor who could check out a vehicle from the motor pool, which might not be possible with heightened security after today. She really didn't know this base's procedures.

She took a sip of her tonic as she watched a group of sailors playing pool. Far too young. She couldn't flirt to start a conversation with a boy in his late teens or early twenties. She was thirty-one, and the thought of flirting with a boy who couldn't drink legally gave her the heebie-jeebies. Like *she* was the creepy old guy doing the tongue wagging. No, thank you.

Anyone over twenty-one was fair game. At least then she wouldn't feel like a pervy professor.

A soldier like Pax would be perfect. He was old enough—she guessed he was in his early thirties—and she wouldn't even have to fake interest. Except he'd sided with the general, which put him on her blacklist for all eternity. The look Pax had given her in the captain's office had been her father's final humiliation.

She tightened her jaw when the object of her thoughts stepped into the crowded room. Her gaze met his, and she cast him a glare before turning back to the bar. *Shit.* She should have started a conversation with a sailor to either side of her. The one to the right stared unabashedly at her chest. His gaze was of the trying-to-decide-if-the-twins-are-real variety.

She could feel Pax approaching and didn't like the tingle of anticipation that started at the base of her skull. She did *not* want to be attracted to the man.

"Morgan," he said, slipping into the narrow space at her side.

She met Pax's gaze straight on. "Dr. Adler," she corrected. Damn, he looked good in a short-sleeved button-down shirt and slacks. He loomed just as large without the pack, combat gear, and helmet.

He raised a brow. "I'm pretty sure you invited me to use your given name earlier."

"I changed my mind."

Those thick brows lowered. "Care to share why?"

She leaned back to get a better look at him. He stood so close, filling the scant space next to her barstool, she had to crane her neck to meet his gaze, putting her in a weak position she didn't care for. "Not really," she said as she slid off her stool. She'd head over to the pool tables and start a conversation with the guy leaning against the wall who had a bored expression on his face.

Pax caught her arm. "What the fuck, Morgan?"

She shook off his hand. "I don't need your judgment, Pax. I grew up with that bullshit, and I'm done."

His head cocked. "This is about your dickhead father?"

"Of course it's about my—" She stopped short, realizing what he'd said. "What? Dickhead?" She frowned. "But you agreed with him. You think I'm a coward."

"Why the fuck would I agree with that asshole? And what gave you the idea I think you're a coward? Jesus. You tried to run back to a car with a bomb in the undercarriage." His brows came together. "I'd never call you a coward."

"But I don't want to stay in Djibouti. I want to go home."

"That doesn't make you a coward. That makes you smart. Now, assuming I'm a judgmental prick...I'm not sure I can let that one pass."

"I saw the way you looked at me. In Captain O'Leary's office."

"Sweetheart, what you saw was outrage—directed at your old man. He sounds like a piece of work." He nudged her back onto the barstool. "Why don't you buy me a drink to apologize for insulting me, and we'll talk?"

She'd been so rude to him, a drink would never cover it. "I'm sorry," she said as she waved the bartender over.

Pax's drink was served in a flash, and he chuckled. "I've never been served here that quickly." His gaze flicked over her chest.

She gave a sheepish smile. "Putting the girls on display does have advantages. But, in my defense, this was the only clean shirt in my CLU, and I didn't pick the size."

Pax snorted. "If you were my sister, I'd be glued to your side with my weapon handy."

"And if I weren't your sister?"

He took a sip of his drink and gave her the exact right kind of appreciative look. Nothing creepy, just a sweep of his eyes that said he liked what he saw. "Same position, different weapon."

Morgan laughed as heat pooled in her belly. Maybe Pax would help her after all. She leaned into him, inhaling deeply and enjoying the musky scent that her brain registered as pure testosterone. "Pax, will you come back to my CLU with me?"

He grinned. "You don't waste time, do you, *Dr. Adler?*"

"Morgan," she corrected, again feeling chagrined. "And I didn't mean that in the way it sounded."

His voice dipped to a sexy rumble. "That's...disappointing."

The heat in her belly radiated outward. "Then maybe you can convince me otherwise."

It was ridiculously difficult to keep his eyes on her face. He was a grown man and had been intimately familiar with his fair share of breasts over the years, but Morgan Adler's centerfold figure had caught him off guard. He'd known she had curves, but nothing like this.

Earlier, she'd downplayed her figure with her baggy top, and odds were she'd been wearing a sports bra then, whereas this one fit her like a push-up—for a woman who clearly didn't need the boost.

He wondered if the skipper's aide had picked up a small shirt for her on purpose, to prevent her from leaving her CLU. Morgan's dad was career military. She'd likely grown up on bases and knew what deployed soldiers were like.

He was outraged at the sexist manipulation and battling his own lust. The guy to her right had his gaze locked on her breasts, and a possessive side of Pax wanted to stake a claim on this view for himself, which was straight-up wacked. He barely knew her.

But that didn't stop him from planting his hand at the small of her back. The tight shirt rode up just enough that his palm straddled both shirt and bare skin, and the contact was electric. He leaned into her and said, "I don't care *why* you invited me to your CLU; we're going. I don't like the way every guy in this room is looking at you."

She cocked her head and a faint smile played around her full lips. She leaned slightly forward, causing his hand to slip closer to her ass. Their lips were only inches apart. "I can take care of myself. Besides, you're looking at me the same way," she whispered.

The adrenaline that had hounded him hadn't been dispelled by the hour he spent in the gym. If anything, pounding on the bag had only ratcheted up his aggression.

He wanted to fuck, and Morgan Adler was just about the sexiest woman he'd ever seen. That might be the adrenaline thinking, but he doubted it.

The funny thing was, she looked nothing like his type. With her long blonde hair, blue eyes, spectacular breasts, and nearly cropped top, she looked like a waitress from one of those restaurants that served beer and chicken wings to guys watching football. He'd always felt sorry for the waitresses. Treated like brainless sex objects, they had to put up with groping, drunken customers while sporting falsely cheerful smiles in response to asinine jokes.

His type was the shy, bookish nerds, which was exactly what *he'd* been until he joined the Army. He'd been a late bloomer, hitting a second growth spurt after nineteen, when he'd shot up six inches in two years and packed on the muscle that made it possible for him to do his job. But the external changes hadn't changed who he was inside, and he was still the sci-fi- and fantasy-loving guy who read scientific journals for fun.

But then, Dr. Morgan Adler might not *look* like his type, but with a PhD in archaeology, she was most definitely a geek girl in a cheerleader package.

"Does it bother you? The way I look at you?" he asked.

She licked her lips. Her voice came out husky, as if he'd made her throat dry. "No. From you, I like it. I just wish I didn't."

He picked up his gin and tonic and knocked it back, then set the glass on the bar. "Let's go." He guided her across the room with his hand at the small of her back. His free hand curled into a fist as every sailor they passed between the bar and the door leered at Morgan.

He slid his hand along her bare skin, cradling her hip to pull her snug against his side, making it clear she was taken. They were in a room full of alpha sailors, soldiers, and marines, but Pax's height and build put him bigger than ninety percent of the men in the room. Eyes shifted from Morgan's body to Pax's possessive hold, to finally meet his glare. A few, the men he knew, tipped their heads in acknowledgment as they passed.

Outside, it was a quick walk from the club to CLUville. Her unit was at the far end. Hers was deluxe—a wet CLU—meaning she had her own sink inside her private unit and shared a toilet and shower with the adjacent CLU. Because Pax's mind was bent on getting her naked, that private shower immediately brought to mind ways they could conserve the most precious resource in this water-starved nation.

He shut the door and leaned back against it, his eyes scanning her from head to toe, reminding himself she hadn't invited him here for a screw.

But still, that didn't mean he couldn't have a taste. He caught her wrist and pulled her against him, slid his hand down her back until he cupped her butt.

Her body molded to his. He clenched his jaw against the lust that ripped through him.

He shouldn't be doing this. He had no idea how much she'd had to drink before he got to the bar. She *seemed* fine, but what if she held her booze really well? There were rules against that sort of thing. "How much have you had to drink?"

"Nothing. Just tonic."

Relief rippled through him. "Okay, then. Tell me right now if this is what you want."

She gripped his shirt in her fists. "What I want and what's going to happen are two different things. I want your cock"—she ground her hips into his erection and he gritted his teeth as fierce want made him even harder—"inside me. I want to lose myself, lose this insane, awful day in hard, wild animal fucking."

Aww, shit. She'd just described his favorite way to end a crap day.

His grip on her butt tightened. "But that's not what's going to happen here."

"No. Not after I tell you what I need."

"What do you need?"

"I don't know if I'm going to stay or go, but I can't possibly make a decision like that without talking to my crew, without checking on Linus. I'm trapped here. I need a ride off base."

Chapter Six

Pax's grip on her ass loosened. She stepped back, missing his heat, hating herself for being honest. She could have screwed him first, then asked. But that wasn't how she operated. Work first, then play.

No results, no cookie.

He pushed off the door and paced the tiny floor space between cot and locker. "It's not that simple, Morgan."

"Can you get a vehicle from the motor pool?"

He stopped and scrubbed a hand across his face. "Possibly, but I need—even *you* need—signed orders to exit the base."

"Signed orders?"

"This isn't like the bases you grew up on pre-9/11. We're in a hostile environment. Outside that gate, people are trying to kill us."

She pursed her lips. "I'm aware of that."

"I'm not sure you are, if you think I can just whisk you off base. It doesn't work that way. I'd need signed orders from my XO."

"Would your XO need approval from O'Leary?"

"No. Different tenant command. I'm in Special Operations—SOCOM."

"Do you agree with O'Leary? That I should stay?"

"O'Leary is doing his job. His job is to command the base, and we need an airstrip. Desperately. Your project can make that happen."

"So you think I should stay."

"No. I was just saying O'Leary isn't wrong in wanting you to stay. *I* want you on the next flight home. Djibouti is no place for a woman like you."

She stepped back and crossed her arms. "A woman like me? What the hell does that mean?"

"A fool who thinks fossils are worth dying for."

Cold shot to her core. "A fool. You think I'm a fool."

"You sure as hell acted like one earlier."

"No. I think I acted like one *tonight*." Why did she think he'd be any different from her father? "Do you have any idea what those fossils could have meant? Tests could have been run—potassium-argon dating. Analysis of the fauna—I don't even know *what* Linus was butchering the day he died. Combined with what we'll learn from Linus' cranium, we have a chance to understand the connection between australopithecines and the first homo genus in a way we never have before.

"So yeah, I was blinded for a moment at the idea that one of the greatest scientific finds of the new millennium was about to be lost, and I tried to save it. I'm sorry I endangered you because it was my risk to take and my risk alone, but if you'd let me grab it in that first moment, I *could* have saved it."

"We didn't know how much time we had." He ground out the words through a tight jaw. He was angry. Well, that made two of them.

"I know that. I don't blame you. I'm sorry I risked your life. But I don't regret the impulse I had to save a piece of prehuman prehistory nearly so much as I regret the loss of it."

She pulled at the hem of the T-shirt, suddenly feeling exposed in a way she hadn't wearing the skimpy shirt in the bar. She'd been used to men thinking she was an idiot when she waited tables in the tight tank tops and short shorts, but at least then she took solace in the knowledge that her IQ probably outdistanced the drunken frat boys by a mile. Their opinion didn't matter because they didn't *know* her.

Well, Pax Blanchard didn't know her either. She stepped to the door and grabbed the handle.

"Where do you think you're going?" he asked.

"Back to the club. If you won't help me, I'm going to find someone who will. I *need* to know what happened to my crew today. For all I know, Desta's men went after them. They could be dead. I will *not* make a decision to stay or go without knowing what happened to my crew."

"Why don't you just call them?"

"Aside from the fact that my phone is broken, none of them have phones."

Pax cursed. "You can't go back to the club like that."

"Like what? Pissed?"

"Dressed like that."

She glared at him. "You're right. The pants are too long. Do you have scissors on you?"

He whipped off his shirt, revealing a washboard stomach that ten minutes ago would have had her salivating. What a waste for a complete ass to have such a perfect body. "Put this on."

She couldn't help but smirk as she pulled off the tee, giving him a prime view of her overflowing bra, then slipped on his button-down shirt. But she didn't bother with the buttons. She tied the tails together right below her breasts, making his shirt far more revealing than the ridiculously small T-shirt had been. "Is that better?"

She met his gaze and took satisfaction in the shocked look that transformed to pure testosterone-fueled lust. He advanced on her, backing her into the wall. "You're not going to the club like that."

"Why not?" she asked. She was dead serious about going back to the bar and using every asset she had to find someone to help her. She would find out what happened to her crew, and Sergeant Pax Blanchard would either help her or get out of her way.

"Because every man there will want to do this." He thrust his fingers in her hair and pulled her face to his. His tongue invaded her mouth in the hottest, angriest kiss she'd ever received.

She made a soft noise at the back of her throat when he palmed her breast and slid his thumb over the nipple. She wanted his mouth there. *Now.* But she also wanted his mouth to remain right where it was, his tongue sliding against hers. Damn. He tasted like heat. Smelled like desire. Felt so right.

She ran a hand over the hard planes of his bare pecs. Perfect sculpted muscle. She traced his shoulder, those biceps that had carried her to safety.

He lifted his mouth from hers. She opened her eyes to meet his gaze. There was no softness in his eyes. Desire? Yes. Anger? Yes. Tenderness? Not even close.

"I'll talk to my XO," he said. "Stay here. I'll be back in less than an hour."

The sun sets quickly at eleven degrees north of the equator, and it was dark by the time Pax returned to Morgan's CLU, orders in hand. He was glad to see she'd untied his shirt and it was neatly buttoned. The tails flapped loosely, almost reaching her knees.

She looked like she'd borrowed his shirt after a fuck, triggering another wave of possessiveness. He wanted to see her that way. Wanted to claim her.

He felt strangely caveman about her. An ironic notion considering tomorrow she was going to take him to see her very own caveman, Linus.

"We leave tomorrow at oh-seven-hundred." He shoved the signed orders in her hands, then turned on his heel and left. He could feel her staring at his back as he headed to his own CLU at the far end and around the corner.

He wouldn't spend an extra minute in Morgan Adler's company, because if he did, he had no doubt he'd end up buried deep inside her, which would be a huge fucking problem. Not only would he be taking her beyond the gates and into what amounted to a war zone tomorrow, but also his damned CO had just made him her bodyguard for the duration of the time she was in Djibouti.

While his A-Team was out doing the job they'd been sent here to do—molding the locals into guerilla fighters—he was going to be Indiana Jones's fucking sidekick.

Chapter Seven

"So this is how we're going to do things on the other side of the gate," Pax said as soon as Morgan settled in the passenger seat of the SUV. "You will do what I say, when I say it. No argument. Got it?"

"But—"

"What I say. When I say it. Or we'll come straight back to the base."

He still hadn't told her that if she decided to stay in Djibouti, she would be stuck with him for the duration. It wouldn't be an issue because he intended to convince her to leave, which should be easy considering she already wanted to go home.

She glared at him but gave a sharp nod.

She'd washed most of the blood from her field clothes and looked shiny and beautiful in the morning sun. She'd pulled back her blonde hair in a neat French braid, the kind his little sister made him learn how to do when she was eight because she couldn't braid behind her head herself. The weave revealed the layers of highlights in her long hair, a rainbow of gold and yellow with darker amber streaks thrown in.

Last night, he'd buried his fingers in the silky soft strands as he'd taken her mouth in a hot, angry kiss that had kept him awake half the night. He frowned. "Do you have a hat?"

"It blew up."

"You don't have a spare at your place in Djibouti City?"

She shook her head. "No."

"We'll get you one today." Great. He'd just added clothes shopping to the to-do list. No. Forget shopping. She didn't need a new hat, because she was getting the hell out of Djibouti. Period.

It took a full twenty minutes to be processed through security and drive through the serpentine gate. "I've never been on a base with this much security," she said after they finally cleared the last checkpoint.

"We're a stone's throw from Somalia and Yemen, and neither country is pleased with the drones that may or may not originate from here." He glanced sideways at her. "Somalis have developed a nasty habit of abducting Westerners and dragging them over the border, and American military personnel are considered the ultimate hostages. Successful extraction is nearly impossible. For that reason, no one leaves the base unless it's absolutely necessary."

"How did you manage to convince your XO to sign the orders to take me off base?"

"There's been friction between Major Haverfeld—our commanding officer—and the skipper."

"Skipper?"

"Sorry. Base commander Captain O'Leary is also referred to as the skipper. Because of that friction, I told Captain Oswald—my XO—this would show cooperation between the two commands and make our Special Forces team in particular look good." But then Oswald had brought the CO into the conversation, and Major Haverfeld had liked the idea so much, he'd seized control over Morgan's heretofore nonexistent security detail and made Pax the head of the team.

Pax had no qualms with the idea she needed security. Yesterday had proven that. But marines should be assigned to protect her, not SOCOM. He told Morgan none of this and wouldn't until after she'd made her decision. If she knew she had a Special Forces operator providing security, would she choose to stay?

"I'm sorry if I caused problems for you."

She didn't know the half of it. He just gave her a curt nod in reply. "Will your crew have gone to the site today?"

She shrugged. "I have no idea. I hope so. We should look for them there first."

He reached back and grabbed a map from the backseat and dropped it on her lap. "Where is the site?"

She pointed to the location, but he only glanced briefly, keeping his eyes on the road. He could have requested an escort but hadn't wanted to draw attention, not when no one knew they'd be heading out, let alone their itinerary. If she stayed in Djibouti they'd need to switch up the routes. Bravo one day, then Charlie, then Alpha. There were four routes onto the base. They'd utilize them all, randomly.

Except that wouldn't happen, because no way in hell would Morgan Adler stay in Djibouti. She was going home, and he was returning to his team to do the job he'd come here for. Planning tomorrow's route and security detail was a waste of mental energy.

They neared her rental car—a shattered heap that had been pushed to the side of the road. It would be picked over for salvage by the locals, but otherwise would likely remain there, a reminder of Etefu Desta's ruthlessness.

He drove past without slowing.

"So what kind of name is Pax for a soldier anyway?" she asked after a long stretch of silence.

He cut a glance sideways. "No one wants peace more than a soldier."

"True, although I sometimes wondered if my dad was the exception there." She turned in her seat, so she faced him more than the road. He kept his focus on the ruts in front of him. The fact that he wanted her was a dangerous distraction outside the gate. "But seriously, is Pax your real name? Is it short for something?"

He debated telling her the truth. Ah, hell, why not? "The name on my birth certificate is Pax Love Blanchard."

She let out a sharp laugh. "You're shitting me. Your name is Peace Love?"

He nodded.

"Oh my God. You had hippie parents, didn't you?"

"Yep. My sister is named Gaia Love."

"How does the son of hippies become a Green Beret?"

"How does the daughter of a hard-ass general become an archaeologist?"

"In my case, rebellion." She turned in her seat again, facing the road. "My father had dreams of me being the first woman on a special forces team. I can shoot—"

He coughed politely at that.

"Hey! I'm out of practice. And I *did* hit him." She paused. "How is he doing?"

"He survived the night. That's all I know."

She turned silent.

Pax missed her chatter. He wanted to know more about her relationship with her father, especially if he was going to convince her to go against her dear daddy's wishes and leave Djibouti. "What else can you do—besides shoot with questionable accuracy, I mean?"

She snorted. "Martial arts training began in elementary school—before the shooting lessons started. I can defend myself in a fight. I did ROTC, but it became pretty clear that while I had skills, I didn't have the strength necessary to keep up with the big boys if I was going to make it through any kind of special forces training. I also lacked the drive." Her voice lowered, losing the upbeat tone. "At the same time, I realized my dad would never be proud of me if I didn't achieve his goal for me. Nothing I did was ever enough for him. Becoming a soldier in his Army but falling short of special forces would've been viewed as a failure, forget that no woman had ever done it. It would have been yet another disappointment after the massive blow of his only child being born with a vagina. So my freshman year in college, I quit every activity he'd insisted I do. I dyed my hair pink and pierced my nose."

He glanced sideways and saw the faint divot on the side of her nose.

She caught his look. "I'm a wuss, and it hurt too much. I decided rebellion should only hurt my father, not me, and let it close a week later." She tilted her face toward the sunshine streaming through the window. "The general cut me off financially when I dropped ROTC, but I had financial aid and a willingness to take on a massive debt load, so for the first time in my life, I was free to study what I wanted. Anthropology was like finding home." She offered a faint grin. "Plus the anthro majors were the closest things to hippies on campus, guaranteed to make my dad shudder in horror."

He smiled. "I wasn't allowed to play with toy guns growing up. Any toy that I made into a gun became forbidden. Sports were discouraged because they rewarded aggression."

"I was the Western Pennsylvania Bullseye Confederation junior champion when I was fifteen," she said with more than a hint of pride, telling him she'd quit shooting to anger her dad, not because she didn't enjoy it.

He flicked a glance sideways. "When we get back to the base, we can go to the practice range and have a little competition of our own."

Her laugh was throaty. Sexy as hell. "Oh no. I wouldn't want to embarrass you."

Her cocky words turned him on even more. He was in trouble.

She's an officer's daughter. He'd made that mistake once already.

"So how did you end up in the Army?" she asked.

"On my eighteenth birthday, I told my parents that I loved them very much, but it was time for me to be who I am. I think they hoped I was coming out, but no such luck."

She snorted. "No way would anyone think you're gay."

"Don't underestimate the blinders of wishful parents."

"Do they accept you? As a straight soldier?"

"Yeah. My parents had their rules and their beliefs, but the core of their philosophy has always been about loving people for who they are. If they'd rejected me, they'd have been denying everything they stood for. I'm not saying it was easy for them to accept having a soldier for a son, but their love never wavered."

"I'm envious," Morgan said with raw honesty.

He placed a hand on her knee. It was supposed to be a casual, comforting gesture, but he'd forgotten about the combustion factor of touching Morgan.

He removed his hand without a word, glad they neared her project area. The sooner they completed the site visit and got back on the base, the better.

She gave him directions that took them deep down unmarked tracks that passed for roads. She gasped when they rounded a bend and a vehicle parked to the side came into view.

"Is that good or bad?" he asked.

"Good. It's Ibrahim's car. Three of my five crew members don't have cars. They give each other rides. So at least Ibrahim is here, but there might be more."

Pax parked the SUV and caught her hand as she reached for the door handle. "We're doing this my way, remember? Just because one car is here doesn't mean they're here."

She frowned. "True, but if you walk out there looking all intimidating—"

"Tough. That's what I'm here for. I will intimidate. I will menace. I will scare the ever-loving shit out of them if I have to, and I *will* find out if they had anything to do with that bomb being planted under your car yesterday."

"You wouldn't—"

"I would and I will. You're going to wait here while I check out the site. Get in the backseat, where you'll be harder to see." When she didn't move, he added, "If you don't cooperate, we'll go back to the base right this minute."

She glared at him but said, "Fine," and climbed over the seat.

"Where will I find them?" he asked.

She settled in the back. "There's a trail between those boulders." She pointed through the windshield and described the path.

With a sharp nod, he pressed the car key and a two-way radio he'd acquired for her from the base into her palm. "This is set on the channel I'll use. If it's safe for you to come to me, you'll hear me say 'Peppermint Patty' three times. If I want you to go to the base immediately, I'll say, 'Snoopy.'" He'd decided to use Peanuts-related code words with her. She'd remember them, and they wouldn't be confused with other chatter on the airwaves.

"If you hear gunfire," he continued, "I want you to get in the driver's seat and drive a klick east. Pull over and listen to the radio. 'Woodstock' means all clear. If it's safe for you to return, I'll say 'Woodstock' three times. Again, if I want you to go to the base I'll say 'Snoopy.' Snoopy always means return to the base. If you don't hear from me at all within five minutes, hightail it back to the base."

She frowned. "I can't leave you."

"You will. You'll promise me right now, or we're heading back. Swear it."

The way she glared at him with flaring nostrils made him want to kiss her, but today he was a soldier, not a randy teenager, and he had a job to do.

"I swear." Her jaw was tight, but she said the words without flinching.

"Good. Okay, repeat the code words and what they mean."

She recited the instructions back to him.

"Perfect." He pointed to the radio frequency. "Don't change the setting, but remember it. I will always use that channel frequency with you."

She nodded. He climbed out of the vehicle and opened the rear door to grab his gear.

"You're going to scare them if you go down in full gear with your M4."

He grinned and donned his helmet. "That's my plan." He then gave in to the stupid impulse and cupped the back of her head, pulling her to him for a quick kiss. Where the hell had his self-control gone? He closed the door and faced the trail.

Time to find out whose side Morgan's crew was on.

She never should have agreed. Mouktar was nervous enough. After yesterday's scare, he might've returned with a weapon and could shoot first and ask questions later. But maybe Mouktar wasn't here at all.

She was tempted to follow, to stop Pax from intimidating the crew, but that could backfire when everyone was jumpy. Plus, she didn't doubt his threats for a second. He'd haul her back to the base, and she'd lose her chance to make an informed decision. After seeing firsthand the rigmarole required just to exit the base, it was clear she wouldn't have another opportunity.

Five minutes ticked by, and she dripped with sweat. The windows were cracked and there were open side vents, so she wasn't quite up to baking temperature yet, but she'd probably only last another few minutes before she'd have to turn on the air-conditioning.

The radio crackled. "Peppermint Patty," was repeated three times. Thank goodness.

She opened the door and jumped out of the SUV. Making a beeline for the narrow path between boulders, she muttered under her breath, "Please let everyone be okay. Please let everyone be here." Yesterday had been terrifying; she didn't blame the men for fleeing. But she hoped they came back.

She slipped into the slot between boulders. Her braid caught on something, forcing her to an abrupt halt. She reached back to disentangle her hair, when she felt fingers—not hers—snarled in her long braid.

A hand gripped her throat.

Adrenaline pulsed through her, slowing time. Slowing breath. Eclipsing thought. Muscle memory thanks to years of martial arts training kicked in. She used leverage to dislodge the hand from her throat and twisted sideways as she let out a scream that echoed down the trail and she hoped into the wide canyon below. She smashed the arm into a boulder. Before he could withdraw, she kicked backward, landing a blow on the man's knee. He grunted in pain.

His hot breath on her ear told her his position. She elbowed him in the windpipe and twisted around to finally see her attacker.

She'd never seen the man before; he wasn't one of the men who'd run her off yesterday. She kicked him in the chest, and he fell backward, landing on the AK-47 that was slung over his back. He must not have expected she could fight him, or he would've used the gun instead of a barehanded grab. But then, she'd always counted on men underestimating her. Twice she'd been attacked behind the bar as she walked to her car after a late night waiting tables, and twice she'd sent her attacker to the hospital.

The man flailed for his gun, so she charged him, kicking him in the chin. His head snapped up, then flopped to the side. He was unconscious or dead. She was breathing heavily and staring at him as a chill settled over her.

Holy hell, what would have happened if she hadn't been able to fight him? What if he'd used the assault rifle instead of simply trying to grab her?

Footsteps sounded behind her and Pax shouted, "Morgan?"

She didn't dare turn her back on the downed man. What if he was faking? There'd been others yesterday. Where were those men now? "Pax! Help!"

"I'm coming!" His reply bounced off the boulders that defined the narrow passage.

She pressed her back to a boulder, her gaze fixed on her assailant. Was he breathing?

At last Pax was by her side. She wanted to thrust herself into his arms, but that was stupid. She'd just saved herself. Why turn all damsel-in-distress needy now? Besides, if Pax had his arms full of her, he couldn't be checking to see if the guy was dead or alive.

She nodded toward the man and said, "He grabbed me from behind. So I, um, fought him."

Pax's gaze went from her, to the man, then back to her. He circled the body slowly, then let out a low whistle and said with a little awe in his voice, "How many years did you study martial arts?"

"Only twelve."

"Only. Twelve."

"Well, only twelve when I was advancing and taking belt tests. I quit that when I was eighteen along with everything else, but I've kept up practicing kata and sparring in the thirteen years since then. It's how I exercise."

"So you've really been studying martial arts for...*twenty-five years?*"

"I wanted to do gymnastics when I was five, but my dad wanted me in karate."

"Right now, I'm glad your dad got his way." He unhooked the AK-47 from the guy's back and slid it out from under him before checking for a pulse.

"What's your belt rank?" he asked as his fingers pressed the guy's carotid artery.

"Black. Third dan." She rarely told men this—guys, when they knew her rank, would often challenge her, either to see if she was boasting or to see if they could take her. Third dan had been a damn high rank for an eighteen-year-old.

Twice she'd made the mistake of agreeing to a sparring match because a guy wouldn't let it go. The first time, the guy had been mortified. He'd never called her again.

The second time, the guy had gotten enraged when he started to lose, and he'd turned violent for real. She'd broken his arm to escape a hold that had the potential to seriously hurt her and never called him again.

She had a feeling Pax would believe her, and given his build and badass Green Beret bearing, he didn't have the need to prove himself to her.

"He's got a pulse," he said.

She let out a breath, relieved. It was self-defense but she still didn't relish the idea of killing a man. Possibly two, given that the guy she'd shot yesterday wasn't out of the woods yet.

On the negative side, they had to figure out what to do with this guy now. Pax rolled him over and slipped plastic flex-cuffs, which he'd grabbed from his pack, around the man's wrists. Then he sat back and stared at the prone form.

"He's a local, and he assaulted you, a civilian. Technically, this should be tossed to the local authorities. But they're not really great at following up, and odds are this man will walk tomorrow. He could come after you again."

"But if he'd assaulted you?"

"Then the US military could label him an enemy combatant and detain him."

She gave him a crooked smile. "First you take credit for my shot, and now you want to take credit for beating the crap out of this man."

"Believe me, I don't *want* credit for that lousy shot." He grinned. "But you did good here."

"What happens when he wakes and tells people what happened?"

"You think he's going to admit you kicked his ass?" He winked at her. "Even if he does, it's a done deal. Hopefully we'll get intel from him that will make holding him worthwhile."

He called the base with a satellite phone and explained the situation. They agreed to send a Humvee to collect the man. She'd been watching him closely and could now see the steady rise and fall of his chest. He was breathing fine.

She'd merely knocked him out.

Pax tucked the phone in his pack, then scooped the man up and tossed him over his shoulder. "Grab his gun. I want you in the lead, with his weapon. Anyone jumps out at you, shoot first, ask questions later." Pax turned and gripped his M4, which was draped over his shoulder, one-handed. "I'll cover our six."

"How is my crew?" she asked as she picked up the AK. A quick check showed the weapon was in working order.

"No one was hurt. Let's move."

She nodded and led the way back up the narrow trail. She scanned each new section for henchmen hiding behind the boulders that littered the landscape before saying, "Clear," and moving forward. At last they reached the flat open area where the vehicles were parked.

Pax dropped the man by the tires of the SUV. "I'm going to search the perimeter, make sure this guy is acting alone. You good standing guard over him?" he asked.

She nodded.

"You see anyone you don't know, lay down a short burst of fire to hold them back, then wait for me. Okay?"

"Will do."

She got a little thrill from the respect in his gaze. He set out for the uneven landscape to the east, the most likely place for this guy to have hidden a vehicle, while she stood sentry over the unconscious man, wondering why he'd attacked her. What the hell was going on?

Ten minutes later, Pax returned. "There's an old wreck of a truck around the bend. Fresh tire tracks. Looks like he drove in this morning, probably hoping you'd show up. No other footprints leading from the vehicle. Appears he was acting alone."

Morgan set down the Kalash and rolled her shoulders. "Can I go down and talk to my crew?"

He shook his head. "We'll head down together after this guy"—he probed her attacker with the toe of his boot—"is taken care of. I fucked up in letting you walk that path alone. I won't make that mistake again." He met her gaze and his nostrils flared. "You did good. Really good."

She gave him a short nod in acknowledgment and stared at the unconscious man. Dark skinned with short-cropped hair and a wispy beard, the man could be from Djibouti, Ethiopia, Eritrea, or Somalia. Like the man yesterday, he was malnourished. Dark yellow teeth indicated years of chewing khat. Everything about him spoke of poverty, of a harsh life she couldn't begin to imagine.

Was he rotten like Desta, or just desperate?

She bit her lip. "When I first arrived in Djibouti, I was shocked to see malnourished children languishing on the side of the road, begging for water. Ibrahim warned me not to give them any. He said if I did, the next day there would be five more, and the day after that two hundred."

"He's right. They're Somali refugees, and if the begging gets out of hand, the government removes them."

She nodded. "Ibrahim said no one knows where they go."

"I saw it happen, not long after I arrived in-country. The group of kids that hang out around one of the entrances to Camp Citron vanished one day. Dozens of kids. Gone."

Morgan shuddered. Having been warned by Ibrahim, she'd ignored the pleas of children who looked like they'd never had a decent meal in their lives. It was her sixth day on the job before she'd been able to drive by the begging children without sobbing.

"Do you think this guy is like the kids? Not evil, just desperate?"

"There's a fine line between evil and desperation. One easily leads to the other. I've seen boys under age ten take up weapons and kill. The child isn't evil. The person who arms a child, the man who sells a child into sexual slavery, is."

Perhaps Pax was right. Djibouti was no place for a woman like her.

"I was wrong."

She looked up sharply. Had she said that aloud?

No. He was still looking at the man she'd fought. It had been ridiculously easy, when it came down to it. The man was weak and malnourished. His only advantage, the Kalash, he'd had on his back, not in his hands. Because he'd underestimated her. Because she was five-four and didn't look threatening.

She met Pax's gaze. "What do you mean?"

"Last night. When I called you a fool. I was an ass. I'm sorry."

"Thank you," she said.

"I still want you to leave, though."

She couldn't help but shake her head even as her lips formed a faint smile. He couldn't leave a perfectly nice apology alone. Why did guys always have to muck up the best apologies? She decided to give him enough rope to hang himself. The more he showed his true colors, the less attracted to him she'd be.

And she *really* wanted to stop being attracted to him.

"I'll bite. Why is that? Does a woman who can fight and shoot nearly as well as the big boys intimidate you? Are you secretly afraid of getting your ass kicked by a woman?"

He laughed. Even better, he didn't assert that he could take her—although he certainly could—or offer up any sort of macho challenge. Instead, a smile played about his lips as he approached her. "No, Morgan, I don't care if you can kick my ass. In fact, I'd prefer it, because it would mean you could protect yourself in this frigging tinderbox. No, there's one reason and one reason alone that I want you to go home."

"What's that?"

"If you stay, it's only a matter of time before we fuck. Hell, right now I want you even more than I did last night. It's ridiculous how caveman I feel. But there it is."

"And why is that a problem? I'm not married, not seeing anyone." Then she stepped backward as the truth dawned. Shit. He was *married*. Her gaze darted to his left hand. No ring. But then, did soldiers wear rings on combat deployments? "Are you?" she asked in a hard voice.

"No. Divorced. Not seeing anyone."

Relief fluttered through her. "Then why is consensual sex a problem? Was the divorce recent?"

"No. Not recent. But last night, when I convinced my XO to let me take you out today, he and my CO took it one step further. They reassigned me, making me your bodyguard for as long as you stay in Djibouti."

She sucked in a sharp breath. "Why would they *do* that?"

"If the skipper gets his airstrip thanks to your project, my CO and XO will get to claim a piece of that success. Saying it was all possible because SOCOM provided security. So you see, if you stay, we're stuck together. Anytime you leave the base, my job is to cover your ass." His hands found her hips and slid around to cup the aforementioned body part. "How long do you think we'll be able to last without screwing?"

They stood chest to chest with his hand on her butt, she was still riding adrenaline, and he exuded hot, stimulating testosterone from every pore. She wanted to lick his throat, wanted him to take her up against the SUV. *Now.* "About ten minutes."

"Exactly. But sex would be a dumbass idea when my job is to protect you. It'll get in our heads. Invite mistakes. And the risk to your safety is very real." His gaze flicked to the man at their feet. "Christ, right now, I'm being stupid. My attention is on you, not the threat lying on the ground three feet away." He took a step back and began pacing. "I've *never* been stupid on the job before. Stupid is a fatal condition for a soldier."

"Maybe we can get Captain O'Leary to change the order."

"And piss off my CO? No, thanks." His gaze jerked back to her face. "Does that mean you're staying?" A sharp edge had entered his voice.

"I don't know. I *still* haven't talked to my crew. I don't even know how many of them are here." She frowned. "Why aren't they here? Why did they stay at the site instead of coming when I screamed?"

Pax frowned. "There's a…uh…there's a problem with the site."

"Problem?"

"Linus's skull is gone."

Chapter Eight

Yeah, that might have been the news he should have led with, but Pax had forgotten in the midst of discovering she was some sort of badass ninja fighter.

She'd flattened a guy who had an AK-47 on his side.

After he'd digested that, he'd had other concerns, like searching for accomplices.

"What do you mean, his skull is *missing*? It was still in the ground yesterday. Rock embedded in rock. Not easy to pry out."

He shrugged. "That's what Ibrahim told me. There was definitely something chunked out of the ground."

Morgan stepped away from the vehicle blindly and looked like she was about to hyperventilate. Or maybe faint. "I think I'm going to be sick," she said and pressed her hand to her mouth. She paced with sharp, quick steps, one arm holding her belly. Anger and horror radiated from her in waves. "The skull. Without it, we can't estimate cranial capacity. We won't know how big his brain was, how he fits on the spectrum…"

"I assume the skull would be valuable."

She shot him a sharp glare. "The value lies in the information it contains. There is no value if it can't be studied. If Desta sells it, if it disappears into some asshole's private collection—"

"My point is, Desta won't destroy it if he believes it's worth money."

"No, but ISIS, the Taliban, or al-Shabaab might. It doesn't fit with their beliefs. ISIS and the Taliban have destroyed several World Heritage Sites."

"But both groups also sell artifacts to fund their terrorism. They only destroy if it's too big to move and sell."

"True." She glanced toward the trail. "I want to talk to Ibrahim."

"You will. As soon as this guy is carted away."

"How many are down there?"

"Two. Ibrahim and Mouktar."

"The others—were they harmed?"

"No. Ibrahim said all three are fine. Just scared."

She nodded and paced, saying nothing for the twenty minutes it took for the MPs to arrive. The man was still unconscious, and one of the MPs frowned. "We might need to airlift him to the ship medical facilities." He glanced askance at Pax. "I heard about the guy yesterday. What is it with you and injuring enemy combatants? We can't afford the medical bills."

Pax shrugged. "They attacked me. Knocking him out was better than killing him."

"Bullets are cheaper than blood transfusions," the MP muttered.

"And intel is more valuable than oil," Pax replied.

"Does this guy know anything?"

"No idea. But the guy yesterday promised to give us Desta's location. Maybe this guy can give us even more."

As soon as they drove off, Morgan made a beeline for the path. Pax caught up with her. "We go together."

She nodded, and he took the lead down the narrow trail that led to an ancient eroding canyon. As they walked, Morgan explained the terrain. "This landform doesn't even count as a wadi, as water hasn't flowed through here in thousands of years, while a wadi can carry water during the rainy season. Not that Djibouti has much of a rainy season."

Pax reached the canyon floor and turned to give her a hand as she stepped over low boulders that littered the floor, preventing easy walking.

She took his hand and continued talking. "Months ago, a geologist dated the lower layers of stratigraphy visible in the canyon wall. That red layer"— she pointed to a thick band of rock—"has been dated to over one-point-five-million years old. And our site is below it, meaning it's older. A lot older."

Her voice had changed. Her demeanor had changed. She was reciting facts she knew well, seeing a landscape she'd visited every day for the last few weeks, but still, her voice had filled with wonder. As if this was new magic she was seeing and describing for the first time.

She released his hand and darted over to an area where orange pin flags were stuck in the ground. She picked up a triangular rock and jogged back to his side to press it in his hand. She wrapped his fingers around the warm stone. "You're holding in your hand a tool that was made by either *Homo ergaster* or *Homo habilis* around one-point-five-million years ago."

Even after all the shock and horror of the last twenty-four hours, she was sharing this—her site—with him with awe and enthusiasm.

He squeezed the rock and studied its sharp edges and broken surface. "*Homo habilis*? Prehuman?"

"Yes. Of the genus *Homo*, which modern humans—*Homo sapiens sapiens*— are a part of, but earlier. Some even think *habilis* should be in the genus *Australopithecus*. Put simplistically, the living creature that made that tool was akin to a hairless, bipedal chimpanzee."

One thing was clear about Morgan Adler: she loved this site. It wasn't about the fame and recognition she'd gain from this discovery. No. She was enthralled by the knowledge that could be unlocked. That she could display this passion, even now, was a testament to what it meant to her. And it made her even more appealing than before.

She'd been kidding herself when she'd said she would leave Djibouti. No way could she walk away from this. No way could she abandon Linus.

He no longer believed he could convince her to leave. No. Now he had a bigger, much scarier task—to convince her to leave the australopithecine skull in Desta's hands.

M organ wanted to throw her arms around Ibrahim and Mouktar, but neither man was the hugging sort. Ibrahim repeated the information that the other three workers were fine. One was too scared to return, while another hadn't liked the job. The third, Serge, had quit because he had family on the Ethiopian side of the border and was worried Desta would target them if he continued with the project. "Serge says he's very sorry, but he can't risk his family."

She nodded. "I understand, Ibrahim." She glanced toward Pax. "Do you think the others would return if…the US military provided security for the fieldwork?"

Mouktar shifted nervously from foot to foot as he glanced toward Pax, then away. "I don't think so," he said in a soft voice, confirming Morgan's belief he feared soldiers. But then, maybe Pax had scared the hell out of him earlier. She had no way of knowing.

She felt Pax's heightened tension at the hint she was considering staying and walked over to the excavation, where there was now a gaping hole where an australopithecine skull should be. "When did you discover this?" she asked Ibrahim.

"About an hour ago," he said. "I'm sorry we didn't return to the site last night—"

"Oh. No." She faced both men, gave in to the impulse, took one of each of their hands, and clasped them together in both of hers. They were likely uncomfortable, but she was a toucher, and this was an important point. "I'm thankful you weren't here." She squeezed their fingers. "There's nothing you could have done, and you might have been hurt by Desta's men." She cast Pax a chagrined smile. "I tried to save Linus's dinner bones from an explosion yesterday, and it's been pointed out that wasn't a wise decision."

Mouktar's eyes widened. "The bones have blown up?"

She released their hands, realizing Pax hadn't had a chance to tell the men anything of what had happened yesterday. She dropped to the ground next to the excavation and grabbed her trowel from the shallow pit where she'd left it yesterday when she fled the site, feeling strangely grateful the tool had survived. She still had her Marshalltown, the trowel she'd gotten for field school ten years ago and that she'd used on every project she'd worked on since then. She'd lost so much in the explosion, but not her trowel.

As she told Mouktar and Ibrahim about what had happened outside the base yesterday, she poked at the hard ground with the dull tip of her trowel. She needed to sharpen it, but then, that was the least of her chores if she was going to stay.

She stared at Linus's long bones, still embedded in rock, then glanced in Pax's direction, before facing what was left of her crew. "After yesterday, I considered leaving Djibouti." She shrugged and reminded herself to own her actions. "Okay. I didn't just consider it—I'd have left right then if I could. So I understand completely why the others have quit. They get no judgment from me. But for myself, I've changed my mind. I'm staying to see the project through."

She touched a three-point-five-million-year-old bone that lay exposed just inches from her fingers. "There isn't much more we can do for Linus. We'll leave what's left in situ. I'm sure the Leakey Foundation and other scientific organizations will fund grants to ensure the work is done properly and no more data is lost. Tomorrow, I'm going start surveying the alternate route. I hope you both will consider continuing on the project, but will understand if you don't wish to stay."

Ibrahim flashed a wide smile. "I came back today, Dr. Morgan, because you have infected me with archaeology. I like the job. I like what I can do for Djibouti."

It had taken weeks to get the crew to stop calling her Dr. Adler. The compromise was Dr. Morgan, which now made her smile. "Thank you." She turned to Mouktar and raised a brow in question.

He nodded. "I will work. Desta has already taken my sister—my only family. He can't hurt me anymore."

She squeezed his fingers again. "I'm sorry."

He shrugged. "It was years ago. She is probably dead." The words were delivered in a flat, matter-of-fact tone that warned her not to ask more questions. There was so much about Ibrahim's and Mouktar's lives she didn't know, and she wondered if they resented her privilege. Mouktar's sister had been taken by a warlord and likely sold into sexual slavery, while Morgan was given a Green Beret to protect her.

She released his hand. "Maybe the militant who attacked us in the wadi will give the US Navy Desta's location. He can be captured." Although really, if they knew where he was, his operation would be bombed if it could be done without harming civilians. His drugs and weaponry would be destroyed along with the man. Swift and efficient, because bullets were cheaper than blood transfusions, and it was the only way to ensure the man's militia was disarmed and defunded. She knew it, and likely Mouktar knew it.

"I will hope for that, Dr. Morgan," Mouktar said.

She turned to face Pax's brooding stare. He wasn't happy she'd decided to stay, but she'd expected that.

She stood and dusted off her pants. The decision to remain in Djibouti expanded the day's to-do list by quite a bit. "I need to pack up my apartment for the move to the base." Her apartment in Djibouti City was free—provided by the local government—but she wasn't about to question the offer of lodging that came with protection from the US military, not after her car had been bombed. And she was thankful to have her own personal Green Beret for security, even though that meant she had to keep her hands off the man.

"We'll do that next," Pax said.

She frowned. "Actually, first we should meet with Charles Lemaire, the Djiboutian minister of culture and discuss how they're going to deal with Desta and the theft of Linus's skull."

He gave a sharp nod.

"Plus I need field notebooks and to replace my camera and computer."

"You can probably get the skipper to sign off on purchases at the base store and sort the contract out later. I'm going to ask SOCOM to issue you a gun."

She nodded. "I'd like Mouktar and Ibrahim to have cell phones."

"That can be arranged," Pax said.

"But cell phones don't work out here, Dr. Morgan," Ibrahim said.

"But they work where you live, and I'd like to be able to reach you should something go wrong again." She shaded her eyes as she looked across the valley toward the alternate Area of Potential Effect where she would begin surveying tomorrow. That APE was more open than this one. Fewer rocky outcrops to provide even minimal shade. She turned to her reluctant bodyguard. "And I need to buy a hat."

Much as he wanted out, Pax wouldn't consider asking his XO to rescind his order. Aside from the fact that a request like that would damage his standing within SOCOM, he had a secondary concern. What if the request was granted and his replacement wasn't up to the job? What if something happened to her?

What if I fail?

He never thought about failing. It wasn't an option. The fact that he considered it now was another sign that she'd gotten in his head in a dangerous way.

He was so fucked.

"Is the embassy still in lockdown?" Morgan asked as he drove through the busy city streets on the way to see the minister of culture.

"No. Lockdown ended sometime overnight."

"I wonder if we should go there before we meet with the minister. We need to tell them about the skull."

"Who is your contact there?"

"The community liaison, Kaylea Halpert."

Pax grabbed his cell from the center console and handed it to her. "She's in the address book."

She stiffened. "Kaylea's in your phone."

"Yes."

"I'm almost afraid to ask why. Kaylea knows about the bets. She's not amused."

He understood what Morgan referred to. Kaylea Halpert was stunning, with flawless brown skin, big brown eyes, and Beyoncé's curves. Recently divorced, she wanted nothing to do with the American military personnel who found excuses to parade through her office. There was graffiti about the US embassy employee in the CLUville showers, because sailors were basically adolescent boys, although he supposed the soldiers were no better. He too had heard talk of the bets placed on attempts to get a date with the woman. "My A-Team is training locals to be American-style guerilla fighters, and while we work more with the force protection detachment officer at the embassy, there's also a community outreach component. She's in my phone purely for work purposes." He paused, then added, "Kaylea's attractive, but no, I've never hit on her and don't have plans to do so."

He caught her small smile before she held up the phone and said, "Passcode?"

He gave her his four-digit PIN. "Put it on speaker," he said. When Kaylea came on the line, Pax identified himself and explained he was providing security for Morgan.

"I'm glad to hear it," Kaylea said. "Captain O'Leary said Morgan is in serious danger."

Unease slid down Pax's spine. "O'Leary contacted you?" It was an odd move for the base commander. But then, nothing about this situation was normal.

"Yes, he needed the location of the Linus site. Morgan, why didn't you tell me about Linus?"

"He wanted the location?" Morgan asked in a strained voice, showing she too, was disturbed by the skipper's undue interest.

"Of course, I couldn't give it to him, because I didn't know about it."

Morgan let out a soft sigh of relief.

"But I explained the situation to Charles," Kaylea continued.

Pax took his gaze off the road long enough to mouth, *Charles?*

"Lemaire. The minister of culture," she whispered. "Kaylea, do you know if Charles told Captain O'Leary the site location?"

"I think he did. At least, I hope he did. O'Leary said Desta planned to loot the site, and he would make sure the fossils were protected."

That sounded good on the surface, but there hadn't been a battalion of marines guarding the site today. The opposite, in fact—Linus was missing his head and a militant had been lying in wait for Morgan. Forcing Pax to wonder if "protected," in Captain O'Leary's parlance, meant "yank the fossil from the ground."

Pax could tell Morgan was holding her breath against a stream of curses that could rival yesterday's foul tirade. The hand that held the cell phone between them shook with anger. Pax pulled onto a side street and parked. Into the phone, he said, "Thanks, Kaylea."

"No problem." She paused. "Sergeant? Did I do something wrong? Captain O'Leary is the final authority when it comes to the base. He told me about the explosion."

"You did fine. Captain O'Leary was just doing his job." He hit the End button then took the phone from Morgan's hand and set it on the dash. Without hesitation, he pulled her into his arms.

She let out a low sob as she pressed her face into his shoulder. Her body shook. She finally took a deep, hiccupping breath and said, "I cry when I'm very angry." Her tone was both embarrassed and defensive, which made him want to smile, but he didn't dare because he had a feeling she might break out her crazy ninja skills if she thought he was making fun of her, which was the last thing on his mind.

He cupped her face between his palms and made her look at him. Her face was red and blotchy, and her eyes verged on swollen. "I'm not some asshole who would ever tell a woman—or a man—not to cry. Tears are a way we process emotion. Emotions make life interesting."

One corner of her mouth turned up in the tiniest of smiles. "Those hippie parents."

"They were right about a lot of stuff."

"O'Leary sent a team out to steal Linus, Pax!" Tears started to roll again. "They could have destroyed the cranium! For all we know, they *did* destroy it." She caught her breath. "Plus, they violated about a dozen international agreements and even more US laws—"

She was forgetting that Djibouti was lawless. Sure, those agreements were on the books, but here, they really didn't apply. It wasn't that O'Leary was untouchable, just that the consequences could be far less dire. No reason to make that point now; it would only make her outrage worse. "We don't *know* if they harmed the cranium. We don't even know if US military personnel took it."

"But it makes sense. If they'd gone out to protect the site, they'd have been there when we arrived, but they weren't."

She'd followed the same logic he had. Damn, but he liked this woman far too much.

"The skull was embedded in solid rock," she continued. "It would have been impossible to remove without damaging it. That's the reason I left it behind after Desta's henchmen showed up."

"Do you want to see O'Leary now?"

She wiped the tears from her face with the palms of both hands. "As long as we're here, I may as well talk to the cultural minister."

"And we need to go to your apartment and pack."

She shook her head. "I can't move to the base and live under O'Leary's command. Not if he ordered the looting of the site."

"It's not safe for you off base. And I can't protect you here." His XO would never authorize him to stay in Djibouti City with her, which was a good thing, because Pax couldn't imagine living with her for more than two hours before they became lovers.

"Maybe the threat is over. They used me to deliver a bomb to the base. Maybe I'm out of it now."

"Did you forget that someone grabbed you at the site just a few hours ago?"

"And I kicked his ass."

He narrowed his eyes. "The next guy might lead with the gun."

She stiffened her jaw. "I'm good with a gun."

"But you don't *have* a gun."

She shrugged. "So I'll get one."

"That won't be easy without Captain O'Leary's approval—which he won't give if you refuse to live on the base."

"Let's table this discussion for now and go talk to the minister."

Charles Lemaire greeted Morgan warmly and immediately called in two other ministers to join their discussion—Minister of Natural Resources Ali Imbert, and Minister of Tourism Jean Savin.

Pax stood by the door, doing his best wallpaper impersonation as Morgan was introduced to the ministers. He wanted all three men to view him as a bodyguard and nothing more. Someone had told Etefu Desta about Linus, and it hadn't been Kaylea Halpert, because she hadn't known of the find until O'Leary contacted her. Now, the question was, did one of these ministers tell Desta? And if so, why?

Lemaire, the culture minister, a black man and, from his accent, Pax guessed either a French national or educated in France, was eager to discuss Linus. "I trust he is protected now that your captain has sent out a team to guard him?"

Pax stiffened. *Shit*. The minister didn't know what O'Leary had done. If, indeed, O'Leary had done it. Was it possible O'Leary had sent guards, but they'd misunderstood and collected what they could instead of patrolling?

Morgan's back had stiffened, and Pax wondered what she'd say. If she was right, if O'Leary had given orders that broke international law, Lemaire was the one man in Djibouti with the power to do something about it. It was possible Morgan held Captain O'Leary's military career in her hands.

"I don't think the US military will provide around-the-clock security," she said, neatly sidestepping the issue. "I'm also not entirely certain I'd like them to." She leaned forward, conspiratorially. "You know how the US military is. Always trying to take control." She laughed to soften the statement, and he had a glimpse of the businesswoman who knew how to bring others to her side. "I would be much more comfortable with Djiboutian security. Can your office provide guards for the site?"

The minister raised his hands in defeat. "Of course, I will try, but my men are no good against a warlord like Desta. Their job is to defend cultural heritage sites against looters who would sell trinkets to tourists in the market, not a warlord who wants to overthrow our government."

Savin, the minister of tourism, joined in. "With more tourists, we'd have a larger budget for security, but without security, we cannot lure tourists who are leery of the perpetual unrest in Somalia and Eritrea and fear Issa warlords like Desta in Ethiopia."

Pax spent his days in Djibouti with locals and was versed in the factions of the deeply ingrained clans and resulting political divide. In Djibouti, where tribalism ruled, men were quick to identify themselves as Issa or Afar. Issas were of Somali descent, while Afars were related to the neighboring Ethiopian Danakils. But even those regional boundaries weren't as steadfast as the tribes themselves. Etefu Desta, an Ethiopian warlord, was Issa, a fact that the obviously Afar tourism minister managed to slip into his speech.

Imbert, the minister of natural resources, stiffened, making Pax think he too was Issa and didn't appreciate being reminded of his notorious clansman.

The first job for Pax's A-Team had been to get their Djiboutian trainees to identify as Djiboutians first, clan second. Soldiers who couldn't do that had been booted from the program.

Imbert leaned into Morgan, a little too close for Pax's liking. If Morgan's rigid spine was any indication, she didn't like it either. "If you could convince your military to guard the site," Imbert said, "Djibouti would be most grateful for the assistance."

"I'll talk to the powers that be, but I'm afraid it might be better if you go through official channels," Morgan said. "I'm not in the military. I have no power there."

"But isn't your father a general?" Imbert asked.

Pax stiffened. How the hell did the natural resources minister know General Adler was Morgan's dad?

He didn't like this development at all.

Morgan cleared her throat. "He is, sir, but his work and my work have no connection."

Imbert gave Morgan a cold smile. "Perhaps we don't need the US military's help at all. China is always looking for ways to help Djibouti. Soon they will break ground on the desalinization plant in Eritrea, and have promised to build us a pipeline for the water if we allow them to further expand their military presence at Obock."

Pax kept his face blank to mask a surge of anger. The US military was recently forced to vacate the small secondary base at Obock, so the Chinese could station ten thousand soldiers there. China was dumping money into Djibouti at a rate with which the US couldn't compete, and the Djiboutian government took their money, not caring that they were opening the door to a country that was likely arranging for the overthrow of their government with Eritrean or Ethiopian allies.

China didn't care who they backed, so long as they held the reins of power when the governments fell.

Like hell would China protect Linus. Morgan had explained earlier that China had destroyed many archaeological sites on the west end of the rail line until Lemaire got wind of the resources being lost. He was one of the few men in the country who understood how valuable those sites could be to Djibouti's tourism industry, and had pushed for an archaeological survey of the rest of the rail line, which led to Morgan's contract and the US military's agreement to expedite the survey in exchange for more land—to counterbalance the foothold China was gaining in the region.

It was a convoluted tangle that involved high-level bribes and may well have included threats of military action. Through it all, Pax was training soldiers to defend a government that might not exist in a few weeks or a few months. Who would the trainees fight for if the government fell? Issas or Afars? Or Eritreans over Ethiopians? What would happen to the Djiboutians?

Camp Citron was the only permanent US military presence in all of Africa, and the US could lose their base of operations on the whim of a president whose grip on power was loose at best. Meanwhile next door, people fled Eritrea in boats due to horrific human rights violations, while China just stirred the pot and waited for it to boil over.

The entire region inched ever closer to the flashpoint.

"China has done a terrible job protecting Djibouti's cultural heritage sites," Morgan said in a hard tone. "I wouldn't count on them to protect Linus."

"I want to know when we can announce this find," the tourism minister said. "A site like Linus will do wonders for our tourism industry."

"We're waiting for the potassium-argon dating results," Morgan said. "Announcing a find of this kind without a solid date is the equivalent of skipping peer review before publishing in a scientific journal. It would make the find suspect, as if we weren't confident in our analysis to hold it up to scrutiny from the expert community. I'm a contract archaeologist. I know what I'm doing and am good at my job—and my job is to find sites along the proposed railroad corridors—my job *isn't* to provide the full spectrum of paleoanthropological analysis. For that, you need an expert. Once the experts have weighed in, we will announce the find. We should have a definitive date for the fossils in two to three weeks, and two of the experts I've contacted have said they could work from photos for the preliminary evaluation but would prefer to see the bones in situ."

Pax wondered what that missing skull would mean for this, and hoped to hell the US military *did* have it, and it hadn't been damaged.

Or China might be given point on protecting Linus after all.

"In the meantime," Morgan said, shifting her attention to Lemaire, "I plan to start surveying the other APE tomorrow. We'll leave Linus alone, and tell no one the site location, while we wait for the date and experts."

The minister nodded. Pax respected that Morgan had just bought time for O'Leary to get the skull back in place. *If* it hadn't been damaged. And if it had been taken by the US military in the first place.

Chapter Nine

Pax unlocked the door to Morgan's apartment in Djibouti City. He shoved it open, then stepped back. He wouldn't leave her alone in the hall, so he had to scan what he could see of the room before stepping inside.

This kind of security sweep was usually done with a handgun. Pax had opted for the M4, but then, he wasn't in the mood to dick around. If anyone was inside Morgan's apartment, they'd be sorry.

The one-bedroom unit was empty of invaders, and he shut and locked the door, then turned to face Morgan. "Has anything been moved?"

She frowned as she scanned the room. Her beautiful eyes were hooded as if she were using X-ray vision to detect changes.

Her eyes at half-mast like that were very, very sexy.

"Yes. My papers have been gone through."

"What?"

"That stack of books, next to the desk. They're in the wrong order. I was reading the *Rickety Cossack* book, but it's second in the stack. I don't remember the last time I cracked open the physical anthropology textbook, but I know it's been weeks, yet it's on top." She stepped forward. "And the human evolution coloring book, my mom sent that. It arrived just two days ago. It shouldn't be with the reference books. It should be with the dictionary coloring book and crayons. They're gifts for Hugo." She pointed to a second coloring book and box of crayons that sat on the desk by a cup full of pens.

"Hugo?" Pax asked.

"His father owns a restaurant down the street. Hugo is one of the only people who speaks English in the neighborhood. I've been teaching him to read."

She frowned again as she looked at the books. "One of the geology studies is gone. It wasn't even mine. Broussard left it here for me to use as a reference—it was a rare monograph, a geologic survey of French Somaliland done by the Vichy government during World War II. Broussard will be upset that it's gone."

"Who is Broussard?" Pax asked. He was beginning to think he should start writing these names down. A chart might be necessary.

"Andre Broussard is the French geologist who initially dated the strata in the valley where we found Linus. He's the one who told China to stop destroying sites and paved the way for my contract. He conducted a geologic survey of the proposed railway APE, and recognized that artifacts littered the ground all along the route."

"Pretend I don't remember what APE stands for."

She smiled. "Sorry. Area of Potential Effect—the project footprint where everything will be destroyed by construction. Broussard's geologic study has been an enormous help for my survey. The government provided this apartment, and Broussard lived here before me. He returned to France in January, but knowing I'd need them for my survey, he left behind several reference books and the monograph. I'm supposed to mail the books to his home in Paris when I'm done."

"So the monograph is missing, and books have been moved. Anything else?"

A cell phone began to ring and vibrate.

"Is that your ringtone?" Morgan asked, turning toward the sound.

Pax glanced behind him. There was a phone on the tiny kitchen table. "No. That phone isn't yours?"

She shook her head. "My phone was smashed yesterday."

No time to flee the building, so Pax pushed her into the bedroom—as far from the phone as possible. It could be the trigger for a bomb.

The phone stopped ringing, and nothing exploded.

Twenty seconds later, it began to ring again.

"Should we answer it?" Morgan asked.

Pax was at a loss. This wasn't his specialty. She needed someone who was trained to protect VIPs. What the fuck was his XO thinking?

I requested this. It's my own damn fault.

"Stay here," he said and stepped into the kitchen. He picked up the vibrating cell and swiped a finger across the touch screen, then hit the speaker button. He said nothing.

"Dr. Morgan Adler," a male voice said, "leave Djibouti."

Chapter Ten

M organ wanted to snatch the phone from his hand and ask who the hell the caller was, but Pax disconnected and ripped the battery from the phone before she had a chance. "You have thirty seconds to pack. You handle clothes, I'll grab your papers. No time to grab all the books, so pick three. Give me a bag."

She plucked a canvas bag from the closet and threw it at him. "My field notebooks are more important than any of the books."

In her bedroom, she filled a second bag with clothing and a third with boots and her secondary dig kit.

She was at least thirty seconds over her time limit when he stood in the bedroom doorway. "Time's up. We're leaving."

She hesitated in the main room. Did he get the USB drive from the desk drawer? She turned toward the desk but he caught her arm. "Nope. We're leaving. You can come back later. Maybe."

She followed him out the door. He tossed the bags in the rear of the SUV. In moments, they were peeling out of the parking lot. He drove a twisted route through town, taking side streets she never would have explored on her own.

"It's a waste of time looking for someone following us when they'll easily spot us on the road to the base," she said. *Shit.* The base. It looked like she was moving there after all. In spite of O'Leary's horrific move, she had no choice but to accept his offer of protection.

"We aren't going to the base. At least not yet."

"Then where are we going?"

"I have no fucking clue." He took a sharp left, then an even sharper right. His eyes darted from the road to the rearview mirror. "Gotcha, asshole."

"There's someone behind us?"

"Yep. White Toyota Land Cruiser. There had to be someone watching, someone following. They knew we were at your place. Someone knew it was time to call, that you were there. Whoever it is probably followed us from the minister's office."

His turns were erratic. The large SUV swerved and skidded, and a few times, she thought he might lose control. "You aren't...trained for high-speed chases, are you?" The words came out high-pitched, having been forced through a throat tight with fear.

He glanced sideways and grinned. "Why do you ask?"

She screeched as they took a turn on two wheels. "No reason!" she shouted over the loud, rapid drumming of her heart.

"Don't worry, babe. I got this."

And then, as if he'd been faking the erratic, poorly executed maneuvers, he slipped through a tight hole in traffic and changed lanes with smooth precision, quickly distancing them from the white Toyota, which was stuck in a traffic snarl he'd created with his horrible driving.

She caught his smug grin. She rolled her eyes and hoped he didn't notice her heart was still in overdrive. "Not a bad bit of rescuing," she said as nonchalantly as she could muster.

He laughed. "Sometimes I even amaze myself."

It was her turn to laugh. A guy who could quote Han Solo might just be her catnip.

He flashed a grin but kept his focus on the road. They were heading away from the base.

"Where are we going?" she asked.

He shrugged. "Not sure. I need to call my XO, update him on everything. I can ask what he knows about Linus."

"Good idea." She'd like to know exactly what O'Leary had done before she faced him. She pointed to a turnoff that would take them to a public market. It was early afternoon. The market would be busy with the sun past its zenith. "We can park in the large lot at the edge of the market. Plus, I can buy a new hat."

He followed her advice and crammed the oversized SUV into a tiny parking spot that meant they'd both have to exit from the driver's side. The lot was a sea of battered cars and trucks, but mostly void of people, who would all be milling around the crowded market.

Pax glanced down at his combat uniform. "I'll stand out here in my camo, and this is one place we want to blend." He unbuttoned the outer shirt. Underneath, he wore a T-shirt that had "US ARMY" emblazoned on the front.

"I've got a tee you can wear. It'll still be obvious you're US military, but at least you'll look off duty." She climbed between the seats and leaned over the backseat to root around in her bag of clothing. She pulled out a men's extra-large Washington Redskins T-shirt she used as a nightshirt, then climbed back to the front and handed it to him.

"The Redskins?" He made a face. "Don't you have a shirt from a good team? One without a racist name?"

"Sorry, the DC area has been my home base for the last eight years."

After the sneak peek she'd had last night in her CLU, she watched with interest as he peeled off the Army shirt. He had a beautiful chest. Wide, thick delts. Hard, cut pecs covered in just the right amount of coarse hair that faded over his abs but gathered again around his belly button and arrowed downward in a thin line.

She didn't know if she'd ever seen a finer display, and the lust she'd been trying to keep in lockdown broke free. Her hand moved of its own volition, and she touched his ripped abs. He jolted away, but now her brain was on board, and she followed, running her fingers over the smooth skin that covered taut muscles. Liking the feel, she shifted from fingertips to palm, sliding across his flat stomach. His muscles tightened as she explored.

She traced the line of hair downward, but he caught her hand and brought the palm to his mouth. He pressed his lips into her skin. "Don't do this, Morgan. Don't start when you know we can't finish."

She wanted to slide her hand back down his chest, over his stomach, and follow that line into his pants. She wanted to grasp his growing erection and slide her hand up and down the shaft. She wanted to watch his face as she stroked him. She wanted to bend her head down and take him into her mouth. To run her tongue over the tip of him. To taste his arousal, and then to wrap her lips around him and take him deep into her throat.

He would come hard and fast the first time. He'd pulse into her mouth, and she'd suck until he had nothing left to give. And then, after he had time to recover, she'd straddle him and he'd fuck her deep and hard. He'd suck on her sensitive nipples as he thrust into her. She'd tilt her face upward and shriek with release.

She could see it all in his eyes, sitting there in the front of the SUV as people passed behind the vehicle, heading to the market. He wanted it too. As badly as she did. This wasn't the time and certainly wasn't the place. But it would happen. It had to. Every moment they spent together was like the ocean after a large quake, before the tsunami. Slowly, the tide pulled the water out, but eventually, that wave would come in. The longer it took for the water to retreat, the bigger the wave would be.

The trick would be keeping her head above water as the wave engulfed her. She could lose herself in Peace Love Blanchard.

It was that damn adrenaline. That damn need for release. Today had been almost as horrific as yesterday and her body was an adrenaline factory working overtime.

This level of arousal from a simple touch was insane. They barely knew each other. She wasn't familiar with adrenaline-fueled lust but was starting to believe it should be a controlled substance.

She slipped her hand from his. "Where are you from, Pax?" Her words were husky. As if they'd just done everything she'd imagined and her voice was hoarse from crying out during orgasm.

"Oregon."

She smiled. "Right. Those hippie parents. Portland?"

He shook his head. "Eugene."

"How long have you been in the Army?"

"Don't do this," he said again. "We aren't going to share our life stories. This isn't a first date. We aren't going to have sex." He paused, then added, "Ever."

"Ever?" she challenged. "Not even stateside?"

"Morgan, when you leave Djibouti, we'll never see each other again."

"That's how you roll?"

"That's how I roll. But with you, I won't even roll. You are my job. My assignment. And I don't fuck on the job."

She'd be hurt by his rejection, except his pants bulged with an impressive erection. He wanted her just as much as she wanted him. He just didn't intend to act on it.

He grabbed the Redskins shirt and pulled it over his head. "This is how we're going to do this. We'll head out into the market. You'll look at hats and tourist items. You will hold my arm, like we're a couple."

"Won't that be a problem? Given that this is a Muslim country?"

"They're used to seeing Americans acting American in the marketplace. They might frown, but I'm big and mean looking, and I'm not willing to take a chance on being separated. I'll make some calls as we stroll, like I'm talking to close buddies. We stay together every moment. The crowd swarms and tries to separate us, you will *not* let go of my arm. Understand?"

She nodded. "You sure you want to leave the SUV?"

"Yes. We'll be looking for familiar faces in the crowd. Tell me if you recognize anyone."

"Okay."

He reached for the door, but then paused. He met her gaze. "I've been in the Army since right after I graduated high school. It'll be fourteen years this June. A soldier is the only thing I know how to be."

That damn inevitable tsunami. The retreating tide before the wave was pulling him out too. He was just better at fighting the undercurrent than she was.

As instructed, Morgan held his arm. She even leaned against him and gazed up at him with doe eyes, causing him to laugh. She enjoyed being silly in the midst of such bizarre circumstances. Yesterday was a terrifying memory, and today had brought new and strange horrors. She'd been assaulted, and someone had invaded her apartment.

They'd called her and told her to leave Djibouti.

Was Etefu Desta behind that phone call?

They really had no proof Etefu Desta had done anything. Just the word of the militants who'd shown up at the site yesterday. It was pure speculation that his henchmen were behind the IED and sniper attack.

What if the warlord was the scapegoat for someone else? How would they possibly know?

Had the man she'd shot woken up from surgery? She didn't even know the poor guy's name. Today she'd sent another man to the infirmary, but he'd also had it coming.

Why had he returned to the site alone? Had it been an abduction attempt?

That made her wonder if she'd been grabbed because she was a woman, or if it had to do with Linus. She'd been told blondes drew more interest on the auction block. Before she came to Djibouti, one official had offhandedly remarked she might consider dying her hair.

She wished she'd listened, but she'd never expected to get on anyone's radar. Her project was low-key. A blip on the railway construction calendar. Notable only because the US military was eager for completion of the rail line.

Clever of the Djiboutian government to tie the two together as they had, giving the military motivation to expend funds they wouldn't otherwise allocate.

The natural resources minister had known of her father, which made her wonder if they'd known her gender all along and only feigned surprise. Had they selected her not because she had a PhD and a willingness to travel to an unstable region, but because they hoped threatening her would draw in her father and the might of the US military?

The idea was ludicrous. A conspiracy that would have had to go back to the early contracting stage, when no one had any idea of what she'd find. She was officially losing it to even have followed that train of thought. Her grip on Pax's arm slipped, a side effect of her thoughts going off the rails. She took his arm again, and they resumed walking.

The market was crowded, a mix of Djiboutians, Somalis, and French nationals who wandered through the heat. Buses were parked at haphazard angles throughout the market, with stalls set up before them. Some vendors sold their wares from blankets spread over the hard ground.

At the edge of the market was a woman with a burlap sack full of different currencies: Ethiopian birr, euros, US dollars, Kenyan shillings, and Djiboutian francs. Most vendors at the market preferred the Djiboutian franc. A check of the stash of money she'd grabbed when she packed her clothes revealed no francs amongst the euros and dollars, so she pulled Pax in that direction.

Exchange complete, she left the food stalls, which were fragrant and colorful with fresh fruit imported from other lands—Djibouti had no crops of its own—and headed toward the textiles to find a hat.

People bumped and jostled them, and a few tried to cut between them, but she kept her word and held on to his arm. It had been awkward during the money exchange, but rules were rules. She didn't always like them, but she did know how to follow them.

Holding Pax's arm, however, was no hardship.

She glanced up to see a frown marring his handsome lips and guessed his phone conversation had triggered it. She kept up her pretense of distracted shopping and tried on a scarf that was the color of a Djibouti sunrise. The scarf was lovely, sheer with lace edging, but not practical for her needs.

She turned to make a beeline for a vendor who had a stack of boonie hats, but Pax stayed rooted to the spot. She turned to see him tuck his phone away, then dig out his wallet. He handed the vendor two thousand francs and took the scarf.

"A beautiful scarf for a beautiful woman," the vendor announced in heavily accented English as Pax draped the scarf over her head.

"My thoughts exactly," Pax said to the vendor.

His words and action sent a thrill through her, and she wished she could see his eyes, but they were covered with dark lenses. "Thank you," she said.

"It's a trade. For the Redskins shirt." His voice was gruff, telling her he already regretted the impulsive purchase. He probably was worried she'd take it the wrong way.

Had she?

It was a sweet gesture, sure. But she knew it didn't change a thing about their situation.

He lowered the scarf to her shoulders. "I suppose you still need a hat for the field."

She nodded, and they made their way toward the boonie hat stall, where she purchased the first hat she could find that was the right size. Pax scanned the crowd over her head, making it look like he was admiring the hat, but she knew his eyes behind the dark shades were taking in everything, everyone.

He took his job seriously, and for that she was grateful. She had a feeling he'd never provided private security before, but he was good at it. Maybe, when he left the Army, he'd get a job in the security field.

She pulled her brain back from that thought. Aside from feeling an irrational surge of jealousy toward his imaginary female clients of the future, she also mentally had him leaving the Army, which he'd made clear he had no plans to do.

And after growing up a military brat, she'd sworn off being a military girlfriend or wife. If she and Pax did end up in bed together, sex was all they could have. She would never get seriously involved with an Army man, no matter how perfect his abs.

They resumed walking, reaching a gap between two empty stalls. "What's the word?" she asked.

He leaned down to speak softly, his lips a scant inch from her ear. "Not here." He tucked a lock of her hair under her new hat, playing his part.

She must remember that this was all a role. A disguise of sorts.

But that didn't mean she couldn't have fun. She pressed close to him. Standing as they were, with his large form between her and the rest of the market and an empty stall at her back, she was shielded from view. Feeling wicked, she ran her tongue over the suprasternal notch of his manubrium. She supposed there was a non-technical term for the groove at the base of the throat, but she didn't know what it was. She could, however, name every process and tuberosity on human—and hominid—bones.

"You're a bad girl, Dr. Adler."

"You should probably spank me."

She felt the intensity of his gaze even though she couldn't see his eyes behind the sunglasses. "Do you like spanking?"

"It depends on the timing. As I'm coming—yes. Pretty much any other time—no."

"Ah, fuck," he whispered. "How the hell am I going to get that image out of my brain?"

She grinned. "I can think of one way."

His brows lowered under the sunglasses frames. "For that, I'm only going to spank you in ways you don't like."

She licked her lips. "As long as your hand and my butt are bare, I'm game."

He took her arm and pulled her between the empty stalls until they were tucked and hidden in the back, next to one of the buses that littered the market. He pressed her back to the dusty side of the vehicle. "You keep this up, and I end up fucking you, I will *not* apologize for crawling out of bed five minutes after I come. You got that? I will fuck you and walk away. No emotions."

"Works for me."

She thought he was going to kiss her, but he didn't. He grabbed her hand and turned to drag her back through the crowd. "Let's get the hell out of here."

It took her a moment to realize he was pissed. She dug in her heels, stopping him.

"Don't, Morgan. I've made the rules clear."

He had, but she kept on pushing until he admitted to having cracks in the shield he'd erected to defend himself against her. The only thing she'd get from him—*if* he gave in—was angry sex. Well, the angry kiss had been hot as hell. Could she settle for angry sex?

Fiery, angry, animal fucking with the hottest man she'd ever met?

Was it wrong that her first thought was, *yes, please?*

Chapter Eleven

She'd treated his statement like a thrown-down gauntlet, which pissed him off no end. He wasn't playing games. He'd spoken the truth, and she was after the challenge. But Morgan Adler had no idea what she was signing herself up for.

"You've got your hat. I'm done with my calls. Let's go. We're rendezvousing with marines in ten minutes."

They were three-quarters of the distance to the Toyota when he saw a man who looked familiar. He'd seen him earlier, chewing khat on the street in front of the minister's office. The man scanned the crowd, looking for someone.

Pax had changed shirts, but Morgan hadn't, and her beautiful long French braid would be easy to spot.

He tugged down the brim of her new hat as he pushed her into a gap between two buses. He could just see the market and the man through the windows of a bus.

Pax cupped her cheeks and planted his mouth on hers. The kiss was meant to hide her face, but, true to form, the woman slid her hands around his neck and her fingers stole into his hair. She thrust her tongue into his mouth, and he sucked on it like the gift it was.

This kiss was all he could have. This soft slide into paradise. He plundered her mouth, taking everything he wanted, knowing there'd be no more where this came from.

His XO had signed him up for a little slice of hell. Daily proximity to the sexiest woman he could imagine, but not only did he need to maintain his focus, he also shouldn't forget that she was a general's daughter. It didn't matter that her father was an ass. If they screwed around, the general would almost certainly find out. Some asshole with an ax to grind would rat him out. It was never a good idea for an enlisted man to get involved with an officer's daughter.

He'd played that game once already, when he was young and stupid. After spending three years busting his ass to get into the Special Forces Qualification Course—a goal he'd shared with his ex-wife on their very first date—his then father-in-law tried to put the kibosh on his acceptance in hopes of steering him into the Green to Gold program, because an enlisted soldier wasn't good enough for a colonel's daughter. Worse was learning Lisa had encouraged her father's action because she'd wanted him to get into the officer program. She'd felt enlisted was beneath her too.

His marriage had lasted less than a year, and divorce papers were signed a month after Pax entered SFQC. An experience like that tended to make a soldier wary of the next officer's daughter who came along.

He ended the kiss and whispered in her ear, "There's a guy at my four o'clock, other side of the bus. He was at the minister's office. The kiss was to hide your face. Nothing more."

His words were both true and a lie. The intention had been to hide her face. That he'd gotten more in the bargain was for him to deal with in silence.

She glanced toward the bus, keeping her head down. He shifted so his body hid most of her face.

"Did you see him?" he whispered.

"Yes."

"Was he looking this way?"

"No." She looked again. "He's heading toward the fruit vendors. Away from us."

"Good. Let's get out of here."

They had to backtrack to get to the SUV, but managed to avoid the man searching for them. And now they had a description to give to the MPs who would follow up on the day's events.

They arrived without incident at the rendezvous point—an abandoned gas station on the edge of the city. An armored Humvee arrived minutes later, and he and Morgan slipped into the backseat. Two marines took over the Toyota SUV and would drive around the city until Morgan was safely within the fence of Camp Citron.

On base, Morgan made a beeline for the skipper's office, while Pax met with his XO, Captain Oswald. He turned the cell phone he'd taken from Morgan's apartment over to his superior, and gave him a rundown of the day's events. An hour later, he found himself in a large conference room as Morgan met with the top brass to determine how best to deal with her archaeological project that had just become both a priority of and a major fuckup for the US military in Djibouti.

In the center of the table lay a three-million-year-old cranium. It was mostly intact, but even his untrained eye could see the left side had fresh breaks along the cheekbone and pieces of the heavy bony brow lay in a pile next to the skull.

Captain O'Leary didn't even appear chagrined at what his orders had wrought upon a singular and spectacular find that could alter what was known about human evolution.

Pax smiled wryly at the thought. Clearly, he'd been suckered in by Morgan's enthusiasm.

He would have loved to see Morgan face down the captain, but then, for the sake of his career, he had a feeling it was better she'd faced the man in his office alone. He just hoped for the sake of her argument she'd been able to keep the angry tears to a minimum, because O'Leary would view them as a weakness to exploit.

For now, Morgan sat quietly at the far end of the table saying nothing. She met his gaze, but her face remained carefully blank.

He had to wonder where her stoic mask came from. To the casual observer, they'd look like strangers, not two people who were fighting a losing battle with attraction.

He had to admit he preferred her passion and anger to this reserved façade. She lived life full of emotion. He liked that about her.

But then, he liked almost everything about her.

From the ideas being tossed across the table, it was clear the Navy intended to seize control of Morgan's project, riding roughshod over her just as she'd feared. It was equally clear that the powers that be in this room didn't know fuck about archaeology. The Navy had specialists on staff who'd visited and consulted on sites in the past, but they were currently stateside, and getting civilian employees to Djibouti in a hurry wasn't a specialty of the bureaucrats at home who managed travel orders.

Aside from Morgan, there was another civilian woman at the table who remained silent. It was an open secret that Savannah James was CIA, and the fact that she'd been invited to this meeting raised all sorts of questions for Pax. What was the CIA's interest in Morgan?

The CIA was certainly gathering intel on Desta, but was James working the China angle? This might not be about Desta at all. It was entirely possible the warlord was nothing more than China's scapegoat.

Finally, after sitting in silence for nearly forty minutes as men who knew nothing about archaeology expressed how Morgan's project—and she— would be handled, Morgan cleared her throat. "I don't care if you *can* get Navy archaeologists here tomorrow," she said softly, the words drifting under the sounds of ignorant men making foolish assumptions.

The low tone worked in a way a shout wouldn't have. Silence fell as Morgan rose from her chair. "You are not importing a man to take over my project. *I* hold the contract. I'm in charge."

O'Leary launched into his excuses. "Desta might not treat a man—"

She faced the skipper, fixing him with a blank expression, but Pax had glimpsed the contempt in her eyes. "He thought *I* was a man." Her voice remained level. Even. "Don't use a drug- and sex-trafficking warlord as an excuse for your sexism, Captain. I'm damn good at my job and have the fieldwork under control. Right now, *you*"—she gestured toward Linus's skull—"have done as much damage to the find as Desta. If the site needs protection from anything, it's from your ignorance. If you try to steal my project, I'll tell the minister of culture exactly what you've done."

A fierce pride shot through him. His woman recognized the source of her power and knew how to wield it to hold the big dogs at bay.

His woman?

It appeared the caveman was back.

"Morgan," the skipper said, "you're being emotional instead of logical—"

"Dr. Adler," she corrected. "I have a PhD in archaeology. What archaeology degree do you have, Captain O'Leary?" She leaned on her fists on the table. "And since when is it *emotional* to demand the person with the most expertise, who in fact is contractually bound to perform the work, remain in charge of the project? How is that not *logical*? I know you're trying to put me in my place, Captain, but you see, my place is at the head of my project, and no one, not even the almighty US military"—her gaze flicked to the only other woman in the room—"or the CIA, can shove me out."

So Morgan had noticed and identified Savannah James too. Interesting.

"I refuse to work this project in name only," Morgan continued. "It's obvious you want a rubber stamp on the route to rush construction of the railroad without serious evaluation of the cultural heritage sites that can and will be destroyed. First of all, no archaeologist in their right mind would agree to that—so forget importing one of your own. I guarantee they'll side with *me*. But more important, you *can't* bring in someone else to work the project, because you lack the authority. You may be the mayor of Camp Citron, but my project is outside the confines of the base. It's not your call to make. This project is, and shall remain, *mine*."

She took a deep breath, then continued, "I'm staying in Djibouti. I will do my job. You'll get your airstrip. But if you try to prevent me from doing what I came here to do, I will tell my client exactly how many international and US laws you broke when you sent a team of marines who know nothing about paleoanthropology to rip Linus from the ground. Do you think you'll get your airstrip then, Captain?"

She met the gazes of each of the men at the table one by one, finally landing on Pax. He allowed his mouth to curve slightly, letting her know he approved and was on her side, for all the good it would do her. As a master sergeant, he was the lowest rank—and the only enlisted—in the room.

She returned her attention to the skipper. "To do my job, I need a phone, a computer, and a camera. Mine were destroyed by the explosion. I expect one of each to be delivered to my CLU this evening." She again gestured toward the skull. "Linus will be stored in a secure facility here on base. I will contact two of the world's foremost paleoanthropologists and ask if they would be willing to come to Djibouti to examine the skull. They will say yes without hesitation, and you will fund their visit and house them while they are here. You broke the skull, you will find the budget to fix it. When they ask, you will acknowledge full responsibility for the condition of the skull. That will *not* fall on me. Fortunately, both are experts in fossil reconstruction, so as long as none of the pieces were destroyed, there will be no data loss, and perhaps Linus's head will be back together in time for the presentation to the media.

"Finally, I need to be at my project area by oh-seven-hundred tomorrow. If you won't provide me with a vehicle and a security detail, then I'll be returning to my apartment in Djibouti City and finishing my project with no further interference from the US military. If you try to keep me prisoner here, I will make sure everyone associated with my contract knows what you are doing and why, including your plans for me to blithely disregard cultural resources because you find them inconvenient. Make no mistake, Djibouti may be poor, but they know damn well what their cultural resources are worth. They won't take your interference lightly."

With that, the beautiful and diminutive woman who had been disregarded, talked over, and minimized throughout the meeting, turned on her heel and left the room.

Pax leaned back in his chair and smiled. It appeared his woman was a black belt third dan in dealing with ignorant, sexist military leaders as well.

Chapter Twelve

There was a knock on Morgan's CLU door at six thirty a.m. sharp. She opened it, expecting to see Pax, but instead found a young marine she hadn't met before. His name patch said SANCHEZ, and he looked about nineteen with a sweet, boyish face. He wore desert camouflage and sported a belt full of military gear. "I've been assigned to your protection duty, ma'am. Are you ready to go?"

"Yes. Let me grab my field kit." She gathered the gear she'd need for the day and locked her CLU behind her. As she followed Sanchez to the vehicle, she wanted to ask where Pax was, but odds were the boy wouldn't know details, and there was no point in advertising her unhealthy interest in the Green Beret.

As it was, an air of melancholy entered her mood, making her aware of how much she'd anticipated working with Pax by her side, how she'd felt secure in the day's work, knowing she'd have her own personal Green Beret providing protection.

The workday progressed as the survey had in the weeks prior to finding Linus, except two armed marines accompanied her, and she had three fewer crew members.

The marines looked like they should be studying for finals and asking girls to the prom rather than out in one-hundred-and-five-degree heat in full gear, providing protection in Djibouti. But it was clear after an hour these were men, not boys, and she was grateful for their protection.

At the end of the day, they'd walked and cleared a small section of the alternate APE. Morgan conferred with Ibrahim over the planned grid for the following day's work. With each day, they shifted farther east, necessitating new meet points and the moving of equipment. This wasn't like the Linus excavation, where they'd stayed in one place for over two weeks.

The survey would take longer with the smaller crew, but Charles Lemaire had indicated that finding men eager to work would be difficult now that Desta had threatened the project along with everyone who worked on it.

As far as the warlord went, she didn't know if the Navy had learned anything from the cell phone Pax had taken from her apartment, or if either man she'd injured had provided any actionable intel. She was out of the loop, which was fine by her, considering being in the loop would mean giving up her project to men who'd stated flat out during the meeting the previous night they wanted her to lie and say there were no significant sites in the second APE after just a cursory search. And when that balloon didn't float, they'd discussed bringing in their own experts who, they believed, would sign off on the project.

Morgan had met her share of Army and Navy archaeologists over the years, and she had a hard time believing any of the professionals she knew would ever sign off on a project in a place as culturally rich and prehistorically significant as Djibouti. People went into archaeology because they had a passion for the subject and wanted to protect the resource. Not to become rubber stamps.

But that didn't mean she'd relinquish control just to prove that point.

She'd looked forward to talking about the meeting with Pax, but he was AWOL today and no one had said a word about why.

She felt bad for the marines, out in the heat in full gear. She and the crew took frequent breaks, setting up a shade canopy when necessary, but the marines were only allowed to take their breaks one at a time. Someone was always vigilant. She and her crew worked in the same conditions, but at least their work was interesting. Every moment held the potential for discovery. This was true in Djibouti more than in any place she'd worked.

She'd never in her life expected to hold artifacts in her hands that had been created by precursors to modern humans one to three million years ago. It was mind-blowing. And then finding Linus, well, she didn't even have the words to describe what that discovery had been like.

Back at Camp Citron at the end of the day, she received a summons to the captain's office. Dread settled in her gut. Had he found a way around her blackmail over the damage to the skull? It was possible he'd come clean with Charles Lemaire in an attempt to convince the minister to pull her from the project. It would be ironic if he got her fired, considering O'Leary had been the one who'd put pressure on her to stay. She had no regrets about her decision, and might even have made the same choice without the pressure from O'Leary, but she resented his methods nonetheless.

Coated with dirt and sweat after hours in the field, she took a shower, spending all of her allotted three minutes of running water before meeting with the captain.

Clean and presentable, she braced herself to face O'Leary. He was on the phone when she was admitted to his office. He waved her forward and bade her to sit with a gesture. She complied and folded her hands in her lap, being careful not to fidget or show white knuckles.

After a lengthy interval, he hung up the phone and met her gaze. Silence settled between them, and she wondered if he was counting to some predetermined number prior to speaking, if that was a technique taught in intimidation school.

She'd graduated summa cum laude from the general's school for facing down authority and could outwait him without breaking a sweat.

Finally, he said, "We got off on the wrong foot, Morgan."

"Dr. Adler," she corrected. If she had to call him Captain O'Leary, he would damn well call her by her title as well, even if it was pretentious.

He inclined his head in acknowledgment. "Dr. Adler. You've highlighted my point. I've made a few mistakes."

"A few. Mistakes. Why don't I list the highlights for you?" She raised a finger to tick off the numbers. "One: you seriously damaged a fossil that isn't just *rare*, it's singular. The only one of its kind." She held up a second finger. "Two: you made a power grab for my project with a complete disregard for the data that's at stake. And three: you used my father to put pressure on me, essentially ending my relationship with him. That's the view from where I'm sitting, so forgive me if I'm not ready to simply say 'mistakes were made' and move on."

He leaned back in his chair and stared at her. His expression was closed. What did she expect? An apology? Foolish, since he was probably cut from the same cloth as the general, and Morgan knew she'd be downhill-skiing in hell before her father ever uttered the words "I'm sorry" to his lone offspring.

All at once, the man let out a heavy sigh and slumped in his seat. "I screwed up. Every step of the way."

His words were so completely not what she expected, it took her a moment to take them in, to see that he'd dropped the command posture. She straightened her spine and waited for him to elaborate.

"I'm sorry, Dr. Adler."

From his sincere tone, she was tempted to tell him to call her Morgan. But this could be a ploy. She cocked her head in question.

"I want to give you my perspective. I don't expect you to forgive me, but I hope you'll understand." He stood from behind his desk and turned to the window. "This room is the center of the US fight against terrorism in Africa and the Arab Peninsula. It's my job to run the base and work with the different commands that have operations here. As you said, I'm essentially the mayor of Camp Citron." He cast a smile at her over his shoulder. "I'm not the highest-ranking officer on base, but my focus is, and must always be, on the base itself. Other officers must look out for their commands, while I look out for our physical presence on the Horn of Africa.

"The job, the needs of the base, can, at times, make me myopic. But lapses on my part can mean terrorist organizations have a chance for success in their strikes. They grow and gain power. Al-Shabaab has committed atrocities here in Africa as bad or worse than what ISIS has been doing in Iraq, Iran, Turkey, and Syria. Al-Shabaab attacks have been as devastating as what al-Qaeda has done in the Middle East, yet many Americans don't even know al-Shabaab exists. I'm fighting a war invisible to most Americans—except for the part where they're pissed about the drones."

She stiffened at that. She had her own issues with drones. "Well, the drones are killing civilians. Families. Children. Machines delivering death without accountability."

He nodded. "Yes. More mistakes. But we can't share with the world the real reasons we target certain individuals. For example, we've suspected for over a year now that China is arming Etefu Desta, which brings the threat he poses to a whole new level. A well-armed Desta could seriously gut our fight on terror on the African continent. He needs to be taken out. Soon. And when we find him, we'll do everything in our power to only kill members of his organization. But I shouldn't have to justify the use of drones to kill Desta to you, considering you've been targeted by the warlord."

"Yes. I'll admit to being a hypocrite. I'm against drones on principle, but I'd cheer if you sent one after Desta, and I'm hoping the man who was shot in the wadi can provide his location."

He turned away from the window and faced her. "Which brings me to the reason I asked you here. He was murdered this morning before he was able to tell us where Desta's base is."

Shock filtered through her. "Murdered? Isn't he on a Navy ship in the Gulf?" She'd seen him fly off in the helicopter. How could he be murdered on a Navy ship?

Captain O'Leary nodded. "Another patient at the medical facility—also a detainee—overwhelmed his guard and slit the militant's throat with a scalpel."

She gasped. "Is the guard okay? Was anyone else injured?"

"The guard has a concussion but is otherwise okay."

"What happened to the detainee with the scalpel?"

"He was shot and killed as he tried to escape the medical facility." The captain paused. "You should know, the killer was the man who was taken into custody after assaulting you and Sergeant Blanchard at your Linus site yesterday."

She sucked in another sharp breath, feeling pummeled by each fact the captain revealed. "Did he plan it somehow? Attacking us at the site so he'd be captured and taken to the ship?"

The captain shrugged. "We'll never know if it was a crime of opportunity or exceedingly well planned. The man had to know escape was unlikely. His willingness to sacrifice himself to keep Desta's base of operations a secret is worrisome.

"Desta has never utilized suicide bombers before, and we'd believed it was because his followers want to overthrow the government of Eritrea—due to political ideology, not religious. Simple greed for power combined with a pedigree that has China betting on him to succeed."

The captain turned back to the window. "But this...this is different. Intelligence indicates the man who killed the militant on the ship might be from al-Shabaab, which means either Etefu Desta is now aligned with the terrorist organization, or al-Shabaab is using the warlord as a cover for their own activities. Either way, they don't want us to find him, and we've got an uphill battle taking down this threat.

"There've been other signs of Desta's cooperation with al-Shabaab, and Monday's coordinated assault on the base that included the bombing of your vehicle may well be indicative of things to come." He faced her again. "When we met on Monday, I was viewing the situation with a much bigger picture in mind. My base had been under attack. My convoy pinned by a sniper. An explosion on the main road to the base. With our own airstrip, we can react more quickly and bring in supplies and new personnel more easily. As the mayor of Camp Citron, I need to look out for my citizens."

She nodded. She *did* understand the importance of gaining an airstrip to aid the US fight in the war on terror in Africa.

"Marines were sent to retrieve Linus because the same person who called in the tip that resulted in Sergeants Blanchard and Callahan stopping you before you reached the base contacted us again and said Desta was going to smash and grab the fossils. The first tip proved true, as you know. I don't regret taking action to prevent the second."

Her stomach flooded with acid. "Why didn't you tell me that yesterday?" When she'd met with him prior to the meeting, he'd offered no explanation. In disgust, she'd attended the meeting and gazed with horror at Linus's shattered zygomatic arches and the broken bits of his glabella—bones that had protected an australopithecine brain that could make and use tools. A male who had hunted with those tools on his very last day. His bones had survived intact for three-point-five-million years, only to be broken within hours of the US military learning of their existence.

That was the attitude she'd brought to the meeting. A little explanation from Captain O'Leary would have gone a long way.

"I didn't tell you because we have reason to believe the tips are coming from someone within Desta's organization, making everything about the tips and the information highly classified." He gave her a faint smile. "Not to mention that *I* don't answer to *you*."

"So why are you telling me now?"

"Because today we received another tip. And this one involves you."

Fear unfurled in her belly. "Me? Like the package delivery tip?"

"This one is more personal. It appears Desta is…*interested* in you."

Fear became full-blown terror. "Interested?" Her voice was little more than a squeak.

"He has expressed the desire to make you his fifth wife."

Her breath left her in a rush. When she could finally speak, she said, "You can't be serious."

The captain shrugged. "There is no way of knowing how serious the notion is, but we can't ignore it."

She jumped to her feet and tried to ignore the spin of the room. This could be a lie. This *had* to be a lie. She really wanted it to be a lie. "You can't use this to remove me from the project or keep me prisoner here—"

He held out a hand. "No, Dr. Adler. I will not attempt to interfere again with the management of your project. Also, it might appear suspicious if you didn't show up in the field, and we don't want to risk revealing we have an informant."

"So business as usual?"

"Not completely. We'll be issuing you a gun, as Sergeant Blanchard requested. I understand you know how to use it?"

She nodded.

"Good. There's another precaution we can take. One Desta won't know about." He crossed the room, opened the door, and signaled to someone in the waiting area.

The woman who'd attended yesterday's meeting entered the room carrying a heavy-duty black case. She set it on a side table and pressed her thumb to a small blank square. A rectangular panel on the top opened, revealing a numbered keypad. She pressed several buttons, and the case lid rose. "We haven't officially met," she said. "Savannah James."

"CIA?" Morgan asked.

The woman offered a tight smile and said nothing.

"Dr. Adler," Captain O'Leary said, "We'd like permission to inject a subdermal GPS transmitter into your arm."

Sweat dotted her brow, as if she were back out in the Djiboutian heat, not in a nice, quiet air-conditioned office with an insane officer who'd just suggested implanting her with something that couldn't exist. "Aren't subdermal trackers science fiction?" she asked.

James answered for O'Leary. "The kind they had in *The Hunger Games* are fiction. No one has made a tracker that transmits continuously. The battery required would be the size of a deck of cards, and would need constant recharging. What we have is highly classified because it's only useful as long as the enemy doesn't know it exists." She held out a two-millimeter wide, fifteen-millimeter long strip that looked like copper-coated vinyl. "It's flexible, so it will move with you. After the insertion point heals, it's painless. A chip this size can emit a signal for four hours. It requires an active cell phone within ten feet; it hops on the signal and transmits to the base station, which is here on Camp Citron."

"What good is it, then?" Morgan asked. "Four hours isn't very long, and cell towers out here are few and far between." The item looked harmless enough. Except that they wanted to *implant it under her skin.*

"It can remain dormant for up to two months. It only wakes when activated. Four hours is plenty of time if the abductee waits to trigger it until they're certain they won't be moved for enough hours for a rescue to be planned and executed."

It still sounded like a narrow hope, but it was certainly better than no hope. Or rather, better than becoming the fifth wife to a sex-trafficking, drug-dealing warlord. "How do you activate the transmitter?"

"The easiest method is direct pressure on the chip for ten seconds. Massaging the spot will activate it in only five seconds. For that reason, we try to put it in a location that's not likely to be pressed while sleeping, but also an area of the arm that can be reached when hands are tied together in front or behind."

The woman had Morgan hold her wrists together and touch her left arm with her right hand. She drew a red line in the easiest places to apply pressure for ten seconds. Morgan repeated the process with her hands behind her back, and her arm was marked again, this time in blue.

"Okay, now nose," James said.

"Excuse me?"

"Raise your hands above your head as though they're bound above you, and press your nose into your arm, applying as much pressure as you can, aiming for the red and blue intersections."

"The name Savannah doesn't fit you," Morgan said. "It can't be your real name."

"It's not," the woman said.

"You wear it like an ugly Christmas sweater. Awkward. Possibly itchy."

The woman laughed. "I do give most of the personnel on base hives, but I'm curious why you say that."

"You're no Southern belle, for starters, and I've only met one Savannah who wasn't from the south—but her parents were. More important, the way you said it when you introduced yourself was flat. Either you aren't connected to the name Savannah, or you don't like it."

She shrugged. "It doesn't matter. Everyone here calls me by my last name anyway. Now press your nose into your arm."

Morgan did as instructed, and the location for the chip was selected. Midway between her armpit and inner elbow, near the deltoid tuberosity of the humerus. Behind her back, she could reach the spot with her index finger, in front with her thumb, and her nose would work if the others failed.

Not-Savannah moved with smooth efficiency as she pulled a gadget that looked like an ear-piercing gun from the case, but it had a wider, flat needle. She inserted a cartridge with a sterile chip into the chamber and said, "This will pinch for a moment, but that's all." She set the gadget aside and reached for an alcohol swab.

Instinctively, Morgan covered the spot on her arm where the tracking device was to be injected. "So, what are the health risks? Will I be getting arm cancer in five years?"

Not-Savannah shrugged. "The long-term effects are unknown, but it's not recommended the implant remain in place for more than two months. Removing is a quick surgery—like pulling out a big splinter. Are you allergic to any metals?"

Morgan pursed her lips. "No. But I've never been implanted with any before."

"If you have a reaction, it will occur within the first twenty-four hours, and we'll remove the implant."

"And what if I set off the transmitter accidently?"

"If it's reset within thirty minutes, the implant can remain, but the transmission length is reduced by the amount of time it was active."

"How do you reset it?"

The CIA agent picked up an item that looked like a TV remote control from the case. "With this. It scans the chip and realigns the settings. It's like a factory reset button. We'll do a test once we have the chip in place."

"And if I accidently trigger it when I'm in the field? I couldn't get back within thirty minutes."

"At that point, we'd have to replace the implant. But these are insanely expensive." Not-Savannah frowned. "So don't do that."

Morgan took a deep breath and presented her arm. This was crazy. She wasn't being injected with top secret technology by a CIA agent—or whatever this woman was—because an Ethiopian warlord wanted to make her his fifth wife. But the sharp jolt of pain at the injection told her it was all too real. And Not-Savannah had lied about the injection not hurting. It had gone right into the muscle and hurt like hell.

"It will be tender for the first day or so. We ask that you keep a bandage over the injection spot for at least five days."

"How will I know if it's working?"

"You won't. There can't be any outward sign you've got a transmitter on you. Too dangerous. But we'll test it now to make sure it's active. Press the spot for ten seconds."

A few curses escaped her lips as she pressed on the fresh injection site. Cold sweat broke out on her brow.

Not-Savannah looked at a screen in her box. "Nine seconds and it's on. Good."

She waved the remote over Morgan's arm and pressed a few buttons. Morgan had the insane urge to power down like C-3PO.

"Okay. Now I want you to massage it," Not-Savannah said.

Massaging hurt even worse than pressing had. The woman was a masochist and Morgan was being Punk'd by the CIA.

"Four seconds. Perfect."

Again the woman reset the chip, and Morgan prayed she was done with the testing as her arm throbbed. "What's the fail rate?" she asked as she cradled her poor arm. It would hurt like a sonofabitch when she dug test probes tomorrow.

"In clinical trials, twenty percent."

"That's high."

"It's also better than not having an eighty percent chance of being rescued."

Not-Savannah had a point.

"And in the field, how many failures?" Morgan asked.

"There's no way to know. MIAs who'd been fitted with a tracker may well have died before they could activate it, or there were no cell phone signals available. There are far too many variables to know if it was the device itself that failed."

Her throat went dry. "How many? How many have disappeared with trackers in their arms?" Holy shit, what had she *done*? There was a tracker implanted in her arm, and this woman had to be a robot to answer these questions so coldly.

"I'm sorry, that information is classified." With that, she picked up her case and walked to the door, where she paused. "I hate sparring with military assholes," she said. "The guys all have something to prove when sparring with a woman, and the fact that I give them hives only makes them worse. I hear you're good, and we both need to stay sharp. Tomorrow evening in the gym?"

Morgan considered the offer. She was always exhausted after the field, and her daily workouts had become weekly at best, but the spook was right, she needed to be in top form if she planned to finish out this project. She also suspected the woman had asked because she wanted to pick her brain like a true spy. "Sure…Savvy. Seven p.m."

"Don't call me Savvy."

Morgan smiled and clutched her throbbing arm, glad to have annoyed the woman, even if only a little bit. "Would you prefer Vannah?"

The agent shuddered. "No. Call me James, like everyone else."

Morgan shook her head. "You should have picked a better alias."

"Fine. Call me Savvy," she said with a sigh. "See you at nineteen hundred." She closed the door behind her, leaving Morgan alone with Captain O'Leary.

"When this project is over and you return to the US," the captain reiterated, "you're to tell no one of the tracker."

She nodded. Weariness settled over her as she left his office. She'd planned to go to the cafeteria for dinner, but her arm ached, and she found she had no appetite. She wanted to roll up on her cot like a roly-poly bug and wait for someone to comfort her.

But her mother was in the US, oblivious to Morgan's situation. Her father had never cared enough. And the man she wanted had disappeared without a word.

The days strung together. Her evening sparring matches with Savvy turned out to be fun—Morgan appreciated having someone to hang out with after a long day in the field, plus she realized how much she'd missed workouts that included taking out aggression on punching bags or other people.

Savvy wasn't exactly a warm teddy bear, but Morgan liked her for her forthright manner and lack of soft edges. In a different time and place, they'd have made good drinking buddies. Except for the fact that Savvy refused to talk about anything personal. Or professional, for that matter. Instead, she peppered Morgan with questions about the project and everyone involved, from the US embassy employees to the Djiboutian ministers, down to the lowly field workers who'd been hired by Charles Lemaire before Morgan ever arrived in-country.

Morgan knew she was being analyzed and her brain picked for intel, but she didn't mind. She had nothing to hide and every reason to aid the CIA's intelligence-gathering efforts. Plus, Savvy had a wicked, acerbic sense of humor, and Morgan desperately needed the escape of laughter.

The only time Savvy's carefully controlled expression slipped was when Sergeant Cassius Callahan came up in a conversation. There was something there, but when Morgan pressed, Savvy's game face returned, leaving Morgan to wonder if she'd imagined the break in the CIA operator's cool façade. Savvy claimed she didn't know where Pax and his A-Team had disappeared to, but Morgan wasn't sure if she believed her.

The injection healed quickly, and the pain faded. By the fifth day after receiving the tracker, Morgan's arm was no longer sore, and she was able to forget it was there. There had been no more tips from someone within Etefu Desta's camp, and her workdays progressed as before: unrelenting heat, walking for hours a day in the desert, conferring with Ibrahim and Mouktar, recording sites, and moving on. Test pits were dug to determine if newly located sites had depth. A new normal settled in, and she could almost forget the crazy two days that had started with henchmen toting AK-47s at the site and ended with a hot kiss at a local market.

Well, she supposed it ended with the tense meeting at HQ, but she preferred to remember the kiss.

She'd seen no sign of Pax since that meeting and had begun to wonder if he'd shipped out. Perhaps his team had finished training the locals and he'd been sent home. But if that were the case, why didn't Savvy confirm it?

Deep down, she knew he must've asked to be relieved from leading her security detail, and while it was the wise choice, it still stung—if "sting" meant it hurt like being shot in the groin. But then, she was feeling melodramatic and rather pissy about the whole thing because she couldn't ignore the stark facts: she wanted Pax; he knew exactly how she felt; he was no longer in charge of her security; and he'd disappeared without a word.

As a Green Beret, he likely had free range over the base. The fact that he knew where she lived and hadn't sought her out in the intervening days was a special layer of hurt she'd never guessed would bother her so deeply.

Six days after being injected with the tracker, she, Ibrahim, and Mouktar took their scheduled day off. Before the explosion, her days off had been spent in the city, exploring the markets, meeting locals, and teaching Hugo to read. But now she was trapped on the base and didn't think she could get orders and a vehicle for an unnecessary shopping trip, especially because Captain

O'Leary insisted she have security every time she exited the gate, and given that Desta had taken an unhealthy interest in her, she wasn't about to object.

Stuck on the base, she wondered how to fill the day. There was a library. She could check out a book and read. It was hard to imagine focusing on a novel, but then, she was so exhausted after the week's labor, she couldn't imagine doing anything other than hiding out in her air-conditioned CLU. Even heading to the cafeteria for breakfast sounded tiring.

Regardless, she made up her mind to grab breakfast, then explore the library. She'd just begun to braid her hair in preparation for being seen in public when there was a knock at her door.

Her fingers were thoroughly entangled in the French braid. If she let go, she'd have to start over. She frowned down at the yoga pants and tank top she'd slept in, then glared at the door. It was probably the captain's aide expecting another update on her progress. The man had been a daily visitor over the past week, but he hadn't showed yesterday evening. If he was uncomfortable seeing her braless, it was his fault for visiting so early on her one day off. She flipped the dead bolt switch with her foot and said, "Come in," then turned back to the mirror to finish the braid.

The door swung wide, letting in a rush of heat. She glanced to the side to tell him to come in again but was struck speechless by seeing Pax in a skintight Under Armour T-shirt and workout shorts.

His gaze raked her from head to toe, pausing on her breasts, which were barely covered by the tight tank top. Her nipples tightened, a reaction she felt and he couldn't help but observe. She turned back to the mirror and tried to appear nonchalant, a challenge given her racing heart and traitorous nipples.

"Come in before you let the AC out." Her fingers worked down her scalp, crossing strands and adding new locks to the weave from rote memory, because her brain had fritzed out at the sight of his chest. The shirt hugged his skin, tracing every glorious muscle.

He did as she bade and leaned back against the door. She'd managed to collect all her hair into the braid and had reached the task of simply crossing the three sections repeatedly to the end. She faced him as she finished. "I was starting to believe you'd been sent home."

"No. My team was busy with the locals we've been training. We did a three-day in the western hills, got back late last night."

Three-day. Meaning he'd been around last week but had avoided her. "I hope that went well," she managed, though her throat was dry.

He shrugged. "No one died."

"A success, then." She grabbed a ponytail holder from the nightstand and tied off the braid. She crossed her arms over her chest and waited for him to speak.

A slow smile spread across his handsome face. He was a giant of a man. Imposing. Intimidating. But his smile undermined that. It was sexy and approving. The light in his eyes could warm her on a winter day in Barrow, Alaska.

"Get dressed," he said. "We're going shooting."

"We're going shooting? I haven't heard a pip from you since that awful meeting, and now we're going shooting. Just like that?"

He nodded. "Just like that."

"I haven't had breakfast."

"I picked up a breakfast burrito for you from the mess. You can eat in the car."

She gave him a tight smile. "A picnic at the shooting range? How romantic."

"This isn't a date, Morgan. Sanchez said you haven't been wearing a sidearm like you're supposed to. We're going to the range to refresh your skills, and you're going to start wearing a damn gun in the field."

She narrowed her eyes. "You sound like my father when you boss me around, which, contrary to what Freud believed, is a huge turnoff."

"Good, because I don't fool around with general's daughters."

"Bullshit." She planted her fists on her hips. "You knew about my dad when you kissed me the first time."

"That was a mistake."

"No kidding."

He raked her with his gaze again. "Get dressed, Morgan. I haven't got all day."

"What if I want to wear this to the range?" Jesus, she wasn't entirely certain where the anger was coming from or why she was baiting him. She just knew that she was angry. Which didn't make sense. What the hell did she have to be angry about? That she'd thrown herself at the man, he'd denied her for a logical reason, and then, when that reason was no longer an issue, he'd avoided her for days.

Yeah. That might have something to do with it.

She didn't deal well with rejection.

And she sure as hell liked to push his buttons.

"Get real," he said. "You're not going shooting in a Double D tank top."

Plus, she might have a bit of an exhibitionist streak. "Fine." She pulled off the tank and tossed it on the floor. She turned to grab a bra from the locker, when hands landed on her shoulders. He turned her, pressed her back to the cold container wall, then grabbed her wrists and pulled them together above her head. He held both wrists in one of his massive hands, holding her exposed to his slow perusal.

She loved the way his eyes raked across her bare breasts. She loved being trapped in his hands, unable to do anything but accept the caress of his eyes. Her nipples formed tight buds she wanted him to lick, to touch, to squeeze. But all he did was look.

"You have fucking beautiful breasts, Morgan. The most perfect I've ever seen. I want to taste you, suck on your tits, lick your clit. I want to fuck you blind."

None of the pro-estrogen activists she'd dated would ever use the word "tits," making the word shockingly sexy. It was as if he had inside, secret knowledge of what turned her on and had zeroed in on a trigger she herself wasn't aware of.

"Do it, then," she said, her words a breathy plea.

"No. I won't lick you. I won't touch you. I won't slide my tongue inside your wet pussy. I won't fuck you. What I will do is take you to the range and shoot at some targets. When we're done, I'll drop you off here and go back to my CLU. As soon as I'm alone I'm going to close my eyes and picture your perfect breasts, and I'm going to jack off."

"Why?" Her throat was so dry, her voice was hoarse.

"Because I'm *still* head of your security detail. Tomorrow, I'll be back with you in the field." His grip on her wrists loosened. "Now get dressed."

"You're still—? But you were gone—I assumed—" He had her so addled, she couldn't finish a sentence.

"My team needed me for the three-day. My XO agreed to let me see that through." He turned and ran his hand over his short-cropped hair. "After the meeting, he gave me direct orders not to get involved with you."

"How can he do that? I'm not in the military. Not part of your chain of command. How is it any of his business?"

"I'm in the Army. My private life isn't mine, and it isn't private. Especially when I'm deployed and living on base, and assigned to protect a civilian who happens to be a general's daughter. Don't for a minute think the brass won't get up in my business if we screw around. I won't sneak, and I won't lie to my XO. I won't fuck up my job." His eyes flattened. "My job is every bit as important to me as Linus is to you."

She gave him a sharp nod as she reached for a bra. His words drove home exactly what was at stake for him. She'd stop baiting him, wouldn't take his rejection as a challenge. It was time to start acting like the professional she was.

Chapter Thirteen

The coming weeks would be a special slice of hell, playing bodyguard to the hottest woman Pax had ever encountered. He'd wondered if the attraction would still be there without the adrenaline booster. Today he had his answer.

Morgan wore sensual like some women wore faded, ripped-up jeans, and she was so comfortable in her sexuality, she didn't need to don makeup, stilettos, or a fancy dress to display it. Hell, he hadn't seen her wear anything other than sturdy leather field boots, doubted she'd even brought basic makeup to Djibouti, and would take a plain T-shirt on her curves over a sexy cocktail dress any day.

She wanted him with an intensity that matched his, and he had to keep his hands off, for so many reasons.

Fuck me.

At the firing range, he laid out a series of weapons to test her. "You said you're good. Time to put your money where your mouth is."

"Bring it," she said with a cocky smile.

He shook his head and picked up his M4 to demonstrate how the first target worked: a direct hit on the round disk on the end caused the arm to swing from left to right. Hit it again and the arm would swing back. "Don't feel bad if you miss. I won't tease you too much."

She took up the rifle, and the metal arm swung back and forth as if she were flipping switches.

"Rifles are easy," he said, unable to suppress an impressed grin.

She laughed. "I forgot how fun this is."

He had a strong urge to kiss that satisfied smile, but instead left her to set up smaller targets down range. Clearly, the closer ones wouldn't be challenging enough.

"Why didn't anyone tell me where you were this week?" she asked when he returned to the firing line.

"Trainings like the one we were on—three days outside the security fence with forty-plus local trainees—are top secret. If al-Shabaab or al-Qaeda got wind of our location, we could have a bloodbath. Not even the trainees knew where we were going. If you were confined to base, you'd have been told, but you interact with locals every day and are in regular contact with various government ministers. The decision was made not to tell you. It wasn't my choice."

She frowned. "I suppose that means being pissed at you was unfair of me."

They had the range to themselves, but still, he lowered his voice. "Considering you showed your anger by flashing me, I'm not complaining."

"Wait till you see me *really* mad."

"Sweetheart, my career wouldn't survive that." He pointed to the various guns on the counter. "Better to take out your anger on helpless targets instead of this helpless soldier."

She picked up each weapon and made the shot. Sometimes it took her a few tries, but she knew exactly how to dial in, adjust, and find the target. No matter how ridiculous the shot—golf ball on a post at twenty-five yards, then again at fifty—she nailed it in five shots or less. He put a Q-Tip at twenty-five, and she got it in one. He was tempted to put a Peanut M&M at a hundred to see if she'd blow the hell out of it too.

Dammit. He wanted to be inside this woman.

My woman.

Which was a screwed-up thought in so many ways.

She picked up an AK-47. "I'm comfortable with the 9mm I was issued. Why bother practicing with these?"

"I want to be sure you're prepared for anything. AKs are the weapon of choice for militants." It was his own private hell that each bull's-eye ratcheted up his desire another notch.

"It's been quiet. There hasn't been a peep from Desta since Wednesday. This is probably a waste of time," she said.

"You had better plans for the day than going shooting with a hot Special Forces operator?" he asked.

"Oh, is Cal coming?"

He laughed. This was okay. They could joke. It would relieve tension that wasn't going to be jettisoned any other way. He grinned and lifted his shirt, showing off his abs. "Are you forgetting about this? I've seen what this does to you."

She shrugged. "Eh. I've been hanging out with cut marines all week."

Behind him, he heard Cal laugh. "You're losing your touch, Pax. I'd have gone with something more subtle."

Pax smiled at Cal but stiffened when he saw who accompanied him. "That's because you don't have the abs for it."

Cal flashed a wide grin. "What I lack in abs I make up for elsewhere."

Morgan choked on a laugh as she set the Kalash on the table, then greeted

Cal with a hug. He introduced her to the other members of their A-Team.

Tension crawled up Pax's spine when Bastian the bastard took her hand in both of his. Things hadn't been the same since Yemen. It would be just like Bastian to pursue Morgan simply because Pax wanted but couldn't have her.

The caveman reared his head again. *Mine*, the brute repeated, *all mine*.

Except she wasn't and couldn't be.

Cal asked about her survey, and she answered with animation that confirmed Pax's assessment a week ago: Morgan loved her job. "You guys should come out to the survey area this week."

"We're busy training a team of locals," Cal said.

"Bring them. Odds are, they'll end up protecting cultural heritage sites at some point. Providing protection from looters is one of the primary expenses of the Djiboutian military."

"You can show them what to look for, talk about what they'd need to know?" Bastian asked.

"Sure."

"What do you think, Pax?" Cal asked.

"Couldn't hurt. Run it by the XO."

Cal nodded, then he caught Pax's pointed look and moved down to the far end of the range, taking the others with him. Pax didn't like the way Bastian's gaze lingered on Morgan before he followed Cal down the firing line. That he'd overheard Pax flirting with Morgan was like blood in the water to a shark.

She shot the crap out of another target, and Pax figured it was time to pack up and go back. After he dropped her at her CLU, he made good on his word and jacked off in the shower while imagining her gorgeous body entwined with his.

Morgan was eager for the coming workday like a kid on Christmas morning. She didn't know if the other Green Berets and their trainees would show up at the site, but that was only a contributing factor to her excitement. Today, she'd have Pax at her side all day. It wasn't good how happy this thought made her, considering they'd never be more than bodyguard and guarded body. But still the feeling was there, and she was energized by it.

She met Pax at the Humvee. Sanchez was there as well, but the other marine had returned to his previous assignment. She slid into her usual spot in the backseat.

"Dr. Adler, why don't you bring me up-to-date on the project?" Pax said.

She met his gaze in the rearview mirror and read his silent message not to correct his use of her name. She nodded in acknowledgment. They needed barriers, and names were a starting point. After all, she'd insisted on calling Savannah the nickname Savvy to break down a barrier and bring them to the same level. She and Pax needed to go in the other direction. She would try to think of him as Blanchard, no different from Sanchez, who had told her his first name but she'd forgotten it from lack of use.

"We've been surveying the alternate APE and have found several sites and a few isolated artifacts. Nothing like Linus, though."

"How long will the rest of the survey take?"

"Two weeks—three at most. It's a long corridor, and this country is rich in prehistory."

"And poor in everything else," Sanchez commented, his gaze on a cluster of children who were picking over a debris pile on the side of the road.

Pax rode the lip of the dirt track as he gave way for a truck loaded with camels heading in the opposite direction. Portions of her project area would only be accessible by camel. She'd been assured the Djiboutian government would provide them when the time came, but with the US military's involvement, she was no longer certain exactly who would provide the camels.

The concept made her smile. She was involved in some serious camel trading. But then, one of the nicer things about having a US-supplied security detail was that some of the project logistics could be passed to them, leaving her to focus on the job. So that made Pax her camel trader.

Ibrahim and Mouktar were already at the project area when they arrived. They set off to work, nothing different in spite of Pax's—or rather, Sergeant Blanchard's—presence on the team. He'd slipped into the role of security chief with ease, the quiet professional promised in glossy Army recruitment brochures.

Damn. All she had to do was look at Pax, and she was flooded with want.

The day was relentlessly hot, as usual. At eleven a.m. Mouktar and Ibrahim took their customary break from the heat that would last until one p.m. The men usually napped in the shade of a pop-up canopy, while Morgan settled into a low beach chair and fleshed out her notes from the morning's work.

Between the canopy, chair, and sun, it was just like being at the beach, except for the excessive lack of water. Really, it was shocking anyone survived in this country now, let alone through the millennia, as lack of water had been a problem for tens of thousands of years.

Yet she'd found a site this morning that had all the earmarks of being only five thousand years old, which didn't make sense for this area. It was baffling how humans could adapt even without the most basic resource.

Pax dropped down, taking a seat beside her on the hard, rocky ground. She smiled at him distractedly as she placed a dot on her field map, marking the location of an isolated artifact. "There's another chair in the back of the Humvee if you want it," she murmured, keeping her focus on the map.

"It's unwise to get too comfortable."

She nodded. That had been their first mistake—they'd gotten too comfortable with each other. It had opened dangerous doors that they now needed to keep firmly shut.

A warm breeze rattled the canopy cover, negating the refuge of shade. Sweat gathered where her back met the chair; she leaned forward to release the heat.

He picked up her water bottle and held it out to her. "Drink, Dr. Adler."

She took the bottle and nearly drained it. It was impossible to carry enough water for an entire day of fieldwork, but they had several gallons in the Humvee.

"What are you working on?" Pax asked.

She showed him the map and pointed to the sites they'd found. "I was just thinking how strange it is that there are so many sites along here, considering the lack of water."

"I thought you said this area was loaded with freshwater lakes two million years ago. Isn't that why Linus survived?"

"Two or three million years ago, sure. But the stuff we're finding today looks recent. Too recent for this kind of occupation. We're talking five to seven thousand years, tops. Meaning people lived here long after the water was gone."

"So? People live here now."

She thought back to the children by the road. "Sure, people survive here, but no crops are grown in Djibouti, so much of that survival involves living off refuse from the port operation. Plus, there's infrastructure—they import much of what they need. Including, when the desalinization plant is constructed, water."

She glanced up along the narrow corridor that was her project area. "I don't know if you heard—I received an email from the natural resources minister a few days ago. China is fast-tracking the Eritrean desalinization plant build. They're hoping my survey will also clear the pipeline route. They want two for the price of one environmental compliance—pipeline and railroad—and offered me a big bonus if I finish my survey in less than a week."

"Will you?"

"It's impossible. I'd have to lie and sign off on large sections. Maybe if Desta hadn't scared off half my crew, but now, no." She frowned. "I know what the pipeline means. Potable water will run right through this corridor. It'll change the living standards of all Djiboutians. But it's going to take a year to build. They can wait another two weeks for an ethical report." She shook her head. "If China had their way, my survey wouldn't happen at all."

"China has their own agenda when it comes to Djibouti, and it's not to be benevolent water suppliers," Pax said. "They're looking for a proxy war, and when all is said and done, they'll swoop in and take the territory. That's why we need Camp Citron. A bigger base means a bigger presence. Less maneuvering room for China."

She nodded. "Is it wrong that I want Djibouti to have the water pipeline, even though China is picking up the tab?"

"It's never wrong to want thirsty children to have water, or starving children to have food. I just wish we were building the plant, and that it was here in Djibouti, not Eritrea." Pax sifted his fingers through the dry dirt. "But US taxpayers would never foot that bill. Not when we've got our own water problems in California and on the Navajo reservation. So China gains a foothold."

He rose to his feet. "But back to the site you found this morning. You're saying it was impossible for people to live here five thousand years ago?"

"Not impossible for individuals and small groups. They could survive with a nomadic lifestyle, but the site we found today has the earmarks of being a village—meaning longer-term occupation by a larger group of people. Even if occupation was seasonal, it doesn't make sense given the lack of water. One of the basic tenets of archaeology is if you want to find a site, look next to the water source."

"And you're certain there wasn't water here five thousand years ago?"

"I'm not a geologist, so I really couldn't say, but Andre Broussard, the geologist I mentioned before, he came through here months ago." She took a long drink of precious water before continuing. "Broussard sent me his in-progress findings, to keep me up-to-date as the contract was being finalized. He sent the results of auger samples he'd taken across the entire route. The blue pin flags we've been seeing along the route are his—marking where he took core samples.

"About two weeks before I arrived, he sent me an email—really excited about something, but light on details. Then a few days later, he sent me what amounted to 'never mind.' When I found Linus, I emailed him, wondering if that's what he'd been excited about, because there was a blue pin flag near the butchered bones. I thought maybe I was wrong about the age of the fossils, that maybe he'd done some tests I should know about. My email bounced, so I tried to call him—but his phone was disconnected. Charles Lemaire promised to contact him for me, but with everything that's gone on, I forgot to follow up."

"Broussard lives in Paris, right?"

"Yes. As far as I know, that's where he is now."

"We can check in with the minister after work if you'd like."

She frowned at the map. "That might be a good idea." She rose from her seat, studying the contour lines. "It's just…the shovel probes Mouktar dug today—the deposits looked like alluvium. But I can't fathom how river silt could be here. Broussard's geologic report indicated the last time water flowed through this valley was two hundred thousand years ago. Alluvium should be long gone."

She left the shade of the canopy to return to the site. She wanted to see the smooth, round gravel Mouktar had pulled from a meter below the surface.

She knelt by the open probe hole. The diameter of a shovel head, it was a quick window into the past. So much of this country was rock. So little soil. So little water. But occasionally, they got lucky and had softer soils to dig through.

A hat was pressed on her head. "You forgot your hat," Pax said. "A bad idea with your fair skin."

She glanced sideways to give him a smile. The hard planes of his face grew more handsome every time she looked. She turned back to the ground, feeling as blinded from looking at him as she was by the sun. "Thanks." She frowned at the puzzle of the river gravel. "It's entirely possible these pebbles are anomalous."

She picked up the shovel Mouktar had left by the hole and crossed to one of Broussard's blue pin flags. She pulled out the flag and started to dig, removing the loose dirt Broussard had augered out months before.

His auger had gone several meters deeper than Mouktar's shovel probe, but mixed with the backfilled soil, she found the same river gravel. He'd encountered the gravel too, but she couldn't be certain at what depth.

Again, it could be an anomaly. It could well be what the geologist had been excited about, but then came to nothing.

Pax brought her a new water bottle as she backfilled the auger hole. "Thanks," she said again. "You take good care of me."

"Somebody has to. You get so focused on your work you're blind to everything else."

Except him. She was aware of Pax on a cellular level, but it wouldn't do to tell him that. Instead, she drank a large gulp of water and splashed a little on her face to cool down.

"You were the same way when shooting yesterday."

She touched the pistol holstered to her hip. "It's how I dial in, I guess."

"You loved target shooting, didn't you?"

"Maybe... Probably. Yes."

He smiled. "But you quit. To spite your dad, you gave up something you loved."

"Eighteen isn't the most logical of ages. I also became a vegan to piss him off."

He raised a skeptical brow. "You had a club sandwich with cheese and extra bacon for lunch."

"True." She grinned. "But my dad hasn't seen me eat meat or dairy for thirteen years."

"Stubborn."

"I resemble that remark." They were dangerously close to sharing a moment. She turned back to the pit and ran her foot over the top to even out the overfill. She planted Broussard's pin flag back in the center. "Can I use the sat phone to call the minister? I'd like to get in touch with Broussard, and I'd rather not wait until after work."

"Sure," Pax said.

Her project budget hadn't afforded a satellite phone. Given that cell coverage dropped off dramatically outside the city, it was a definite bonus that the US military had provided one to her security detail.

The minister answered immediately. When she asked if he'd been able to locate Broussard, the cheer in the man's voice dimmed. "Can you come to my office after work today?"

She relayed the question to Pax, who nodded. She set up the meeting and disconnected, unsettled by the man's caginess. After handing the phone back to Pax, she glanced at her watch. "Another hour until break's over."

"I'm going to scout the survey area up ahead. Stay here with Sanchez."

She nodded and settled back in her chair under the canopy, her gaze on Pax as he disappeared downslope.

Sex had been taken out of the equation, but did that mean enjoying his company was off-limits too? Was friendship not allowed?

Somehow, she thought so. Because friendship would only lead to frustrated desire.

Pax's Special Forces team arrived with the trainees in the late afternoon as the day cooled from one hundred and five degrees Fahrenheit to a chill one hundred.

Upon their arrival, Morgan asked Ibrahim and Mouktar to give the locals the tour. She stood back with Pax while the men spoke in French and Arabic. Ibrahim was more animated than Pax had seen the man, clearly proud of the work he was doing, the contribution he was making.

"Is he an archaeologist?" Pax asked her.

"He is now," she said with a grin. She watched the group of men, her face showing her pride. "He didn't know anything about archaeology two months ago. The culture minister hired him, Mouktar, and the three who left, to work as laborers. They were chosen because their English is better than my French—my Arabic is nonexistent—and they were willing to dig and clear acacia in the hot sun. They're *good*. Smart. And they know this land far better than I ever could. Finding sites is more about knowing the landform than anything else. I just taught them the key signs to look for. And they've been reading up—I gave them e-book readers loaded with reference materials when they first started. I hope they'll stay on with the Cultural Resources Department when this project is over."

"This could be a career for them?" Pax asked, realizing their jobs were similar. He was teaching locals how to be soldiers. She was teaching them how to be archaeologists. Djibouti needed both.

When the tour of the survey area was complete and his Special Forces team left with their busload of trainees, he took Morgan to the minister's office as arranged. Sanchez guarded the front entrance, and Pax stood sentry inside the man's office.

The minister greeted her warmly, although it was clear he was troubled. He dropped behind his desk and folded his hands together on the surface. His French accent was more pronounced, as if he wasn't making the effort to sound more Djiboutian than French. "I received a response just this day to my inquiries into the whereabouts of Monsieur Broussard. It seems he is missing."

Morgan stiffened in her chair. The shift was slight, but Pax was far too in tune with her physical reactions. "Missing? For how long?" she asked.

"That is an excellent question. It appears no one has seen him since the Christmas holiday. However, he filed his final report of findings for the railway project in late January."

"I received an email from him with the final report attached," Morgan said, her voice wary.

"Yes. As did I. Authorities in Paris will trace the emails I received to see where they originated. He was supposed to have returned to France to finish writing up his report, but we can find no record of his flight, no indication he ever left Djibouti, however the hard copy of the final report was mailed from

Paris."

"So the report was…a fraud?"

"It is possible. I have asked his university colleagues to examine the report for inaccuracies or phrasings a geologist wouldn't use. I have also given the Paris *Police Nationale* a copy to run through a program that will determine if it is consistent with his work."

"And why is this just being discovered now?" Morgan asked. "No one noticed he wasn't in Paris?"

"He had taken a year sabbatical to complete this project. Before he left Djibouti, he emailed his colleagues with the news that he planned to finish the report from a villa in Morocco, where he intended to holiday for a few months to finish out the sabbatical."

"So everyone in Paris thought he was in Morocco, and everyone here thought he was in Paris?"

"Yes. It wasn't until his rent lapsed that the landlord started making inquiries. His phone had been disconnected due to lack of payment. His email account was suspended due to inactivity."

"You said Paris's *Police Nationale* are investigating. Are authorities in Djibouti involved?" Morgan asked.

Lemaire's shoulders lifted in a resigned shrug. "We don't have the resources the authorities in Paris have. It is my hope that *Police Nationale* will send an inspector. After all, a Parisian has gone missing. Our local gendarmes won't complain over *Police Nationale* interference."

"All leads must be cold," Morgan said. "Broussard has been missing for more than two months."

Pax stepped forward. "Dr. Adler, you said earlier that Broussard emailed you, and he seemed excited about something. Do you believe that email was really from him?"

She glanced over her shoulder. The light from the window framed her gold hair, giving his angel a halo. "I do. He was eager to discuss something he'd found, but he was going to take more samples to confirm. I can't imagine why someone else would send such an email when the next message said to disregard the previous."

"So he might have disappeared between messages."

"Yes."

"Do you know the dates he sent them?"

She frowned. "The first was a week—no, two—before I left Virginia."

Pax took another step closer. "How many days between emails?"

"I was in the waiting room to receive my final vaccination when I read it on my cell. I'd have to check my calendar, but I think it was eight days before my flight. So maybe five days apart?"

"Still a big window," Pax said. Did the geologist's disappearance have anything to do with Desta or the bombing a week ago?

"The local gendarmes will be eager for any information you can provide," the minister said, then he cleared his throat and spoke the real truth. "Or at least it might spur them into action. It is entirely possible you, Dr. Adler, were the last person to communicate with him."

That statement sat with Pax like a tuna and mayo sandwich left out for hours in the Djibouti sun. What if Morgan's observation of the anomalous alluvium was somehow related? He thought back to those blue pin flags. "There was writing on the pin flags. What did the flags say?"

"Broussard noted the auger test number, depth, and date he did the test," Morgan answered.

"So we can compare the dates written on the flags to the date of his excited email and figure out where he'd been working when he emailed you?"

He could see a subtle frisson of excitement course through Morgan. "Yes. Absolutely. Brilliant."

He was used to women admiring his body—Morgan was no different in that regard—but times like now, when she showed equal admiration for his mind, set her apart. Many of the women he'd known—hell, even his ex-wife—didn't look beyond the big soldier exterior. But today in the field, Morgan had explained her work to him without using dumbed-down words or assuming he didn't grasp basic geology.

She knew he hadn't gone to college, while she held a PhD. She was wicked smart and yet treated him like an equal. Given his line of work, that was unpleasantly rare. As if he needed another reason to want her.

If he were a different sort of man, a different sort of soldier, there could be hope for something between them when this was all over, but his work was his life, and as long as he was in Special Forces, his job, his team, was his number one priority. Anything less could be fatal, for him or for team members who counted on him to have their backs.

Morgan deserved better than coming in second.

They asked Lemaire to keep them informed and left. At the base, they collected Morgan's laptop from her CLU, then walked to the building that had Wi-Fi Morgan could use. Pax planted his hand on the small of her back as they climbed the steps to the front entrance. She looked at him askance, and he quickly withdrew his hand.

Shit. He was slipping. On base, no less.

They settled at a desk, and Morgan booted up the laptop. They wrote down the dates of the two emails from Broussard—both had been sent in January, just as she'd remembered.

Task complete, he glanced at his watch. They'd been working in one capacity or another for twelve hours straight, much of it in the Djibouti heat. "You hungry? We can go to Barely North for a bite."

She shook her head. "I'll just go to the cafeteria."

She was being wise, but a perverse side of him couldn't help but press. They couldn't have sex, couldn't have a relationship, but at the very least he could enjoy her company for another hour. "You've earned a beer with your dinner."

"I don't think that's a good idea, Sergeant Blanchard."

It was the first time she'd used his rank and title all day, and he found it didn't sit well with him, that distancing formality, even though he'd wanted it earlier. "After hours, you can call me Pax."

"No. I don't think I can." She grabbed her computer and strode to the door. "Have a good evening, Sergeant. I'll see you at oh-six-thirty sharp." She was outside before he could utter another objection.

Chapter Fourteen

"The notation on the pin flags changed," Morgan said. "The date is above the auger test number, and the number six is...off." She pointed to the number. "I've read enough of his handwritten notes to recognize his writing. Broussard's sixes aren't always closed. I think he started with the bottom loop, making one curved stroke to form the number. Whoever wrote the number on this flag started at the top, rounded the loop, then crossed the line. Like a curl."

She glanced up at Pax, who had accompanied her on the long walk to inspect Broussard's pin flags, while Ibrahim and Mouktar stayed back with Sanchez in the survey area to start the day's fieldwork. "Broussard didn't mark this flag."

He glanced back down the line they'd followed. "But he marked the others?"

She nodded. "I think so."

She poked at the loose soil in the hole with the narrow, flat-edged shovel dig bums often called sharpshooters. After a moment's hesitation, she dug out the auger hole. It wasn't as if she was messing up forensic evidence that would be collected. "I wish Djibouti had the resources to really investigate this," she said as she removed the dirt. "It's so unsettling, the idea that a man can disappear and nothing really will be done about it—locally, anyway." She wiped sweat off her forehead with a gloved hand. "Two weeks after I got here, I found a woman's pelvic bone on survey. She'd been dead at least six months, and it was definitely female—so it wasn't Broussard. I reported it to the gendarmes, and they shrugged it off. *People die*, they said."

"Welcome to Djibouti," Pax said.

"That's exactly how it felt."

"One of the first things I ever said to you was that Djibouti is pretty much lawless."

"Yeah. It's finally starting to sink in." She dug in with the sharpshooter and hit something solid. She scraped out the hole and reached inside to touch the bottom. "Solid hardpan, thirty centimeters below the surface." She frowned. "Broussard might've stopped an auger test when hitting hardpan, but the flag says this was a two-meter-deep probe with a bucket auger. This isn't even a third of a meter deep."

She dropped down next to the hole. "The auger hole is a token, dug just deep enough to look real on the surface, with a pin flag planted in the loose soil at the right interval." She slipped off her gloves and opened her water bottle. She splashed the cold liquid over her face before drinking. "He's dead, isn't he?"

"Most likely," Pax said.

"Broussard found something out here that got him excited. But we know from the dates it wasn't Linus. He worked in the area where Linus was found in December, two weeks before he flew home for the holiday. He returned right after the New Year. The last place we can be certain he worked was the area we surveyed yesterday. He dug those tests on January eleventh, and this auger test, dated January sixteenth, is bogus."

Pax dropped down to sit on the dirt beside her. "Yesterday, you noted something that made you curious and want to talk to the geologist who went missing after working in that very area."

A chill ran up her spine. Who would have thought she could be chilled when the heat index was a hundred degrees?

"Could this be about mineral rights?" Pax asked. "He might have found signs of valuable deposits."

"It's possible. This area has never really been surveyed by a geologist before—which is why that World War II monograph for the Vichy government was so important. Until Broussard came through here, they didn't even have a basic soil map for the western half of the country." She scooped up a handful of dirt and sifted it through her fingers. "For all we know, Djibouti could be sitting on a massive diamond mine." The dry silt wouldn't stick to her fingers. She blew on her open palm, sending the fine coating of dirt floating into the hot air.

"But I don't think so," she continued. "Given the alluvium deposits, it's possible Broussard found something even more valuable to Djibouti." She glanced down the wide, ancient valley. "I think there was water here, more recently than anyone ever realized. It's hard to imagine, but glaciers cut through this area once upon a time. When they melted, there would have been lakes, even springs."

"If there was water here in the recent—geologically speaking—past, what does that mean for Djibouti today?"

"Over the millennia, lakes could have seeped down, and the springs cut off. It's possible Djibouti is sitting on a deep aquifer capped by anticline rock. Given the lack of geologic survey, no one would know." She bit her lip. "I'm no geologist, and I'm definitely no expert in arid environments. But what if?

What if Djibouti is sitting on an untapped supply of water? Lack of water is the one thing that keeps the country dependent upon Ethiopia and Eritrea—and the US and China. Water would change everything."

"Could you find the aquifer, if there is one?"

She shook her head. "No way. We'd need a geologist. We'd need Broussard." She frowned. "If it's there, it could be hundreds of meters deep. Broussard would have merely seen the signs on the surface."

"If Broussard made a find like that, who would he have told?"

"Natural Resources Minister Ali Imbert, certainly. I'm not sure if he'd have told Lemaire."

Pax's gaze scanned the landscape. "Let's get you back with the team. We'll use the sat phone to call the local gendarmes and tell them what you learned from the pin flags, and hope they care enough that a man went missing to look into it."

She nodded and used the flat edge of the sharpshooter to scrape the dirt back into the hole, then replaced the pin flag.

In the end, Pax made the call, because the officer on the phone didn't speak English. He translated her words into French, then hung up, a dissatisfied frown marring his handsome face. "They won't do shit," he said.

"It will come down to *Police Nationale*, then."

He nodded. "If this ends up being connected to Desta, Interpol will get involved—they investigate drug and sex trafficking. But for now, all we've got is *Police Nationale*."

"I'll call them when I get back to the base tonight." In a way, contacting the French police would be easier. Geology wasn't her specialty, and it was unwise to dangle the hope of fresh water to people in lawless, dry, impoverished nations.

Part of the problem was Broussard had been *the* expert on the region. Others could be called in to examine the area, but they didn't have his experience, his knowledge of this part of the world. He'd worked in Ethiopia and Eritrea. If there were a deeply buried aquifer, its location and volume would likely remain a mystery without someone with matching expertise retracing Broussard's steps.

Fortunately, Broussard's breadcrumbs were metal pin flags that held up to the heat.

That evening, after speaking at length with a *Police Nationale* inspector, Morgan decided to go to Barely North for dinner. Savvy had canceled their nightly sparring match—being typically cryptic as to why—leaving Morgan free. Concern over the missing geologist had her belly in knots, and a beer might help her relax. Unfortunately, Barely North risked a different kind of tension. She might run into Pax.

Having him by her side in the field was a delicious, torturous pleasure. She'd wanted him before, but now she knew him better and enjoyed his company. His mind. His humor. His quiet competence. Like a reduction sauce simmering on the back burner, the flavor of desire had intensified.

But the connection she felt with him, this intensity, this flavor, could never be tasted. Could never be savored. Maybe another man in Barely North would catch her fancy. A fling could be just what she needed to get the Green Beret out of her mind.

As if a fast food burger could satisfy a hunger for French cuisine.

Business in the club was light, with fewer than half the tables and barstools filled. She settled onto a seat at the bar and was quickly pulled into conversation by a group of sailors. They were fun and lively, but her heart wasn't in it. She wasn't in the mood for fast food.

A man from Pax's team slipped onto the barstool to her right. "Can I buy you a drink, Dr. Adler?"

"Morgan, please." She tried to remember the man's name and came up blank. The names on their uniforms were so convenient, but in the bar, everyone had to wear civvies.

"Chief Warrant Officer Sebastian Ford," he supplied. "Call me Bastian."

Right. He was one of the two officers on the A-Team, the assistant commander—just above Pax in the team hierarchy. Flirting with this man would be a seriously dumb-shit idea. "Thanks, Bastian, but I'm all set for drinks."

"I have it on good authority you aren't involved with Pax."

She appreciated his directness, because it meant she could be equally direct. "Yes, but I'm also not an asshole."

He tilted back his head and laughed. He was handsome; she'd give him that. Black hair and hooded eyes that hinted at Native American or Asian heritage. Fine, chiseled features. Nothing like Pax, who had a darker, southern European complexion and a face of hard angles. Pax wasn't easily handsome like this man, but Pax was hot in a different way.

"I take it I'm the asshole?" Bastian asked.

"Only if you intend to hit on me."

"Then I guess I am."

She picked up her drink. She'd find another place to sit.

He caught her hand to stop her. "Stay, please? I won't do anything to make you uncomfortable."

"I'm not going to be the target in a pissing contest between you and Pax."

"He's told you about me, has he?"

"No. He's never mentioned you at all. But I'm the daughter of a general. I spotted your swagger at fifty yards."

He laughed again and waved the bartender over and ordered a drink. "Tell me about your project, then. I hear you've been finding really old shit."

She was tempted to say no, they hadn't found any coprolites, but odds were he wouldn't get the joke and explaining it would take all the funny out of it. So she told him about the village site and the alluvium and the missing geologist, and he pretended he hadn't heard the story in a debriefing already.

"Want to play pool?" he asked when the conversation waned. He nodded toward an empty table.

"Sure." She slid off the barstool. She hadn't ordered dinner, but the truth was, she wasn't hungry. Low-level nausea had settled in her gut when she acknowledged Broussard had probably been murdered. A beer, she could handle. Food not so much.

Bastian was a typical guy when it came to playing pool. Lots of strut and swagger and just decent enough to back it up.

But Morgan was better. She botched her first two turns to let him get complacent, a little sloppy, so he'd go for the difficult shot to show off, thinking there was no way she'd catch up. But he messed up the shot, and it was her turn. Time to reset his ego. She picked up her pint glass and downed the last quarter of her beer, then grabbed the stick and proceeded to run the table.

Around the time she sank the fourth ball, Bastian started to catch on. "Aww, shit. You're hustling me."

"It's only a hustle if you put money on the game." She turned back to the table and lined up her shot. It was long, and she had to bend across the table to reach the cue ball. Bastian would have a prime view of her ass, but there was no helping that. This was pool. She played to win. Always.

No sooner had she sunk the ball than she heard a low snarl behind her and turned to see Pax up in Bastian's face. Hell. He must have arrived just in time to assume the worst.

Sonofabitch. This was exactly what she'd wanted to avoid.

She dropped the cue. She didn't think Pax had touched Bastian, but his stance was pure intimidation. "Pax, back off," she said in a low voice. She glanced around the room. Only a few people were paying attention to the drama by the pool table. Maybe she could get him out of here before they had a full-blown scene that would tank his career. She grabbed his wrist. "Outside. Now."

She took a step for the door, but he didn't budge. She dropped his hand and kept walking. He could self-destruct if he wanted to, but she'd be damned before she would stay around to watch.

Outside the club, she took a deep breath of the humid air. It didn't ease the pain in her chest.

"Morgan, wait!"

She glanced over her shoulder to see Pax had followed her from the club after all. She didn't break stride and rounded the building, too upset to speak.

He caught up to her and grabbed her arm, pulling her to a halt. "Mad that I ruined your fun with Chief Ford?"

White-hot anger flashed through her. "You ass," she said, her voice shaking with rage. "Do you really think I'm so vile I'd mess around with someone on your team? When you're all I can think about? All I want?" She broke free of his grip and kept walking.

Tears surged. Stupid angry tears. A reaction she'd never been able to control, which only pissed her off more. Her dad had believed the best way to get her to stop crying was to shame her for the tears. God, how she hated that his tirades had found fertile ground in her psyche, that she was ashamed of the tears, even now.

She hated even more that she wanted a Neanderthal like Master Sergeant Pax Blanchard, who thought the worst of her and cornered his superior out of stupid, unfounded jealousy.

How could she want a man like that?

And why did it hurt so much to know she'd never have him?

She reached her CLU and jerked the door open. But she wasn't alone. Pax followed her inside and slammed the door closed. She whirled to face him, her hands covering the shameful tears that stained her cheeks—but before she could move or utter a word, he pressed her against the wall. He lifted her hands from her face and pinned them above her head, then his tongue was in her mouth, stealing her breath with an urgent, angry kiss.

She groaned and slid her tongue against his. She pulled her wrists from his hands so she could thread her fingers through his hair. She wrapped her legs around his waist, and he slipped an arm under her ass, supporting her with her back pressed to the wall.

The kiss was fire: hot and feral. Pure Pax. He plundered her mouth, nipped at her lips, and squeezed her breasts with an urgency that bordered on pain.

She kissed him back with the same pleasure-pain need. She bit his tongue, then sucked it deep into her mouth.

This. *Yes*.

She'd fantasized about this for days. She pulled his hair and ground her crotch against his erection. "Fuck me, Pax." She didn't want to talk about the scene in the bar. She didn't want to talk at all. She wanted sex, and he was the only man she wanted for the deed.

He gripped her hips and pressed his cock against her. She groaned with the sensation, sucked harder on his tongue, then reached for his fly.

All at once, he froze.

His hands dropped from her hips, and her legs slipped to the floor. He lifted his mouth from hers and slowly stepped back, until no part of their bodies touched.

"Shit, Morgan. I shouldn't have done that." Remorse ran deep in his voice. He took another step back and ran a hand over his hair. "Any of it." He shook his head. "Bastian stared at your ass as if he owned it, and I lost it. Fuck, I want you so bad, the idea of another man even looking at you makes me insane with jealousy."

"You don't own me, Pax. But even so, I'd never screw around with anyone on your team. I'm insulted that you believed I would."

His brown eyes burned with emotion. "You didn't see the way he was looking at you."

"I don't give a fuck. You're insulting *me*. Besides, he's a *guy*. I was bending over a pool table. Normal guy reaction. Hell, he probably wasn't the only one. And I wasn't doing it on purpose. I was trying to make my shot."

"Yeah, but Bastian and I…we're gas and flame. Have been since an op went sour in Yemen. He blames me, and I…hate him for being right."

"And neither of you can admit shit happens? Especially in combat?"

"Not this time." He raked a hand through his hair. "But you're right. I insulted you. I'm sorry." He took another step backward. "All I know is I look at you, and I feel this primal possessiveness. You're *mine*."

"No. I'm not. You've made it clear we won't happen."

"*Can't* happen. I have orders I can't blow off."

She straightened her shoulders. "Now, sure. But what about when this is over? When you're no longer protecting me?"

"You'll leave Djibouti, and I'll go God-knows-where for my next assignment."

"Surely you'll be stateside sometime. Aren't you home at least six months of the year?"

"My life is the Army, Morgan. I made a decision years ago—when I attended one too many ceremonies where a buddy's wife was given a flag folded into a neat triangle—as long as I'm active duty Special Forces, I won't get involved—not seriously—with anyone. My team comes first, and I won't leave kids behind with a flag to hug instead of a father. So if you're up for a fuck the next time I'm stateside, then game on. But if you want anything more than that, I'm not your man."

"You want me to wait around for months on the off-chance we'll have a stateside hookup that goes nowhere?" If he truly wanted her as much as he said he did, he'd give her a reason to be patient. An appetizer at the very least. This wasn't even fast food. This was a shriveled, overcooked convenience store hot dog.

"That's all I can offer."

She crossed her arms over her chest, unsure why this hurt so much. All they were doing was ending something that had never started. But then, he'd just told her she wasn't worth the wait, wasn't a reason to change his rules, and rejection always hurts. "Then you aren't my man."

"Fine," he said with a sharp nod. "My only request is that you stay away from the men on my team."

She narrowed her gaze. "Screw you. I wasn't flirting with Bastian. He *knew* I wasn't interested. How could you think I'd be that shallow?" Her stomach soured. "But you can't tell me who I can and can't be friends with." She stepped toward him and jabbed him in the chest. "And if I hook up with someone who is not on your team, you have no say in the matter. Not when you've given me the 'not now, not ever' blow-off speech. I am *not* yours. You have zero say in what I do, who I date, and who I fuck. Are we clear?"

His eyes hardened, but he nodded. "We're clear. Good night, Dr. Adler."

"Good riddance, Sergeant Blanchard." She closed the door behind him and slumped to the floor, holding her breath against shame-inducing tears.

Chapter Fifteen

Pax wasn't surprised to find a summons for his XO's office posted on his CLU. It had been too much to hope his jealous display might've been overlooked in Barely North. He also wasn't surprised to see Bastian already there. But instead of the expected look of glee in the man's eyes, he saw contrition. Bastard. The prick had baited him, knowing he would snap.

"Are you two aware we are in the middle of a fucking war zone?" Captain Oswald said in a low tone that carried more anger than a shout. "Djibouti may be friendly to us, but we're spitting distance from Somalia, and ISIS is gaining ground in Eritrea and Ethiopia, not to mention we've got al-Shabaab and al-Qaeda to contend with right beyond the fucking gate, and you two dickheads argue over a *woman* in the middle of Barely North?" He pinned Pax with a glare. "You have orders to keep your hands off General Adler's daughter."

Pax suppressed the urge to point out that the woman had her own name and identity that was quite separate from her father, but instead he stood at attention and said, "I'm not involved with Dr. Adler, sir."

"I didn't ask if you're involved, I'm asking if you've fucked her in violation of my orders."

"No, sir."

The man stared into Pax's eyes as if to determine if he were lying. Anger boiled inside Pax at the insult. This was probably akin to how Morgan had felt when Pax made assumptions about her interest in Bastian—outrage over her integrity being questioned.

He'd fucked up. In every way possible.

Oswald gave a sharp nod, then turned to Bastian. "And you. Given that you all gossip like teenage girls, you knew Sergeant Blanchard has a hard-on for Dr. Adler. Hell, I hear she goes into heat every time he gets near her."

Pax bristled at the insult to Morgan. She'd been nothing but professional in the field. He was the one who'd screwed up.

"What the fuck were you thinking hitting on her? That kind of shit gets in a soldier's head, and I shouldn't have to remind you you're on the same damn team. Don't fuck over the guy watching your back."

"I didn't hit on her, sir." Bastian paused, then added, "She shut me down before I tried and called me an asshole. We were just playing pool after that."

Pax's right hand curled into a fist. *She'd* just been playing pool, while Bastian stared at her tits and ass. And shit, hearing what she'd said to Bastian was further proof Pax had royally screwed things with Morgan, letting the caveman loose as he did.

"I don't want to hear any fucking excuses, Chief Ford. It was a dumb-shit thing to do. Own it."

"Yes, sir."

The XO fixed Pax with another glare. "You're off her security detail effective immediately. Sergeant Ripley will take over. Debrief with him at oh-six-hundred, then return to your regular assignment under Chief Ford."

"Yes, sir."

"The order to keep your hands off her remains in place, Sergeant."

"Understood, sir."

"Dismissed."

Pax left the office, trying to tell himself he'd gotten what he wanted all along. Ripley was a good man—and a devoted husband and father. Morgan would be protected, and Pax wouldn't have to see her day in and day out. But the truth was, Morgan was so deep under his skin, he had a hard time believing anyone could protect her as well as he would.

Morgan wasn't surprised Pax had been replaced. She knew how the Army worked and just hoped the scene in the bar didn't result in worse punishment. Even though it had been his own stupid fault, she didn't want his career to suffer. It was for his career that she was suffering, so it would be a shame if his work were compromised either way.

Sergeant Ripley took command of the security detail with ease. Sanchez said nothing, but Morgan had no doubt he was aware of the details. The resulting ride to the project area was long and silent. Once there, she, Ibrahim, and Mouktar settled into their routine while the marine and Green Beret patrolled their work area. They left the prehistoric village site and continued along the proposed route for the railroad, calling out isolated finds as they surveyed by walking in parallel lines ten meters apart.

Isolated artifacts were recorded in situ and left on the surface. If more artifacts were found, it was deemed a site, and they'd walk the area to determine site boundaries on the horizontal plane with shovel probes to determine depth. Just like she'd always done archaeology back home, except the tools she found here had the potential to be hundreds of thousands of years old, not hundreds *or* thousands.

This project, these sites and isolated finds, meant something. Her work would add to the scant but essential knowledge of how humans came to be. She still wondered if Linus was the catalyst for the explosion and coordinated assault on the base, but couldn't for the life of her guess why—or how—considering the find had been a secret.

And if ISIS or the Taliban had gotten wind of the find and had attacked in an effort to crush knowledge that didn't fit with their interpretation of Islam, they would have gone after the site directly. Not Camp Citron.

She couldn't help but think this was about water. Possibly water that had been here five thousand years ago. Because if she'd seen the signs, as untrained as she was, then there was no doubt Broussard had seen the same thing. And he'd told someone.

Then he'd disappeared, and his report was cleansed of all information relating to the presence of water in this area in the recent geologic past.

She could think of only one reason someone would cover up such a find, and it was the one she'd told Pax. The water had gone somewhere, but it hadn't gone away. What if Djibouti sat on a very deep aquifer, the kind that could sustain a country for generations?

Whoever controlled the water would be more than a warlord or even king. That person would be a god.

She considered going to the cultural or natural resources minister with her theory, but that was exactly what Broussard would have done, so she settled on Captain O'Leary, who might be able to bring in a US geologist. But when she returned from the field that afternoon, O'Leary was unavailable. She was no longer high priority. Her project was moving along, and there'd been no more threats from Desta.

She was shuffled off to his aide, who feigned interest, quizzed her mercilessly on her expertise in making such a wild assumption, and promised to pass on the information to the captain, who would decide if it was worth the expense of importing a geologist.

From O'Leary's office, she went to the gym, but Savvy wasn't there. She worked out with the punching bag, then returned to her CLU. She flopped on her cot and tried to figure out what to do.

She didn't want to go to Barely North. After the spectacle of the evening before, it would be a few days before she could face anyone there.

The cafeteria had the same nonexistent appeal. But she needed food. Moments like this, she wished she were back in her apartment in Djibouti city. It was hot, run-down, and noisy, but it was private. Plus, there she'd been able to explore a city and country that was so utterly foreign.

She thrived in foreign settings, because being a stranger in a strange land forced her to learn. And there were few things she enjoyed more than the firing synapses of a brain processing new information. Taking in new sights and sounds. The cadence of foreign languages. The smell of unfamiliar spices. Watching interactions between individuals of a different culture.

Military bases were the exact opposite. They were insular, designed to make GIs feel at home anywhere in the world. She'd lived on bases growing up that had felt more American than Lebanon, Kansas, the geographic center of the contiguous United States.

In her apartment in Djibouti City, she'd been happily immersed in a foreign world, with only a ten-year-old boy to act as translator.

All at once, last week's visit to her apartment in Djibouti returned to her. *The missing geology monograph.* She'd thought of it before, of course, but not the fact that it had been taken, while the other books that belonged to Broussard remained. More important, Broussard had lived in her apartment, which was in fact where he'd been living when he disappeared. Which meant someone else moved him out, but they knew enough about her communication with the geologist to know he'd agreed to leave the books for her, which meant his murderers had read his email.

Not earth-shattering news, considering they'd used his account to send emails, but whoever was behind his disappearance had been very careful, ensuring two months passed before anyone noticed the man was missing.

Why was the Vichy monograph taken but not the others?

She wanted to return to her apartment and claim the remaining books. Had anything else of Broussard's been left in the apartment?

She sat up straight. Had the cell phone in the kitchen belonged to Broussard? Pax had turned it in to his XO so they could mine the data to see if the phone had ever been in proximity to Desta. But did they bother to trace ownership, or had everyone just assumed it was a prepaid burner phone?

She should probably find out who was examining the phone and what they'd learned. Would they bother to coordinate with *Police Nationale*? She couldn't imagine the US military would share information on their search for Etefu Desta with anyone, unless there was a proven direct connection between Broussard's disappearance and the cell phone.

Would Ripley's XO—Captain Oswald—authorize a trip to her apartment? There was only one way to find out. She knew where the man's office was located on the base. She would shower, then search for him there. As long as she was out, she might as well get dinner at the cafeteria. Maybe there she'd run into someone who could point her in the right direction, or at least give her a phone number for Captain Oswald.

She didn't even have Pax's CLU or cell phone number.

But that was probably a good thing.

Chapter Sixteen

Pax grimaced as the woman of his dreams entered the cafeteria. At the same time, his heart kicked up a notch, and he silently admitted he'd been hoping for a Morgan sighting. Because he was a dumb-shit fool.

Cal glanced from Pax to Bastian the bastard and shook his head. Then he picked up his empty tray and left the table, demonstrating exactly how much faith he had in Pax's ability to not be a dickhead. But then Pax had earned Cal's low opinion.

Morgan glanced toward their table of a half-dozen Special Forces operators without meeting his gaze. She frowned, then turned for the food line.

Bastian grunted to the group and, like Cal, grabbed his tray and crossed the room. Pax couldn't help but stiffen as the man walked in Morgan's direction, but he merely gave her a sharp nod, then sorted the items on his tray into the compost, dish, and garbage bins.

Slowly, the others on his team vacated the table. They didn't seriously believe Morgan would join him, did they? Maybe they feared being called as witnesses if Pax made an ass out of himself again.

He stayed rooted to his seat at the now-empty table, waiting for Morgan to exit the food line, eager yet dreading to know where she'd choose to sit.

At last she stepped out of the service area with a laden tray. She glanced in Pax's direction and came to a dead stop. She frowned in obvious indecision, then took a deep breath and walked his way. She paused next to the seat across from his at the empty table.

He nodded toward the chair. "Have a seat."

She shook her head. "I need to talk to your XO. He's not in his office. Can you give me his cell phone number?"

"Sit, and I'll text it to you."

"I don't think I should."

"Sit, Morgan. I'll behave. I promise." He smiled at her. "Do you really want to eat alone?"

"Who says I'd eat alone?" She flashed a smile as she set her tray on the table and sat.

She wore cocky well, and she was right. No chance would she be alone at a table for long. That might have something to do with why Pax wanted her with him.

He had a few issues to sort out when it came to Dr. Morgan Adler.

He pulled out his cell phone and found Captain Oswald in the address book. He attached it to a blank text. "What's your number?" he asked.

She recited the digits. He entered them in his phone and hit Send. "Done." He tucked his phone away. "Why do you want to speak to my XO?"

She outlined her questions about the cell phone recovered from her apartment and the missing monograph. "Also, I'm trying to remember if Broussard left anything else. The apartment was furnished, and there were a few items in the cupboards in addition to books on the shelf. I want to go over everything. I want Oswald to authorize Ripley to take me there."

"Sounds like a good idea, but you shouldn't go. It's not safe. Have someone pack everything and bring it to you."

"But they won't know what's mine and what might be Broussard's. And they wouldn't recognize if things have been moved."

"You think you're CSI?"

She snorted. "Hardly. But we both know the gendarmes aren't doing anything. And who knows if or when *Police Nationale* will get here. I need to do *something*. What if I'm right and Broussard found something as valuable as water?"

"What if you're wrong but you put yourself back in Desta's sights? He's been quiet. Leave it alone. Stay on base. If I were still in charge of your security, I'd lock you in your CLU at the end of the day."

"You'd make me a prisoner when I'm trying to do my job."

"It's not your job to figure out what happened to Broussard."

"Maybe not, but at least I'm human. At least I care that a man disappeared."

"I care that Broussard went missing." *But I care about you more.*

She glared at him. "Don't you dare tell your XO not to let me do this. It's *my life*. You are no longer head of my security detail, and you've made it clear we will never be a *thing*, so you have no say in what I do."

He took a deep, calming breath, and told himself not to screw up and make a scene *again*. He gave her a curt nod and tried to smile. God, she was beautiful. Her long blonde hair was loose and free, and he wanted to dive in, wrap it around his wrists, and pull her to him for a hot deep kiss.

Instead, he took a bite of his cheesecake. It didn't come close to satisfying his hunger.

He'd woken up with a painful hard-on this morning after a night of frustrating, never quite fulfilled sex dreams featuring Dr. Morgan Adler and her perfect body. He pulled out his cell phone and found the last number texted. He tapped out a quick message: *God, you're beautiful.*

Her phone chimed. He smiled, realizing the sound came from her breasts. She'd tucked her phone in her cleavage again. She reached into her top.

He shook his head. "Don't read it now."

Her brow furrowed in question.

"Later. Eat your dinner."

She stared at him for a moment, her expression quizzical, but then she shook her head and resumed eating.

He typed another message: *You have the sweetest fucking lips. The things I want to do to you.*

And another: *Which is why I go insane at the idea of you taking risks. But I have no claim on you or right to interfere. So I won't.*

Followed by: *But know that I want to protect you, because just being near you brings out the caveman in me.*

And finally: *You're so fucking beautiful. I hate it that you're completely off-limits. But you are.*

He hit Send on the last message, stood, and picked up his tray. "Have a good evening, Morgan."

She studied his face, then nodded. "'Night, Pax."

Pax's phone vibrated on the nightstand. He groped for it in the dark room, groggy from sleep. The call couldn't be about an urgent mission, or Cal's phone would be going off as well. He cracked open one eye to see who his caller was.

Morgan.

Alarm filtered through him as he stabbed at the answer button. It was two a.m., something had to be wrong. "Morgan? Are you okay?"

"If having frustrating sex dreams is okay, then I'm fine."

He wanted to be annoyed she'd woken him, but part of him couldn't help but smile. He'd been deep in a dream that was all about arousal with none of the payoff himself. "I can't help you there," he said softly. He glanced over at Cal, who grabbed his pillow and rolled over on the bed.

"Thanks for the texts," she said.

He'd wondered if she'd reply. He'd sort of hoped she wouldn't. But at the same time, hearing her voice with that husky, whispery lilt was a pleasure he was glad he hadn't missed. Hell, he was already sporting wood thanks to a dream that featured her gorgeous ass.

"I meant every word. Including the part where I said you're off-limits."

"I know. I was thinking we could...*talk*. You wouldn't be violating orders if we're just on the phone."

"I can't. I share my CLU with Cal."

On the cot next to him, Cal made a noise that sounded mildly irritated.

She made a harrumphing sound. "I take it he's there right now."

"He's trying to sleep. I can give him the phone so you can apologize for waking him."

She let out a soft laugh. "Don't you dare." She paused. "Okay. If you aren't alone, then you can just listen as I describe all the things I want to do to you. Starting with licking your abs and working my way down."

Aww, shit. She wasn't going to play fair. "Don't do this, Morgan." How many times had he said those words to her already?

"First I'll strip to the waist, because I know you like my tits as much as I like your abs, and I want to slide my breasts against your bare chest and abs as I work my way down to your cock."

He closed his eyes against the mental image. "Stop," he whispered.

"You mentioned my lips. Can you imagine them wrapped around your cock? The pleasure you'll feel as they slide against your thick, hard prick and I take you deep into my throat? I've been fantasizing about going down on you since we were at the market together."

His phone vibrated as she spoke. He glanced at the screen and realized she'd sent him a text. Like a masochist, he opened it. She'd sent a picture of her lips with the note: *Sweetest fucking lips? You got the fucking part right.*

Holy hell. He was done. He couldn't listen to her without jacking off, and he couldn't jack off with Cal trying to sleep on the cot next to him and probably wishing he could shoot his dumbass roommate.

"I need to go, Morgan."

"Do you want to slide your cock between my tits, Pax?"

Well, now that you mention it…

He shook his head. She was singing some sort of siren song, calling him to the rocks that would crush his career.

It's not like sex with Morgan would be a Uniform Code of Military Justice violation.

The fallout would be more like a reprimand. But it would look bad on his record, and he was already on Captain Oswald's shit list for the scene in Barely North.

Her father's a general with the power to make my life hell.

The phone vibrated again. Powerless as a moth to a flame, he opened the text, and there were the breasts he'd been thinking about since she stripped for him that morning in her CLU.

Every man had a breaking point, and Morgan Adler had just found his. He kept the phone to his ear and pulled on sweatpants over his boxer briefs and listened to her whisper about all the dirty things she wanted to do with him. He slid his feet into a pair of shoes and grabbed his key. He was at the door when he remembered condoms. He grabbed a box from his locker, then covered the mic on the phone with his thumb as he gently opened the door and slipped outside.

Morgan's unit was on the back side at the other end of CLUville. Less than a two-minute walk, during which she described sucking on his cock in great detail.

Finally, he stood before her door and interrupted her titillating bedtime story. "Open the door, Morgan."

"What?"

"I'm about to make your fucking dream come true." He paused, then added, "Literally."

Chapter Seventeen

Morgan jolted upright on her cot. "You're here?"

"Yes. Now open the damn door before someone sees me."

She leapt from the bed and lunged for the door. She fumbled with the lock. How did the mechanism suddenly turn complicated? She disengaged the bolt and yanked open the door. Pax, big, beautiful, sexy, tall Pax, stood right outside. He stepped into her CLU with authority and closed and locked the door. Then he took the phone from her hand, hit the disconnect button, and set both their phones and a box of condoms on the desk next to the door.

Finally, hands free of unwanted objects, he took her breasts into his palms and stroked his thumbs across her nipples. She'd stripped down to her panties for the selfie and hadn't bothered to put her T-shirt back on, now she berated herself for not taking off the underwear.

Pax dropped to his knees and took her nipple into his mouth.

She gasped as pleasure flooded her.

When it came to her breasts, she liked a hard suck, and Pax didn't disappoint. But then, she'd been describing what she liked on the phone. Apparently, he'd been listening.

He dropped lower, bringing his face level with her crotch. He took a deep breath, and she knew he was taking in the scent of her arousal. "I'm wet and ready for you, Pax. But you aren't going to be inside me until after I've had your cock in my mouth."

He slid a finger against the wet fabric of her underwear and hooked it under the edge to slide the crotch to the side. He leaned in and licked her, then he dipped his tongue inside her vagina, and she bucked against him.

"Wrong. I was just inside you." He yanked the scrap of fabric all the way down, then he spread her legs and gave her swollen clit attention that made her dizzy. His fingers slipped inside her and stroked as he slowly rose to his feet.

His mouth met hers as he scooped her up and pressed her against the only open section of wall, where he'd pinned her twice previously. He grabbed both her hands as he had before and pulled them above her head, holding them in one hand. He supported her with one arm and the pressure of the wall at her back. But this time, he abandoned her mouth and sucked on her tits, and she was ready to combust with the intensity of how good everything he did to her felt.

He raised his head and met her gaze. He released her wrists, freeing his hand to slide between her thighs and stroke her clit. He slipped two fingers inside her. "This is how we're going to do this. I'm going to fuck you blind. You can suck on my cock to your heart's content, but you aren't calling all the shots. I'm a little angry that I'm even here, because I told you the rules, why we can't do this, and you pulled the stunt with the phone. So now that we *are* doing this, it's going to be my way. I'm not some meek boy you can boss around.

"Tonight is all we get. I'll fuck you until I've had my fill, then I'll slip out of here before the base gets active. If I get caught, I'll own it. I will not lie. But otherwise, this is don't ask, don't tell, all over again. Tomorrow, if we see each other, you will act like you did in the cafeteria tonight, and I will do the same. There will be no further texts or phone calls between us. If my cold attitude will hurt you, speak now and end this. If you can accept my terms, say yes, and we'll fuck."

He stroked her clit through his entire speech, rendering any answer but yes impossible, but then, she had no problem with his terms. At least they'd have a few hours.

He lowered her feet to the ground. She slipped a hand into his sweatpants and pulled out his hard cock. "Yes," she said and dropped to her knees before him. She stroked the length of his shaft and grinned up at him, then pressed his penis between her breasts for a brief moment before opening her mouth, licking the tip, then taking him deep. She sucked with the tip in the back of her throat, eliciting a groan from him.

He pulled off his T-shirt and kicked off his shoes, while she dropped his sweatpants and briefs to the floor.

Once he was fully naked, she gave in to the fantasy that had sustained her for days. It was a simple fantasy, really. She slid her mouth up and down his shaft, while he threaded his fingers in her hair and slowly disassembled. She sucked, he enjoyed. Simple gratification.

She brought him to the brink, then looked up at him. His face was tight with pleasure, but even more mesmerizing were those brown eyes and the way he looked at her. As if he'd never seen anything more incredible than her going down on him. She released him from her mouth but continued to stroke his prick with her hand. "Do you want me to swallow, or do you want to come on my chest?"

From the way his eyes widened, she guessed that coming on her chest held more appeal than he'd realized. Well, he did say he was a caveman when it came to her, and nothing said "mine" more than that. And she wanted to be his. She wanted the caveman. He had all the testosterone she'd been missing over the years combined in one man.

"Neither," he said, surprising her. "I'm going to come inside your hot, wet pussy, but first I'm going to lick you and make you even wetter."

He scooped her up and tossed her on the cot. In one smooth motion, he grabbed her calves and spread her legs, pressing back, pinning her legs open as his tongue found home. She bucked when the pleasure got too intense, but he pressed harder against her legs, giving no quarter, making her take the intensity until a fast, hard orgasm erupted from within her.

She screamed, and he reached out and covered her mouth, reminding her that the containers had thin walls.

But even so, he didn't let up with his tongue, and her orgasm continued, finding new heights. Finally, he released her, and she panted from the pleasure. He grabbed the box of condoms and slipped one on. Then he pressed against her vagina and slid home. The feel of his cock inside her mixed with post-orgasm sensitivity was intense. Hot. Amazing. The friction of his thrusts awakened dormant sensations. She'd had good sex before, but somehow, she didn't remember it being quite *this* good.

It was that damn tidal wave. It had finally come in, and the buildup made it all the more powerful.

Pax Love Blanchard lived up to the hype she'd built in her mind.

She wrapped her legs around his hips, loving the slide of his skin against hers. His mouth found hers for a long, hot kiss as he thrust within her. She was wrapped in a feast of sensation, enjoying the rich flavor of a long-simmered reduction. There was no way one night with Pax would ever be enough.

She wanted to possess him as fiercely as he wanted her. Her man. Her Green Beret. *Mine. Mine. Mine.* She chanted the words in her head as her orgasm built, but then the word slipped out. "Mine," she gasped as she came a second time.

He muttered a curse as his muscles tightened. He arched his back as he came, making a soft grunt that was followed by a low pant that told her the orgasm has been as powerful for him as hers had been.

He didn't collapse on top of her or take a moment to relax. Not her Pax. He placed his hands on her hips and rolled until he was on his back and she straddled him, still inside her. He met her gaze. "Yours. For a few hours," he said in a husky voice as he thrust upward with his hips.

Given the choice between a few hours or never, she'd take this and try to be satisfied. She could fall in love with Pax, if he gave her half a chance. It was a good thing he'd made the rules clear.

He rolled with her again and slid from her body. He left the cot and disposed of the condom, then returned to her a few minutes later with a cloth he'd dampened in the sink. "I'm going to go down on you again, but I don't like the taste of spermicide."

She grinned at his practicality. "I'm the same way, so you need to wash too."

"Already did." He then proceeded to use the cold washcloth to tease her clit.

"Holy fuck," she panted, unable to believe he was able to elicit a response from her so quickly.

His tongue followed the cloth, then he grazed her clit with his teeth, triggering a harsh jolt of pleasure. "You are so fucking beautiful," Pax said, his gaze locked on her center.

"My pussy is beautiful?" she asked with a laugh.

"Hell yeah. It's a goddam masterpiece." He met her gaze. "And the view of the landscape from here is magnificent. Your blonde curls, the indentation of your belly button, and those full, gorgeous tits." He stroked his tongue across her clit, then slipped it inside her vagina. "The slick feel of you against my tongue, your tangy taste, the sexy smell of your arousal, and the noises you make when you come. Fuck. It's almost too much. My senses are on the brink of hedonistic overload." He scooted back. "Roll over and put your ass in the air."

She did as instructed. He stroked her ass, then licked her again. She pressed her face into the pillow and let out a hard groan.

He positioned himself behind her and slid his hands between her breasts and the mattress. He pinched her nipples, then cradled their heavy weight. "Next, I'm going to fuck you like this, while holding your tits."

She whimpered. She loved that position, loved it when hands lifted the heavy weight of her breasts, loved the wild animal feel of it. "Now."

He twisted a hand in her hair and pulled gently, so she turned her head to the side, facing the edge of the cot. "Suck me until I'm hard, and I will."

She nodded and rolled to her side, and he moved and knelt before her, presenting the feast of his half-mast cock to her mouth. She took him in, and he was full-mast in moments. He tried to move away, but she wrapped her hand around the base, keeping him in her mouth. Just a minute longer. Tonight was all they would have. She would give herself—and him— memories that would last.

He stroked her clit as he slid in her mouth. He brought her to the brink of orgasm, and she pulled back, releasing him. She had only so many orgasms left before she'd be oversensitized, and he was going to take her from behind like he'd promised.

"Get a condom on," she said. They didn't need it for birth control—she was covered by a three-month shot—but since tonight would be singular, there was no need for the health history questionnaire. They were exchanging enough bodily fluids that the conversation was probably warranted anyway, but with only a few hours, she didn't want to.

Pax slipped on another condom. Morgan scooted up the bed so she knelt on the pillows at the top with her hands pressed to the wall. This would give him better access to her breasts.

As he positioned himself behind her, she asked, "Are you still angry with me? For calling and texting you?"

"Yes," he said as he thrust inside her.

She gasped against his thickness. His cock set off ripples of sensation inside her.

"We shouldn't be doing this." He thrust deeper. "This could ruin me." He cupped her breasts just like she'd hoped, and thrust again. "And yet I can't stop."

"Don't stop," she said.

"Never."

His hands slid over her breasts, to her side, then up her shoulders. He braced one arm on the wall and wrapped the other in her hair. He twisted and pulled it to the side, then his mouth was on her neck. Stubble abraded her skin in the most pleasing way as he nipped at the sensitive intersection of neck and shoulder. He moved to her ear and whispered, "I'm angry that I'm fucking you and grateful for it at the same time."

He released her hair and slid his hand along her shoulder, up the arm braced against the wall. "I love touching your soft skin." The hand that supported his weight against the wall returned to cup her breast, while his other hand slid along her arm.

He pinched her nipple, causing her to groan and clench down on him. Another orgasm started to build.

His breathing changed, and she felt his body tighten against her. He was coming too. She crested while he grunted, and the pressure of his hand on her arm increased. They came together as he cupped her breast and leaned into her.

Alarm bells clanged in her mind even as she rode the hard, fast orgasm. What was wrong? His weight shifted. She rocked with pleasure. Finally, the position of his hand on her arm registered. *Oh fuck. The tracker.*

Chapter Eighteen

"Stop!" Morgan said, her voice low and breathy. She twisted, dislodging his hand, and Pax realized he'd been putting his weight on her as he had another mind-blowing orgasm.

"Shit, babe! Did I hurt you?" He slid out from her body and turned her to look at him, cupping her face. "I'm sorry."

"No. It's not that." Her gaze darted frantically to the door. "It's the tracker. In my arm. If you press on it for ten seconds, it goes off."

All the blood in his body charged straight for his heart. "You have a subdermal tracker?"

"Yes."

He reared back, dizzy from the lack of blood. "Those things are top secret and only for seriously valuable VIPs." Shit, exactly who *was* General Adler, anyway? He grabbed her arm and searched for the injection site. He only knew about trackers because his team had been sent to rescue a man in Yemen. But they'd been too late.

He found the faint white line on her arm. "How long ago did you get this?"

She ignored him and jumped from the cot. "You need to hide!" She grabbed the washcloth and ran to the sink. "Shit! I smell like sex and they could be here any second." She ran the wet cloth over her skin, focusing on her crotch.

"I can't believe you have a fucking tracker in your arm and you didn't warn me."

"I didn't think of it! I guess I assumed you knew." She ran to the door and flipped off the lights. She whirled to face him and pushed him toward the bathroom. He could just make out her features in the green glow of the alarm clock. "Get in the bathroom! Hurry!"

He remained frozen in place as the full scope of this disaster sank in. How long had he pressed on the tracker? Was there a chance he hadn't activated it?

Not fucking likely.

"I'll act like I was sleeping with my head on my arm." She plucked her panties from the floor and slipped them on, then grabbed a tank top and pulled it over her head.

A cold, calm anger settled over him as he watched her try to make up for her massive blunder that could well ruin him. He'd made it clear they couldn't be together. She knew exactly why. And still, she'd called him. Talked dirty on the phone and sent him selfies.

Shit. His phone. Without a word, he grabbed it from the desk next to the door and then scooped his clothes from the floor and headed for the shared bathroom. If he made it through this humiliation undetected, Morgan might well wish she'd turned him in.

She settled into the cot as he stepped inside the bathroom and locked the door to the opposite CLU. He leaned his forehead against the door and tried to control his breathing so he could hear.

Not thirty seconds after he was inside, there was a knock on Morgan's unit. She called out, groggily and took her time unlocking the door. Her words were muffled, but he thought she did a convincing job sounding like she'd been deeply asleep. Too bad she—and the whole damn CLU—smelled like sex.

Her voice rose with alarm, and her words became clear. "I set off the tracker? Shit, I was so tired from the field today, I was dead asleep. I must've had my head on my arm. No wonder it's half-numb."

Another voice uttered indistinct words.

"Just let me throw some clothes on and I'll go with you." He heard the door close and a locker open. A minute later, she reopened the door. "Okay, let's go." The door shut firmly, telling him he was alone in the CLU.

It would take about two minutes to drive to the building where someone would reset the tracker—and they would drive instead of walk, because timing was critical to battery life on those things.

Jesus, triggering a tracker—which were ungodly expensive—because of careless sex was yet another layer of trouble that could land at his door. As if sex with her weren't bad enough.

He considered going back to his own CLU while the getting was good. But he decided against it because this would be his only opportunity to have this particular conversation with Morgan Adler.

He slipped out of the bathroom and grabbed her cell phone, which he found on the nightstand, not the desk. He deleted his number from her address book and the text messages they'd exchanged. He then deleted her selfies from his phone. Surprise ripped through him when he saw she'd sent him another text—probably when she was in bed, waiting for the knock: *I'm sorry. So sorry.*

Yeah, he didn't think sorry would cut it with this one.

He returned to the bathroom to wait for her return, hoping like hell she'd be dropped at her door and no one would find an excuse to enter the unit.

How humiliating to be reduced to skulking in a bathroom like a teenage boy who'd sneaked into a girl's bedroom.

Ten minutes later, he got his wish. She walked straight to the bathroom and tapped softly on the door. "Pax?" she whispered.

He opened the door.

Those big, beautiful blue eyes gazed up at him. "I'm sorry, Pax."

"You fucked up, Morgan. And your fuckup could well have put my role on my Special Forces team in jeopardy. Disobeying a direct order—even if it's about my personal life—is bad."

He stepped out of the bathroom. "I shouldn't have texted you, but I wanted to let you know how I felt, while underscoring that you are *off-limits*. My texts weren't an invitation." His gaze landed on the cot. Sweet Jesus, being inside her body had been as intense as he'd imagined. He looked away. "But you called, and I came—that's my fault, I should have hung up on you and stayed the hell in my CLU." He finally met her gaze again. "But once I was here, why the fuck didn't you warn me you had a high-tech tracker in your arm? What the hell were you *thinking*?"

"I wasn't. I was just...playing. I thought it would be fun to talk dirty to you. That it wouldn't go anywhere. We wouldn't violate your orders."

"Yeah, well, while you're *playing*, I'm trying to do my job, which is training Djiboutians to be guerilla fighters. You may not think much of the Army because of your asshole father, and you may not give a crap about my role in it, but it's damn important to me. The work we do here is important. You've seen what it's like out there. There are fucking warlords who traffic in young girls, starving refugees from Somalia, and countries all around gunning for what little precious resources these people have. They need an *army* to defend their borders and their children, and I'm helping them build one. So you can play all the fuck you want, but I'm out. I've got a job to do and don't have time for bullshit games."

He grabbed the knob and jerked open the door. Outside, he marched down the row of containers without looking back. Her security was someone else's problem, and now that they'd had sex, he had her out of his system. In every way that mattered, Morgan Adler was now out of his life.

Chapter Nineteen

Morgan plastered a fake smile on her face for the guard as the Humvee passed through the last checkpoint and entered the base. It had been a long-ass hot, miserable day in the field, and she was exhausted from her sleepless night. All she wanted was a shower and bed. She'd have dinner tomorrow. Or maybe never. Food no longer held appeal.

She feared Pax hated her, and she couldn't blame him. Even worse than his anger was knowing she'd lost his respect. He saw her as a foolish, selfish woman, with no knowledge or care for the problems of Djibouti.

Worse, she feared his assessment wasn't far off. Not that she didn't care about Djibouti, but the foolish and selfish part. She'd been so caught up in her desires, she'd gone blind to the risks. Blind to what it meant to Pax. Blind to the fact that this was neither the time nor the place to indulge in a selfish fling. No matter how badly she wanted him. No matter how badly he wanted her.

He'd made the stakes for his career clear, and she pushed anyway. Because she'd been hurt by his rejection. But taking something just because you wanted it was a spoiled child's reaction. She'd never considered herself spoiled, but now she had to examine her emotions and actions. Pax probably saw her as an overindulged general's daughter, which was an especially bitter pill, because something had happened to her as they made love, and it wasn't the three orgasms that had rocked her crumbling foundation.

She could fall in love with Pax. She might even be halfway there. He was everything she'd never wanted: a soldier, bossy, downright domineering in bed, a possessive caveman at the wrong times and in the wrong place, and her father's dream son-in-law.

So why the hell had she wanted him so desperately, she'd made that damned booty call, even when he'd made it clear he couldn't cross that line?

And why did it hurt so much to know she'd never make love with him again?

"Morgan?" Ripley asked from the driver's seat.

She opened her eyes, which she hadn't even realized she'd closed to relive another memory from the night, and saw the Humvee was stopped in front of her CLU. Home sweet home.

Except she wouldn't be getting that shower or bed anytime soon, because standing in front of her unit was none other than her dear old Dad.

Oh one damn day. All Pax wanted was twenty-four damn hours without having to see Dr. Morgan Adler. Of all the days in the world, this one—a mere fourteen hours after he'd left her bed—would've been the perfect day to be Morganless for an entire rotation of the earth. But he'd been called to a meeting at command destined to involve the very person he wanted to avoid. He had no doubt the woman in question would be front and center.

Initially, he'd feared he'd been found out, but that would have been a confrontation with his XO, not the base commander. And one thing he knew about his XO, the man would handle such a breach privately. He'd make Pax's life a living hell, but he'd deal with his anger and disappointment in an off-the-books sort of manner, unless he intended to seize on the excuse to boot Pax off the team. A possibility, given the tension between Bastian and Pax since Yemen—but again, that action wouldn't involve Navy brass. That was Special Operations Command all the way, and SOCOM didn't air dirty laundry in front of other commands.

He took his three-minute shower in the public facility, feeling envious of Morgan's private shower not for the first time. In a different world, if he were no longer in charge of her security detail and without orders to keep his hands off, he could have pursued something with her, and he'd have made good use of her private shower and private CLU. The tracker in her arm wouldn't be an issue. He'd put a bandage on the spot before sex as a reminder to avoid it.

It was too easy to slip into sex fantasies involving Morgan, and he snapped off the shower in frustration. She was out of his system. Done.

Except he had to face her in a few minutes. With a towel around his waist, he stepped to the mirror and proceeded to shave, bracing himself for the coming encounter with the centerfold with a PhD.

Twenty minutes later, he was presentable, wearing a clean ACU, and climbing the steps to enter command, Cal and Ripley with him. Cal hadn't been summoned to a meeting involving Morgan since the first one in the skipper's office, making Pax wonder what was up now.

Odds were high Cal knew Pax had slipped out of their unit last night, but he hadn't said a word, which Pax appreciated. If Cal ever learned Morgan's tracker had been set off during sex, he'd laugh his ass off, but for now, fortunately, that remained a secret.

All subdermal tracker use was top secret. Special Forces found out about them only when they were sent in to save someone's ass. In this area, that job usually fell to SEALs. Yemen had been an exception.

Most of the seats around the conference room table were taken when they arrived. Given that Morgan and the skipper weren't present and there were only three seats left, Pax opted for a seat along the wall. Cal and Ripley followed suit. They were the only enlisted in the room and didn't warrant seats at the table.

Pax met Savannah James's gaze as low murmurs of conversation buzzed around the room. She wore that speculative expression he wasn't fond of, as if she knew all his secrets. He wondered if she practiced that unsettling look in the mirror.

From the whispers that flitted around him, he gathered that no one—not even his XO—knew the purpose of the meeting.

Finally, Captain O'Leary arrived with Morgan and an older man wearing a crisp ACU. Someone called out, "Attention!"

Pax stood along with the others. He scanned the Army officer and caught the two stars in the middle of the man's chest. *Shit.* A major general.

"At ease," the general said as he took his seat.

A glance at the name tape could confirm his worst fear, but all he needed was a glimpse of the man's familiar, wide blue eyes.

Ah, hell. Pax dropped into his chair. Just when he thought his day couldn't get any worse, Morgan's daddy had arrived.

Morgan took the vacant seat to her father's right and grimaced. Pax was in her direct line of sight. She could do without seeing his every reaction to her father's never-ending condescension. But then, she could do without seeing Pax at all.

Captain O'Leary stood. "Officially, General Adler, the commanding general of Intelligence and Security Command at Ft. Belvoir, is here to inspect and confer with INSCOM's subordinate command at Camp Citron, but the timing of his visit was moved up due to the recent threats to his daughter, Dr. Adler." O'Leary nodded in her direction. "The purpose of this meeting is to bring General Adler up-to-date on the search for Etefu Desta and the security arrangements that have been made for Dr. Adler and her archaeological project." He turned to her father. "General, did you wish to speak before we begin?"

Her father stood and cleared his throat. Morgan braced herself, knowing exactly where dear dad would start. "Sorry we were late. My daughter insisted on taking a shower first, as if you all have nothing better to do than wait on her, when you've been out fighting the good fight all day, and all she's been doing is looking at old rocks."

Yeah. Because that was what she did, she *lived* to waste the military's time. She took a deep breath. Anger would only cause tears, which in this room was *not* an option. Her father knew damn well that anger was her trigger, and he was trying to diminish her right out of the gate so he could ride roughshod over her.

She fixed her gaze on the wall and thought about last night with Pax. How he'd called her beautiful as he made love to her. She found a serene smile as she remembered the feel of his mouth on her neck as he cupped her breasts.

"First off," her father said, "I'd like to thank Sergeants Blanchard and Callahan for saving my daughter. She's a handful, I know, and not always prone to making the wisest choices. It couldn't have been easy for them, and I'm grateful for their professionalism."

The only thing missing from his description of her was the word incompetent, but at least he'd captured it with his tone.

She tried not to let it bother her. When that failed, she fixed her gaze on Pax and imagined going down on him while he still wore his combat uniform. This might not be the time for blowjob fantasies, but it was a defense mechanism to save her from tears and she wasn't about to give it up.

For his part, Pax's eyes were blank. Vacant. He was the solider she'd met by the side of the road who took her passport and ordered her from the car.

Well, that was who he should be. So be it.

"I'm told Sergeant Callahan single-handedly took out the sniper who kept the convoy pinned. Excellent work." He nodded to Cal. "Although my guess is Sergeant Callahan had the easier job, given that he didn't have my hysterical daughter to contend with along with militants lying in wait in the wadi." Her father laughed, and a few men at the table joined in.

Savvy fixed the general with a hard glare, winning her friendship for life.

Cal cast her a sympathetic look.

Morgan shrugged. This was her dad in all his glory.

Her father continued, "Sergeant Blanchard is to be commended for shooting two militants in the wadi and saving the life of one when it became known the dying man had valuable intel."

Pax cleared his throat. "Dr. Adler deserves credit for that, sir."

She looked up sharply. Surely he wasn't tanking his career for all time by announcing he'd given her his gun?

"Excuse me?" her father said.

"Dr. Adler stopped the man's bleeding. All I did was apply the bandage. Dr. Adler saved the man's life. Not me."

She suppressed her sigh of relief. He was merely giving her the only credit he could. Which was nice, considering her father never gave her credit for anything.

"I'm glad to hear it, Sergeant. I guess I raised her right after all." Every condescending word her father said cut deeper than the last.

His gaze shifted to her. "It's my understanding you've resisted the Navy's efforts to aid your project by bringing in their own experts, both a poor business decision and a poor tactical one."

And at last they'd arrived at her father's agenda. He was putting her in her place to pave the way for the Navy to swoop in and take over the project. Except...she and O'Leary had reached an accord. The Navy no longer wanted control.

By all accounts, her father was an excellent officer, devoted to the US Army. He'd earned his rank and deserved the respect that came his way. Where he fell short was as a father. But right now, his rotten father-ness was bleeding over into his professional life, making him a lousy general.

If she were removed from the equation, she'd bet her father would be running this room, but as it was, only a handful of officers seemed to be on board. She cleared her throat. "I will take your feedback under advisement, General, but at the moment, I have my project well in hand. Awaiting assistance from Navy archaeologists would only delay the fieldwork."

She gave him a tight smile and continued, "I'm touched more than I can say that you would travel all this way to ensure my safety." She was proud she kept the sarcasm from her voice. "With approval from my security team"—she nodded toward Ripley—"tomorrow morning, I'd like to show you the Linus site, so you can see for yourself what an astonishing find it is. Tonight, I suggest you read up on the Ethiopian Lucy skeleton, so you'll have context for the value of Linus to the paleoanthropological record. The Djiboutian government wants to announce the find very soon. We should have the potassium-argon date from the lab any day now, and the minister of culture has been arranging security for the site, which will be necessary twenty-four seven after the announcement.

"We've also been waiting on analysis from one of the world's foremost experts on paleoanthropology. He was unable to visit immediately but has been examining photographs, and his preliminary assessment matches my own—a three-point-five million-year-old australopithecine male with a complete tool assemblage. He intends to visit as soon as he's free—late next week, at the earliest. His daughter is getting married, and he was told in no uncertain terms that he couldn't miss her wedding, not even for a find like Linus." She smiled at the room at large. "Don't think he wasn't tempted."

Chuckles met her statement, and she felt the tension in the room ease a notch. She dipped her head toward her father. "I hope you'll still be in

Djibouti when the find is announced. It should be quite an event."

And maybe, just once in your life, you'll find a reason to be proud of me.

She shoved the bitter thought aside. "I'm afraid that, after tomorrow morning, I'll be unavailable to show you around because I've a project to finish. To that end, I must escape this meeting. I have hours of work to do tonight, as I'm writing the report concurrent with conducting the field survey in order to meet my deadline."

She turned to Ripley. "Sergeant Ripley, when you're done here, I'd like to discuss security for tomorrow's tour for General Adler and a necessary visit to Djibouti City. I'll be in my CLU."

Ripley nodded. She turned on her heel and left the meeting.

The righteous anger Pax had been nurturing with great care began to crumble as soon as General Adler started to speak. It shattered when Morgan stood and defended herself with grace.

The man had an amazing woman for a daughter, and he couldn't see her accomplishments, brains, or fortitude. Where the hell did Morgan's belief in herself come from? Because she sure as hell hadn't gotten unconditional love, support, and a girl-power message at home. He imagined her mother must be the meek sort to have put up with General Adler all these years, assuming her parents were still married.

That thought caught him short. He'd made love to the woman but didn't know a thing about her except she lived in or near DC and her dad was a hard-ass two-star general. Her childhood had been shaped by trying to please him, while rebelling against him had shaped her adulthood.

What else did Pax know? She was a black belt third dan. She could shoot a jellybean off a thimble at fifty feet. She loved her work. And she was utterly beautiful as she took him deep inside her body.

The meeting fell apart without her, considering the general's purpose had been to force her to accept Navy oversight of her project, control the Navy no longer wanted. Captain O'Leary adjourned the meeting and escorted the general out of the conference room suggesting they have dinner at Barely North. Times like this, Pax wished the base had an O-club for the old guard. But at least it would be safe for Pax to grab a meal from the cafeteria.

He could only hope Morgan was in her CLU, because one thing had become uncomfortably clear as he watched her throughout the unpleasant meeting. He was falling stupidly in love with the stubborn, proud, and persistent archaeologist, and with her father on base, she was more off-limits than ever.

Chapter Twenty

The tour of the site was conducted with great fanfare. Camp Citron's commander of SOCOM and another commanding general joined her father and Captain O'Leary for the tour. O'Leary brought with him a foam-lined case, which he'd had constructed to protect Linus's skull.

The Navy had issued cell phones to Ibrahim and Mouktar, making it possible for Ripley to inform them they needed to be at the Linus site for the tour. If nothing else, the tour was good practice for her team to prepare for the unveiling for the international press.

At the site, Morgan asked Mouktar and Ibrahim to lead the tour, as she'd done when the Green Berets had visited the survey area. This was their country; they should be the face of the find, not her. It might have been an opportunity to strut her knowledge and skill for her father, but she'd given up on pleasing him so long ago, it no longer mattered. As it was, she was there to answer questions when her crew couldn't, and that, too, was good training for both men.

Pax's Green Beret team and accompanying busload of trainees arrived in time to watch as Morgan placed Linus's broken skull back in situ. Both the damage to the skull and Pax's arrival triggered anguish. It made sense that the locals would get to tour this site as well, given that some of them might be assigned security in the days to come, but she wished she'd been warned she'd see Pax again. As it was, she felt the same irritating flutter in her belly she always had when she saw him, but now it mixed with heartache.

As Ibrahim and Mouktar answered questions, she couldn't help but look his direction. A frisson ran through her as she met his unabashed stare. The anger had left his eyes, as had the stone-cold glare. He was Pax again, his eyes serious but conveying a hint of lust he couldn't quite hide.

The crack in his shield didn't give her hope. Far from it. With her dad here to underscore the risks for him, there wasn't a chance he'd yield. The chasm between them only grew wider.

When all the questions had been asked and answered, Linus's skull was again packed up and secured in a Humvee. Ibrahim and Mouktar repeated the tour for the belated trainees, and Morgan thanked her father and the other officers for their visit. She turned to rejoin her crew, longing for this to be over, so she could escape the scrutiny of the two men who had the power to hurt her the most.

"Wait," her father said. He gave the Navy captain an apologetic smile. "I'd like to speak to my daughter alone for a few minutes."

Sure, it was fine for *him* to waste the captain's time, but when all she'd wanted was a three-minute shower after a day in the hot sun, she was being selfish. She shrugged the bitter thought away. There was no salvaging her relationship with her father, and her hostility served no purpose other than to burn a hole in her stomach lining.

She followed the general to a patch of shade next to an acacia tree. He was silent, and she knew better than to speak before being spoken to. He'd trained her well.

He cleared his throat. "As you suggested, I read up on the Lucy fossil last night."

She startled. That was just about the last thing she expected him to say.

"It was…interesting." He shook his head. "Okay, it was boring as crap and I didn't understand much of it, but I can see why it was—and your Linus will be—a big deal. I still think you made a mistake pursuing archaeology instead of putting your sharp mind to use for the military. You could've gone far in the Pentagon in military intelligence or another branch."

Sharp? Her father thought she was smart? The heat must've gotten to him.

"You never mentioned anything about a career in the military that didn't involve me being the first woman on a special forces team. Not because you think women are up to the job and needed a trailblazer, but because then you'd finally have the son of your dreams."

He reared back, as if struck. "What makes you think I wanted a son?"

It occurred to Morgan this might be an opportunity for a real conversation with him. Not a one-sided lecture that left her in angry tears and hating her weakness. "I don't know, maybe the way you would say—no matter what my achievement—that I could have done better, and I needed to work harder, usually accompanied by the words, 'if you only had balls.'"

"That's just a phrase!"

"It's a phrase with a specific meaning. I don't have balls, General. And I'm not sorry about that. And I don't agree that I'm a failure if I'm not the best either."

"I never said that."

"You did, sir. Every damn day."

"I was being encouraging. Pushing you."

"No, sir. You were being a drill sergeant, when what I really needed was a father." Her eyes teared, and she knew, much as they needed this conversation, she couldn't have it here. Not now. Not when Pax stood twenty meters away and she had a crew to manage with hours of work ahead of her.

"I'm sorry, General. I've got work to do. There's an A-Team and a platoon of guerrillas-in-training waiting." For the second time in as many days, she left her father's company without waiting to be dismissed. She made a beeline for her team's Humvee, avoiding Pax's gaze.

She hoped her dad wouldn't insist on them dining together tonight, because she wanted to drown her sorrows in a big, very unhealthy, very unvegan chocolate milkshake.

P ax was the last one on the bus. Most of the team rode in Humvees ahead and behind the bus of Djiboutian trainees, but Pax and Bastian the bastard were stuck together, playing the role of teachers controlling students on a field trip.

The bus was owned and operated by the Djiboutian government, providing steady work for at least one citizen. The US military hired Djiboutians whenever possible, a laudable practice that sometimes made his job more difficult, but this driver, at least, was well trained.

It was fortunate also that these students took their studies seriously. The men were all young, strong, and eager to defend their country, but that didn't mean a break from the guerrilla training wasn't welcome, and they'd seemed to enjoy the excursion to see Linus before the world learned of his existence.

He heard the banter as they claimed the little chimp as Issa or Afar, but the tribalism was a joke. These men had learned to set it aside. Like the others on his Special Forces team, Pax had the language skills to work with the locals, but his fluency was in French, not Arabic, and the conversation drifted from the French he could understand to the Arabic he couldn't. Not a concern, because Bastian the bastard was fluent in Arabic and could monitor what was said. Their complementary fluency was why they were paired on the bus.

It was a relief for Pax to sit back and close his eyes, tune everything out, and try to forget how fucked up this deployment had become.

Except every time he closed his eyes, he saw Morgan, naked and beautiful, giving her body to him with an uninhibited boldness that left him weak and wanting more two days later.

He didn't like it that Linus was about to go public, but he was no longer in charge of Morgan's security, no longer had any say in her life. Not that he ever had.

His cell phone vibrated, and he answered without bothering to check the ID, thankful for the distraction. "Sergeant Blanchard."

The man spoke rapid French, and Pax changed mental gears. "This is Charles Lemaire, I need to speak with Dr. Adler. It's urgent. News of the site has leaked. Our intelligence minister has just informed me that ISIS has put out a call for volunteers to destroy Linus."

Shit. As if they didn't have enough problems. "Do you have the resources to protect the site?"

"No. I was hoping the US military could assist. Our president is contacting your Navy captain as we speak."

It would probably fall to SOCOM, maybe a team of SEALs if the threat were imminent; otherwise, marines would be set to guard. His guerrilla trainees might be defending the site far sooner than anyone had expected. He shook his head. This wasn't his battle. Not his mission. "To reach Dr. Adler, you have to call the new head of her security team." He gave the man Ripley's phone number.

Call complete, he tucked away his phone and trudged down the center aisle of the bus to Bastian's seat. He told the chief—second in command of their A-Team—the news. Bastian's gaze swept over the forty trainees who were ready and eager to defend their homeland. "I'll radio our XO. We should head back. Plan the defense of the site."

Pax nodded. He'd been hoping that was what the chief would say. He was still a bastard, but he was a smart bastard.

Morgan's workday, already cut short due to the tour, was utterly demolished by the phone call from Lemaire. She was forced to leave Ibrahim and Mouktar to work unsupervised while she and the security team went to the minister's office.

Upon arrival, Minister of Tourism Jean Savin led her to a small conference room, where Charles Lemaire waited along with Minister of Natural Resources Ali Imbert. Ripley stood guard at the door, while Sanchez covered the building entrance, same as when Pax had accompanied her.

Imbert, a native of the country who, according to Lemaire, was one of the old-school ministers who'd been upset to learn Dr. Adler was a woman, studied her critically, then said, "Your government spends money protecting a woman while our site remains vulnerable. We asked you at our last meeting if they would protect Linus, but they have only protected *you*."

"Without this woman, you'd have no site to protect," Morgan replied. "But I didn't ask for the protection. It was offered after a warlord bombed my car, and I'm not a fool, so I accepted."

Lemaire said something in rapid French to the other minister, and she had a feeling he was admonishing the man. In English, he said, "I have been informed Captain O'Leary has promised guards—Marines, he said—and even as we speak, there is a detachment of your soldiers—the ones who are training our men—who are coming up with a defensive plan for the site.

Morgan met Ripley's gaze. The man gave her a quick nod with an even quicker smile. His A-Team was on it.

A flicker of warmth spread through her at the notion that Pax might be behind that action. Foolish because he wouldn't be doing it for her. Linus wasn't *hers*. The australopithecine belonged to Djibouti, and protecting his fossilized remains was in America's best interest because goodwill between countries would lead to a US-controlled airstrip. Which would give the US an edge in the war on terror in East Africa.

That was all there was to it.

But deep down, she wondered if he felt as protective of the little old hairless bipedal hominin as she did.

After the tourism and natural resources ministers left, Lemaire stayed behind to discuss the investigation into Broussard's disappearance. She wasn't surprised to learn the inquiry had barely moved forward because the gendarmes weren't really investigating and *Police Nationale* had made no move to send anyone to Djibouti. She kept to herself her plans to return to her apartment, knowing from her discussion with Ripley that he wanted no one informed that she'd visit her old neighborhood ahead of time. Instead, she simply begged the minister to keep her in the loop through Ripley.

Giving out her cell phone number would require disabling the GPS tracking function, so she wasn't permitted to use the phone with the minister or even with her crew. Basically, she could only use the phone to contact US military personnel. Making it a rather useless device as far as she was concerned.

It was late when she finally returned to the base at the end of the extra-long workday. She went straight to the cafeteria and got a milkshake to go. She'd spend the evening in her CLU. Hiding. Because she was a coward.

Some would say she didn't have balls, but she was inclined to tell those people to fuck off.

Shake in hand, she settled at her desk to work on the survey report. Except for the anomalous village site, the second corridor was proving to be the better route for the railway. It would take a find equal to Linus to prevent bulldozers from going through. Sites would be lost, but in the grand scheme it would be better for Djibouti. China was paying for the line, Ethiopia would pay a fortune annually to use the dedicated railway to the port, and plans for the water pipeline to follow the same route were moving forward.

Add Linus to the other benefits, and Djibouti had gained a national treasure that would bring the same degree of prestige as Lucy brought to Ethiopia, making her contract a huge bargain all around.

If it weren't for the warlord and new threats from ISIS, she'd be flying high from her work on this project. As it was, she was worried. What would ISIS do when photos of Linus were spread across the web? Would the publicity renew Desta's interest either in the project or in her?

Desta had been quiet. In one of her debriefings, the captain's aide had indicated they thought there was infighting within the organization. It was possible the tipster had been identified and eliminated. From what she'd gathered, no one thought the new threat from ISIS was related to Desta. He was aligning with al-Shabaab, not ISIS.

She missed being able to discuss this with Pax. He understood her suspicions and questions about the strange site with recent alluvium. What if Broussard really had found something?

She picked up her cell phone—not to call him; she'd never do that again—but to read the texts he'd sent her as he sat across from her in the cafeteria. To feel a connection to him again. With each moment that passed, she was more and more certain she'd been falling in love with him. If she'd behaved, if she hadn't called him, hadn't sent those selfies, would they have had a chance, later, once they were stateside? Or would he have stuck to his rules about no officer's daughters and no serious relationships as long as he was a Special Forces operator?

She had no reason to think he'd have changed his mind. In which case, that one night was all they ever would've had. The thought eased her regrets a small amount. At least this way, she had the memory of what it had been like to be utterly possessed by Sergeant Pax Blanchard.

She opened the text menu on the phone. He was the only person she'd texted since she got the cell, so it should have gone straight to that thread. But there was nothing there. His beautiful notes were gone.

He must've deleted them when she was having the tracker reset.

She understood why. She couldn't be trusted with his number. But still, knowing he'd taken away those precious texts broke her. The precarious grip she'd held on her emotions since Pax walked out of her CLU shattered. This time she didn't cry because she was angry. She cried out of sheer and utter heartache.

Chapter Twenty-One

For the first time in weeks, there were clouds in the sky. Well, one. But Pax welcomed the sole puff of white, hoping it was the first of many. Even the locals seemed lighter, happier at the sight. As if seeing one cloud reminded them clouds were indeed real, not a fictional invention like dragons and unicorns.

The day's training with the locals was being conducted at a firing range Pax's team had set up, complete with an obstacle course they had to maneuver through prior to taking their shot. A grueling test of skill and determination due to the hot sun and heavy packs, but also fun. A contest. The mood was light among the group as they traded barbs and boasts over who had the worst time or the most accurate shot. Pax usually loved this, but everything about the last few days had soured his mood.

Shit. *This* was why he hadn't wanted to get involved. It was screwing with his focus. With his job.

He'd never been such a screwup before.

A dust cloud in the distance warned of an approaching vehicle, and like good trainees, the men used their riflescopes to identify the vehicle. "Humvee," one shouted. They called out everything they could see that might be valuable intel in an ambush situation, but it was clear this was a visit from the brass and not a threat.

Dread settled in his gut. He knew exactly who would be in that vehicle. The general, being Army, had shown an interest in their Special Forces team. He was here for the requisite inspection.

The A-Team captain ordered the trainees to line up at attention. Once assembled, Pax and the rest of the team mustered as well.

"At ease," General Adler said after receiving the perfunctory salute. He then performed a rote inspection, walking down the line. He paused in front of Pax. "Sergeant, it's my understanding you requested removal from my daughter's security team."

Pax practically choked. *Requested?* Well, at least his XO had given a kind misstatement. He supposed a dumbass public scuffle with a superior could be interpreted that way.

"Yes, sir."

"May I ask why?"

"Because I'm needed here, sir."

"More so than Sergeant Ripley?" The general looked up, seeming to remember the other Special Forces operators and guerrilla trainees who were listening. "Dismissed," he announced.

Pax didn't bother to hope the order included him.

"Walk with me, son."

In Pax's experience, it was never a good sign when a superior adopted fatherly words. But he nodded. Orders were orders.

"I've seen the way she looks at you," the general said. "And you're good at hiding it—better than she is—but I've seen the way you look at her too."

He could deny it, play dumb, or remain silent. He opted for silent.

"Is that why you requested reassignment?"

Pax considered his response carefully. "I'm in Djibouti to train Djiboutians to be soldiers." He paused, then added, "Sir."

"You can drop the 'sirs,' this is a personal conversation."

"In my experience, there is no such thing as a personal conversation with a superior officer I've only just met, sir."

"I can see why she likes you. You're as stubborn as she is. Did you know my daughter has been pretending to be a vegan around me for over a dozen years, just because she knows it irritates me?"

Pax kept his face blank, but deep down he wanted to laugh. "It sounds like you're equally stubborn, sir, if you haven't let on that you know."

"Morgan is an amazing woman."

"Yes, sir. She is."

"I'm not certain you're good enough for my daughter, Sergeant Blanchard."

"And I know for a fact I'm not. Now, if you'll excuse me, I have soldiers to train." Pax gave the man a crisp salute, then turned back to his team.

Pax had just returned from the shower when his cell phone vibrated. Caller ID indicated it was his XO. He braced himself. These days, any communication with the commander set him on edge. Invariably, it had to do with Morgan.

He answered brusquely, glad Cal was still in the shower. They were on the waitlist for single wet CLUs like Morgan had, and he couldn't wait to have privacy at the end of a long day.

"This is an unofficial call," his XO said without preamble. "General Adler just left my office. He requested you be transferred to Fort Belvoir, Virginia.

His post."

"SOCOM doesn't have a command at Fort Belvoir. He's trying to yank me from Special Forces?" *Sonofafuckingbitch.*

"He requested a TDY for six months to a year. Nothing permanent. He said he thinks you have potential."

Yeah. Potential son-in-law. He gripped the phone in a tight fist. "Am I being sent to Virginia?"

"No. I told him you're needed right where you are. When this deployment is over, you're returning to Fort Campbell with the rest of the team. But Pax, if he keeps pushing, there's only so much I can do."

"Got it. Thanks for the heads-up." He hit the End button and stared at the phone. His entire body was tight with anger. He didn't think Morgan had put her father up to this, but she sure as hell would put a stop to it.

Chapter Twenty-Two

Morgan jolted at the angry pounding on the door. Her gaze dropped to her arm. No. She hadn't accidently triggered the tracker again, so the urgent knock couldn't be about that. She frowned. The entire container shook with the force of the pounding. The shade was pulled down on the window inset in the door. "Who is it?" she asked.

"It's Pax. Open up. Now."

Given the anger in his tone, she found it irritating that she felt a giddy flutter. She was pathetic.

She unlocked the door and pulled it open. He stood there, his beautiful, angry, massive self filling the doorway and blocking the low evening sun. "What a pleasant surprise to see you, Pax," she said with sugar-laden sarcasm. "How may I help you this lovely evening?"

His eyes flattened. "May I come in?"

"No."

His jaw clenched. "We need to talk."

She cocked her head. "Why, do you have a burning sensation when you pee? You didn't get that from me." She started to close the door. He thrust an arm in the gap and pushed the door wide.

"I'm not in the mood for games."

She flinched at the reference to his parting words from the other night.

He stepped forward, menacingly, and like the fool she was, she retreated. Inside, he slammed the door shut, then advanced on her. "Did you ask your father to transfer me to Fort Belvoir?" His voice shook with rage.

She took another step back as shock filtered through her. "No! *Sonofabitch.* Pax! You have to believe me. I would *never* do that. How did he even—" She stumbled, both verbally and physically, unable to speak and retreat at the same time.

The first wave of his anger diminished, but hot behind it was another set rippling toward shore. "Fine. You didn't put him up to it. But you *will* call him off. Because, you see, he's a fucking general, and I'm fucking enlisted, so *I* can't tell him to back off."

"Of course, I'll talk to him! Are you—that is, have you—been transferred?"

"Not yet. But if he pushes, he'll get his way. It's what generals do." He glared at her. "*This* is why I don't get involved with officer's daughters."

Dear old Dad had screwed her over good this time. If there had even been the slightest chance of them getting together someday, her dad had just taken that faint hope, doused it in gasoline, then thrown a grenade on it.

"I'm sorry, Pax. I'm just as horrified as you are."

"Are you really? Because you aren't the one who's being threatened with having everything important to you yanked away because an old fool wants to indulge his baby girl. I already went through this shit with my ex-wife."

"Your ex-wife was a military brat? Why the hell didn't you tell me that before?"

"It has no bearing on you and me."

"*Bullshit!* It's framed the way you've viewed me from the start." Dammit. Not only was he holding her responsible for her father's action, it was also possible she'd been unknowingly shouldering the burden of his failed marriage.

She clenched her jaw as she stepped closer to him, no longer cowering or feeling guilty over something she'd had no part in. "You know what? Fuck you, Pax. I didn't ask my dad to give you to me for my birthday. I wasn't even aware he thinks there's something between us. But screw you if you think I'm the type of woman who would use him to try to get you."

She planted her fists on her hips. "I don't know what kind of relationship your ex had with her father, but in case you haven't noticed, my father and I aren't exactly close. Certainly not a relationship where I could—or would—convince him to meddle in your career so we could be together. And I'm hardly so desperate to land a man that I need my daddy to pull strings. I do just fine on my own. I could replace you in a heartbeat if that's what I wanted."

His eyes flared with heat, and he took a step toward her, angling her into what she now thought of as his favorite section of wall. "You think you can replace *me*?" His voice was low, menacing. "Do you think another man could make you come apart like I did? Do you really believe another man would satisfy you now?" His voice dropped lower and lower until the last words were no more than a sexy rasp.

Her back was to the wall, and he leaned over her. Intimidating. Dominating. And under the cloak of anger, she saw the true fuel behind his words. Desperation.

He feared she *could* replace him.

She ran a hand over his crotch. He hardened instantly. "No, Pax," she whispered, voicing her own desperation. "I don't want *this*"—she stroked his erection—"from anyone but you."

He groaned as she slipped her hand into his pants and wrapped her fingers around his thick cock.

"Suck me off," he said, opening his fly. "Now. Take me in your mouth."

She dropped to her knees and freed him from his boxer briefs and took him just like he'd demanded. She knew damn well this was nothing more than a convenient blowjob for him, and she didn't care. Didn't care that he hadn't kissed her. Didn't care that he wouldn't return the favor. Right now, she was doing exactly what she wanted to do, storing away another memory to savor later.

He braced his hands on the wall above her as he thrust into her mouth. He muttered as she sucked. Only some words were intelligible between curses and groans. "…fuck, babe…yes… Mine, babe… *Mine*."

She sucked and stroked and loved every moment. His orgasm built, and she toyed with the idea of taking off her shirt so he could come on her chest. Not something she'd ever been into before, but the possessiveness she felt toward him, and the need she had to be possessed by him, made it a powerful urge. But the logistics of getting the shirt off when he was so close defeated her, and he pulsed into her mouth with a groan, and she swallowed and kept sucking.

His hips stopped thrusting, and he slipped gently from her mouth, then grabbed her shoulders and pulled her to her feet. She braced herself for anger, for regret that he'd given in to impulse again. But he surprised her by kissing her tenderly, whispering the word "Mine," repeatedly as he did so.

She kissed him back, and when his mouth moved to her neck, she said, "I'm yours, Pax. I don't want anyone but you."

"This can't go anywhere. This can't happen again." His voice was husky, pained.

"I know. But still, I'm yours."

"You won't hook up with anyone else while you're here?"

"No. How could I when you're all I want?" She smiled sadly, then pulled his mouth to hers and kissed him deeply. When the kiss ended she said, "You're mine, Pax. My caveman. Even if you never touch me again. You're still mine."

A knock sounded on the door. *Oh hell, not again!* She glanced at her arm, but they hadn't touched the tracker.

Pax tucked himself in and zipped his fly. She glanced around for other signs of what they'd been up to, but doubted her hair was even mussed.

Another knock. "Morgan? It's your father."

Pax's eyes hardened, and dread shot through her. He must have caught her reaction, because he shook his head and whispered directly into her ear, "I'm not mad at you. At him."

She'd been mad at her father her whole life. She could relate to that. They could handle this one of two ways. "Do you want to hide, or face him?"

He pressed his lips to her neck, then said, "Face him."

Pax stood stiffly in the background as Morgan invited her father in. The general's eyes flashed in surprise at seeing him. This should be Pax's worst nightmare come true, yet he felt strangely free. He'd been in this situation before, except on that occasion, the daughter in question had requested her father's intervention. It wasn't his ex-wife's father who'd triggered the end of his marriage. It was his wife herself.

General Adler glanced from Pax to Morgan. "I was hoping you'd have dinner with me at Barely North. Of course, Sergeant Blanchard, you're welcome to join us."

"No, thank you, sir."

The general nodded. He'd clearly expected that answer. "Morgan?"

"Sure. Let me just get my shoes on." She faced Pax. "Thank you for your input," she said smoothly.

He found it hard not to snicker at her choice of words. He should be thanking her. "You're welcome. I want to know when you hear from *Police Nationale* about Broussard."

"I'll text you." She fixed him with a pointed look. "But I need your number."

She'd noticed the deleted messages. He probably shouldn't have done that. He nodded. "I'll send it."

Morgan sat on the cot to slip on her shoes, and Pax had his opportunity to leave. And yet, he took one look at the beautiful, composed woman who'd just rocked his world, and he couldn't simply walk away.

He turned to the man who had the power to crush his career and decided to face him head-on. "Sir, I understand you've requested I be assigned to your post in Virginia for temporary duty."

"Yes, I did."

Pax forced himself to relax his posture, which had been inching toward attention. "I'm speaking to you now not as a subordinate, not as a soldier, but as a man." He didn't wait for permission. He didn't need permission, not for this. "I have feelings for your daughter."

Behind him, Morgan sucked in a sharp breath.

"But given the situation, this is neither the time nor place to pursue those feelings. It remains to be seen whether the future will present a better time and place, but your machinations are not welcome. I am a Special Forces operator. Do not take that away from me. Not only would you be doing the country you have sworn to serve a disservice, but the harm you do to your relationship with Morgan might be irreparable."

The general's expression remained unchanged, but Pax didn't really give a damn what the man thought. He turned to Morgan, who sat on the cot, frozen with one shoe on and the other in her hand. Her full, sexy lips were open, her jaw dropped in shock. He wanted nothing more than to slip his tongue in that mouth and make impossible promises. Instead he gave her a sharp nod. "Enjoy your dinner. By the way, he knows you aren't a vegan."

Her jaw snapped closed, and her eyes widened.

He winked at her. "We'll talk later."

She flashed a brilliant smile. "Send me a text."

He intended to. He'd start with a picture of his abs.

Dinner with the general wasn't the ordeal Morgan feared, but it also wasn't a joyous reconciliation that magically fixed years of resentment and rebellion. But it was steak night at Barely North, so she was thankful Pax gave her the heads-up on the fake vegan front.

"Your mother doesn't know you were in danger," her father said as he sliced his steak.

"How did you explain your trip, then?"

"She doesn't know I'm here."

"And you're just telling me this now? What if I'd called her?"

He cocked his head. "When was the last time you called your mother out of the blue?"

"Actually, it's not *Mom* I don't call." It was refreshing, speaking frankly to him.

His mouth tightened, and his gaze dropped, surprising her. Her words had hurt him. It had never occurred to her she had the power to hurt her father's feelings, because he'd never expressed regard for her opinion. The notion she'd upset him triggered guilt, but she dampened remorse with the reminder of all the pain her father had served her over the years. Hell, the humiliation he'd inflicted his first evening in Djibouti.

"Sergeant Blanchard has an exemplary record."

"I won't discuss him with you, General. I don't want or need your approval."

He frowned. "You've *never* wanted or needed my approval."

"That's not true. I wanted it. I just never received it. I've learned to make do without." She pushed her baked potato across her plate. She was rapidly losing her appetite.

"Well, it's hard to approve when you're throwing your life and money away on useless degrees."

It had been too much to hope he'd change. She took a deep breath followed by a sip of wine. *He'd tried, at least. Give him credit for that. He just reverted quickly.* "Why did you come to Djibouti?" she asked.

"Because you were going to screw everything—"

She slid back her chair and stood. "Good night, General."

He caught her hand, preventing her escape. His face pinched as he took a deep breath. Finally, he said, "I came because I was worried about you. I was terrified you'd get hurt, and it would be my fault because I'd insisted you stay. I came to convince you to come home with me. That's why I wanted the Navy to take over the project, why I belittled you at that meeting and tried to make you sound incompetent. Because I want you safe at home."

Morgan dropped back into her seat. She curled her fingers around his, no longer captive, now holding on. She didn't think she'd held his hand since she was eight years old. "You aren't the reason I stayed. That phone call had nothing to do with my decision. I stayed for Linus. I couldn't just walk away from a find like that."

His fingers tightened around hers. It was a start.

Chapter Twenty-Three

Morgan settled on her cot with her cell phone and a bowl of rocky road ice cream. She'd skipped dessert with her dad so she could enjoy the cold treat in the privacy of her CLU.

She smiled. Pax had texted her. Her heart fluttered when she saw the picture of his perfect abs. She held the phone to her chest with eyes closed and took a deep breath against the rush of emotion. The selfie was as much a declaration as his words to her father.

She typed out a quick reply: *Nice photo of #4.*

His response was immediate: *#4?*

She took a bite of ice cream, savoring the flavor. Savoring the moment. *Your abs are #4 on my list of things I want to lick.*

Pax's reply: *Ah. Well, convenient, because you've already sent me pictures of my #2 and #3.*

She grinned, thinking of her earlier selfies: breasts and mouth, giving her a good idea of what his number one was.

He sent another message before she could reply: *How was dinner?*

She responded: *Awkward and painful, but also good. We're talking, at least. Also, I think he approves of you.*

Pax's reply: *And how much does that bother you?*

She laughed. He already knew her so well. *You have no idea. You're screwing up 13 years of excellent rebellion, because you're too damn perfect, you bastard.*

His next text included a photo of his neck, chin, and lips. *My official title is Sergeant Bastard, Dr. Adler.*

She stared at the photo for a full minute before responding. *Sergeant Sexy Bastard. Nice combo shot of #2 and #3. I just licked my phone.* She sighed and sent another message. *I suppose I have to make do with pictures?*

He responded: *Yes. Your father's approval or not, I still have orders. And I also have a job to do here that requires 100% focus, and you are distracting.*

She nodded even as she typed: *I understand. I should be done here in the next two weeks. Then I'll return to DC.*

She finished her ice cream while waiting for his response. Wondering if the idea of them ever getting together was simply impossible.

She set the empty bowl aside when her phone chimed with his reply. *Maybe*

I can get a few days leave when you finish. We can rendezvous in a hotel in Rome. I'll start at #42 and work my way up to #2…then down to #1.

She replied: *Yes to Rome or wherever you want to meet. What is #42?*

His response made her laugh out loud: *The answer to life, the universe, and everything. Also, the back of your left knee.*

She touched the spot behind her knee, wondering if she'd think of Pax now every time she touched that particular spot. *My right knee is now jealous.* She sent the message, attaching a picture of the named body part.

It shouldn't be, it's #38. Crap. Cal just came in. I should go.

She replied: *Good night, Pax. Thank you for facing my father.*

She'd set the phone on her nightstand when it chimed one more time. *I meant what I said. I have feelings for you, Morgan. I don't intend to run from them.*

M organ dropped into her beach chair in the shade and pulled her field notebook from her backpack at her feet. She'd spend today's siesta expanding on her notes from the morning's survey. The sun was nearing maximum hot, and Mouktar and Ibrahim had settled down for their two-hour heat break.

Ripley closed the Humvee door—he must have finished calling in his midday report—and approached her. "The brass has given permission for you to return to your apartment. Does now work for you?" He nodded toward the field notebook in her hands. "Or do you need to finish that?"

She set down the book. "Now is good. The notes can wait." She dug around in her backpack and found her wallet, cell phone, and apartment key. She tucked the wallet and keys into her back pocket and slipped the phone down the front of her jog bra. She grabbed her hat and water bottle and said, "Ready."

She climbed into the back of the Humvee. Sanchez had the day off, replaced by a young marine named Jeb Holloway, who took the front passenger seat. Holloway was all of twenty years old and had been eager to escape the base for the day. Morgan felt a tension in her gut—which she hadn't realized she carried—unfurl as the project area faded from the rearview mirror. She'd wondered if this moment would ever come.

She wanted to slide open the window and feel the hot breeze generated by the vehicle bounding down the rough road at forty miles per hour. But open windows were forbidden according to everyone who'd guarded her in the last two weeks.

So air-conditioning was the only breeze she felt, and the cold air had the same artificial American feeling she felt on base.

She wanted to experience Djibouti in all its uncomfortable glory. If she was going to drive by starving children in an air-conditioned, armored Humvee, she should be able to give them food or water. Didn't privilege come with responsibility?

That was why she'd cried during her first week in Djibouti. Here, she had enormous privilege. Unable to share it with the locals who were horrifyingly less fortunate, the riches sat heavily upon her shoulders, threatening to suffocate her.

Every instinct in her body wanted to scream, "Stop!" when she saw the children digging through the roadside trash heaps, which were as ubiquitous as McDonald's restaurants in the US. But she held her breath against the scream, knowing the impulse to stop would do more harm than good.

They drove on in their luxury, and when the view from the window was too much, she averted her gaze.

This country wasn't for the weak or idealistic. As far as she could tell, the only creatures that thrived here were the Northeast African carpet vipers.

They reached her apartment without incident. Holloway stayed with the Humvee while Ripley escorted her inside. Nothing had changed since her last visit. "I want to grab the rest of my clothes and the research books," she said. "And look to see if Broussard left anything besides books behind."

Ripley nodded. "I'll box up the books for you."

"Thanks. After I'm packed, there's a restaurant down the street where we can grab a bite. My treat."

He frowned at her. "No can do, Morgan."

"It's a tiny place. Locals only. Good food."

He shook his head.

"Can we at least bring Hugo the coloring books?" From the desktop, she picked up the two coloring books along with the box of crayons her mother had sent. They'd arrived the day before the explosion, which was why she hadn't given them to the boy yet.

"Hugo?"

"His father owns the restaurant. He's ten years old. I've been teaching him to write English." She could see Ripley's face soften. "How old is your son again?"

He laughed. "You know he's eight."

She flashed a toothy grin. "Guilty."

"We can bring Hugo the gifts, but that's all."

"If Desta really wanted to grab me, he could get me at the site."

"Yes, but this area is populated. Too many unknowns. Your survey area is wide open and vacant. Visible. I don't have to worry about a shot taking out an innocent bystander."

"This must be so boring for you." She was still, all these days later, getting used to the idea of having to ask for permission for everything she did. In a way, Desta had already made her a prisoner.

But at least this was her choice. It occurred to her that if she told Ripley she didn't want his protection, he'd have no recourse. He couldn't force her to return to the base with him. But she wasn't a fool.

Packing went quickly. She decided to leave behind the souvenirs she'd gathered. If all went well, she'd return here and pick up the keepsakes for her mom and friends before she left the country. If it didn't go well, she'd hardly regret the loss.

She didn't find anything that might've belonged to Broussard other than the books she knew were his. Tonight, she'd flip through his remaining books and see if any notes or papers were tucked inside. It was a long shot, but what could she do? Spending time with Pax was out, and she could only take her father in small doses.

Packed, they loaded the boxes into the Humvee with Holloway's help, then, coloring books in hand, she walked with Ripley to the restaurant at the end of the street. Ripley made an effort to look off duty, and she tried to look relaxed. In all probability, they both failed.

The proprietor greeted her warmly. He spoke no English. She spoke no Arabic and little French, but she'd learned the menu and he knew her preferences. He took one look at her companion and held up two fingers, asking if she wanted her usual for two. She glanced at Ripley with pleading eyes, but he shook his head. "No time, Morgan."

She nodded, then turned to the proprietor and declined the food order. "Is Hugo in?" she asked hopefully.

No sooner had she said the words than Hugo entered from the back. His face lit up when he saw her, and he gave her a polite bow. He knew enough English to help foreigners, and while she'd been teaching him to read English, he'd taught her some Arabic. He was a far better student than she was.

She wanted to give him a hug but wasn't sure how the gesture would be received. There was so much she still had to learn about the culture in Djibouti.

"Mogon! You back," he said.

"I've missed you, Hugo."

"I have been making the words. Just like I promised." He glanced back toward the kitchen. "Don't go." Then he darted into the back before she had a chance to offer him the coloring books.

Ripley shot her a questioning look, and she shrugged.

A few minutes later, Hugo returned, waving a stack of papers. "See! I have made all the words." His gaze fixed on her with utmost seriousness. "All. Of. Them." He placed the bundle in her hands, and she smiled, seeing he'd been practicing his writing. The pages were filled with random words, far more than she'd taught him. It appeared he'd cracked the code and understood the basic phonetics of the alphabet. He'd tried to write every word he could speak.

Her heart ached to see words like gun, wor, deth, and drone, intermixed between momma, syster, and famlee. "You've done very well, Hugo." She flipped through the pages, keeping her expression cheerful and proud. Her eyes teared at seeing Mogon on one page. She slipped it from the stack and handed him back the other pages. "Can I keep this one?"

He nodded as he beamed with pride. "And now that you are here, the Somali man will pay me five thousand francs!"

Morgan stiffened and met Ripley's gaze. His eyes were equally wide with alarm.

"Somali man?" she asked.

"Yes. He has been in every day asking for the yellow-haired American woman and said he'd pay me if I let him know when you are here. He wants you to teach him to make the words too."

Morgan opened her wallet and pulled out ten thousand francs—worth a little more than fifty US dollars. "Hugo, I will pay you if you don't tell him."

The boy's eyes widened, and his mouth formed an O when he saw double the payment in her hand. He frowned. "I cannot take your money." His expression said this pained him. "I have already told him."

"I'm sorry, Hugo. I have to go." She shoved the money, books, and crayons into his hands as Ripley grabbed her elbow and pulled her toward the door.

"Will you be back?" Hugo asked.

"No. I'm sorry!" She dropped another five thousand Djiboutian franc note on the floor as Ripley dragged her from the restaurant.

"Get to the Humvee!" he said as he pulled her down the narrow street. He cursed under his breath, and Morgan couldn't blame him. She'd fucked up in going to the restaurant, complacent in the knowledge no one expected her.

It never occurred to her they knew of her fondness for Hugo.

She slid into the backseat as Ripley took the wheel, explaining the situation to Holloway. There was only one route to the main road from where they'd parked, and it would take them right by the restaurant. They rounded the corner, bringing the tiny business front into view.

"Get down!" Holloway shouted.

But she couldn't. Shock and horror had her frozen as a man stepped out of the restaurant, gripping Hugo's arm, holding a gun to the young boy's head. Hugo's eyes were wide with terror. Tears streamed down his face. In one hand, he still gripped the pages he'd written on, and in the other, he held the coloring books. The crayons slipped from his fingers and landed in the street.

"STOP!" she shouted.

"No," Ripley said.

"Stop the fucking car!"

"I can't!" Ripley yelled back.

Her life wasn't worth more than that little boy. She would never be able to live with herself if they drove by, allowing him to die so she'd be safe. She wrenched open the door and tumbled out, into the road. Adrenaline surged, masking the pain of the abrading gravel as she rolled on the ground. She staggered to her feet as she heard the Humvee come to a screeching halt.

She didn't look back. She needed to get to Hugo.

The man clutching the boy tightened his grip, pulling up Hugo's arm at an awkward, painful angle, but he no longer held his gun on the boy's head.

"Don't hurt him. You can have me."

She knelt before Hugo, aware that the militant's gun was now pointed at her head. "Go inside, Hugo. Go to your father."

"I'm sorry, Mogon!"

"It's not your fault, Hugo. You are good. You did nothing wrong." She pulled him to her and hugged him fiercely. She pressed a kiss to his temple and whispered, "Go now. Protect your family. I'll be okay. I promise." She shoved him toward the door.

The militant made as if to grab him, but she kicked his arm away. "NO! You can have me, but you will leave the boy alone."

Hugo ran for the restaurant and disappeared inside.

The man grabbed her wrists and wrenched her arms behind her back, turning her as he did so. In the street, Ripley fought one militant and Holloway another. The Americans were fit, while the militants had none of their strength, training, or health. In moments, they each had their man in a headlock.

"Let her go!" Ripley shouted as he increased the pressure on his captive's throat.

Escaping now would only endanger Hugo again. She had to see this nightmare through, or the boy would suffer. "No, Ripley. Go to the base. Tell them what happened. Tell them I *chose* this. It's not your fault. It's one hundred percent mine. I can't let them hurt Hugo."

The Green Beret's face pinched. "I can't do that, Morgan." The man he held collapsed. Unconscious or dead, she didn't know.

The man holding her didn't seem to care. He gripped Morgan tighter and stepped backward down the street.

"If they don't take me now," Morgan said, pleading with Ripley, "they'll come back for Hugo. I can't live with that. Can you?"

Hugo wasn't a child of war, taking up arms against US soldiers. She'd brought this nightmare to him.

But there was another reason for her to do this. "They'll take me to Desta," she said firmly.

Ripley knew about the tracker. After the fiasco with Pax, she figured the head of her security team should know all the security measures that had been taken and had told him. To hell with O'Leary's insistence on secrecy.

You'll get the location of Desta's base. The words were a silent chant. She willed Ripley to accept that as reason to let her go. To keep Hugo safe.

Ripley's jaw tightened. He released the unconscious militant. The man dropped, landing prone on the pavement.

"Go back to the base," she said as a cargo van came careening down the small side street. It skidded to a halt next to her and the gunman. "Tell them they're taking me to Desta!" she shouted.

Ripley gave a sharp nod, his nostrils flaring. His body seemed to puff outward, like an animal preparing to attack, but he did nothing to stop her from being shoved into the back of the van.

Ripley was going to catch hell for this, and it wasn't his fault at all. Worse, Pax, caveman that he was, would lose it.

She was shoved face-first to the floor of the van, a knee pressed to the small of her back. They took her holster and gun, then tied her hands with old, thick twine. She could see a small section of street through the open rear doors, which flapped as the van turned the corner. The last thing she glimpsed of her quiet neighborhood was the lone box of crayons on the pavement.

Chapter Twenty-Four

Her abductors were in a hurry to get away, and after she was tied, they didn't bother searching her beyond taking her wallet and keys. The man looped the rope on her wrists through a metal tie-down mounted on the side of the van in the cargo hold. Once she'd been secured, he yanked the rear doors closed and settled down across from her, pointing her own gun at her face.

She'd expected him to conduct a more thorough search, but maybe he'd decided to wait and do the full strip search away from the city. They'd have to untie her for the search and would need to be certain the Humvee wasn't following.

She still had her cell phone in her bra, and it was on. While they were in the city, it was pinging cell towers, and the phone's internal GPS was active, which was good because it was far too early to trigger the tracker in her arm now. The four-hour window meant it could stop transmitting before she reached her final destination. Odds were Desta's lair was in Ethiopia. She had to wait.

But what if she was wrong? What if they weren't taking her to Desta? What if they were taking her to one of the markets where they sold young girls into sex slavery? She'd read in horror how they stripped the girls—some who hadn't even reached puberty—and stood them nude upon auction blocks.

She lay in the back of the truck as it tore through city streets, trying to keep a grip on her fear. Reminding herself she'd done the right thing in protecting Hugo.

But if they didn't take her to Desta's base, then her sacrifice could gain the US military nothing.

As the minutes ticked by, her plan to go meekly to her kidnapper's destination so they could pinpoint Etefu Desta seemed…impossible. She had to fight. Because the possibilities that awaited her were nightmarish.

She wore an emergency paracord bracelet around her wrist. It looked like a friendship bracelet with thicker string and had a cutting edge on the fastener. A small survival tool she always wore in the field, but which she'd never needed.

Tied as she was, her guard couldn't see her hands. He faced her, but his cold, hard eyes stared off into the distance, and her hands were behind her back. She scooted slightly so her back pressed to the side of the van, where she was attached to the tie-down. She twisted the bracelet so the edge met the rope that bound her. Slowly, silently, she sawed with that tiny blade.

Small movements, invisible with the bouncing of the van, but that meant it would take a long time to cut through the layers of rope. How long before they stopped and searched her?

Would the search happen in town, or would they wait until the city was long behind them and her cell phone no longer of use?

All she could do was saw. It wasn't as if she had anything to lose by trying. She was in deep shit whether they discovered her escape attempt or not.

The van bounced, and the cutting edge slipped and nicked her skin. The ropes became slick with blood, but she kept sawing. This pain was nothing compared to what awaited her.

The motion evened out, and she wondered if they'd reached the edge of the city. She sawed with renewed effort, risking alerting the guard. They would pull over and search her soon. She was sure of it.

The last fiber snapped, and the tight rope went slack. Keeping to small movements, she unhooked the paracord bracelet. She would use the cutting edge as a weapon.

A very tiny weapon, versus the much more lethal gun the guard held in a slack grip, but she had surprise on her side.

The driver of the vehicle said something to her guard in Arabic. Only two men—the driver and the guard—were in the van. The other two were back in the city with Ripley and Holloway. They'd be interrogated on the base and could provide information on where she was being taken. And she still had her cell phone. They were tracking her.

Ripley would have called the base. Blackhawks could be searching for her even now. The van would be easy to spot on the open road.

The vehicle made a left turn, then a right. It lurched after hitting a pothole at speed. The driver yelled something to the guard. He said something sharp back. Then she heard the driver talking to someone—not the guard—in a muted voice. A cell phone?

That meant they were still in range.

The van slowed to a stop.

She met the gaze of her guard, backing up against the side of the van, letting him see her very real fear. He spoke to her in Arabic, but she had no clue what he said except it was likely derogatory.

He gestured for her to sit up. She hooked a finger through the tie-down loop so she wouldn't accidently reveal she was untied as she changed position.

The man pulled out a knife. She sucked in a sharp, terrified breath and told herself it was probably to cut her binding.

But possibly he meant to use it to cut off her clothes. It might be time for the strip search.

Just a strip search.

The knife is for the rope and my clothes. Nothing more. Maybe if she repeated those words enough, they would become true.

The driver had stopped talking into the phone. In the silence that followed, his door opened, then slammed closed. She had maybe ten seconds until he reached the rear double doors.

She waited until her guard was practically upon her—out of reach of a head butt, which he might anticipate, but not out of reach of her arms. With the cutting edge between her fingers, she swung out her right hand and used the appropriately named knife-strike blow, aiming for his eye, followed by a hammer fist with her left.

The man screamed and lunged with the knife, even as he covered his wounded eye. Blinded by pain and the cut, there was no force in his strike and she easily claimed his knife for her own. He raised the gun, and she slashed with the blade, opening his neck.

She had no time to take in the horror as he made a gurgling sound and blood spurted from his neck, spraying her. She grabbed her gun.

It took only the length of a heartbeat to realize the driver hadn't opened the rear door because it was locked from the inside. Her guard had secured it when he closed the doors, but the driver had left the keys in the ignition.

She bolted for the front of the van, desperate to get to the driver's seat before he returned. She scrambled for the lock as the door wrenched open. She stumbled forward, momentum carrying her through the opening. The driver grabbed her by her braid, letting out an incomprehensible yell of rage as he yanked her forward and swung her around. The gun slipped from her bloody fingers, but she still had the knife.

He pointed his gun at her, but she kicked out. Twenty-five years of training meant her muscles knew exactly what to do, even if her brain wasn't keeping up. The gun flew from his hand. She punched with her left as she brought the knife around. He blocked the punch but didn't see the blade coming. It sank into his chest, and he fell to the ground.

She'd hit him center mass. Pax would be proud.

She collapsed and scooted backward, breathing heavily. Her entire body shook.

She twisted to the side and vomited, then staggered to her feet, lurching toward the van and the empty driver's seat. She climbed inside and pulled the door closed, then locked it and buckled her seat belt out of habit.

She turned the key. She'd get the hell out of here. Drive back to the base. She'd be safe.

A weak noise emitted from the engine, but it didn't turn over. She pumped the gas and twisted the key again. Again it made a sound of struggle, but no purr. No rev.

The third time it wouldn't even gasp for life. Just the click of the key, then nothing.

Shit. They'd pulled over not to search her, but because the van had broken down. The damn pothole.

She grabbed her phone from her bra and hit the last number dialed.

Pax answered immediately. "Morgan?" His voice was urgent, hoarse.

"I killed them, Pax. They're dead. But I'm stuck. The van won't start. I don't even know where I am."

"We're locking in on the cell phone GPS now. A team of SEALs has been mobilized. They'll be in the air in seconds."

She burst into tears.

Chapter Twenty-Five

"Stay with me, Morgan." Pax's voice came out smooth and even, betraying no hint of the tremors that quaked inside. At least, he hoped that was the case. "Tell me what you see. They're trying to patch my phone into the command center so everyone at SOCOM will be able to hear you."

On the other end of the line, Morgan took a deep, hiccupping breath. "I think we're on the western edge of the city. The driver pulled the van over, and I thought it was so they could search me, but now the van won't start. He took a pothole really hard. It must have damaged something."

Like everything else at Camp Citron, SOCOM was housed in a temporary structure. Kit built, the command center was a hybrid between a tent and prefab construction but was filled with technology that belied the humble exterior. All around Pax, members of a Special Forces B-Team scrambled to extract every bit of data they could from Morgan's phone and relayed that data to the SEAL team that was piling into a Blackhawk as they spoke.

"Is there anyone around on the street?" he asked.

"No. The area is wide open. There's a series of old, run-down houses about a hundred yards behind me. Ahead is open road that winds through the desert. I'm surprised I have cell coverage."

Next to him, his XO and one of the SEAL team commanders discussed whether or not she should leave the van and take shelter in one of the houses. To Morgan, he said, "Can you make a run for one of the houses?"

"Maybe. I don't know. I don't have my gun. It's on the ground by the driver. But I can grab it if I leave the van."

The back wall of SOCOM HQ was covered in monitors. One showed an aerial map of the location where Morgan had been grabbed with lines indicating possible routes the van had taken. Another monitor showed the cell towers that had been pinged, while a third showed a tech's efforts to zero in on the phone GPS location. Finally, the faint red blip, which had been darting all over the map, solidified, indicating a lock on her location. As she'd guessed, she was on the western perimeter of the city.

Satellite images zoomed in. These were static images, not yet from a live satellite feed. Now that he had the location, the tech was working to bring a live camera online, even as he transmitted her GPS coordinates to the

Blackhawk that had just lifted off.

On the third monitor, Captain Oswald pointed to a row of houses near the red dot that represented Morgan. "These must be the houses. What's the intel on this area?" he asked another tech.

"So far all I have is that it's an Afar neighborhood. Possibly abandoned after an attack by Issa militants some months ago. That edge of town is rough."

"Stay in the van," Pax said to Morgan. He needed to keep her talking. They needed more information. The SEALs would be going in blind. They needed to know about every potential threat to themselves and to Morgan. "You said you killed your abductors. You're certain?"

"Yes. I got a knife from the guard in the back and cut his carotid." Her voice was steady, with only the slightest waver on the last word. "He's definitely dead."

Pax closed his eyes as he imagined the shock of what she'd had to do, utterly thankful she didn't hesitate, but horrified by the scars she'd bear. This wasn't her world. "And the driver?" he asked, hating that he had to delve further, that he wasn't there to hold her as she relayed the story.

"I stabbed him in the heart. I can see him through the window. He's not moving, not breathing." Her voice dropped to a whisper. "Is Hugo safe?"

"Yes. His family is being moved. They'll be protected until Desta is neutralized."

"Thank you. Tell everyone there I said thank you." Her sob played in stereo over the speakers as his phone was finally synced with the command console.

"You're on speaker, Morgan," he said. "Everyone can hear you now."

"Thank you," she repeated. She cleared her throat. "Is my"—her voice broke on a hiccup—"dad there?"

"Not yet. He was on a ship in the Gulf when Ripley called. He's on a copter now. Should be here any minute."

"Tell him I'm sorry," she said. "Just…sorry."

"You'll tell him." He studied the map showing the Blackhawk. "The SEALs are five minutes out. You'll be back at Camp Citron in no time."

He held his breath against the words he couldn't say. He couldn't tell her that he'd been fighting a losing battle against falling in love with her from the day they met. That all his crazy, caveman possessiveness was because his heart had known—even when his head was too damn stupid to catch on—she was his and there was no going back to his solitary, single-minded existence.

He wanted to give her everything he'd been holding back. But this was so very public, and he'd be locked out of the op to take out Desta if he made it obvious how personal the mission would be for him. Hell, odds were he'd be locked out anyway, but he wasn't about to make it an easy decision for his XO. He wanted to kill Desta with his bare hands. He'd been a guerilla fighter for years, but he'd never felt bloodlust for a particular human enemy before. Until today, it had been about protecting his country against faceless enemies.

This was protecting his woman.

His throat was full of all the words he couldn't say. He gripped the phone, and one slipped out. "Mine," he said in a low whisper.

She made a noise that sounded like a choked sob. "I killed them, Pax."

"You had to."

"I know…" She cleared her throat. "It's not Ripley's fault. I had to protect Hugo."

Adrenaline pulsed through him. *Morgan was taken.* The words kept hammering through his brain. He'd failed her. She'd fought and killed two abductors. She was miles away. In danger. His body shook with the need to go after her.

He hadn't prevented this. Hadn't protected her. He could have told his XO his concerns about allowing her to return to her apartment. He could have ensured Captain Oswald would deny her request. He could have stopped this from happening.

Morgan was taken.

Morgan gasped, then said, "Is that Ripley in the Humvee?"

Pax looked over at his XO, then glanced at the screen that showed the neighborhood where Morgan had been abducted. Ripley had been searching for the van and had been directed to patrol the north end of the city. He was miles away from Morgan's position.

Sickening dread filled his belly.

He met the gaze of his XO. The man's horrified expression likely mirrored Pax's.

Into the phone, he said, "No! We don't have any Humvees in the area." Shit. Desta had a Humvee?

Morgan let out a strangled gasp. "The damn van won't start!" There was thumping in the background as she let out a sob. "No. Dammit, no!"

He guessed she was hitting the steering wheel in frustration. "Stay with me, babe," Pax urged. "SEALs are on their way."

"I'm going for the gun." Her voice sounded distant, as if she'd dropped the phone.

"No! Stay in the van. Hide in the back." Shit. She was dead if she stayed. But going for the gun…

He wanted to puke.

The phone went silent. He guessed she'd left it in the van as she grabbed the gun.

A spray of gunfire was projected in stereo for every man in the room to hear. Had Morgan grabbed a machine gun from one of the dead militants? Had Ripley seen machine guns in their arsenal? He couldn't remember. He could barely even think as he waited to hear her voice, waiting for her to say she'd fired the gun, that he hadn't just heard someone shooting at her.

The room went silent. He met his XO's gaze. The man gave him the signal to mute his end of the call.

Pax did as directed, and the soundless seconds stretched on as they all waited to hear from Morgan.

A single gunshot sounded, followed by a stream of curses that was pure foul-mouthed fairy. Pax smiled even as tears came to his eyes. *She's alive.*

In trouble, but alive.

"Why are you doing this? What do you want from me?" Morgan asked.

Pax couldn't make out the muffled response.

A primal, blood-curdling yell sounded. The yell became Arabic curses.

She shrieked, and there were several thumping sounds. Was Morgan fighting the man?

A few male grunts played over the speakers, and Pax hoped that meant Morgan got in some good hits. A loud whack was followed by a shriek from Morgan, which abruptly cut off.

There was nothing but silence for several seconds, then Pax's phone chimed. The screen flashed with the red symbol that indicated the call had been cut off on the other end.

Pax glanced at the map. The SEAL team was three minutes out.

The hands around Morgan's throat tightened. She was going to pass out. The man had gone berserk after seeing the body in the back of the van, and he'd lunged for her after letting out a primal yell. She'd fought him off, but she was shaken from everything that happened and slipped, allowing him a window to gain the upper hand.

She bucked against the clawlike hand. She needed air.

Blood rushed in her ears, blocking out all other sound. His grip on her right hand was loose, and she broke free and jabbed him in the eye. He recoiled but didn't release her throat.

She grabbed at the hand, desperate.

SEALs were coming. If she could just keep these men here long enough, the Navy team would save her. Just as that thought formed, the man who had her pinned by the throat was yanked backward. She coughed as she took in air, wheezing in a shallow breath through her bruised windpipe.

Her vision was blurred. Had a SEAL saved her?

A man scooped her up by the shoulders and dragged her backward. Toward the Humvee. Not a SEAL, then. One of the other militants. She gasped, trying to take in dusty, hot air, which scraped her throat and seared her lungs.

She was shoved in the back of the Humvee. A man followed her inside, practically sitting on her. She fought against him, and he grabbed her hands, then slapped her across the face, a harsh blow that had her head spinning. "Enough!" the man yelled. "Or I will tell Desta that François killed you." He leaned out of the Humvee and fired a pistol.

Through the doorway, she saw the man who'd choked her. His forehead sprouted a red dot, then he dropped to the ground. Another man—the one who must've pulled her attacker from her—stepped over the body of his former comrade and climbed into the front seat of the Humvee.

"That was François," the gunman said. "He attacked you because you killed his brother."

She said nothing. She was too busy reeling, trying to take in all that had happened. She leaned over and vomited on the seat between her and the gunman, surprised to discover there was any food left in her stomach.

The man glared at her, and raised his hand, as if to strike again, but maybe he realized another blow would just make her puke again, because he lowered his hand and shouted to the driver to move.

The heavy vehicle surged forward. She slapped a hand over her mouth, fighting a different kind of nausea.

This was really happening.

Her gaze darted around the vehicle. It was old, battered. A remnant from an earlier conflict. She never would have mistaken it for the armored ride Ripley drove, except she'd been out of sorts.

She decided to focus on the fact that a team of SEALs was in the air and would likely spot them. They knew she was in a Humvee. This vehicle would be hard to hide. They'd find her. She glanced backward, watching Djibouti City fade into the dust. They rounded a bend and came to an abrupt halt.

Another vehicle waited. This one an ancient SUV. She was dragged from the Humvee and shoved into the back of the old Land Cruiser.

"Don't vomit in this one," the gunman said as he bound her hands. "We'll be in this truck for a while."

In minutes, they were off. The Humvee went one direction, the Land Cruiser another.

The Blackhawk wouldn't find her. Not now. These men would take her into Ethiopia and straight to Desta.

But she had the tracker. Once she was settled, she'd trigger it, and the Blackhawk would come. She would be found. She would be rescued.

Pax stared at the monitor that carried the live feed from a camera strapped to one of the SEAL team members. His heart pounded as he took in the carnage at the abandoned cargo van. One man with a slit throat, another with a knife in his chest, just as Morgan had described. It was the third body that caused his blood to run cold. A bullet between the eyes. But who had fired that shot?

Where was Morgan?

Ripley had arrived in his Humvee five minutes after the SEAL team landed. He'd grabbed two SEALs and taken off after the active GPS signal from Morgan's cell phone. Pax watched monitor three as they closed in on the cell phone's red dot. A direct line to Ripley had been patched into the command center, and the Special Forces operator's voice carried over the speaker.

"The only vehicle on this road is a small pickup truck, heading deep into the desert." Ripley switched to Arabic and Pax assumed he was commanding the driver of the pickup to pull over, using the Humvee's loudspeaker. Feedback from the microphone caused a piercing tone, and the radio was shut off.

Pax waited, knowing in his gut Morgan wasn't in that truck. It wouldn't be that easy, not when the phone call had been deliberately cut off by someone on Morgan's end. They knew about the phone, and if they didn't want it followed, they'd have pulled the battery.

But still, it was a lead that had to be followed.

Long minutes later, Ripley radioed the base. "Negative on Dr. Adler. We've recovered the phone, which was in the back of the pickup. The driver didn't know it was there. It was probably tossed in the back. The driver says he passed an old Humvee five klicks back, on the edge of the city. Also, the US should probably buy the guy some new tires. We shot out two when he didn't pull over."

Pax's vision tunneled. He'd expected this report, but still, the reality of it had him reeling.

Forty-two minutes had passed since he'd last heard her voice, and they had no fucking clue where she was.

The truck drove in the shadows of a ridge, which would make it hard to see from the air. Morgan tracked the sun, well aware of the time of day. She didn't need her compass to know what direction they drove.

The plan had been simple. She'd trigger the tracker; the US would get Desta's location. They'd send a team to save her, and they'd take out Etefu Desta in the process. The US had agreements with the Ethiopian government. They might not want US interference, but they'd tolerate it, because it would be lucrative for them, and Desta was a thorn in their side as well. But after an hour of driving, the problem with the plan became alarmingly clear.

They weren't driving west toward Ethiopia.

No. They'd been heading steadily southeast, which meant they were taking her to the one place the US military would have the most difficulty entering. The one place no American in their right mind would willingly go given the current situation.

Her abductors were taking her into Somalia.

Chapter Twenty-Six

Miles short of the border, the SUV pulled over. She'd managed to pick up two of her captors' names from listening to them argue. The driver, Saad, demanded she strip, then she was given a plain, traditional buna dress to wear without bra or underwear. Considering they'd skipped the cavity search, she wasn't about to complain. But then Kaafi—the man who'd shot François—told Saad to gag her in addition to binding her hands and feet.

She recoiled. "No. Please," she said to Kaafi, who was clearly the leader. "If I vomit, I might choke."

The militant merely glared at her. "Then don't vomit."

A new wave of fear washed through her, worse than when she'd realized she was being dragged into Somalia. She held her breath against the sobs that wanted to break free as she was bound and gagged and forced into the rear footwell of the SUV. A coarse blanket was draped over her. The heat was suffocating under the wool covering, and she wondered if it would be her burial shroud.

She'd assumed they'd cross the border using one of the panya smuggling routes that were rampant in Somalia, so why were they hiding her? But even if they did go via the main road, ransom payments were a major portion of Somalia's gross domestic product, it was hard to believe border guards would bother to halt them.

Was this a simple abduction for ransom? Or was this about Linus or Broussard?

The battered SUV bounced along the pitted road. She suffocated beneath the hot blanket and tried not to fall apart.

Months ago, after reading through the various warnings put out by the US embassy regarding work in Djibouti, she'd said to Staci, a close friend and fellow server at Double D, that she'd make a suicide pact with one of her field workers before she'd let herself be dragged into Somalia.

She'd only been partially kidding. She'd known the risk was real, but somehow, not *that* real. Yet here she was. The jokes had proven to be both horribly unfunny and terribly naïve. Following through with a foolish, poorly considered suicide plan hadn't been an option. She was being taken into Somalia. Odds were, tracker or not, she'd die there. And her death wouldn't be easy.

The SEALs couldn't save her. Not inside Somalia. The US military would have Desta's location, and eventually the drones would come. They'd take out Desta and everyone inside his compound. That was the *best* death she could hope for. At least then Desta would be gone, unable to hurt more people.

She should have told Pax she loved him. To hell with all the SOCOM personnel listening in. She should have told him that their one forbidden night was the best night of her life, that she'd never felt such a connection before. It had been so much more than sex.

He'd likely guessed how she felt, but there was power in hearing the words and in saying them.

She loved him. He was her soldier. Her Green Beret. Everything she'd never known she wanted wrapped into one perfect, flawed caveman.

The truck slowed to a stop, and Kaafi placed his boot on her head and uttered a sharp warning for her to be quiet.

They must be at the border. Not a panya route, then.

The driver spoke with someone—likely a border guard—in Arabic or Somali. She debated making a noise to get the guard's attention. The measures Kaafi had taken to hide and silence her told her they did have something to fear, and she wondered if the US military had put out the Djiboutian equivalent of an Amber alert, and if that would even matter in the lawless region.

Pressure on her temple increased. In spite of the fact that he'd clearly been ordered to take her alive, she didn't doubt Kaafi's willingness to kill her.

She bit down on the gag in her mouth and thought of the look on Pax's face when he'd draped the scarf over her hair in the market the day after they met. She held on to that image and remained silent.

She had to survive until she got to Desta's. After she'd triggered the tracker she could take risks. Until then, she'd be an obedient prisoner.

Pax stared at the monitor that showed the flight path of the search helicopters. They worked in a grid, clearing one section, then moving on, much as Morgan did on her archaeological survey. Soon the search would be called off. Morgan's abductors had plenty of time to cross the border into Ethiopia. She was long gone, out of their searchable range.

General Adler dropped into the empty seat next to him, but thankfully, the man remained silent. Pax didn't think he could find words to try to comfort the man. They shared a similar agony, but beyond passing on Morgan's apology, Pax was at a loss for what to say.

And he was still pissed at the way the general had humiliated Morgan during the meeting on his first night in Djibouti.

They sat in silence as the men around them discussed options, and finally the CO gave the order for the search helicopters to return. Pax had known it would happen, but still, the order was a blow.

Unless they received a signal from the tracker or had a tip she was being held in a particular area, active searching would cease. Pax wanted to kick the walls, to smash the nearest object. He hadn't found it this hard to hold back a violent outburst since he was a hotheaded nineteen-year-old out to prove himself.

He debated going to the gym, but then he wouldn't be here. And what if a transmission from the tracker came in?

The searchers returned, and Pax remained in the control room, staring at the monitors that were now blank.

Cal appeared at his side and dropped a plate of food in front of him. "I figured we wouldn't be able to convince you to go to the cafeteria."

Pax nodded and said thanks. He dutifully ate, because he knew he needed the calories. His body was used to being pushed to the limit and would perform as required, as long as he did his part and provided fuel. He didn't pay attention to the meal before him. Couldn't smell or taste it. It was fuel, nothing more.

He could well imagine the horrors she faced, and the idea that she would suffer—could be suffering even now—caused his vision to tunnel. His fear for her was unlike any he'd ever experienced before.

Dimly, he was aware this could be the thing that broke him. Not since his divorce when he was twenty-one had he seen himself as breakable. He'd spent the intervening years denying that fragility, out to prove that no mere relationship had the power to take him down. He'd built a mental wall against commitment. He'd made rules that justified his solitary life.

The intense attraction to Morgan was part of the reason he'd attempted to resist her. He'd known she'd be a weakness. A vulnerability. Not just to his focus or his job, but to his content isolation.

He should have told her he loved her. Was crazy for her. That he'd never be the same because of her. But all he could do was hope thoughts of the crazy wonderful intensity they shared would carry her through the coming nightmarish hours.

Moving forward, he needed to turn off those thoughts. He needed to shut down the emotions that threatened to tear him apart, because he needed to remain whole. He needed to fight for her, and his XO would only let him stay in the game if he saw a Special Forces operator in prime mental and physical condition.

Only then could he go after Desta. Only then could he save her. And he would save her, or he'd die trying.

M organ was pulled from the suffocating footwell after they cleared the border. They drove onward over rough roads, deep into Somaliland. Pax had called Djibouti lawless, but the country was a veritable haven of orderly governance compared to Somalia and the self-declared state of Somaliland that bordered Djibouti.

Darkness fell, and she stared out the rear window, orienting herself with the position of the stars. The angle of the North Star from the horizon gave her latitude. If the star was straight above her, or ninety degrees, she'd be at the North Pole. If it looked like it was sitting on the horizon, she'd be on the equator. Midway between, she'd be at forty-five degrees latitude.

She was somewhere south of eleven degrees north of the equator now, with the north star so low on the horizon, she rarely was able to spot it through the rear window, but when she did see it, it confirmed her fears that she was being taken deeper and deeper south into Somaliland.

They drove late into the night, but she'd lost her ability to gauge time, as each minute felt longer than the last. At some point, adrenaline gave out, and she escaped into the oblivion of sleep.

Ten minutes or two hours later—she had no idea which—Kaafi dragged her from the back of the SUV, without bothering to wake her first. Her shoulder hit the side of the vehicle, and she staggered to get her feet beneath her before she landed on her face.

She was taken into a run-down house and wondered for a moment if this was Desta's compound. But the house was too small for an operation as large as his must be. Kaafi led her around the back of the small structure so she could squat to pee. As this was likely the least of the indignities she would face, she offered no objection even though his piercing glare ratcheted up her fear another notch higher. At least the buna dress provided covering.

Bladder voided, she wondered if they'd return to the vehicle, but instead, Kaafi led her into the main living area, where he tied her to a heavy metal ring bolted to the wall. "We will all sleep," he said. "You try to escape, you will be shot between the eyes."

She shuddered, realizing the purpose of the wall-mounted ring was to tie up prisoners. A kidnappers' rest stop.

She lay on her side with her back to the wall, her arms stretched above her head, parallel to the hard ground. Her nose could reach the tracker, and Kaafi pulled out a phone and dialed, indicating cell coverage.

They'd be here for a few hours. Long enough for a team of SEALs to fly in. But this was Somaliland, meaning they'd need more than a few hours to plan, and this wasn't her final destination. Desta wasn't here.

Decision made, she closed her eyes and released a slow breath. Kaafi grumbled and tucked away his phone. It appeared there wasn't a cell signal after all. This was a lesson in making slow, reasoned decisions. She couldn't be rash. She had to exercise patience. She'd have one chance to call for help, and that was all.

She dozed fitfully. Not really sleeping yet not quite awake either.

Dawn arrived, and she was stiff from the floor and dehydrated with a fierce headache. Kaafi gave in to her plea for water, then again took her outside so she could empty her bladder. She'd had precious little fluids in the last twenty hours, making the excursion largely unnecessary.

"How long until we get where we're going?" she asked as he escorted her back inside.

Kaafi merely grunted, making it clear he had no intention of answering her.

They stayed at the house for the rest of the day, Kaafi leaving periodically and returning. She suspected he was driving to a location that had cell coverage. From his manner, she figured he was waiting for instructions.

It seemed these men weren't followers of Desta, but hired freelancers. Kidnappers contracted to deliver her to the warlord, part of the local economy.

She imagined their résumés: a list of the number of victims they'd abducted; the number of successful payouts; a boastful paragraph listing their skills with knives and guns and the ability to terrorize convincingly. They might include a fee schedule. Kidnapping without injuring the victim probably cost more. Did they bill for overtime on jobs like this? Was there a bonus for avoiding Imperial entanglements?

Several times throughout the long, hot morning, the third abductor, who'd rode in the front of the vehicle, paced the small house and argued with Kaafi and Saad. Early in the afternoon, the angry abductor left with Kaafi but didn't return. She wondered if the man had completed his part of the job, or if Kaafi had decided he didn't want to split the bounty three ways. He'd killed François without hesitation. She had no doubt he'd kill another partner.

There was no food at the kidnapper's layover, just water. Late in the day, Saad left and returned with bread and beans. He gave her a small portion, and she forced herself to eat, knowing she should be starving after over twenty-four hours without food, but she had no appetite and just prayed she'd keep the food down.

The sun was high in the sky the following day when Kaafi returned from another of his trips and announced they were leaving. Back in the SUV, Morgan settled in her seat, not bothering to ask how long the drive would be. No one had answered any of her questions so far. She'd given up asking.

This time, they drove north. She gathered this from the angle of the sun and was baffled as to why they'd backtrack, not daring to hope they were returning to Djibouti.

It was several hours after sunset when they arrived at yet another ramshackle house in the middle of nowhere. They hadn't crossed the border, but they'd driven long enough that she'd wondered if they were close. They repeated the bathroom ritual, followed by being tied up inside. This kidnapper's nest, however, lacked a built-in restraint system, so she was bound to a heavy chair. She slept sitting up, but after two nights of fitful sleep, she was just tired enough to at least drift in and out of consciousness.

Throughout the ordeal, she thought of Pax. His training was such that he could probably sleep standing if he had to. Her headache worsened with each minute, and she was beginning to think she was actually feverish, not just overheated from the stagnant, unrelenting humidity.

Was Pax losing his mind now that she'd been gone for over sixty hours and the tracker hadn't been used? Was he running himself ragged trying to find her, or trapped on the base by his XO?

Did he know she loved him? Would he find any peace in thoughts of their time together, or would her death render him unable to treasure the memories? Had her father told her mother the truth about why he'd gone to Djibouti? She'd give anything to spare Pax, her mother, and her father the agony they must be feeling.

Her head throbbed even as her belly churned. She tried to tell herself the fever was really a heat rash, but she didn't believe it.

Hopefully, tomorrow they'd reach Desta's—perhaps he was in Ethiopia after all, and the excursion into Somalia had been an attempt to throw off any followers. Maybe tomorrow she'd reach her final destination and could wake the tracker, giving her parents and Pax one glimmer of hope. Perhaps she'd find hope again too, because at this point, she'd left all hope of survival at the border.

Cal dragged Pax out of the command center sometime after midnight on the second day, reminding him that he'd be shut out of everything if he wasn't functional. It didn't help that he'd made his feelings for Morgan so obvious.

Pax feared once he left the room, he'd be shut out and wouldn't be allowed to return, but Cal had a point. Pax needed sleep so he could present himself as ready for action. He needed his XO to see him as a Special Forces operator, not a man who was falling apart because his woman had been taken.

So he slept—a full, deep six hours—then worked out, showered, and ate. During that time, Cal planted himself in the command center, ready to alert Pax if there was news, good or bad.

A soldier again, Pax walked to the command with renewed energy. The workout had done as much good as the sleep and meal to rejuvenate him. Morgan had been gone sixty-eight hours. Surely the tracker would ping soon. It had to.

He knew the stats, provided by Savannah James. Every tracker involved in a successful extraction had been triggered within seventy-two hours. A few—including Yemen—had been triggered between seventy-two and ninety-six hours, but none of those abductees had survived. For the odds to remain on Morgan's side, the number crunchers believed they needed a lock on her location within the next four hours.

But Pax wasn't a number cruncher. He was a soldier. He didn't give a fuck about the odds or how these scenarios had played out in the past. If—*when*—they got Morgan's location, nothing would stop him from bringing her back alive.

Some young officer who was probably fresh out of school stopped Pax at the entrance to the command center. "I'm sorry, Sergeant, you aren't on the approved list."

Shit. This was what he'd feared would happen. He'd been locked out. He glanced into the room and met General Adler's gaze. The man's look was shuttered. Pax wondered if he'd tried to intervene but had been denied.

Generals were rarely denied, but then, this general's admittance into the room was also tenuous. His daughter had been taken, and he had no intel to bring to the conversation. This was one hundred percent emotion for him. It was a testament to his rank that he was in the room at all.

Behind Pax, a woman said, "Step aside, Lieutenant, and let Sergeant Blanchard in." Pax turned to see Savannah James giving the young officer a steely stare.

"I can't," the lieutenant said.

"You can, and you will. He has valuable intel on the inner workings of Dr. Adler's project. We need him at the table."

Pax wondered why the woman was lying to get him in the room, but he was grateful. He knew she and Morgan had sparred in the gym more evenings than not in the past weeks—Pax was the one who'd suggested they work out together in the first place—and Morgan had described her as a developing friend. Not that any spook allowed real friendship.

As far as this mission went, James held no rank, had no tangible authority. Yet, it was her chip implanted in Morgan's arm. CIA technology, under CIA control, giving Pax the feeling the CIA operative was calling more shots than he knew.

He didn't even know if the woman was an analyst or a case officer. He'd originally assumed analyst, and yet he thought she managed assets outside the base, which was a case officer's job.

The lieutenant manning the door looked to the SOCOM commander for help.

The commander frowned at Savannah James. "He's out, James. This is too personal for him."

James crossed her arms. "He's in. One of the mercenaries Sergeant Ripley detained during the kidnapping finally broke. He admitted one of Dr. Adler's field workers was an informant. Sergeant Blanchard knows the guy from the days he was in the field with her. I need to know everything I can about Mouktar Clouet so we can find him and bring him in."

Mouktar?

Ah shit. When Morgan learned of his betrayal, she'd be devastated.

Pax nudged the lieutenant aside and made a beeline for the conference table at the rear of the room. "Get Ripley in here too," he said to James. "He might know where the weasel lives."

"I've already summoned him," James said as she dropped a stack of files on the table. "Mouktar ditched the cell phone the Navy gave him, which tells me he knew we'd figure it out eventually. But odds are he slipped up somewhere. We'll find him and shred his ass along with his brain."

"We need to talk to Charles Lemaire," Pax said. "He's the one who hired Mouktar and all the field crew."

James gave Pax a calculating smile. "I was thinking after this meeting, you and I should pay Lemaire a visit. You've met him a few times. I want your take on his demeanor."

At last, he was being given a job. A purpose. He'd been drowning from the moment Morgan's desperate phone call had ended, and Savannah James had thrown him a lifeline. "That would be my pleasure, Ms. James."

She smiled, but it wasn't the calculating smile he was used to seeing. This was her true smile, the person behind the agent. "Please, call me Savvy."

Chapter Twenty-Seven

Charles Lemaire looked like he hadn't slept in three days. A point in the bureaucrat's favor, in Pax's mind. The man raked a hand through his hair after he settled behind his desk. "I'll do anything I can to help you find Dr. Adler," he said. "Everyone in the department has been devastated to learn of her abduction."

"Even Imbert?" Pax asked. "Ripley said your natural resources minister was irritated our military was providing her with security."

"Ali Imbert is sexist, but he's no traitor," Lemaire said.

"What makes you say that?" Savvy asked.

"He is Djiboutian. He cares about his country."

"In my experience," Savvy said, "the most successful traitors are the ones who believe their actions are patriotic. In Djibouti, that means clan first, then country." She paused and leaned forward, her calculating smile fixed on Lemaire. "What clan is Imbert?"

"Issa," Lemaire said.

"Etefu Desta is also Issa," Savvy said.

"As is half of Djibouti," Lemaire said, clearly angry. "*I* am Issa. But I put Djibouti before my tribe."

"Which makes you unique," Pax said.

"You don't believe me?" Lemaire glared at him. "Who are you to judge me, Sergeant? You are an American Green Beret, touted as having the best military training in the world, and yet you and your team couldn't even protect one woman."

Pax held back the snarl and refrained from going for the minister's throat. Charles Lemaire had no idea what hornet's nest he toyed with in taunting Pax. It didn't matter that Ripley had been in charge of Morgan's security detail when she was taken. Pax blamed himself, for the simple reason that she was his. He should have protected her. Period.

What kind of soldier couldn't protect his woman? He wasn't worthy of the woman or his Special Forces tab.

"How did you find and hire Mouktar Clouet?" Savvy asked.

Lemaire faced the CIA operative. "Why do you ask?"

"Just answer the question, Charles." The way Savvy said the minister's first name could give a man chills. And not the good kind.

"His name was given to me as someone who spoke English and wasn't averse to hard labor."

"Who gave you his name?" Savvy pressed.

Lemaire let out a heavy sigh. "Ali Imbert." He glared at Savvy. "As the natural resources minister, he maintains a list of field workers who work with foreign contractors. There was nothing untoward."

Savvy gave the man a tight smile. "I don't think that's for you to decide, Charles."

Morgan guessed her fever ran around one hundred and three by the time she reached Desta's base of operations, making her entrance a blur as Saad and Kaafi dragged her inside, not because she resisted, but because she was too weak to walk.

Neither man seemed to believe she was ill, and they clearly weren't versed in nursing enough to recognize that she couldn't fake a fever of this magnitude, but she was too sick to care.

One thing about being grossly ill, it squelched her fear over having been kidnapped to a negligible level. She couldn't think about fear when all her energy was focused on the agony of being dehydrated with a stomach bug. She was too sick to give a damn what sort of harm they intended to inflict upon her.

She was led to a stark cell. No windows. A cot. No blanket, no pillow. A hole in the floor in the corner to serve as toilet, while a large bolt in the center was attached to a long, thick chain with a metal cuff at the end.

All Morgan cared about was the cot. It was stationary, unlike the SUV. It was softer than the chair she'd spent the night in. She lay on the cot as the woman who'd led her to the room attached the cuff to her ankle.

She closed her eyes and promptly lost the battle with her belly. She tripped over the chain and didn't make it to the hole in the corner in time.

The woman said something to the guard in an angry tone. The man argued back.

Morgan crawled over the chain and finally reached the hole, where she emptied her stomach.

Spent, she made her way back to the cot and collapsed again. Several minutes later, the woman reappeared. She placed a damp cloth on Morgan's forehead and cleaned the mess on the floor.

A bowl to catch the vomit, should she suffer another bout of vomiting, was placed next to her. She promptly filled it.

At some point, the cuff on her ankle was removed. The woman must have won the argument with the guard. The woman came and went, bringing Morgan water to drink and more damp rags to cool her head.

Dimly, she was aware she should trigger the tracker now that she was in Desta's lair, but she had just enough brainpower to know that she needed to be certain the man was here and that there was cell coverage.

She had no idea if she had a simple flu bug or something more serious. Her breathing was shallow as her eyes drifted closed. She could only hope she would wake again and would have the energy to do what needed to be done.

Ninety-six hours passed without a signal from Morgan. Pax continued to work the government angle, trying to find Mouktar, determined to find out who was really behind Morgan's abduction and why, but he was aware that Savvy, who had great faith in statistics, was losing hope.

Morgan was now outside the successful range. If she were rescued now, she'd be an outlier. Unquantifiable.

Savvy wasn't the only one with doubts. Pax knew ninety percent of the SOCOM brass had mentally written off Morgan as dead.

Pax would never do that. He didn't know a combat soldier who would take statistics over eyes on the ground.

He had to give Savvy credit for going after Lemaire and Imbert like a bulldog. Pax learned she'd long suspected Imbert of playing for either Desta, the Chinese, or both. He wondered if she'd latched on to Morgan to get access to Imbert.

It was hard to guess the woman's motivation, but her goal, in this at least, was pure: to bring Morgan back.

"Why did you fixate on Imbert?" Pax asked, early on the fifth day. "Nothing in his background stands out."

"He has a sick kid," she said in an emotionless voice. "The boy needs Western medicine or he's a goner. If I were the Chinese, he's the one I'd target."

Pax met her gaze. "You mean you did target him, but he didn't bite, no matter what carrot you dangled. So you figured the Chinese beat you to him."

She shrugged. "I'm good at my job, but the Chinese probably locked him up before I was in-country. Blame my predecessor."

"How is Imbert's son?"

"No one has seen him in months. Either he's in China or he's dead. Given that Imbert hasn't betrayed his handler, I'm thinking the boy's in China and responding to treatment."

Imbert's loyalty would last as long as his son's health. "What makes you think he's not aligned with Desta?"

"I think he is, to a certain degree. But Desta can't cure cancer. Hell, Desta can't cure a hangnail. The warlord is nothing but a weak puppet with big dreams."

"According to my CO and everyone in charge at Camp Citron, Desta is the next great evil. The Osama bin Laden of East Africa."

She shook her head. "He aspires to that. His end game is simple: he wants Eritrea back in the Ethiopian fold. And he wants to be the dictator at the helm. If that happens, my job is to bring him in line. Akin to Saddam Hussein in the eighties—before the Iraqi dictator invaded Kuwait."

"Back when he was the US's bitch?"

"Exactly. Right now, Desta is a wannabe dictator up for grabs. His army is thin and supporters in Ethiopia weak. His only hope is to recover Eritrea, giving Ethiopia a coastline again, so they won't be dependent on Djibouti for their port. But Eritrea is no closer to being annexed by Ethiopia now than it was five years ago. Desta is looking for a foothold, and aligning with China is one way he could achieve his goals. I think China is arming him and gave him that nonnuclear electromagnetic pulse generator you found in his Yemen stronghold last year."

Pax did a double take. "You know about that?"

"It was our tracker in the hostage's body. I know everything about Yemen and that success."

"That mission was a failure. The hostage died."

"That mission was a success because you found the EMP, and it was destroyed in the drone strike before Desta could use it to obtain highly advanced US equipment and sell it to China. The hostage knew finding and destroying the EMP was the end goal."

Pax reared back. "He was bait? Why weren't we *told* this?"

His anger didn't faze her in the slightest. "It was classified."

"Is Morgan bait? Was this planned all along so you could get Desta's location?"

"No, but that doesn't mean we won't seize an opportunity here." She spread her arms wide to encompass the command center. "And don't think I'm the only person in this room who feels this way. If Desta has taken Morgan, this is our chance to save her and make the power-hungry asshole our bitch, not China's."

"If he's taken Morgan, the asshole is going to die," Pax said.

Savannah James fixed him with that chilling, calculating stare. "No, Pax. If Desta has Morgan—and she's still alive—the warlord will come out of this situation more powerful than ever. The only question is, will it be China or the US pulling his strings?"

Morgan guessed she'd been in Desta's stronghold for well over a day when the fever broke and she finally kept a meal down. She was weak but figured that after a shower, she might even feel human again.

The woman who had tended her in her illness spoke very little English, just a few keywords, and Morgan wished again she'd learned more Arabic. The woman led Morgan to a bathroom where she was presented with a bar of soap and hot and cold running water.

She took the longest shower she'd been allotted in months, but was too weak to stand for the entire ten-minute water smorgasbord. A single window was high in the bathroom wall, and the light changed from day to night in the short time she was in the room, giving her an estimate as to the time of day.

She ate an entire bowl of beans after her shower, and her stomach didn't rebel at the influx of food. Given the rapidity of her recovery, she guessed she'd suffered food poisoning, and wondered if it had been deliberate, or if being a foreigner had caught up with her and she'd come across a bug the locals were immune to.

Bathed and fed, she wondered if she'd at last meet the warlord, but instead she was returned to the cell she'd occupied in her illness. She'd gathered that, given the time of day, she was expected to sleep.

Shockingly, she did, and she woke the following morning with renewed energy. She guessed that six days had passed since her abduction. The lack of windows in her cell made estimating time difficult, but she was certain most of the people on the base would have given up on her by now.

Did Pax believe she was dead?

What about her father? Had he given up hope?

She sat up on her cot and pulled her knees to her chest. Six days. She touched the back of her left knee. Number forty-two on Pax's list. She wanted desperately to have Rome and the promise that rendezvous implied. For that to be possible, she had to trigger the tracker, but even more important, she needed to look for her own way to escape. She'd begun to wonder if relying on the chip was the real danger. Instead of trying to escape sooner, she'd allowed herself to be taken here, waiting for an opportunity to trigger the tracker. En route, she'd only had two guards, while she now had no idea how many men guarded Desta's compound. It was entirely possible the fail rate of the chip was because those who had been taken before her had relied too much on being rescued and hadn't sought their own escape.

Not that she blamed other victims. There was likely nothing they could do, especially if they were bound. Tortured. And maybe there was nothing she could have done on the journey either.

But right now, she wasn't bound. Cruel Kaafi and menacing Saad no longer guarded her. For all she knew, the mercenaries had moved on to grab their next victim for another client.

She was weak from her illness, but that could work to her advantage. The chain had been removed when she was sick. If she let her captors continue to believe she was ill, perhaps she'd remain unbound.

She had nothing to fear from the ruse, and everything to gain.

Her secret power had always been that men underestimated her. It was time to take that to the next level.

Chapter Twenty-Eight

Hours later, a man with an AK-47 appeared at her cell door and insisted she get up and follow him. She moved slowly, as if weak—not faking nearly as much as she'd like—and as she'd hoped, he didn't bother binding her.

She eyed his gun, wondering what it would take to get it from him. He held it casually, the way women held purses: an everyday accessory, there if needed but not something clutched tightly except when walking down a busy city street.

He didn't expect her to be a threat.

Good. But it was too soon for her to act.

She only exaggerated her shaky legs a slight amount as she was escorted down a hallway and a flight of stairs. By Somali standards, the place was a palace, with multiple rooms, electricity, and hot and cold running water, but in the US, the dilapidated mansion would be considered squalid.

She was reminded of Osama bin Laden's hideout in Abbottabad, Pakistan. The press had made much of it being an estate and at first had described it as a luxurious mansion. There was no doubt the man had been comfortable, but photos had later proven it wasn't a grand home fit for *Lifestyles of the Rich and Evil*.

Desta's home appeared similar, large, with multiple wings, but sweltering and decayed.

At last she was presented to the warlord, who sat behind a desk in a small office at the back of his estate, like any lord of the manor. The very mundaneness of his office, of the lack of fanfare after waiting for days to face down the paunchy, middle-aged African man, took the wind out of her. She didn't have to fake being weak and grabbing a chair.

Maybe his very normalness was what rattled her. His eyes should be cold, a manifestation of his evil. He should be scarred. If this man were auditioning for the role of East African warlord for a Hollywood movie, casting directors would roll their eyes and send him home.

"It appears you were not faking your illness, as Kaafi and Saad claimed when you arrived," the warlord said.

"They are poor nurses if they can't recognize when a person has the flu."

"Better that they went into mercenary work over medicine, then. However, I hired eight men to collect you, and only two completed the task, so perhaps you have proved they were poor mercenaries in addition to poor physicians."

She stiffened. She didn't want him to see her as capable. "It wasn't me so much as well-trained US soldiers and in-fighting between the men. I gathered Kaafi and François didn't get along."

"Only François's brother could tolerate him. He was an ugly brute."

The audacity of a warlord calling a mercenary a brute was too much. "And you aren't?"

"I am a prince of my people trying to reclaim the throne that was stolen from my father. I am fighting for the liberty of my people, like any of your American founding fathers."

"Yeah. You're a regular George Washington. Except George didn't traffic in young girls or khat."

"Your George Washington owned slaves, as did your Thomas Jefferson. Jefferson even sired slaves with his slave mistress. And both men grew hemp, which was legal in their time, as khat is here."

Dammit, she hated it when warlords were up on their American history. She could argue that hemp wasn't marijuana, but she wasn't there to debate Jefferson's and Washington's legacies with Etefu Desta. "Khat may be legal here, but it's not in the countries where you sell it."

"You have done your homework on me. I'm flattered."

She glared at him. "If you've abducted me for ransom, you're wasting your time. The US government won't pay, and my family is hardly wealthy."

"Your concern is touching. Have no fear, I will be well rewarded for your abduction."

"It's too late to stop Linus from being revealed. I'm not needed for that."

"Your fossilized monkey is of no concern to me. He was simply an irritation because the discovery meant your survey of the alternate route would be intensely thorough, and you might see the same signs Broussard did."

Morgan leaned forward in her chair. The sudden movement made her dizzy, but she couldn't help but wonder if it wasn't due to illness so much as finally getting to the truth. "Is he dead?"

"Most certainly."

"Why?"

The warlord made a tutting sound. "You aren't nearly as clever as I'd hoped. My sources indicated you hypothesized a great aquifer deep below your project area."

The taunt made her bristle. "I'm no geologist, but yes, I wondered if

Broussard found evidence of an aquifer."

"He did."

"And you killed him. Why?"

"I did not kill him. Ali Imbert did."

"The natural resources minister?"

"Yes. He either killed Broussard himself, or hired it done. No matter, the man is gone."

"Why would he do that?"

The warlord sat back in his chair and studied her. "I could warn you that if I tell you, you'll never be released. But you must know I have no intention of letting you go."

She shivered but met his gaze without flinching. "No one will pay the ransom."

"True." He shrugged. "Two years ago, when the Chinese first proposed paying for the railway line from my country to the sea that should be ours, they hired a geologist—one of their own, a Chinaman, who has as much experience as Broussard but isn't granted Western respect, because you are egocentric megalomaniacs."

"Unlike present company," she couldn't help but say.

"I am a patriot."

"As am I."

"You have strayed far from your country, Dr. Adler, if patriotism guides you."

"One could say so have you."

"I am an Issa from Ethiopia. Issa are Somali. Somalia—or Somaliland—Ethiopia, Eritrea, and Djibouti should all be one, under Issa rule. *I* will make that happen, I will complete the dream denied my father with help from the aquifer Broussard found."

"Because you will bring water to the people?"

"No." His eyes flashed with glee. "Because I will use it to bring down my enemies and unite my people." He cleared his throat. "The Chinese geologist saw the same thing you and Brossard did, and under the guise of geothermal testing, his team located the aquifer with deep bore tests.

"With the aquifer found, the Chinese government proposed to fund a privately owned desalinization plant in Eritrea, which will provide drinking water to both Eritrea and Djibouti. This was seized upon as a great generosity, when in truth, Eritrea's plant will pump water from the aquifer, then pipe it back into Djibouti and sell it to the very people they're stealing it from."

The unmitigated evil of stealing water from the dry nation caused her unsettled belly to churn. "And how are you part of this plan?"

"Eritrean law prevents foreign governments from owning vital utilities. Imbert and I, through proxies, own the plant."

"Neither of you are Eritrean."

He shrugged. "I have papers that say otherwise, as does Imbert." He flashed yellow teeth, indicating he'd used khat in the past, but the decay was mild, leading her to believe he hadn't used the stimulant for several years. "I will use the proceeds to increase my army and arsenal, and then crush the very government that allowed us to build the plant. Once I'm installed as the ruler of Eritrea, the rebel state will be reunited with Ethiopia, and Djibouti can have their aquifer back."

Her head spun at the machinations involved. "And you abducted me to stop me from exposing the aquifer? It's not like anyone was listening to me. No one in Djibouti was even investigating Broussard's disappearance."

"Imbert has the police in his pocket, but you would have *Police Nationale* come. You were trying to get your military involved."

"*You* got the US military involved when you planted a bomb under my car."

Again, he made the tutting sound. "That wasn't me. That was Imbert. He was trying to scare you into leaving Djibouti before you saw signs of the aquifer. He never wanted the archaeological survey to begin with. The Chinese were pushing for the railroad to be built without any investigation. It was the damn Americans who insisted, and who pushed Lemaire to make it a condition of construction. Your father, it seems, was trying to get you a job."

Her father had played a role in her getting the contract?

How on earth did this warlord know this, when even she'd been ignorant? Her mind flashed back to the meeting in Lemaire's office, when Imbert mentioned her father. He was telling the truth about Imbert's involvement. "If you and Imbert are allies, why did his henchmen name you when they came to the site and put a bomb under my car?"

"It appears my partner has gotten greedy and is trying to use your government to get rid of me."

"Now that you abducted me, that might be exactly what happens."

"No, my dear. For that, the US military would have to know where I am. No doubt they are looking for you in Ethiopia." He paused. "Do you even know where you are?"

"Somalia, or Somaliland, depending on who you ask."

"Correct. You are, in fact, only twenty-six kilometers from your Camp Citron."

She'd been right about them backtracking on the endless drive. "Why?

Why did it take days to get here, then?"

"I ordered Kaafi to take you far afield, in case you were being tracked somehow. It is known teams of SEALs have located kidnapping victims within three days of abduction, but no one has been rescued after four days. I believe the US military has some sort of tracking system. My guess is a subdermal tracker with a short life—four days at best. My orders were to hold you deep in Somaliland where you couldn't be extracted until four days had passed."

Holy hell. The warlord had detected a pattern in unsuccessful abductions? She'd known Desta's father, also a warlord, had sent Etefu to Oxford, as any king would send his prince to be educated abroad, but she'd never counted on Desta being a good student, of applying analysis to his terror trade. However, everything about this conversation showed he was intelligent and shrewd.

His methodical approach to kidnapping was chilling, but she was grateful he hadn't figured out the truth, that it wasn't the number of hours that mattered, it was access to a cell signal.

Morgan wanted to press the tracker, but she waited for a sign this house had cell coverage. It was the final missing piece.

Did Desta believe he'd get some sort of ransom for her? He'd said he would be well compensated, but there was no way the US government would pay for her release. It would be open season on Americans if they did. And it wasn't as if she'd be valuable to the Chinese or any other government. Djibouti had neither money nor a reason to pay.

A sound emitted from his pocket, and Morgan tried to mask her reaction.

Was that a working cell phone?

He pulled out the device, and she held back a smile at the sight of the wonderful, sweet, beautiful cell phone.

After the warlord answered the call, she reached over and massaged the spot on her arm vigorously, as if it ached. Four seconds should trigger the tracker, but she kept rubbing to be certain, praying Desta would ignore her, so she could sit in proximity to his phone and let the tracker do its job at last.

Chapter Twenty-Nine

Six days, one hour, and seven minutes of nothing. Pax had spent the last few days chasing down fruitless leads with Savvy. He'd spent endless hours on the computer, searching for answers. Searching for Morgan.

But the hard truth was, they didn't even know if Desta had taken her.

The two mercenaries in lockup only gave Mouktar's name. Mouktar led to Lemaire, and Lemaire led them to Imbert.

Imbert was cagey, but a search of his home hadn't revealed a damn thing.

All the while, the tracker remained silent.

The command center, once a hive of activity, was now down to a skeleton staff during the odd hours of the day.

In another day or so, Pax's XO would insist he return to his job training Djiboutians. As if he could simply return to work while Morgan remained missing.

In Yemen, he hadn't known the victim, and in spite of what Bastian believed, they'd done everything they could. Returning to the job after the failed op—and no matter what Savvy said, it had been a failure—hadn't been easy, but he'd done it. But this was Morgan. No way could he run live ammo training when his mind was on her. He'd be booted from the team, from SOCOM. Hell, he could be busted down to private and spend the remainder of his time in Djibouti on KP duty.

And he didn't give a damn.

Pax glanced around the empty room. Most of the SOCOM staff had gone to lunch. Only Pax and one tech who monitored the various phones and computer screens remained. Pax figured he'd grab a sandwich after the others returned. He still didn't have an appetite, but at least he remembered to eat.

As if conjured by his thoughts, a turkey sandwich appeared before him. Pax glanced up to see Cal, bringer of food, enforcer of sleep.

"Thanks," he said.

Cal dropped into the seat next to him. "What's the latest on Imbert?" he asked.

"Savvy is pretty sure he's stealing from the geothermal research kitty. The guy is crooked as hell."

"But no connection to Morgan?"

"None yet. But she's looking into the possibility that the bomb under Morgan's car could be Imbert's work."

"Why would he do that?"

"Not sure. But she's right about one thing. Whoever set up the bomb, the sniper, even the militants in the wadi, made damn certain we'd blame Etefu Desta and look no further. They were planting the warlord's calling card everywhere. Which isn't really Desta's MO. He prefers to fly below the radar, keep his dirty dealings private."

Cal smiled. "Savannah James is a smart cookie."

"When are you going to get off your ass and make a move?"

"Never. Spooks scare me."

"Chickenshit."

"Hell yeah."

"You're a dumbass. Savvy's cool."

"Cold is more like it. And since when does she let people call her Savvy?"

"Morgan started to call her that, and she discovered she liked the nickname."

Cal laughed. "Trust Morgan to blowtorch her way into an iceberg. Hell, look at how she changed you."

"Have I changed?" Pax asked, surprised by the statement.

"Well, for starters you're giving relationship advice. Terrible advice, but still. It's not like you to give a shit about anything but the job."

He grimaced. Cal had a point.

"Before Morgan, you were determined to be a badass Special Forces operator twenty-four seven. Guys used to ask me if you powered down at night in the CLU, as if you were some sort of soldier-bot. Then Morgan showed up, and you hit puberty."

Pax rolled his eyes but figured Cal was right. Morgan had changed him. She'd cut a new facet on his previously single-faceted existence. He grabbed his water bottle to wet his suddenly dry mouth.

"You ever going to tell Captain Oswald you triggered her tracker during sex?" Cal asked with a cheeky grin.

Pax had a mouthful of water, and it took all his control not to spew over the computer in front of him. He glanced over at the tech, relieved to see the guy wore headphones. He managed to force the water down his throat and faced Cal. "Hell no," he said softly. "How long have you known?"

"I figured it out when we all learned Morgan had a tracker. I was shocked you were in such a foul mood after you got laid. It was obvious things were cold between you and Morgan after that, which made no sense, unless you couldn't get it up. But don't worry, I had faith in you."

"Fuck off," he said with faint laugh.

Cal flashed another grin. "Then during the first debriefing after she was abducted, someone asked if James was certain the tracker worked properly. She said it had been tested upon injection and that it went off once in the middle of the night, when Morgan had slept on her arm. James's gaze flicked in your direction when she said that. It was subtle. I doubt anyone else noticed. You sure as hell didn't. You were fixated on the monitors."

Pax shook his head. So Savvy knew. Had, in fact, known this whole time. It didn't surprise him. The only thing that did surprise him was that she'd been the one to keep him in the loop when she could have easily seized on that to shut him out.

Hell, it would have been *right* for her to shut him out.

Pax met Cal's gaze and spoke the words that would get him ejected from the room if he said them to anyone but his CLUmate and closest friend. "Every hour the damn tracker remains silent, I feel like another part of me dies. Pretty soon there won't be much of me left." He tightened his jaw against tears he could not allow. Alone in their CLU, he could break, but not in SOCOM headquarters.

On the other side of the room, the tech, who'd been sitting with his feet on the desk, sat up straight, his feet hitting the floor with a dramatic thump.

Shit. Was he wearing the type of headphones that amplified whispers while cutting out background noise? Had he just overheard Pax's confession?

Stupid of him to have spoken. The words served no purpose.

The tech hit some buttons and a monitor flashed to life. The words ACQUIRING SIGNAL lit the screen. The young man yanked the headphone jack out of the console. "Sergeant, you'll want to hear this."

Pax had been told the transmitter signal was basic Morse code, utilizing the three-letter combination recognized throughout the world: three short beeps, three long, three short, or S-O-S.

Tears rushed to Pax's eyes after the first three short beeps. He surged to his feet and crossed the room. The cycle started again. The beeps were the most beautiful sound he'd ever heard.

Morgan is alive.

"Have you got a lock on her location?" he asked.

"Working on it," the tech said as his fingers flew over the keyboard.

Cal turned on the public address microphone and broadcast the signal to the main buildings on base. Those in the know would understand what it meant and show up at SOCOM.

In minutes, the room was full of special forces operators from every branch of the military. Savvy James arrived with General Adler in tow. Both had damp eyes.

Hell, even Pax's XO swiped at his eyes.

With the signal coming in one hundred and forty-five hours and thirty-odd minutes after being abducted, Morgan was officially an outlier. The statistics no longer applied to her.

His woman was a survivor who'd busted the odds.

"I've got a lock!" the tech said.

Pax's heart pounded as he waited for the monitor to show her location on the map. A satellite image appeared. Rugged desert. Unremarkable terrain. No reference points marked.

"Zoom out," Savvy and several others said all at the same time.

The tech did as instructed, and it took a moment for the image to reform. Another moment passed before the geopolitical markings appeared. Pax's heart went into overdrive as the words on the map became clear.

Morgan was a mere twenty-six klicks away. However, the distance put her firmly inside Somalia.

Chapter Thirty

Somalia changed everything. Sure, SOCOM had run through Somalia drills and planned a Somalia extraction just as they had an Eritrean one, but no one believed that would be the eventual plan. They'd all been counting on Ethiopia. After all, intel had indicated Desta's stronghold was in his home country.

An extraction from Somalia—even a mere sixteen kilometers past the border in the self-declared autonomous state known as Somaliland—wouldn't be simple. It would be akin to Yemen, a much riskier intrusion into a hostile nation.

Pax glared at Savvy James, wanting someone to blame for the lack of intel that led to this surprise. Savvy considered Morgan a friend, but she'd also made it clear everyone was expendable in the big picture.

The tracker had transmitted for three minutes. There were any number of reasons the signal could have been cut off. Morgan could have moved too far from the cell phone. The phone battery could have died. The tracker itself could have failed. They had to assume there would be no further signals and plan the extraction, updating the plan if they caught a break and more data came in.

Within thirty minutes of the initial transmission, a spy satellite captured updated images of Desta's compound. The idea of sending an unarmed drone in to collect better intel was considered and discarded. A drone, if spotted, would alert Desta.

The powers that be at SOCOM formed a plan to send in a SEAL team to extract Morgan. They would kill Desta if he crossed their path. If not, they'd call in a drone strike.

"Where are we with the buy-off on a drone strike?" the SEAL team commander asked.

"We have a joint target coordinating board analyzing the aerials now," the commander in charge of Joint Targeting said. "Given that Desta's compound is far from any population center, I expect the board will give the green light."

"I want Desta captured, not killed," Savvy interjected. She was determined to have her puppet.

She was overruled, and plans for the drone strike were solidified. The strike would give Desta no opportunity to escape. Odds were, the warlord and everyone within his compound would die.

If the SEALs were unable to obtain Morgan, the strike would be delayed, unless they had reason to believe Desta would escape or the SEALs discovered the warlord had advanced or chemical weapons on hand that must be destroyed. In that situation, there would be no canceling the strike. Not even for Morgan.

Pax knew the rules. In Yemen, they'd followed the same protocol, and he'd identified a nonnuclear EMP in Desta's possession. The mistake on that mission was twofold. Bastian had continued the search for the hostage and overstayed in the building after the EMP had been identified. Pax, unaware Bastian hadn't given up on finding the hostage, made the call for the strike.

Bastian made it out of the building. Barely.

Bastian maintained Pax had called for the strike early, and the radio log showed Bastian was right. Pax had shaved thirty seconds from the mission clock. But Bastian had also screwed up, pushing past the evacuation window by a full minute.

Timing on rescue ops was that tight. A minute on one end, thirty seconds on the other, and Pax nearly lost a brother-in-arms. And it would've been his fault, because he didn't have eyes on the bastard when he made the call.

Pax was no different from any other soldier. The real reason he fought was for the men next to him. The brotherhood sustained them. Kept them fighting in the face of defeat. Not to save themselves, but to save each other. Ripley had children who needed a father. Cal had parents and two little brothers who worshipped him. Pax had parents and a little sister. And now he had Morgan.

Reasons to live. People to notify in the event of failure.

Bastian the bastard had a girl in every port and a major chip on his shoulder, but that didn't mean Pax didn't feel a kick in the gut over having made the call that could have killed his teammate.

Things hadn't been the same between them since Yemen, and until Bastian hit on Morgan, Pax had accepted Bastian's animosity as his due. But hitting on Morgan was a step too far, and even Bastian had known it.

Now here they were, a year after the Yemen mission that destroyed their friendship, and the hostage in question was the woman Pax was in love with. One of the SEALs at this very table could make the call that would bring in the bombs that would kill her.

Pax didn't think he could play that kind of odds game anymore. After today, he doubted he'd ever be able to make that call again.

Was that what had happened to Bastian? Had he undergone a fundamental shift when he realized that the bombs were coming for him and his own teammate had—however inadvertently—ordered up the Hellfire?

Satellite photos of Desta's compound filled the screens. Twenty-six klicks to Morgan. Ten kilometers to the border, sixteen on the other side. A total of sixteen miles. He'd driven farther than that from his parents' home outside Eugene to his high school.

Hell, over a panya smuggling route, the drive would take only twenty minutes.

He glanced up at the men around the table. They let him sit in on this meeting as a courtesy, he knew, but that didn't mean he couldn't help. He looked to Lt. Randall Fallon, the leader of the SEAL team, and said, "Do you have intel on the panya routes near Desta's compound?"

"Just aerial photos. We haven't run ops in that area."

"We've got locals we've been training who know the rat routes. Some of our guys were freedom fighters for Somaliland before they joined the officially recognized Djiboutian Army. They might even have been on the ground at Desta's place. They could have intel on the layout."

Fallon sat up straight. "How soon can you get them here?"

"Thirty minutes."

"Do it."

Pax called in his team, feeling renewed energy. Cal and the others would round up the trainees with the most knowledge on the panya routes. The SEAL team would enter from the air, in the same type of stealth Blackhawks used for the bin Laden raid. A quick in and out. But intel on the smuggling routes—likely to be Desta's escape route when things went south for the warlord—could mean the bastard was less likely to get away.

"If we can get intel on the smuggler's routes, why not just go in that way? Why use Blackhawks?" General Adler asked.

The head of SOCOM answered the general. "Six months ago, when Etefu Desta was still in Ethiopia, we learned the location of his stronghold. We also discovered—the hard way—that he protected the perimeter with landmines. Desta escaped, and we've been searching for him ever since. We don't have time to determine if he's surrounded the property with landmines again. If this weren't a rescue situation, we'd send in drones and be done with him. A quick extraction via Blackhawk is the best way to rescue Dr. Adler with the least risk to the SEAL team."

Pax had studied the plan, and he knew it was the best option. It would work. Morgan would be back in his arms in just a few short hours. And later, they'd meet in a hotel in Rome, and he'd work his way up his list of forty-two places on her body he wanted to lick. In order.

The woman who'd taken care of her while she was ill looked apologetic as she locked the cuff on Morgan's ankle.

She really should have learned more Arabic so she could communicate with this potential ally. The woman was another victim of Desta's. She looked to be no more than twenty, but her eyes revealed a different kind of age, making Morgan wonder at the atrocities this woman faced as housekeeper to a warlord.

Was there any way to save this woman, or would the drones take her?

Morgan grasped her hand. "What is your name?" she asked in a combination of Arabic and English.

The woman paused, then said, "Esme."

"Esme. Beautiful name." She studied the woman's eyes, searching for understanding. The lessons with Hugo had taught her what to look for, and she saw it in Esme's eyes. The woman understood more than she let on.

"Esme, if you hear sounds. Big engine noises. You must run. Outside. Far." Morgan made hand motions, trying to convey the whirr of helicopter blades, the motion of running.

The housekeeper's eyes dimmed. "No run. Desta kills she who runs."

Morgan didn't dare tell the woman more. Aside from the language barrier, sharing knowledge of the coming attack was far too risky. "Run. No need to worry about Desta. Just run."

"Desta shoot." She made her free hand into a gun to demonstrate.

Morgan squeezed the woman's fingers. "The guns will shoot him." She hoped trusting Esme with this truth wasn't a mistake, not that the woman would believe her. But still, she needed allies, especially one with the key to the ankle chain.

"Desta die?"

"Yes. They're coming. For him."

A smile spread across the woman's face. "When?"

In all likelihood, late tonight, but Morgan didn't dare say that. "When you hear the big engine noise. Listen for big noise." She touched the ankle cuff. "Can you…give me the key? So I can run?"

Esme pursed her lips. "You run, Desta shoot *me*."

"I won't run until they shoot Desta." She would *never* sacrifice another person to save herself, but this woman had no reason to believe that.

Esme extracted her hand from Morgan's. The crease between her eyebrows deepened. Finally, she said, "No. Now you better, Abdi take key. I no have key to give."

The extraction was scheduled for oh-dark-thirty, because SEALs loved their poetry, even when it was overused. Oh-dark-thirty was a generic term for the start of an op, and in this instance, it meant one in the morning, a little less than twelve hours after Morgan's tracker had reported in.

Four trainees had provided information on the panya smuggling routes. One of the men had, indeed, been to the compound a year before, when a Somaliland rebel leader occupied it. He swore Etefu Desta was not the leader in question. Desta had seized the compound, much as he'd seized territory in Ethiopia.

Thickets of acacia trees surrounded the property and crowded the roads near the house. The trees were what made the rat routes successful. Aside from the brutal thorns that prevented climbing or hiding within the vegetation, they provided cover. There were tracks that connected the rat routes to the compound, some of which were almost certainly peppered with landmines. But Desta would have left at least one route open, one safe exit.

The trees gave way to a deep wadi, another escape route full of hiding places. Odds were, Desta would flee to the wadi when he realized the SEALs were coming for him.

The trainees offered to scout the rat route. They were locals and could get in position before the raid. If spotted, they wouldn't be taken for being part of a US military operation, and they could identify the safe route to Desta's compound, if there was traffic leading in or out. They wouldn't tip off Desta, and the SEALs would have valuable, up-to-the-minute intel.

It was a good plan, and the four men were among the most trusted of the trainees. Not to mention they were damn good guerilla fighters nearing the end of their training.

Plan set, a break was called so the SEALs could prepare. Pax, forced to sit on the sideline, opted to go to the gym and beat the shit out of a bag. He held on to the belief that the mission would go off without a hitch. He had to.

But deep down, he couldn't help but feel like something was off. Like Desta was calling the shots somehow. But that idea was batshit crazy.

He kept coming back to the question of why Desta had abducted Morgan in the first place. If she was right about the aquifer, he'd just called attention to her suspicions instead of burying them. But even so, Djibouti didn't seem inclined to give a damn about the missing geologist. Morgan could have made a lot of noise, and she still would've been ignored.

Then there was the fact that Morgan wasn't the best bet for a lucrative ransom. Her family wasn't rich, and everyone knew the US government didn't negotiate with hostage takers. It was the only way to ensure Americans weren't snatched off the streets of every marginally hostile nation in the world.

Her father was a two-star general, however, and the head of INSCOM—Intelligence and Security Command—and that made her *very* valuable, just in a different way. That same major general had traveled to Djibouti after his daughter had been threatened. Add to that the fact that she was an American who'd been under the protection of American forces, and Desta must be aware that while the US wouldn't pay ransom, they'd do whatever they could to bring Morgan home.

Then there was Savvy's suspicion that Imbert was behind the bomb under her car, which had merit. Imbert made more sense than Desta. The natural resources minister could have been trying to get her to leave the country before she saw the same signs Broussard did. Plus, the warning they'd received over the cell phone in Morgan's apartment had been straightforward: *"Dr. Morgan Adler, leave Djibouti."*

So why was Morgan taken? What was in it for Desta, or Imbert, or whoever was behind it? And how was it that she had beaten the odds and initiated the tracker so much later than other hostages?

Morgan was smart. She knew not to trigger the tracker too soon. Which meant there hadn't been an earlier opportunity. But why? Cell coverage was decent that close to the border. If she'd been there all along, she'd have had plenty of opportunity.

What if Desta somehow knew about the tracker, knew the parameters, and ensured that Morgan wouldn't have a decent opportunity to use it until the US military was well past the point of desperation?

What if Desta had a different payoff in mind?

Chapter Thirty-One

Morgan sat on her cot, staring at the door, wondering if the tracker had worked, if Pax knew she was alive, if a rescue was being mounted, and even if she'd made a mistake in waking the chip. Desta's demeanor when he dismissed her from his presence earlier had unsettled her. She couldn't help but think he *knew*.

He was more cunning than she'd ever guessed.

He was playing a long game with Imbert and the aquifer. Methodical. He knew Imbert had implicated him with the bombing of her vehicle and the coordinated attack on the base, but he gave no hint as to what his retribution for his partner would be. She would guess warlords were like the Dread Pirate Roberts: they couldn't appear soft. Which meant Imbert would pay. Likely sooner rather than later. And then Desta would be the sole owner of the fake desalinization plant.

Desta's endgame was nothing less than being made ruler of Eritrea. How was her abduction part of that endgame? If he wanted to ensure she didn't expose the aquifer, why hadn't he just killed her? The only reason for her to be alive was if he expected ransom and needed her to provide proof of life. Since that wouldn't happen, what did he expect to get from taking her?

What was it about *her* that made risking his methodical endgame worthwhile?

The fifth-wife thing was clearly bullshit. He was no more interested in her than she was in him, and she found the sex-trafficking, drug-dealing warlord utterly repulsive.

A noise at the door got her attention. A piece of paper slipped underneath.

Morgan got up and approached the note slowly, almost fearfully. Afraid to hope she had an ally. Even more afraid Desta was messing with her mind.

She picked up the paper and unfolded it. It took her a moment to figure out what she had. Understanding caused her heart to pound. Esme had drawn a crude map of the house and grounds.

She recognized Desta's office from the route she'd taken. A second drawing with the same footprint but different layout must be the upstairs. The same symbol that marked Desta's office marked a room on that level. His bedroom?

Another symbol became clear. Esme had drawn guns in various locations.

Morgan studied their placement and decided Esme indicated where armed guards were stationed within the house and grounds. Tick marks next to a gun symbol on the side gave her the size of Desta's army: there were at least thirty armed men on the premises.

The final piece of vital information Esme gave her was the locations of all the exits. All Morgan needed was to be free of her cuff, and she'd be able to escape.

Morgan studied the map, committing it to memory. She hoped, if she was rescued, that she'd be able to find Esme and get her out too. She'd been forced to ignore the starving, thirsty children, but she couldn't turn her back on Esme. Screw privilege if it meant she couldn't save at least one person with the blessings that had been bestowed upon her.

Study of the map showed that if she could just get free of the heavy chain, escape would be simple. Desta was a third-world warlord, while Morgan was a first-world woman. In the US, she might have to deal with guards armed with lasers mounted on sharks—or at least motion-activated security cameras in each room—but here, there were no cameras. No electronic surveillance. Cameras required electricity, and while this house did have power, they were in Somaliland. Electricity was intermittent. Certainly not consistent enough to put faith in cameras, or waste the precious resource on their sporadic use. And Desta couldn't afford sharks and laser beams any more than he could afford a helicopter. It was a simple fact that the enemies of Djibouti didn't have the ability to mount airstrikes. That was why drones were so effective. The very people they targeted were defenseless against attacks from the air.

Hours passed slowly. She had no watch, no window, but it had to be near midnight now. Had the mission been launched? Were SEALs even now on their way?

A sound outside her door had her lifting the chain so it wouldn't make noise as she scurried to the hole in the floor, where she dropped the map. She hurried back to her cot and lay down and pretended to have been sleeping.

The door opened to reveal the same guard who'd delivered her to Desta hours ago. "Desta wishes to speak with you."

She faked grogginess. "What time is it?"

The guard ignored her as he bent down and unlocked the ankle cuff. She could take him out right then, while the heavy chain was still attached to her. She could wrap it around his neck or kick him in the head. So very tempting, but risky right before her rescue, especially when the man was about to remove her cuff, which meant better opportunities for escape could present themselves.

The man carried his AK-47 as casually as before. She followed meekly, glancing left and right as she walked the length of the house. The guards Esme had indicated weren't at their posts.

They paused outside Desta's closed office door. Through the thin wall, she heard a man speaking English with a heavy Chinese accent. "The trucks will enter the compound on my command."

Desta responded, also in English. "Call them now, so they will be ready."

"No. We won't risk exposure if you fail. They will come when you have the prize, not before."

Silence met the statement, and Morgan imagined the warlord bristled at the idea he could fail. She wondered what, exactly, the prize was, but was glad their common language was English, giving her at least this scant information.

The radio on her guard's hip issued a command in Arabic, which she heard in stereo as Desta spoke from the other side of the closed door.

It must have been a command to bring Morgan into the room, as the guard opened the door and shoved her inside.

Desta again sat behind his desk. His Chinese visitor stood and scanned her from head to toe before giving Desta a sharp nod and leaving the room.

Morgan watched him leave, then turned to face the warlord. She wanted to stand before him, but remembered that she needed to look weak, beaten. Ill. She dropped into the chair and waited for Desta to speak.

From his frown, she guessed her silence annoyed him. She rubbed her eyes and decided to go with insolence. "Your hospitality is lacking, Etefu. It must be after midnight, I was asleep."

"I would think you'd want to be alert for your rescue."

She stiffened. "My rescue?"

"Yes. But before your SEAL team comes, I will need the tracker."

She didn't have to fake dizziness. "What tracker?"

The warlord's face was impassive. "There is no need to play dumb, my dear. I am certain you initiated the subdermal tracker hours ago. Now that it has played its part, I need the device." He nodded toward the door through which his associate had exited. "The Chinese will pay good money for it. I can kill you and try to find it, but it took us hours to find the tracker from a dead hostage last year, and my men destroyed it in cutting it out. So save us all time and tell me where the tracker is now."

Her instinct was to cover her arm, but she resisted, remaining frozen in the chair. Her throat had gone dry, making her voice little more than a low rasp. "How did you find out about trackers?"

"A year ago, we took a hostage to my operation center in Yemen. A team of your soldiers showed up, and soon after, drones destroyed the building. I lost many weapons, including an extremely valuable EMP device.

"The hostage had been moved prior to the soldiers' arrival. They didn't find him. We tortured him until he confessed about the chip. So you see, I knew to keep you away from cell towers until I was ready. I even knew how to bait you into triggering the signal. A prearranged call at the right time." He patted the pocket that held his cell phone, then nodded toward the guard who stood next to the open door.

The guard pulled a large knife from the sheath at his hip. "Now, you can save yourself some pain and tell me where the tracker is, or Abdi can start cutting until he finds it."

She scrambled backward, stumbling out of the chair, backing away from the man with the knife. "Why did you let me use it? Don't you care that a team of SEALs is coming?"

"Oh, my dear, I am counting on it. I told you I'd be well compensated for your abduction. Your rescue will provide my ransom payment, with your vaunted SEALs as the delivery service."

Her mind raced even as she cowered from the knife. Horror washed through her as his intention sank in. "You're after the Blackhawk."

"Not just any Blackhawk, an MH-X Silent Hawk. The Chinese only got to peek at the one from the bin Laden raid. I'm going to give them the whole bird." His eyes flashed with inhuman light. "You worried your government wouldn't pay your ransom. The stealth Blackhawk, my dear, makes you the most valuable hostage I've ever taken."

"This was your plan all along? Why you placed the bomb under my car?"

"I said that was Imbert. I did not lie. It wasn't until Imbert made a spectacle of you that this plan came together. It was clear your military was eager to protect you, given who your father is and how much they wished to ingratiate themselves in your project. Once I realized how valuable you are to them, I expressed my interest to Imbert, who duly tipped your military that I wished to take you for my fifth wife. I expected they'd chip you then. Just like a dog."

"You'll never be able to take a Blackhawk away from a team of SEALs. You're crazy if you think you can beat them."

"But I don't need to beat them. My Chinese allies have given me another EMP to replace the one I lost in Yemen. With the electromagnetic pulse, I can make the Blackhawk fall from the sky. Any SEALs who survive the crash won't last long, not when the Blackhawk will be surrounded by my men.

He nodded toward the man with the knife again. "Now, we're running short on time. Tell me where the chip is, or I'll have Abdi start cutting."

An attempt to fight now would be useless. The Blackhawk was coming. She needed to give up the chip and figure out an escape. She held out her arm and prayed she wouldn't be killed immediately after they had the chip.

Chapter Thirty-Two

Ten minutes to the start of the op. Pax paced the command center. He paused and met the gaze of Morgan's dad. They'd barely spoken in the last six days. For Pax, he'd been unable to find the words. Now the look that passed between them conveyed the depth of General Adler's fear and remorse.

If Morgan only knew how much her father really cared, how proud he was of his incredible, amazing daughter.

The team of trainees was in position, hidden in the acacia forest along the panya route. They didn't have line of sight on Desta's compound, so they monitored the short-range radio frequencies, seeking signs of activity in the structure. They'd intercepted Desta's security checking in, giving all-clear codes, rote procedure for the night watch team.

Pax's body coiled with tension, almost as if he were deploying on the op. Except, usually he settled into a deep calm before a mission, and tonight he was anything but. SOCOM had been right to exclude him from the op, he was far too emotionally invested, and yet *not* being out there was excruciating.

Everything was in place. All indications were the mission was a go.

He paced as he listened to the chatter on the radio, ignored the low murmurs of conversation between the leaders of SOCOM, and avoided Morgan's father's gaze. Less than five minutes until the SOCOM commander would issue the launch order.

Morgan's arm burned with pain, far worse than when the chip had been injected, but then, the surgery to remove it had lacked proper tools or a skilled surgeon. As soon as the bloody chip had been gouged from her arm, Desta had taken it and ordered her guard, Abdi, to return her to her cell, then report to the field where the EMP was positioned. She wondered if that was where the other guards had gone, if the house was emptied of militants.

Desta made no offer of bandages or anything to tend the gaping wound, but he probably intended to kill her after he'd secured the Blackhawk. She suspected she remained alive only as a bargaining chip should something go wrong with his plan.

As if the US military would give up a stealth Blackhawk for anyone.

She covered the cut with her hand, wincing as she pressed the flap of skin in place. She practiced deep breathing against the pain as she followed Abdi through the house back to her cell.

She had to find a way to call off the raid. She'd be giving up her rescue, but with an EMP, Desta might succeed in taking the Blackhawk. SEALs would die. She couldn't allow the slaughter any more than she could allow Desta to take top secret technology that gave the US an advantage in the war on terror.

She wobbled on her feet, unsure if blood loss or fear was behind the dizzy feeling. Abdi caught her arm—the cut one—before her knees buckled, saving her from collapsing while sending breathtaking pain from her brachialis muscle up to the trapezius. Sweat dotted her brow from the intensity of it.

The militant cursed and tightened his grip on her wounded arm as he dragged her down the corridor to her cell. Inside, he slammed her against the wall, then bent down to attach the cuff to her ankle.

She didn't pause to think; she just reacted. The moment he cinched the cuff around her ankle, she kicked upward, slamming ankle and metal cuff into his neck, knocking him backward.

He let out a rasping sound as he reached for his Kalash. The blow might have broken his hyoid. She twirled her foot around his head, wrapping the thick chain around his throat. She yanked the chain, one hard tug, and his neck snapped. His hand fell away from the gun as his head hit the hard floor.

She grabbed the weapon with one hand and rifled through his pockets for the key. Her eyes landed on the two-way radio at his hip. She abandoned the search for the key and glommed on to the radio.

She heard a faint noise from outside. Rotor wash? Were the Blackhawks near?

With shaking fingers, she changed the frequency to the one Pax had made her memorize weeks ago and prayed there was someone in range who would hear her message. "Call off the raid! It's a trap! This is Dr. Morgan Adler. Repeat, call off the raid. It's a trap." She searched for something she could say that would let them know it was really her, if anyone was even listening. "Pax, if you can hear me, call off the raid. Snoopy! Go back to the base." She remembered that Pax had said to repeat the code three times. "Snoopy, snoopy, snoopy!"

Chapter Thirty-Three

Minutes after the Blackhawks took off, the trainees on the panya route radioed the base. "We've intercepted a transmission that sounds like Dr. Adler. She's calling off the attack."

The commander instructed the Blackhawk pilots to circle the perimeter, move no closer to the compound until they could determine if the message was real. The trainees relayed the frequency number, and a cold calm settled over Pax as he confirmed it was the channel he'd instructed her to use. It was a short-range channel, but SOCOM had the technology to amplify the signal and the techs dialed in. In moments, Morgan's voice played over the room. "Repeat, it's a trap. Snoopy. Snoopy. Snoopy!"

His heart chilled at her words even as emotion surged at hearing her voice. "That's definitely Morgan," he said.

General Adler nodded, confirming it was his daughter's voice.

"Is she being forced to transmit this message?" his CO, Major Haverfeld, asked.

"Call off the raid," Morgan continued over the radio. "Desta is after the Blackhawk! He has an EMP to disable it. Snoopy. Snoopy. Snoopy!"

"Snoopy is the code word I told her to use for 'go back to the base,'" Pax said. "No one else knows that code. She wouldn't use it under duress. She means it."

The SEAL commander took the radio. "Abort mission. Operation Artemis Liberation abort. Repeat, Operation Artemis Liberation abort."

Pax's heart clenched at the order.

"Desta is here," Morgan said, "He has an EMP. Call off the raid. Send in the drones. Destroy the EMP. Snoopy! Snoopy! Snoopy! Send the dro—"

Gunfire sounded over the radio, then the transmission cut out.

A guard filled the doorway. His eyes widened as Morgan shouted into the radio. He lifted his AK-47.

Morgan held Abdi's Kalash loosely in one hand. She cut off her message midword and fired without pausing to aim. Her shot hit his arm, causing his shot to go wild.

She dropped the radio and fired again, this time hitting center mass. The man fell.

She sucked in a deep breath and tried to rein in her shaking as she pointed the weapon at the downed man. She kicked at him to determine if he was dead.

His hand gripped her bound ankle and tugged. She pulled the trigger as she stumbled. The bullet struck him in the back of the head. The hand on her ankle went slack.

She again searched Abdi for the key, finding it in a pocket attached to his belt, and unlocked the cuff with wildly shaking fingers. Freed, she searched for the radio, finding it under the second guard. Her last bullet had gone through him and destroyed the two-way.

The second guard didn't have a radio. She didn't know if her message had been received, but the outside noise that might have been rotor wash was now retreating. She couldn't radio to confirm, but at least she now had two Kalashnikovs.

As she searched both men, she prayed Desta's men were all outside, in position to take the Blackhawk down. She hoped the rotor wash—if that was what it had been—had blocked the sound of gunfire within the house. Regardless, she had to hurry. She needed to get out of here before anyone came looking for Abdi and the other guard.

Her hands shook as she used Abdi's knife—still bloody from her surgery—and cut a strip from his shirt, which she wrapped as tightly around her arm as she could with her teeth and one hand. She took his gear belt as well and holstered the knife at her hip, noting as she did so that he'd carried two small grenades and spare magazines for the Kalash on the belt. Thus armed, she draped the strap of a Kalash over each shoulder and left her cell with an index finger poised near both triggers.

P ax didn't bother to wait for the order to send in the drones. They'd gotten the buy-off from the JAG. Target approved if they had confirmation Desta was there and had advanced or chemical weaponry. It didn't get much more advanced than an EMP, and the man had intended to use it to steal a Blackhawk and take out a team of SEALs.

The order would be given. It was what Morgan herself told them to do, but he'd be dammed before he did nothing while Hellfire missiles intended for Etefu Desta took her out.

He went straight to the room where his team kept their mission-ready gear and grabbed a loaded pack and weapons. Outside the building, he found the

SUV Cal had checked out to round up the trainees and dumped the gear in the back.

He needed orders to get off base, but if his XO got wind of his plans, he'd be detained. The clock was ticking. Even now, they could be arming the drones. He pulled out his cell phone and called Ripley, who was still inside the command center. "Send Morgan's dad out front. Now." He hung up before Ripley could respond.

Thirty seconds later, General Adler stepped outside. Pax didn't bother with preliminaries. "I'm going after Morgan. I need signed orders to leave the base."

"There could be landmines. You don't know what you're facing."

"I'm willing to accept that risk."

"I'm not your CO. I can get you off base, but you'll still be considered AWOL."

"Morgan is all that matters."

"I won't be able to protect you, son. I have no power here. Especially not in this."

"I don't give a damn. We have less than an hour before the drone strike. Get me off base, and I will bring back your daughter."

His future father-in-law gave a sharp nod.

Less than ten minutes after Morgan's frantic transmission, Pax was ready to roll. He'd take the smuggler roads and radio the trainees as he neared. They'd been ordered not to engage, but they were still in position. He'd have allies on the ground.

He'd find Morgan, and if he couldn't find her, he could stay and accept the bombing as his due.

The thought brought him up short.

Shit no.

He wasn't suicidal. He'd sacrifice himself to save Morgan without hesitation, but not unnecessarily so. He wouldn't play Romeo in this drama any more than she would play Juliet.

As far as he was concerned, Shakespeare was an ass for not giving those two a happy ending.

He would save Morgan and seize their happy ending. They'd rendezvous in Rome, and he'd start the next phase of his life, which, since he was going AWOL, wouldn't include an active duty Army career.

So be it. He'd have Morgan and find other ways to serve his country.

He put the SUV in reverse, right as the passenger door was wrenched open and Bastian the bastard tossed a heavy pack on the floor and jumped inside.

No way in hell would Bastian stop him. "Get out."

A rear door opened and Cal shoved his pack through the opening, then climbed in. Both doors slammed closed. "Where we headed?" Cal asked.

Pax was taken aback by the question. Finally, he said, "Djibouti City. I'm paying Lemaire a late-night visit. You're staying here. You don't have orders. So get out."

"Oh, but we do." Bastian set a sheaf of papers on the dash. "I just need to fill in the destination. It didn't seem like writing 'Somalia' would be a good idea."

"Where the fuck did you get orders?"

"That's for me to worry about," Bastian said. "So what's the plan? Meet up with our boys on the panya route?"

"I'm going to see Lemaire."

"Bullshit," Cal said. "You're going after Morgan, and we're going to help you. You can't go in alone."

"I'm going fucking AWOL to save a woman. The Army is going to fry my ass. I won't let them fry yours too."

"You already tried to fry my ass, Sergeant Blanchard," Bastian said. "Besides, it's not your call to make—this time."

"Fuck you, Chief Ford. I don't want your help."

"Tough. You're getting it. Also, I've decided to forgive you for Yemen."

"I don't need your fucking forgiveness."

"Tough. You're getting it," Bastian repeated. "Now, you're wasting time. Let's roll."

Pax had no choice but to accept both Bastian's and Cal's help. Every minute he delayed was risky for Morgan, plus, it was never wise to go into an op without backup. They were guerilla fighters who knew how to work together. Etefu Desta didn't stand a chance.

This time of night, they cleared the gate in no time, and the open road stretched before them. They would be over the border in seven minutes. Another twelve minutes from there to Desta's. Nineteen minutes total. Operation Artemis Liberation plan Bravo was a go.

Chapter Thirty-Four

Morgan glimpsed the silhouette of a man by the back exit. She ducked into the pantry. She'd been lucky up to this point; the house had been empty of militants. They must all have been outside, ready for the assault on the disabled Blackhawks. She thought she'd recognized Desta's Chinese associate, but couldn't be certain in the dim light.

Her heart pounded. She needed to confirm they'd heard her and called off the mission. Otherwise, she'd have to search the grounds for the men and attack their flank in a feeble attempt to help the SEALs should their copter crash. If they'd heard, she could get the hell out and run.

She *should* get the hell out and run. Because drones were coming.

She tried to control the harsh sound of her breathing, hoping the noise wouldn't give her away when the back door opened and voices filled the kitchen. One or two men she could take, but if all thirty of Desta's men flooded the house, it was all over.

"I heard gunshots." She recognized the heavy Chinese accent. "Before the Blackhawks turned." Relief surged through her. *The Blackhawks had turned.* He continued, "Your prisoner could have shot her guard and used his radio to send back the helicopters."

A man—Desta?—said something in Arabic. A third man replied, also in Arabic, then footsteps retreated down the hall. The man then spoke in English, confirming the speaker had been Desta. "He will find Dr. Adler and kill her."

"You waste time when you should be securing the EMP before the drones come. China won't give you a third one. I must go." The door opened, and footsteps retreated.

Curses accompanied the sound of breaking glass. Morgan guessed Desta was taking out his anger on a window. A moment later, he spoke in Arabic into his radio. His voice retreated down the hall, likely heading toward his office as he issued orders to his army.

Morgan clutched both AK-47s tight. She was armed and ready, but fear raced through her. When the bodies in her cell were discovered, they'd no longer underestimate her. They would shoot to kill on sight.

Escaping through the back door was out. That was where Desta had come from and could be where the rest of his army remained. She closed her eyes and considered Esme's map. There was another exit on the ground floor, at the end of a hallway. Esme had drawn several small rooms along that hall. Morgan hadn't deciphered the symbol she'd used for those rooms. Could they be the servants' quarters? Was Esme's room down that hall?

Was Esme sleeping as the US military armed drones? Morgan had called for the drones herself, knowing Desta's unwilling servants would be victims along with his private army.

Slowly, Morgan eased open the pantry door with the barrel of a Kalash. She peered out, ready to pull the trigger at the first sign of movement. The kitchen was empty.

She walked softly down the hall, for once glad for bare feet on the wood floor. Her boots had been taken during the original strip search, and her feet had been bare for the last six days. Now that meant silent steps on an old floor with a tendency to squeak.

She found the hallway Esme had drawn and opened the first door. A glance inside made her heart drop. Six girls huddled together inside. None could be older than thirteen. Girls for the auction block.

This was how Desta funded his army.

She had to get them out.

The girls stared at her with wide-eyed fear. They'd probably woken from the gunshots earlier and now were visited by a bloody woman sporting two AKs. "It's okay," she said. "I'm here to help." She gestured for them to come to the door, knowing they probably spoke no English. "We need to run. Leave."

They stared at her blankly, not moving, and her gaze landed on the chains and ankle cuffs. All six were chained to a single large bolt in the center of the floor. No wonder Esme hadn't been allowed to keep the key once Morgan was shackled again. Was Esme too locked up at night? Was every room along this hall filled with sex and servant slaves?

Six rooms, six slaves per room?

She patted the pocket on the gear belt where she'd initially found the key. She swallowed hard when she found the pocket empty. She'd have to go back to her cell and get it.

She stepped back into the hallway, guns ready. She'd kill anyone who stood in the way of her retrieving that key.

She opened the door across the hall. Four girls huddled in the center. A glance at the end of the hall revealed the exterior door Esme had indicated. Once she had the key, that exit would be their escape route.

She turned. A dark shape filled the hallway entrance. She dove for the open bedroom as the man fired a shot.

Shit. Shit. Shit!

She wasn't trained for this. She could shoot, sure. And she could fight. But she'd never practiced for a firefight. Never fired a Kalash from each hand. Never considered gunning down militants while protecting at least ten young girls.

The girls spoke rapidly in alarmed voices. Speaking Somali or Arabic, Morgan wasn't sure. She gestured for them to be quiet so she could listen for the guard.

The scrape of a boot on the floor. If she leaned out and fired, would he shoot her first? How well trained was he? Dare she hope he was hopped up on khat and unreliable?

She released one Kalash to grip the other with two hands, positioning the rifle. Her wrist brushed against a hard metal item on the gear belt as she shifted position.

I have a grenade.

No time to think. No time to plan. She plucked the explosive from the belt, pulled the pin, and tossed it down the hallway.

She scrambled on her knees deeper into the room, praying the man wouldn't have time to throw the grenade back. She heard a curse followed by a deafening bang.

Anyone still in the house would know she was in the slave wing. Even those in the yard had to have heard the explosion. She darted back into the hall, steeling her stomach against the carnage and searched the man for a key. Fortunately, his utility belt was intact. Her breath whooshed out of her when she laid fingers on the small piece of metal.

Key in hand, she returned to the room of terrified girls. In seconds, she had the girls unlocked. Back in the hall, each doorway had filled with women and girls peeking out, at the limit of their chains. Morgan spotted Esme and tossed her the key. "Unlock yourself and everyone else. Run for the exit! I'll cover the hall!" She didn't wait to see if the woman understood. She turned and positioned herself in a convex depression in the wall created by the grenade, her bare feet slipping in the blood as she settled in, and pointed a Kalash toward the main house.

A moment later, a man appeared. She fired. He dropped, blocking the opening. Good. He served as a warning to anyone who would attempt to enter the hall. Alone, she wouldn't last long if they came at her with a direct assault, but she needed only a few minutes for Esme to unlock everyone and empty the corridor.

Behind her, she heard girls and women entering the hall and running for the door at the end, but she didn't dare look, didn't dare take her focus off the entrance to the hall. If someone attacked from the exterior door, they were screwed.

"We run now," Esme said from behind her.

"Everyone is out?" she asked.

"*Oui*. We run."

Morgan backed up slowly. She was tempted to give Esme a Kalash but didn't know if the woman knew how to use it, and didn't want to give up the spare if she didn't. She saw the dead soldier's Kalash out of the corner of her eye and nodded toward it. "Gun," she said. "For you."

Esme plucked it from the dead man's remains. Morgan dared a glance to the side and lifted hers, showing Esme how she held it. "Like this."

As she backed down the hallway, she slid the selector on her gun to the middle position. "Automatic," she said to Esme. She put it in the lower position. "Semiautomatic." She kept hers in semi, to prevent unloading the magazine too quickly.

They reached the open exterior door. Esme went first, then Morgan turned and left the house.

How much time had passed? How far away were the drones?

The women and girls—nearly two dozen by Morgan's quick assessment—had regrouped at the low stone wall that ringed the property.

Like Morgan, all the women were barefoot. They'd have to run through the thorny acacias, which grew just beyond the wall, or search for a vehicle. Did Desta even have enough vehicles to transport everyone? Were the vehicles guarded, or was Desta's army fleeing?

"Where are the vehicles? The vans?" she asked.

Esme frowned, then said, "Truck?"

"Yes. Truck. Where?"

Esme pointed toward the back of the house. "Trucks there."

Jump the fence or go for a vehicle?

The thorns would be a problem. A huge problem. But what she faced at the back of the house was a great unknown.

Acacia thorns had ruined her best hiking boots in the first weeks she'd been in Djibouti. The long spines could puncture a tire and pierce a bare foot easily, and they'd all be running through thorny trees and shrubs in the dark. It was an effective security system, keeping prisoners barefoot in a house surrounded by acacia.

She turned to Esme. "Stay here. Guard the girls. I'll get us a truck."

They radioed the trainees stationed on the panya route when they crossed the border. The men told of chaos within the compound, if the radio communications between Desta's men were to be believed. Dead guards, grenades in the house, escaping slaves.

Pax felt fierce pride even as fear pulsed through him. His Morgan was a badass one-woman army.

And she's in a shitload of trouble.

"We need to radio SOCOM," Bastian said. "Let them know we're here. They'll have intel we can use."

"Okay by me, but it will end our military careers." Pax said. "Can you both live with that?"

"It sounds like there are at least a dozen girls who'll be killed if we don't get them out. That's the call I can't live with," Cal said.

"Agreed," Bastian said.

Cal set his radio to the frequency Desta's men were using. Bastian translated the mixture of Somali and Arabic communications, making Pax damn glad the bastard had come along.

"Desta is leaving everyone behind and fleeing," Cal said.

"He'll come out this way," Bastian said. "Make a run for Ethiopia through the rat routes."

They were close enough to hear shots fired at the compound, and Pax clamped down on his emotions. The shots were either fired by or at Morgan.

Odds were, they were fighting with Kalashnikovs. That day at the shooting range, Morgan had fieldstripped a Kalash in under thirty seconds to prove to him she knew the weapon. *"It's not my favorite,"* she'd said, *"but I understand it."*

It had made him smile at the time. She *understood* AKs, like they were moles in chemistry, a concept to be mastered. Hell yeah, she'd mastered the assault rifle, and right now, Pax was grateful for her father's pushing her to be a soldier all those years.

Bastian, an officer and the highest rank among them, radioed SOCOM. Their XO rolled with the news. From his tone, Pax figured Captain Oswald had known all along. He'd probably spent the last thirty minutes assiduously avoiding looking at the empty seats around the table. But that didn't mean there wouldn't be hell to pay when they returned to base.

Pax tucked the SUV into a thicket of acacia trees as the official word came down: secure Desta and the EMP, and the strike could be called off. They had twenty minutes. If they failed, they'd have two minutes to clear the perimeter. Desta could not be allowed to retain an EMP.

The mission was no longer to save Morgan. His orders were to capture the warlord.

Morgan pressed her back to the wall in the shadows of the eaves and caught her breath. She'd had to shoot one guard to get this far, expending three precious bullets. She'd sliced her foot on something—likely a sharp rock—as she'd crossed the yard. Adrenaline masked the pain in both her foot and her arm. Her brain barely registered the wounds were even there.

One more corner to round, and she'd know what she was facing at the rear of the house. There could be an army of men, or no one. Even though the first Kalash still had a few bullets left, she switched out the magazine for a full one. Better to reload now than to regret it later.

She wished she'd checked the dead guy in the hall for more grenades. They were handy little devils, and she only had one left.

An engine noise sounded. Time to move. She pushed off the wall and rounded the corner. A cargo van backed out of a barnlike structure that must serve as the garage. The van backed up in an arc. At that trajectory, the headlights would be upon her in a second. She dropped back into the dark eaves, tucking behind a thorny shrub.

The van would be perfect for hauling the girls out of here. She needed that van.

How to stop them without disabling it?

Shoot the driver. In a moving vehicle.

God, how she *hated* today. She'd thought yesterday was bad, but everything that had happened after midnight really, really sucked.

She switched the Kalash to automatic and launched herself out from behind the shrub, catching the arc of the vehicle as the headlights washed over her, firing the weapon as she dove to the side. The magazine emptied, and she landed hard on the unforgiving rocky ground. She grunted with the pain of a bad landing. Not even adrenaline could mask that she'd knocked the wind out of herself. Stupid, sloppy move. She shouldn't have attempted something she'd never practiced.

She tried to suck in air, unable to focus on whether she'd gotten the driver or not. The headlights were out—either she'd shot them, or they'd been shut off.

The rev of the engine gave warning of what was coming.

Still unable to breathe, she grabbed the second Kalash and started firing as the van barreled toward her. She rolled to get out of the way, still firing.

Air entered her lungs in a rush as the van screeched past her and came to a halt. She scrambled to get her feet under her as she heard the passenger door open. Blinding pain shot up her leg. Her ankle gave out, and she collapsed before she was even halfway up. *Shit*. She'd screwed up her ankle.

A man rounded the vehicle. She aimed the Kalash and pulled the trigger. But the magazine was empty.

He approached, holding a small pistol, which was pointed at her forehead. Faint light from the crescent moon landed on his features, and she recognized Etefu Desta.

Chapter Thirty-Five

Pax, Cal, and Bastian left the SUV and slipped into the trees. They had to hope landmines were few and far between given that the thorny trees made the approach difficult enough without adding explosives. The Djiboutian trainees would cut off any vehicle that tried to escape via the mine-free road, while the three Special Forces operators would enter the compound on foot and fight man-to-man. Their specialty.

Their first goal was to take Desta. If they didn't locate him within five minutes, Cal and Bastian would evacuate the girls. Pax would go after Morgan.

They spotted two fleeing soldiers at the perimeter of the property. Cal took out one, Pax the other. Silently, with knives, so as not to alert Desta reinforcements had arrived. Then they followed the men's path of broken branches to the compound. They'd been given a mine-free route by the fleeing militants.

Pax came to an abrupt halt when a machine gun sounded, a long blast that would empty a small magazine. He started to move in that direction, to hell with the slow, careful route. They didn't have time.

An engine revved, followed by a rapid blast from another machine gun. Pax ran full bore in the direction of the sound. He finally reached a low wall and took in the scene. The dome light of a cargo van provided just enough light to see the driver slumped over the steering wheel.

There was no sign of Morgan or anyone else.

He slipped over the wall. Farther down, he saw Bastian and Cal do the same.

There was no cover between the wall and the house, but fortunately, landmines, if there were any, would all be outside the wall. Pax ran along the wall in a low crouch, heading toward Bastian.

Movement near the house caught his eye. From the shape, it was a small woman—not Morgan, he'd know her silhouette anywhere, and this wasn't her—with an AK. One of Desta's slaves?

The woman spotted Cal and raised her weapon. Pax had no choice but to blow their cover. "Hold fire! US Army!" His voice carried, ensuring Desta and his henchmen knew they were here.

The woman startled and raised the weapon even as she pulled the trigger. The shot went wild, and she dropped the AK as if it burned.

Bastian charged across the yard, while Pax and Cal provided cover fire. In moments, Bastian had the woman detained under the eaves. Cal crossed the open space next, with Pax laying down cover fire. When he reached Bastian's side, Pax made his move.

He reached Bastian, who questioned the woman in Arabic. To Pax and Cal, he said, "Desta has Morgan. He grabbed her and used her as a shield when this woman would have shot him to protect her. He dragged Morgan into the house."

Pax stared at the dark structure. Shit. Two floors. Multiple corridors. Who knew what sort of weaponry was inside. Desta had taken Morgan as a human shield.

Pax is here. Morgan's heart swelled when she heard his voice. She was useless as a dead human shield. Knowing the Green Berets were here, there was no way Desta would pull the trigger of the gun pressed to her temple.

"Pax!" she shouted at the same time a gun fired. Her voice was hoarse, and she doubted it carried beyond the walls, let alone could be heard over the shot.

Desta dropped the gun and dug his fingers into the wound on her arm. Her vision tunneled as pain engulfed her. She tried to scream but the only sound that emitted was a low groan.

They'd entered the house through the rear door. Desta shifted his grip and dragged her through the kitchen to the main hall. He turned for the slave corridor. She tried to get her feet under her, but her ankle couldn't support her weight. She grappled for the doorway, stopping him.

He was neither fit nor a trained soldier, and struggled with her weight. She continued to fight him, even as he dragged her over the bloody, grenade-shattered remains of one of his men.

He paused in the open doorway of one of the slave bedrooms. She tried to gouge him in the eyes, but he again dug into her arm, incapacitating her.

He cursed and shoved her into the room. Before she could catch her breath and fight, he slapped one of the open cuffs around her swollen ankle. Unencumbered, he escaped down the corridor.

Cal was sent to round up the women and load them in the van. With Desta unsecured and no knowledge where the EMP was, the clock was ticking for the drone strike. They needed to get the women to safety.

Pax and Bastian would hunt Desta. They had five minutes to secure the warlord and call off the drones, or seven minutes to evacuate completely.

Inside the house, he heard thumping—perhaps a struggle—in another wing. He nodded to Bastian and they raced through the kitchen. He skidded to a halt in the main corridor. Where had the sound come from?

"Pax!"

Morgan.

He didn't reply. Desta could be forcing her to draw him out. He waited and listened.

"Peppermint Patty!" she shouted.

Relief washed through him. Damn, she was smart, using the "it's safe to come to me" code only the two of them knew.

"Peppermint Patty!" she repeated.

He bolted down the hall before she could say it a third time. "I'm here, babe." Not the kind of shout he usually said during an op, but this wasn't the usual mission. He finally laid eyes on her. Covered in blood and looking like she'd been through sheer hell, she was the most beautiful thing he'd ever seen. He dropped to his knees and kissed her. A brief kiss that took only a precious second.

She gripped his shirt. "Desta escaped down the corridor."

Pax turned to see Bastian in the doorway. "Go after Desta. I'll get Morgan out. If you can't get him within a minute, clear the property. Meet at the rendezvous point."

Bastian nodded and bolted down the hallway.

Pax turned back to Morgan. "Can you walk?"

"No. But—"

He scooped her up and immediately saw the problem.

"I don't know what Esme did with the key. It may be in the hall, or she may still have it."

Odds were Esme—assuming she was the woman with the Kalashnikov—was long gone with Cal.

He studied the thick chain, wondering if he could shoot through it, but Desta didn't mess around when it came to locking up people. He'd have to fire at close range, and the ricochet from the bullets would do serious harm. And it still probably wouldn't free her.

He might be able to convince the Navy to call off the strike, but the only surefire way to save Morgan was to get Desta. Now.

He kissed her again. "I love you," he said, then he bolted for the corridor.

Chapter Thirty-Six

Pax radioed the command center as he ran down the hall. "Call off the strike! Artemis is trapped. We can't get her out. Repeat, abort strike. We can't free Artemis."

At the open exterior door, he paused. He radioed Bastian. "Chief, do you have eyes on the prize?"

"Negative. Garage is empty. No vehicles. No tangoes."

The warlord probably couldn't afford more than a few vehicles, and once his men realized a drone strike was imminent, odds were they'd bolted in the only rides available. He'd bet Desta had been in the cargo van because he'd loaded it with his supply of khat and any small weaponry he could grab.

Which meant Morgan had thoroughly disarmed the asshole. Without a vehicle, without an army, without a hostage, where would the warlord go?

Pax raced for the nearest section of wall. Desta would have taken to the trees. He'd be heading for the wadi. And Desta would know the mine-free route. Worked for Pax. Hunting down men in wooded areas just so happened to be one of his specialties. He'd make damn sure the man didn't make it to the wadi.

He paused on the other side of the wall, tugged down night vision goggles, and slowed his breathing so he could listen. He scanned the acacias. The wide thicket had both tall trees and low shrubs, providing decent cover, but at the cost of one's skin. Everything here had barbs, but it was easy to see the broken trail through all the barbs. Add to that the plants were brittle and noisy, and following Desta would be no problem.

Pax wouldn't be able to pursue in silence, but neither could Desta flee without revealing his position. The snap of branches to the east had Pax dialing in the night vision.

There. A lone man. Right height and build.

He raised the M4, but Desta slipped behind a thick tree trunk and disappeared. Pax set off in pursuit. He reached the acacia trunk and paused to listen again. Desta's movements had become stealthy. There was no longer a wake of broken branches to follow. The calm, quiet night belied the battle that had raged and the ongoing frantic exodus of slaves and militants several hundred yards to the south.

A burst of rifle fire in the distance told him the trainees were rounding up Desta's soldiers as they fled on the rat road. But here, in this thicket, it was just Pax and the warlord.

Desta was older, out of shape. He was alone without an army to help him. His silence, the very lack of movement, said he knew he was being hunted. He'd stopped running and had opted to hide.

Pax was low on patience but forced himself to wait. To listen.

Heavy breathing, several feet to the right, on the other side of the low shrubs.

Pax made his move. Desta bolted from his hiding place. The warlord stumbled, caught his footing, and ran. But he was no match for Pax, who was on him in a flash.

He tackled Desta, then rolled to his feet, lifting the man by the shoulders. He slammed the warlord into the unforgiving trunk of an old tree.

Desta's head lolled from the blow, and Pax punched him in the jaw with repeated, rapid blows. Dimly he was aware, as he landed the successive punches, that he'd missed his chance to shoot the sonofabitch, meaning the kidnapping, sex-trafficking, drug-dealing asshole would live.

He turned the warlord onto his stomach, pressing his face into the dirt as he bound his hands. With Desta immobilized, Pax grabbed his radio. "Target acquired. Repeat, Icarus acquired. Call off the drones. I have Icarus in custody."

"Copy that, Sergeant," Major Haverfeld said. "Operation Icarus abort. Target acquired. Operation Icarus abort."

Pax slumped down on the ground and caught his breath. He'd lay odds that they'd have called off the strike knowing Desta wasn't inside the house and Morgan was trapped, but still, it was damn good to have the warlord in custody, ensuring Morgan's safety once and for all.

But he couldn't sit here and rest on his laurels. His woman was chained in the scumbag's house. He stripped all weapons from the unconscious warlord's body, smiling when he found what appeared to be a key to the cuffs. He grabbed his radio. "Tell Morgan I'm coming, and I've got a key."

"Copy that, Sergeant," Bastian said.

He stood and gripped Desta's ankle. He dragged the man through the trees, aiming for every rock and thorn he could find on his route back to the house.

One of the trainees was assigned the job of driving the van full of refugees back to Camp Citron. Bastian loaded the unconscious warlord into the back of their US military SUV, and another trainee rode with him to guard Desta. The remaining two trainees loaded the back of their vehicle with the handful of militants they'd taken prisoner, leaving Cal to requisition the fleeing militants' vehicle for driving Morgan and Pax back to the base.

Bastian had located the nonnuclear EMP in a field below the garage. It was too big to load onto a vehicle, and too valuable to leave unguarded. SOCOM issued orders to set charges on the device and destroy it in place. The glow from the resulting fire lit the night sky as Cal drove them away from the compound.

Pax rode in the backseat with Morgan in his arms. She had numerous injuries, including a possibly busted ankle, and he wanted to call for a medic helicopter the minute they cleared the border, but Morgan refused. She tucked her face into his neck and gripped him tightly. "I can wait the fifteen extra minutes it will take to drive to the base, and I want those minutes with you."

He tightened his grip on her, a dozen conflicting emotions all flooding him. Relief. Joy. Shock and horror for her sake. His breathing was shallow as he tried to take in this moment. She was real. Her ordeal was over. She'd survived six and a half days as a warlord's prisoner, and he again held the woman of his dreams in his arms.

He never wanted to let go.

They hit a large pothole, and the vehicle bounced. Morgan winced at the jolt.

"Sorry," Cal said.

"It's okay," Morgan said. "I'm fine."

Pax cupped her cheek. The backseat was nearly pitch dark as men equipped with night vision goggles drove all the vehicles in their short convoy. No lights until they crossed the border into Djibouti, meaning no headlights penetrated the windows; it was too dark for him to see her face.

He was tempted to put on his own NVGs, just so he could see her. "Did they hurt you, beyond the obvious wounds?" he asked.

"During the kidnapping, I got a little battered, but I wasn't sexually assaulted, thank God. Desta knew about the tracker, and wanted me to trigger it once he was ready, so he gave orders to take me alive. I think the orders included not raping me, probably because he feared the tracker could be triggered in a struggle, which would've ruined his plans."

He ran his lips over her forehead. She smelled of blood and gunpowder, death and pain. She would have scars from her ordeal no matter what, and he'd be there for her through every aching moment as she came to grips with what she'd faced and what she'd done to survive, but he was thankful for her sake she hadn't been sexually violated by the warlord or his henchmen in addition to the other atrocities she'd confronted.

"How much trouble are you going to be in with SOCOM for coming to rescue me?"

"What makes you think we weren't acting on orders?"

"If SOCOM were going to send in Green Berets, they'd send at least half the team—isn't that how the teams are structured, so you can divide into two?"

"Yes."

"Yet I only counted three of you. No way was this a sanctioned mission. So what's going to happen? Will you be brought up on charges?"

"Considering you were rescued, Desta was taken alive, we destroyed the EMP, we didn't waste a few very expensive Hellfires, and twenty girls destined for the auction block were liberated," Cal said, "I think we'll be fine."

"And if you'd failed?"

"We'd have faced court-martial," Pax said.

Morgan tightened her grip on his shoulders and burrowed deeper into his lap. "You risked everything for me."

"Of course I did, babe. I love you."

"I love you too," she said.

He felt the dampness of her tears against his neck. Emotion rushed in at getting to hear her say the words. They'd come damn close to not having this moment. He'd known the emotion between them ran both ways ever since she'd told him she was his, even if he never touched her again. Now he had to wonder what the hell sort of dumb shit he was that he hadn't dropped to his knees then and there and told her how insanely crazy he was about her. How could he have imagined even for a moment he would go through life without Morgan Adler as the center of his world?

"I'm crazy in love with you, Morgan. I'm never letting you go again."

"Don't mind me while you two are having a moment," Cal said with humor in his voice. "I'm just driving the getaway car from the rescue in which I *also* risked my career…"

Morgan laughed. "Thank you, Sergeant Callahan. I'm grateful to you and Chief Ford for everything."

"That's more like it," Cal said. "Save the sappy stuff for when you're alone. And now that you're in my debt, it's time for some ground rules: no more late-night phone sex. I need sleep."

"He's just upset because he hasn't gotten laid in a long time," Pax said in a stage whisper.

"You should go after Savvy," Morgan said, making Pax laugh. "She totes thinks you're hot."

"Not you too," Cal said with a groan. "Why can't you just offer to fix me up with one of the other waitresses at Double D when we're stateside? That's what a real friend would do."

"You were a waitress at a Double D restaurant?" Pax asked. He remembered her wearing the sexy tank top, but hadn't put it together that she'd actually worked there.

"You must've missed when General Adler told the story of Morgan beating the crap out of men who assaulted her behind the restaurant on two separate occasions."

"My dad knew about that?"

"He worried a lot about you working there. Of course, that was nothing compared to this week. He said he wished you were still waiting tables, nice and safe in Virginia."

The thought of Morgan putting her body on display for tips made the possessive caveman surge to the surface. He wanted to shout a firm denial, to insist she never work at such a place again, but reined in that impulse. He had a feeling that wasn't how this relationship would work.

She shifted in his lap. "Are you bothered by the idea of me waiting tables in a tight tank top and short shorts?"

He slid a hand up her side and cupped one of her perfect breasts. She nipped at his neck, giving silent approval of his action in the dark vehicle as they bounced down the road with Cal at the wheel. "Hell yeah, because you're mine, and I don't like the idea of any guy looking at you and getting ideas. But if you want to go back to your old job, I'll deal."

"I don't know what I'm going to do, but I doubt waiting tables is in my future." She pressed her lips to his and slid her tongue into his mouth for a quick kiss, the deepest they'd shared since she'd been freed, and the first one she'd initiated. "I have my eyes on a hot Green Beret who's stationed at Fort Campbell. I'm considering moving my consulting firm to Kentucky."

"You might want to hold off on that. I heard a rumor I'm up for a TDY to Fort Belvoir. It might be good to take a break from Special Forces, see what else the Army has to offer."

Chapter Thirty-Seven

Immediately upon arriving at Camp Citron, Morgan was airlifted to the medical facilities on a Navy ship in the Gulf of Tadjoura. Pax kissed her as she settled on the gurney and promised he'd get to the ship to visit as soon as he could. He hoped he wasn't lying.

It remained possible he'd face incarceration pending trial for going AWOL. He hoped to hell not, but he'd be a fool not to consider it. He, Cal, and Bastian received orders to go straight to their CO's office once the prisoners, refugees, and trainees had been delivered to their various destinations.

Camp Citron didn't have housing for twenty refugees, and the small medical clinic had only a few beds, so cots were being set up in the library. Tomorrow they'd be taken to the US embassy and the search would begin for their families. Sadly, some families wouldn't take their daughters back because of the value placed on purity, and the stigma of rape was extending, like ISIS, from the Middle East into this part of the world.

Bastian voiced this concern as they drove from the medical clinic to SOCOM. "It's possible some of those girls will be executed by their own parents for the sin of being kidnapped. Victimized by their community after being victimized by a warlord."

Pax shuddered at the idea the girls had been saved from the auction block only to face dire punishment from their families. "That's a question for Kaylea Halpert at the embassy. Maybe girls from extremist families can be placed in safer homes here or abroad."

"This place is so fucked," Bastian said. "Too poor to take care of their own. Fucking warlords acting with impunity. Sometimes I hate this job."

"Dude. We won a big one tonight," Cal said. "Take a moment to revel."

"How can I celebrate when there are sixteen more assholes like Desta ready and waiting to take his place in this fucking tinderbox?" Bastian said. "Hell, I bet someone moves into his compound before the week is out. We should have bombed the motherfucking shit out of it so no one else can use those goddamned chains."

Silently, Pax agreed, but for himself, he was celebrating. Morgan was safe.

He didn't even give a damn about the upcoming showdown with his CO and XO. He would accept whatever punishment given because, holy hell, the woman he intended to spend the rest of his life with was safe. That was all that mattered. Any price he paid was worth it to the nth degree.

He'd worry about the big-picture problems of Djibouti, Somalia, Ethiopia, and Eritrea another time.

They reached the SOCOM building. Cal, who was in the driver's seat, turned to meet their gazes. "You guys ready to face the music?"

Pax gave a sharp nod. "Whatever happens in there, know this. I'm grateful to you both more than I can say." His throat clogged with emotion over what these two soldiers had risked for Morgan.

"Just take good care of her, Pax," Bastian said. "And we're square."

Maybe he wasn't such a bastard after all.

Inside their CO's office, they were greeted by Major Haverfeld, Captain Oswald, and, surprisingly, Savannah James and the leader of the SEAL team, Lieutenant Fallon.

Cal, Bastian, and Pax all stood at attention.

"At ease," Captain Oswald said. "I want to thank the three of you for successfully carrying out Major Haverfeld's and my orders to launch a secret, secondary mission, Operation Icarus Capture." The man flashed a sly smile. "As you know, Ms. James and Lt. Fallon were in the loop, aware that orders were in place for Operation Icarus Capture should the mission to rescue General Adler's daughter either fail or be aborted.

"With both Lt. Fallon's and Ms. James's assistance vouching for the mission and orders, the commanders at SOCOM have accepted that there cannot and should not be any action taken against the three of you for any perceived acting without orders. Furthermore, the leaders at SOCOM wish to thank you for exemplary service in your willingness to enter enemy territory as a skeleton force to capture the warlord alive and without a single US casualty. This mission has been and shall remain classified. There will be no press release and no credit taken by the US for separating the warlord from his army and weapons.

"Unfortunately, the top secret nature of the mission means no medals or commendations can be issued for your exemplary service and valor." Captain Oswald grinned again, then added, "But neither will there be backlash for any perception of an unsanctioned US operation, regardless of which level did...*or didn't* issue orders. So I think we're good." He met each of their gazes in turn. "Are we agreed, Chief Ford and Sergeants Callahan and Blanchard?"

Pax couldn't suppress his own grin. "Yes sir," they said in unison.

"Excellent. There will be a debriefing with all SOCOM commanders at oh-eight-hundred. Until then, you are dismissed." Oswald paused, then added, "Blanchard, a moment please, before you go."

The room emptied and Pax faced his XO.

"For the record, both Fallon and James came to me with this plan," the man said.

"I understand why James was on board, but why Fallon?"

Oswald dropped in his chair. "With an EMP and the element of surprise, Desta might have succeeded and taken out an entire team of SEALs along with two Blackhawks. Even if he failed at taking the birds, there almost certainly would have been SEAL casualties. Dr. Adler called off her own rescue to protect men and top secret technology, knowing her chance of surviving the night was minimal. Fallon promised to say whatever necessary to help her. She's one in a million, Sergeant. Don't blow it."

"Can I take this to mean orders regarding relations with Dr. Adler have been rescinded?"

"You're the one who'll have to deal with her father. If you want to risk messing around with a general's daughter, go for it."

Pax smiled. "I think I can handle the general."

Morgan woke disoriented. It took her a moment to remember she was in the medical facility on a US Navy ship, where a SOCOM commander had questioned her until dawn as doctors and medics treated her various injuries.

The wound on her arm had been cleaned and sewn together, but it was possible she'd need a graft if it didn't knit along one edge. She'd fractured the lateral malleolus of her right fibula. For now, her ankle was immobilized with a brace, and the doctor had said she'd get a cast in a day or two, after the swelling subsided.

She had other aches and pains—she'd sliced open her right foot in addition to busting that ankle—but nothing life threatening. The doctor had suggested ibuprofen would be her best friend in the coming days.

Her eyes focused, and she recognized the form of her sleeping father in the chair next to her hospital bed. Okay, he wasn't *exactly* who she'd hoped to see upon waking, but he was her second choice.

She stared at the man whose opinion had, in one way or another, shaped most of her major decisions, good and bad. She'd wanted nothing more or less than for him to see her. When she was younger, she wanted him to be proud of her, and, if she were being honest, that had been her goal as an adult too, even when she'd aimed to piss him off.

It appeared he'd seen her all along, and in ways she'd never imagined. He just hadn't known how to show it. It was time for her to grow up when it came to her relationship with her father. But she needed for him to meet her halfway.

She squeezed his hand. "Dad?"

He woke immediately, sitting up straight, coming to attention, giving her a glimpse of what he might have been like as a young soldier, ready to fight for his country at a moment's notice. Her father's eyes focused, then lit with a smile. "Mornin', princess."

Oh man, it had been twenty years since he called her that. But even more than the nickname, his fond tone made her heart squeeze. They could build on this. She hoped.

He glanced at the clock on the wall. "Or rather, afternoon." He grimaced. "I didn't really sleep last night. Or last week. Guess I was catching up."

"I'm sorry your only sleep has been in that chair. It can't be comfortable." The memory of her night bound to a chair deep in Somaliland caused her to shudder.

His eyes clouded at her reaction, but he pasted on a smile. "I'm fine," he said, then shifted and was unable to hide a small groan. He exaggerated the sound, and she guessed he was attempting to lighten her mood.

She smiled, remembering how he had played with her when she was in kindergarten, pretending to be a grumpy bear. She'd forgotten he was once playful. "Liar."

He laughed. "Maybe. But I don't want to look weak with all these young sailors around. A general needs to look fierce."

She chuckled because he looked anything but. In fact, rumpled as he was, he looked much more like a dad than a general. The laugh caused her ribs to ache. She must have bruised them.

He cleared his throat. "It breaks my heart to realize I've never said this before, but I'm proud of you, princess. I always have been. From your first steps to getting your PhD, there isn't a day I haven't been proud to be your father. You don't need to save a team of SEALs or take down a warlord to earn my awe."

Her eyes teared. She'd never in her life imagined her father saying that, let alone it being true, but the emotion in his voice said he didn't lie. "I love you, Dad." She squeezed his fingers again. "I know I've been a shit since…forever. But even when I was so damn angry I couldn't breathe, it was because I love you."

"Me too, princess. Me too." He cleared his throat again. "I know you don't want, or need, my approval, but I'll do whatever I can to help Sergeant Blanchard if he is brought up on charges."

"Thank you. I appreciate that." She pressed the button to raise the bed to a sitting position. "Expect to see him around a lot, because I'm sort of crazy about him."

"Only sort of?" Pax said from the doorway.

Her body flooded with…whatever it was that inundated a woman when the Green Beret of her dreams arrived unexpectedly and looked incredibly hot in a crisp combat uniform and sporting a fresh shave. Her grin started in her heart and shot north and south, lighting a fire in the southern regions and making her brain swim with giddy light-headedness.

Pax entered the room and stood at attention before her father.

"At ease, Sergeant." Her father stood and held out a hand to Pax, and when he took it, her father pulled Pax to him in a one-armed hug. "Thank you for bringing my daughter back to me, son." Her father stepped back and wiped his eye. He cleared his throat. "From now on, no standing at attention when it's just us family. That's an order."

Pax nodded and crossed the room to the side of her bed opposite her father. He bent down and pressed a brief kiss to her lips. "Good afternoon, beautiful."

She smiled up at him, feeling dopey happy now that he was here.

Her dad leaned over and kissed her forehead. "I'll leave you two alone." He turned for the door.

"Thank you, sir. Also there's no need for you to intervene on my behalf. My XO forgot to inform SOCOM of the orders he gave Sergeant Callahan, Chief Ford, and myself to provide backup for the mission."

"Sloppy, he failed to mention it to me too." Her father winked at Pax. "But I'm glad he straightened it out." He smiled in Morgan's direction. "When I come back, Morgan, we'll call your mother. She's eager to hear your voice."

"I can't wait to talk to her too."

He left the room, closing the door behind him.

Morgan grinned up at Pax, her heart rate steadily increasing as she stared into his beautiful brown eyes framed by those thick lashes. How had she ever found his gaze cold? The man was a walking sirocco. But in a good way.

"You're not in trouble?" she asked.

"Nope. My XO even rescinded the order about not getting involved with you, and authorized me to take the tender here so I can check up on you." He flashed his teeth. "I heard a rumor Lt. Fallon will also be coming to see you. I just wanted to say that I know SEALs are a big deal and all to civilians, but Green Berets…we're the *real* Special Forces. I mean, it's our actual *name*."

She laughed, a full belly laugh that caused her to grab her sore ribs at the pain. She crooked her finger toward him, and he leaned over her. She clutched his combat uniform and pulled him down, until his mouth hovered above hers.

"Kiss me, Sergeant. That's an order."

"Yes, ma'am." His mouth met hers and his tongue slid inside.

The kiss was fully sanctioned by and permitted by the powers that be in the US Army, but more importantly by the two participants. It was sweet, hot, and intense. Morgan couldn't say for sure it was the best kiss of her life—the others with Pax had been pretty damn spectacular—but it was different. A beginning. And a precious gift.

She stroked his smooth cheeks. "I love you, Pax," she said against his mouth. She couldn't say the words enough. Uttered billions of times the world over, the three words felt inadequate. She would just have to show him.

She shifted on the bed, and the movement caused her ankle to bump the rail. Pain shot up her leg. She gasped sharply. Okay, maybe she'd wait to show him physically how she felt until after she had that hard cast.

"You okay, babe?" he asked.

"Ankle," she breathed into the pain, meeting it head-on. "I'll be fine in a sec."

He circled the bed and took her father's vacated chair. "I don't have much time before I have to go back to SOCOM. I know you were up all night answering questions between X-rays and exams and need more sleep, but I wanted to tell you a few things I learned—which I have permission to share."

She nodded.

He threaded his fingers through hers. "I worked with Savannah James last week, chasing down leads for who Desta's inside man was. We hoped once we identified him, with pressure he'd reveal Desta's location."

Dread settled in her gut. She knew so few people in Djibouti, just the idea that one of them might have fed Desta information about her hurt with the power of a thousand busted ankles. "Who was it?"

"Mouktar Clouet."

Her breath left her in a rush. It hurt even worse than she'd thought.

"But there's more to it. Esme Clouet is Mouktar's sister. Mouktar knew she was one of Desta's slaves—she was abducted three years ago. Ali Imbert told Mouktar that Desta would kill her if he didn't cooperate. He never wanted to betray you, but he had to protect his sister."

Just when she'd thought she'd used up all her emotions, a new one hit her. She wasn't sure, exactly, what this one was, but it was a strange mix of relief and regret. Sadness and sympathy.

"Mouktar told Imbert—and through him, Desta—the bare minimum," Pax continued, "and even got things wrong when he could—like not correcting Imbert when he assumed you were a man. It appears Charles Lemaire didn't mention your gender to Imbert, because he knew how sexist Imbert was.

Knowing Imbert wanted to quash the archaeological project altogether, Lemaire feared the natural resources minister would use the excuse of your gender to boot you from the project, and the railroad would go through without a survey, destroying every site in its path. Linus never would have been found."

"So Imbert didn't learn I was a woman until the day the militants showed up at the site. And at that point, it was too late to send me home. Lemaire is innocent?"

"Yes."

She breathed a sigh of relief. After learning of Imbert's schemes, she'd feared the cultural resources minister was also involved. Another hope flared. "Does Mouktar know Esme has been freed?"

"Yes. He turned himself in to the US embassy yesterday, around the time you triggered the tracker. He couldn't take the guilt and wanted to do what he could to save you. He had no idea where Desta's stronghold was. Even if he'd been rounded up on day one, it's unlikely he could have helped."

"Will he be released? It's not right for him to be punished for trying to protect his sister." She glanced down at her ankle and grimaced. "And I can't do the legwork anymore. I need Mouktar in the field."

"I'm glad you still want him, because there's still Imbert to think about. The minister is in bed with China, and Mouktar is a conduit into his organization. He's agreed to keep informing, but this time to us, on Imbert."

"Will that be safe for Mouktar?"

"That's for him to decide. No one is forcing him. The truth is, there's nothing we can do about Imbert—not yet. He's Djibouti's problem. But if it's true the Chinese found the aquifer, and Imbert is at least partial owner of a fake desalinization plant currently under construction, it will come out. The US won't allow Eritrea and China to steal Djibouti's water. After Djibouti learns the truth, China won't be seen as quite so welcome or benevolent. Eventually, we might get our base back at Obock. It's a long game with high stakes."

"With Desta in US custody, couldn't China just build a *real* desalinization plant? The US would look pretty foolish claiming fraud if the plant actually did what they promised."

"Actually, that's exactly what Savvy thinks they'll do. Which would be a win for both Eritrea and Djibouti. But it means we can't touch Imbert. Hell, he can come forward with information on the aquifer and be a national hero."

"What's going to happen to Desta?"

"Either he'll come to heel and become the CIA's toady, or he'll quietly disappear."

"Toady? The asshole was selling girls!" The idea that the man would escape swift and violent justice took her breath away. "He planned to steal a Blackhawk and sell it to China!" The personal affront, that he'd abducted her, didn't even register on the top ten list of the reasons the man should suffer.

"He'll pay for his sins. He'll never be the king he believes he should be. But he might be useful as a puppet."

She tilted her head back and closed her eyes. "Sometimes I hate this place."

Pax kissed her cheek. "As much as I want to see you every day and hold you every night, I wouldn't mind if you got your gorgeous ass out of Djibouti. I don't think I'm going to breathe easy until you're safe on American soil."

"You promised me Rome."

He smiled and lifted her fingers to his lips. "Hell yeah, I want Rome. But after that, I want you to hightail it to the US and wrap yourself in bubble wrap until I get home."

She smiled at that. "I wonder what it would be like having sex on a bed made of bubble wrap?"

"Sounds like something we should research."

He slid her index finger into his mouth and sucked on the tip. Her voice came out breathier than she intended. "How much longer do you have on this deployment?"

He released her finger but held on to her hand. "Six weeks." He pulled a cell phone out of his pocket and pressed it into her palm. "I need to head back. I was told they plan to keep you on the ship for a few days, until they can cast your ankle. I probably won't be able to visit again, so I got you this. At least we can text." He leaned down and kissed her, openmouthed. Mind-blowing. Creating an instant sirocco-like vortex of heat. "I already sent you a few messages to get the conversation started."

Pax waited near the helipad for the helicopter transporting Morgan back to the base to land. It had been five days since he'd seen her. The wound on her arm had shown signs of infection—not surprising considering the initial surgery had been far from sterile—and they'd kept her for as long as they could to be certain the antibiotics were effective. Tomorrow, she needed to be present in the field for the press conference at the Linus site. Immediately after the press conference, she would be whisked away to Landstuhl, Germany, where she would receive outpatient medical care at the US Army hospital while she finished writing her report.

They had twelve hours together before he would report to work, and she would need to pack and get ready for the press conference.

He was strangely nervous, standing in the hundred-degree heat, clutching a bundle of wilting flowers he'd paid a small fortune for. It had been a dozen years since he went on a date that mattered, and that had been with his ex-wife. He'd been all of twenty years old and full of himself.

Now he was older, wiser, and so much more aware of his failings.

He'd had confidence when it came to a fling—hell, it was easy when emotions weren't on the line—but this was the start of something real, and he was fully aware he might not be worthy of the object of his affection.

The wind whipped up, a hot blast on the humid April evening, as the helicopter lowered to the ground. A few of the blossoms lost their heads, causing him to laugh at himself for the attempt at something normal in the world's most abnormal courtship.

Morgan appeared as she was lifted out of the helicopter by a medic and every stupid doubt he carried vanished in the hot vortex created by the rotating blades.

Fuck she was magnificent, his blonde, badass centerfold with a PhD. His foul-mouthed fairy. His woman.

He ducked down and approached, meeting her under the slowing blades as she took a pair of crutches from a second medic and propped them under her arms. She grinned at the flowers but couldn't carry them while on crutches. The medic handed Pax her bag, then shouted under the noise of the engine, "Take good care of her, Sergeant!"

Pax grinned. "Will do."

Morgan waved to the medics, who jumped back inside the bird. Pax walked beside her as she hobbled on the crutches to his waiting vehicle. He dumped her bag and the lame flowers in the backseat as the helicopter took off behind them, whipping her unbound hair in a frenzy. He slipped an arm around her waist and lifted her off her foot. She dropped her crutches and wrapped her legs around his waist. Her bright green cast dug into his hip but he didn't give a damn as he planted his mouth on hers.

Ah God. How he'd imagined this moment so many times over the last five days. Hell, eleven days, as he'd vividly imagined their reunion while she was missing as a way of keeping hope alive.

The helicopter was long gone before he raised his mouth from hers. "Do you want to have dinner first, or just go straight to your CLU?"

"We'd better eat. You're going to need your strength, and once I have you alone and naked, there's no way we're leaving the privacy of my CLU."

"Practical. I like that."

She slid her hand over his erection. "Fuckable. I like that."

He tilted back his head and laughed. He'd been crazy to be nervous. Being with Morgan was easy. The easiest thing he'd ever done. Perhaps that was why he'd never enjoyed dating. Never wanted to get serious again after the divorce. It had never been easy. Not like this.

They went to Barely North for dinner. Pax's A-Team was there, in the center of the room, laughing and talking smack with the SEALs, making him worry they'd made a mistake in choosing the bar over the cafeteria. He didn't want to share Morgan's attention with anyone.

They found a quiet table in the corner. She ordered a tonic with lime, and he realized he'd never seen her drink alcohol. Crazy as he was about her, there was so much he didn't know about Dr. Morgan Adler. "Do you drink?" he asked.

"Sure. I had a beer the night I was playing pool with Bastian. But I won't drink tonight—the doc said alcohol won't agree with some of my prescriptions, and I don't intend to miss a moment of our limited hours together."

He grinned. "We could always get dinner to go."

She propped her cast foot on the seat across from her. "I don't know. I'm sort of enjoying this buzz of energy. The anticipation of what's to come, the agony of waiting."

"You aren't a dessert-first sort of woman?"

"I am. Sometimes. But not tonight. Tonight's about savoring."

Bastian the not-a-bastard-after-all appeared at their table, waving a black marker. "I get to be the first to sign your cast."

She turned to Pax. "Do you mind if he's first?"

He scowled at Bastian. "As long as he goes away, I don't care."

She and Bastian both laughed. "Sign away, Chief Ford."

After Bastian, the SEALs and his Special Forces team came by twos and threes to sign Morgan's cast. She enjoyed the attention, and at one point requested haikus, but he put the kibosh on that idea. Cal alone would spend an hour trying to come up with the perfect poem.

For his part, he felt a special sort of pride as he watched his teammates pay their goofy homage. She was *his*.

Their food had finally arrived when she leaned toward him and whispered, "So. Even though I knew I was clean of STDs, I asked the doc to run tests, just to be sure. The results came back, and I'm good to go."

Pax jolted upright with attention. Other parts of him came to attention too. "My last round of tests—right before this deployment—all came up clean. You're the only person I've been with since then. I'm good. But what about birth control?"

"I'm on the three-month shot and was nearing the end of the coverage. The doc gave me another dose. We're all set to go condom-free."

He pulled out his wallet and dumped money on the table. "Time to go."

She laughed and grabbed her crutches. "I haven't eaten yet."

He plucked their plates from the table. "Two dinners to go."

"You're just going to take the plates?"

"You're right, we need silverware too." He set down one plate and crammed forks and napkins into his pockets, then lifted the plate again. "Let's go."

She hobbled out of the bar in front of him. He caught the laughing grins of half his teammates as he passed their table. He was a damn lucky bastard, and they all knew it.

Because she was on crutches instead of walking, he set their food in the backseat of the SUV, and they drove the short distance to CLUville. When they reached her CLU, he placed the plates on the desk, then locked her door.

He turned to face the beautiful kickass woman of his dreams. "This is how we're going to do this. I'm going to fuck your brains out. You can go down on me all you want, but I get to go down on you first, for like, an hour. Just promise me we won't be interrupted by parents or trackers, and we're good."

She slipped her arms around his neck, shifting her weight from the crutches to his chest. "And if I don't agree to those terms?"

Crap. She was on to him. "Fine, whatever you want. However you want it. You're in charge. You always have been. Just *please* let me be inside you."

She kissed him. "Are you kidding? I love it when you boss me around in bed. I never knew that would be such a turn-on. Every fantasy I've had since we made love involves you telling me exactly what to do to please you."

He sucked in a deep breath and rose to his full height. "Lose the shirt."

"That's more like it." She grinned and sat on her cot so she could use both hands to yank the shirt over her head, her movement slowed as the T-shirt caught on her bandage.

He knelt before her and tugged it free, then ran his fingers over the thick gauze, his touch so light, she wouldn't feel it. He ran his lips over her shoulder and down to the top edge of the white band. "I'm so sorry," he said.

She shrugged. "It's just skin. The rest of me, the important parts, are intact."

He cupped her face. "You're amazing. You know that, right? I'm in awe of you. I want to make love to you, to show you exactly what you mean to me, but I'm afraid of hurting you."

She kissed him, softly at first, then with growing heat. Her tongue slid along his, a taste of sweet, hot paradise. She pulled back and said, "I'm not made of glass. I want this. Hell, I *need* this. It's an affirmation. I'm alive. You're alive. We're together. Good wins over evil. Love conquers all. I don't give a damn what the cliché is, or even that it's a cliché, because it's how I feel. It's real. It's you and me, making love because we belong together, because we survived. Because you saved me."

His eyes teared. "You saved you, Morgan. I just arrived in time to mop up."

"Give yourself credit, you saved my ass. And for my part, I did what I had to do because I had something to live for. I held on to the thought of you the entire time I was captive. Because I wanted this."

He grunted. "No pressure or anything."

She laughed so hard, she grabbed her ribs. "Oh, God. That hurts." And then she laughed some more.

He cupped her cheeks between his palms. "Okay, here's how we're going to do this. I'm going to make love to you slowly. I'm going to look in your eyes as I slide deep inside you. It's going to be gentle and hot, and you're going to come so hard, we might forget about your injuries for a moment and hope endorphins kick in and cover the pain. This will be the second of about a million times I'm going to make love to you, because you're mine, for always and forever."

She pressed her lips to his. "Works for me. Carry on, Sergeant."

Author's Note

My husband's work as an archaeologist for the US Department of Defense has twice brought him to Djibouti. The archaeology of Djibouti has largely been unexplored and could well hold sites as interesting as the fictional Linus site described in this book.

As with archaeology, the geology of Djibouti has yet to be studied in depth. What I describe in this book is fiction but plausible in that in many areas no one really knows what lies beneath the rocky surface.

All descriptions of Camp Citron and Djiboutian government infrastructure and officials are completely fictitious.

Thank you for reading *Tinderbox*. I hope you enjoyed it.

If you'd like to know when my next book is available, you can sign up for my mailing list on my website at www.Rachel-Grant.net. There you can also find links to my Twitter feed and Facebook fan page.

Reviews help like-minded readers find books. Please consider leaving a review for *Tinderbox* at your favorite online retailer. All reviews, whether positive or negative, are appreciated.

Acknowledgments

This book wouldn't have been written if my amazing husband hadn't been sent to Djibouti by the US Department of Defense, so I guess before I thank Dave, I need to thank his colleague for making the trip possible.

Thank you to Dave, for being my partner in life, a wonderful father, and for keeping me up-to-date on the world of archaeology. You keep me sane and make me happy every day.

Thank you to my agent Elizabeth Winick Rubinstein for asking me to start a new series, and for embracing this book. Working with you makes me a better writer.

Thank you to Gwen Hernandez, Kris Kennedy, Bria Quinlan, Carolyn Crane, and Anna Richland for your valuable critiques. Your feedback made the book so much stronger. Special shout out and thanks to Gwen and Anna for helping with the military details. I'd be lost without you both.

Thanks to authors Darcy Burke, Elisabeth Naughton, Jenn Stark, Serena Bell, and Toni Anderson for being there for me online and in person when I have a quick question or just need a friend. You keep this profession from being lonely without the need to put on pants and leave the house.

To my readers, thank you for all the wonderful emails, Tweets, and posts. It means so much to me to know my work brings you joy.

Thank you to my children for making me Lego book trailers, sewing my costumes, making book swag for giveaways, and for being amazing people I'm lucky to share my life with.

Lastly, I again thank my husband for the plotting walks, background information on everything imaginable, and for your endless love and support. Thanks for sharing this life adventure with me.

Read on for a sneak peek at Catalyst (Flashpoint #2)

Chapter One

Camp Citron, Djibouti
March

Sebastian Ford scanned the club, his gaze landing on the woman he was searching for. He'd recognized her the moment he spotted her in Savannah James's office. What the hell was Princess Prime doing at Camp Citron hanging out with the base spook?

He'd questioned James, but she was her usual secretive self and refused to even confirm the woman's name, but an internet search confirmed Bastian's initial suspicion.

Not that he'd doubted his own memory. He would never forget those pretty lips that had spewed terrible lies. Or those wide mocha eyes that feigned sympathy all while calculating how to cheat people of their land rights.

He felt stares as he crossed the room and wondered who in the club had been here last night when he'd stupidly triggered a fight with Pax, a member of his own A-Team. It had been a dumbass move and he would have happily stayed away from Barely North for the rest of this deployment, but instead he'd returned to the scene of his idiocy to pick a fight with an oil company shill whose daddy was one of the richest men in the world.

His XO was going to flip, but he wanted to know what the hell Gabriella Prime was doing in Djibouti. What atrocity did she intend to inflict on people who had even less than the tribal members on the reservation she'd attempted to screw over ten years ago?

He dropped onto the empty barstool next to her and ordered a beer while he figured out how to open the conversation.

The ten years that had passed since he last saw her looked good on her. She had a maturity about her that had been missing before. But then, she couldn't be much older than he was, meaning she must've been all of twenty-two or three when she'd been made Vice President of Screwing Indian Tribes for Prime Energy.

He cleared his throat to speak.

"I'm not here to get laid," she said before he could get a word out. "So you can save your breath."

"Don't worry, Ms. Prime, I'm not interested."

She startled at his use of her name and studied him. She raised an eyebrow. "I think you have me mistaken for somebody else."

"Not at all. Gabriella Stewart Prime. Only child of Tatiana Stewart and Jeffery Prime and the youngest of Prime's three children. Your daddy is the CEO of Prime Energy, and your great-granddaddy was the founder of the company. I'm good with names and faces, and I'd never forget you." His gaze swept her from head to toe. She *was* memorable, and not just because she was a Prime. She'd even done some modeling when she was really young, but that had been before she was on his radar.

"And you are?"

"Princess Prime, I'm your worst nightmare."

Her eyes narrowed. "Don't call me that."

"Fine, I'll call you Gabriella."

She scanned his body with the same degree of assessment he'd just given her. She paused on his face, her brow furrowed. "Did we have sex or something a long time ago?" She bit her lip then said with a wince, "If so, I'm sorry, I don't remember you."

That startled a laugh out of him. Unexpected and strangely pleasing. "Sweetheart, if we'd had sex, you'd remember it."

She snickered. "One would hope." She picked up her drink and took a slow sip, completely unfazed by him. She set the glass down and smiled. "So if you aren't here to rehash or initiate a night of passion, why *are* you pestering me?"

"I want to know what you're doing in Djibouti."

"I don't believe that's any of your business. You haven't even told me your name."

"Chief Warrant Officer Sebastian Ford. Bastian to my friends."

"I think it's safe to assume I'm not one of those. What do your enemies call you?"

"Bastian the Bastard, but that's usually behind my back."

"And what do they call you to your face?"

"Asshole."

She smiled. "I like the straightforwardness of your enemies. Cuts right through the bullshit. But my dear granddaddy would be distressed at my using such foul language, so we'll have to come up with something else."

"We wouldn't want to have the old oil baron rolling over in his grave."

"Oh, not him—Grandpa Prime was a foulmouthed sonofabitch. I was talking about Grandpa Stewart."

Bastian shook his head at how she was controlling this conversation. Plus, she still hadn't answered his question. "Those who are neither friends nor enemies but who must tolerate me nonetheless call me Mr. Ford or Chief Ford. Mister is the official address for a warrant officer, but chief is acceptable."

"Chief Ford it is then. Friends call me Brie. You may call me Ms. Stewart."

"Stewart? Not Prime?"

She shrugged. "I legally changed my last name to my mother's maiden name."

"Like Prime Petroleum changed to Prime Energy a dozen years ago? Obvious and unconvincing greenwashing."

"I wasn't greenwashing, I simply no longer wished to be associated with Prime Energy, and the decision to change my last name sent a clear message to Jeffery Senior."

"You call your father by his first name?"

"He insisted upon it when I worked for the company. Plus, it fit him more." She paused then smiled. "But mostly, I called him asshole to his face."

Bastian couldn't help but laugh. She *still* hadn't come close to answering his burning question, and yet he couldn't resist a follow up. "And your granddaddy wasn't bothered by your language?"

"Grandpa Stewart made an exception for Jeffery. He called my dad names that would make a sailor squirm."

"Why are you here at Camp Citron?" he repeated.

"Why are *you* here?"

Fair enough. He'd even get specific if it would elicit an answer from her. "I'm US Army Special Forces. My A-Team is teaching Djiboutians to be guerilla fighters."

"Special Forces. I'm impressed." Her gaze swept down his body again. "I shouldn't have been so quick to say I'm not here to get laid." She ran her fingertip around the rim of her glass. "But then, it's not like you're a SEAL."

He snorted, irritated his body had responded to her perusal. She was a viper, even if she did amuse him.

He wasn't interested.

He nodded toward a table in the middle of the room, where Lieutenant Fallon and a few other SEALs were gathered. A glance showed they—not surprisingly—were checking her out. She was pretty, in Djibouti, and likely leaving in a few days—the perfect prospect for a no strings screw. "If you're looking for a hook up, a few SEALs are over there."

"I'll keep that in mind after I ditch you." She took another sip then asked, "How did you recognize me? It's not like I flaunt who I am. It's been years since someone recognized me."

He would imagine anonymity was important, given that her father was

CEO of one of the world's largest oil companies and ransom payments made up a large percentage of the economy of Somalia, which was just ten miles away.

It was insane for her to be here, really. Her dad was a billionaire with a B, and for all he knew, she had her own billions tucked away. He took her hand and slid up her sleeve to study her arm, looking for a cut or bandage. But what he saw were track marks. Very old track marks.

She jerked her arm back and pulled down her sleeve. "I've been clean for eight years," she said, defensive. Angry.

"I wasn't looking for that." Guilt trickled down his spine. He'd invaded her privacy without meaning to. "I was looking to see if you'd been chipped by Savannah James."

"No. It would be a waste of resources."

She knew exactly what he was talking about, which was telling in itself. Trackers were top-secret technology, and Savannah James wouldn't have told Gabriella about her favorite spy gadget if she didn't think it was warranted. Which meant Gabriella had refused. "How so? You're a prime target." The pun wasn't intended. He grimaced and let it stand without comment.

"One, because I've been in South Sudan for over six months and there hasn't been an issue because no one there knows who my dad is—changing my name to Stewart had multiple benefits. Two, I'll be there for at least another six months, which is far past the tracker's expiration date, and I can't fly back to Camp Citron every two months to get a new tracker. Three, there aren't any cell towers where I am, rendering a tracker useless. And lastly, there is no way in hell Jeffery would pay any sort of ransom for me, so why bother?"

Bastian's brain froze the moment she said "South Sudan." Princess Prime was hanging out in South Sudan? What kind of con was she pulling here? There was no reason for an oil baron's daughter to be in the war-torn country unless her plan was to steal their oil.

•••

Brie grimaced as she confessed to a total stranger that her dad didn't give a crap about her. But hell, he'd just seen the scars that were her greatest shame, so it wasn't like she could go any lower in his estimation. She picked up her soda and sipped from the straw until it made a loud slurping noise, then caught the bartender's eye and ordered another ginger ale.

She'd changed. She'd pulled herself back from the brink. Chief Bastard could judge her all he wanted, but *she* knew who she was now, and she was proud of herself. Lord knew she had to take pride in her accomplishments, because no one in her family had kind words for her.

"What the hell are you doing in South Sudan?" Chief Bastard asked, his voice more angry now than it had been earlier. Where did his anger come from?

Maybe she really had slept with him back when she'd been using. He could have denied it simply because she didn't remember him. The male ego was more fragile than a soap bubble.

But damn, it was a shame if she didn't remember that body. Or that face. Eyes so dark they were almost black, slightly hooded, indicating Asian or perhaps Native American heritage. His lips looked just right for kissing and other pleasures.

Seated as he was, she couldn't be certain of his height, but guessed he was an inch or two shy of six feet. His build was perfectly proportioned, muscular, with broad shoulders and narrow hips. He wore a T-shirt that hugged his pecs, and she'd be sure to check out his ass in those jeans when he walked away.

He was the Goldilocks of men. Or was he Baby Bear, since it was the bear's things that were just right? She figured he wouldn't appreciate being called Baby Bear anymore than he'd like Goldilocks.

"What are you hiding, Princess Prime?"

The hated nickname pulled her out of her whimsy and rooted her firmly in the here and now, facing down a badass Special Forces operator who didn't like her very much. And it was entirely probable she'd earned his animosity in her Princess Prime days.

"I said don't call me that, Chief Bastard." The bartender set a fresh ginger ale in front of her and she took a sip. "I'm not hiding anything. I work for the US Agency for International Development. I'm an aid worker. I've been helping South Sudanese people who've returned to their villages after being displaced by the civil war prepare for the rainy season, which by all accounts is going to suck elephant dicks this year."

She dreaded the coming rainy season. She'd thought the last six months had been tough? That was nothing compared to what was around the corner.

"You're an *aid worker*?" He said the words with an unflattering amount of incredulity.

"Yes, Chief Ford. You can run a background check if you'd like. Tell Savvy I gave you permission to see my file. Brie Stewart is my name. And when you're done, let me know what intel she's gathered on me. I'm curious to know if she found out what happened in Denmark twelve years ago." Not that anything bad had happened—at least she didn't think so—Brie just didn't remember.

His shock that she had a real job was rather insulting given that she'd always been a hard worker, even when she made a few minor headlines for the exploits of Princess Prime. She'd worked sixteen-hour days for Prime Energy back then. She'd self-medicated over the soul-sucking job with drugs and sex, but no one could call her a slacker.

She regretted the drugs but missed the sex. Hell, she'd take up sex as a hobby again, if South Sudan wasn't such a terrible place for it. The three men she worked with were great guys—she'd most definitely be interested in them in the first world—but she wouldn't screw around with a coworker, not when the job was one hundred percent stress. It was a recipe for disaster.

She cast her gaze in the direction of the SEALs. Maybe she should try to get laid while she was at Camp Citron.

"Oh, I'd love to know what Savannah James has on you," Bastian said, pulling her attention back to him. "I bet she has the same suspicions I do."

Brie rolled her eyes. "And what would that be?"

"You were sent there by your father to ensure Prime Energy locks down the oil rights. You're the closer for a deal certain to screw starving people out of the only valuable resource they have."

She sighed. "Your Google skills are weak if you think I still work for my father. I quit my job at Prime Energy when I started grad school over nine years ago." She cocked her head. "How the hell did you recognize me?"

"Ten years ago I attended a community meeting for an oil transport proposal PE was ramming through the environmental impact process in eastern Washington. I sat in the front row as you defended PE's plan to destroy an important Traditional Cultural Property to build a rail line that would bisect the state from Canadian border to Columbia River. You had no respect for the sovereignty of tribes over their treaty land. Your plan lacked even basic environmental protection for air and water, but you defended it because you didn't give a fuck about air Indians breathe or water Indians drink."

Well, that answered her question about his ethnic background, and it also explained why he hated her. Plus, she had no defense, because he was right. It was projects like that one that had set her on the merry path of self-medicating.

How ironic that it was that very project that triggered the decision for her to go to grad school to study cultural anthropology. After the National Historic Preservation Act and National Environmental Policy Act had been used to kill yet another major transport project, her father had deemed it necessary to show that someone at the top of the company hierarchy had the credentials to address NHPA and NEPA compliance in-house. He wanted her to find ways to skirt doing the necessary remediation, to be an expert witness who could refute evidence of Traditional Cultural Properties. He'd wanted her to be the cultural resources version of a climate change denier.

But in the end, her father had gotten more than he bargained for. Graduate school had been her escape route.

Her fellow grad students had helped her clean up and find the strength to turn her back on her family and Prime Energy. In grad school she'd found purpose and a path to redemption.

But none of this could be shared with a stranger in a club on a US military base in Africa. While she knew she owed Bastian an apology for her actions as Princess Prime, she also knew nothing she could say would mean a damn thing to him. His goal here was to shame her, not find a reason to forgive her.

"PE lost that battle. The Corps of Engineers never granted our permit. You won." She dropped a twenty on the bar to pay for her two sodas, leaving a far bigger tip than she could afford, but she didn't want to wait for change. "Now, as lovely as it's been strolling down memory lane with you, I have an early flight back to the mudpit I call home. Good luck and have a good life, Chief Ford."

•••

Bastian watched her leave, utterly confused as to why he felt like a shit for hurting her feelings, when she'd been the one who'd tried to undermine a Washington tribe's treaty rights so her daddy could add to his billions.

The Kalahwamish Reservation, his tribe's land, was on the Olympic Peninsula. Their rights hadn't been in jeopardy, but tribes from across the state had all come together, much like tribes across the country had rallied to stop the Dakota Access Pipeline.

His belly churned, as it always did when he thought of DAPL. He was in Djibouti, serving his country, and that same country he risked his life for was screwing over the Standing Rock Sioux Tribe. For the last year he'd been asking himself if it was time to get out of the Army and go home to take up the fight to preserve freedom for his tribe and all Native Americans. How could he continue to risk his life for a country that didn't give a damn about his people?

But damn, he loved being a Special Forces operator. After Cece burrowed her way into his family until there was no room left for him, his A-Team had become his family. Who would he be without the uniform? Without his brothers?

He paid the bartender for the beer he'd barely touched and left the club. Night had descended while he spoke with Gabriella, or Brie, or whatever her name was now. It was full dark. The air was muggy and hot and escaping into his air-conditioned Containerized Living Unit—CLU—held no appeal. He was restless. Antsy. Pissed off.

He walked out, beyond the buildings that clustered around the club, beyond the rows of containers that made up CLUville. They couldn't see the Gulf of Tadjoura from this part of the base, but there was an open area that offered prime stargazing.

He'd been stupid last night in attempting to hit on the woman Pax clearly wanted for himself. Pax was on his team, one of his brothers. But it hadn't felt that way since Yemen, and Bastian knew his own pride was the major issue. Just like with Gabriella, he'd held a grudge against Pax. But unlike with Gabriella, both he and Pax had made mistakes.

Princess Prime had crumpled under the shame he'd applied, while it only made Pax stand taller. But then, Pax knew he wasn't alone in the guilt department, that Bastian shared equal blame.

He was such a bastard.

Ahead of him he could see the silhouette of a woman in the dark. She stood in the open with her face toward the night sky. A nearby light post gave just enough illumination for him to see the shine of tears on her cheek.

He shouldn't feel guilty for calling Gabriella Prime—or Brie Stewart—on what she'd done, but somehow, he did.

She was the embodiment of everything he despised. But damn, that body. She wore simple clothes that hugged her slight curves.

The jeans and long-sleeved button down shirt were nothing like the tailored suit she'd worn all those years ago. He'd been a senior in college and had known nothing about women's clothing, and yet he could tell her suit had cost big bucks, as had her hair and makeup. Ten years ago, she'd looked like a glossy business fashion ad in the flesh. From his front row seat he could practically smell the money on her and it had never occurred to him that money could smell so damn good.

Cece had noticed his fixation and called him on it, claiming he had white-girl fantasies, and that he wanted to fuck the daughter of big oil.

He'd been trying to break up with Cece for nearly a year at that point and had wanted to tell her, no, he wasn't having white girl fantasies, he was having anyone-but-Cece fantasies, and the women he dreamed about came in all colors.

Gabriella Prime just so happened to be the latest and whitest.

When he finally managed the breakup a month later, Cece accused him of wanting to track down the bitch from the oil company and become her Indian boy toy. Gabriella had made a strong impression on Cece too, apparently.

Staring now at the woman who'd played a role in some rather hot relationship escape fantasies, it was amazing he'd recognized her. Brie Stewart bore only the slightest resemblance to the polished Gabriella Prime, but she was every bit as compelling. More so now, because she looked real.

She wasn't Oil Company Barbie anymore.

She wasn't particularly curvy, but nicely proportioned. If anything, she was a little thin—likely due to being in South Sudan for six months and not because she'd relapsed into heroin addiction. While he had no doubt plenty of drugs were trafficked through South Sudan, he believed her when she said she'd been clean for years. If she'd been using in South Sudan, she'd look like a junkie. Drugs combined with the place would have hollowed her out.

He'd witnessed the combination of poverty and addiction first hand, and while Princess Prime had been able to maintain a polished façade while supporting a heroin addiction, no way could that be done in a place like South Sudan. He'd also seen enough to recognize when someone was an addict, when they were recovering, and when they relapsed.

And it was clear Gabriella Stewart Prime had gotten her shit together.

He imagined exploring her body, confirming that she bore no recent track marks, but the thoughts were just an excuse to return to favorite spank bank fantasies of ten years ago.

"Are you just going to stand there and stare at me, Chief Ford, or did you follow me out here to tell me more about why you suspect me of wanting to harm the people I work my ass off to help?"

"I didn't follow you. But if those are the only choices, I guess I'll go with continuing to stare at you."

"I'm flattered."

"You're a beautiful woman, it's a simple fact."

She laughed softly. "No I'm not. I mean, I clean up well—I'm not being falsely modest—but you don't live in my world and get to maintain the illusion you're anything special, not when everyone is so eager to point out that my eyes are too wide, my face too round, and that I should have a surgeon take care of my unfortunate nose."

"Unfortunate nose?" He'd never even noticed her nose. It was just a nose. "What's wrong with it?"

"It's giant, obviously."

"White people are weird."

"I'm sure that's true, but in this case you might mean rich people."

"They're the weirdest white people of all." He cocked his head. "So, you still rich? I mean, should I make a play for you because you're loaded?"

She pressed her hand to her heart. "You'd be willing to overlook my unfortunate nose?"

He shrugged. "If you've got money, sure. I can work around the beak."

Her laugh was genuine, and she wiped her cheek, erasing her tears. "Thank you. I needed that." Then she approached him, stepping farther from the streetlight and into the darkness that separated them. She came to a stop in front of him and placed her hand on his chest.

He knew this was nothing more than a tease, and yet his heart rate kicked up, which was insane. Worse, she could feel the rapid beat, and there was just enough light to see her smile.

Damn, she had a smile. Sweet, sexy. He didn't notice her unfortunate nose because he was too busy looking at her perfect lips.

She placed her other hand on his chest and rose on her toes, sliding both hands over his pecs, giving every sign she was impressed by what she felt through the thin layer of his T-shirt. She brought her mouth to within an inch of his. "Do you want to kiss me, Bastian?"

"Strangely, I do."

"You'll end up disappointed."

"Why is that? Are you a terrible kisser?"

"Oh no. I take kissing very seriously. Like everything I do, I give it my full hundred and ten percent. I'm a magnificent kisser."

He laughed. She had a certain crazy appeal. "Then why would I be disappointed?"

"Because then, of course, you'll want to have sex with me. And you'll probably fall in love with me, because I'm also very good at sex."

"I could be willing to take that risk. I don't fall in love easily."

"But in the end you'll be terribly disappointed to learn that I am completely and thoroughly cut off from my family. I live paycheck to paycheck on my USAID salary."

That was the most appealing thing she'd said so far. As if mesmerized, he found himself leaning down and pressing his mouth to hers, unsure if she'd really intended things to go this far. But even that edge of uncertainty turned him on.

Forbidden fruit had always been an aphrodisiac for him, and she represented the ultimate enemy in his world.

Her lips opened under his, and the sweltering night grew hotter as their tongues mingled. She tasted sweet, and she hadn't been kidding about her kissing skills. The bold stroke of her tongue announced she'd absolutely intended this, and the soft sounds she made told him she enjoyed it as much as he did.

Her fingers gripped his T-shirt. His hand slid around the back of her neck. He could get lost in her mouth. He wished there was a wall to back her up against. He wanted to pin her and grind his erection against her spread legs.

His lips left hers to trail along her jaw and neck. He reached her collarbone and licked the salt from her skin, sweat put there by the humid night. He paused, closing his eyes, breathing her in.

Even her sweat smelled good. He wanted to take her back to his CLU and fuck her against the container wall, just like he'd imagined all those years ago, when he'd fantasized about banging Oil Company Barbie.

All at once the shock of what he was doing came to him. He was making out with Gabriella Prime.

Some spank bank fantasies were never meant to become real. He'd lusted after Gabriella when he was twenty-one because she was the ultimate taboo. His parents would never approve of her in the way they did Cece. At twenty-one, it had been mental rebellion. At thirty-one? It was just stupid.

He pulled back and fixed a smile on his face. "Well, I think I survived that without suffering great disappointment. But I'm sorry to say I don't want to have sex with you and won't be falling in love with you. But thanks for giving me the chance to find out. Nice seeing you again, Gabriella." With that he turned his back on her and walked away.

•••

Want to read more? Visit Rachel Grant's website at www.Rachel-Grant.net for release date information.

About the Author

Four-time Golden Heart® finalist Rachel Grant worked for over a decade as a professional archaeologist and mines her experiences for storylines and settings, which are as diverse as excavating a cemetery underneath an historic art museum in San Francisco, survey and excavation of many prehistoric Native American sites in the Pacific Northwest, researching an historic concrete house in Virginia, and mapping a seventeenth century Spanish and Dutch fort on the island of Sint Maarten in the Netherlands Antilles.

She lives in the Pacific Northwest with her husband and children and can be found on the web at www.Rachel-Grant.net.

Made in the USA
Columbia, SC
16 June 2019